Lucy Hawking has written for the *Daily Mail*, *The Times*, the *Telegraph* and the *Evening Standard*. She lives in Cambridge.

Also by Lucy Hawking

Jaded

THE ACCIDENTAL MARATHON

Lucy Hawking

**headline
review**

First published in 2006
by HEADLINE REVIEW
An imprint of Headline Book Publishing

A HEADLINE REVIEW paperback

1

ISBN 0 7553 0697 X

Typeset in Meridien by Palimpsest Book Production Limited,
Polmont, Stirlingshire
Printed and bound in Great Britain by
Clays Ltd St Ives plc

HEADLINE BOOK PUBLISHING
A division of Hodder Headline
338 Euston Road
LONDON NW1 3BH

www.reviewbooks.co.uk
www.hodderheadline.com

G. L. Wilde
In loving memory

Thank you, everyone. More than words could ever say.

The icon is not a picture to be looked at, but a window through which an unseen world looks through on ours . . .

St John Damascene, *On Divine Images*, AD 730

1

The horizon was perfectly still, the endless straight line of the placid sea drawn flat against the clear sky like blue stripes on a brightly coloured beach towel. The sun was blazing down afternoon heat on the azure Caribbean waters, which lapped against the sides of the boat with a self-satisfied, murmuring splosh. Behind the little motor boat, chugging gently out of the mouth of the bay, lay the old stone walls of English Harbour, the port built by Nelson on Antigua hundreds of years before to hide the Royal Fleet from harm. In front of the boat's white-painted prow, pointed straight along the sparkly golden path across the sea made by the dancing reflection of the sun's rays, was nothing but open water, cobalt sky and sunshine.

'Are you sure they went this way?' asked the boat's passenger, a blonde woman who was incongruously wearing a black wool suit and holding a briefcase.

'Lady,' said Elvis the boatman who had on much more suitable attire, given the climate and time of day. His orange and white batik shirt was open at the neck, his shorts lived up to their name and unlike those of his passenger, who wore black leather boots, his feet were happily encased in flip-flops. 'Dey tell me at the port, dey's headed for Barbuda.'

'Right,' said his passenger indecisively.

'And dis is da way to Barbuda,' said Elvis, gesturing to the glittering expanse of turquoise sea. He turned the prow of the boat, sending a wave of pale jade foam rippling out over the smooth surface of the water. To the right lay land, a long strip of blond beach fringed with deep green; to the left, the motionless horizon.

'It's just I can't see another boat,' his passenger pointed out in mild tones.

'I tink dey's a bit faster dan us,' chuckled Elvis, accelerating the engine which in response made busy whirring noises and frothed lots of water at the back without the side benefit of any discernible increase in speed.

'Well, possibly,' said the woman in the boat politely, wondering quite how she had managed to hire the slowest boat out of English Harbour. Admittedly, there hadn't been many to choose from. Her request – that she follow in a motor boat the 72-foot ocean-going cruiser *The Dalai Lama*, recently departed from the secluded mooring at English Harbour – had not found many takers. In fact, it hadn't found any at all – some of those she asked obviously thought she was mad, others had been out early that morning and didn't feel like facing the waves once more and a third lot simply couldn't be bothered. Only Elvis had taken pity on the girl, finding her standing forlornly by the great stone columns in the Harbour, gazing out to sea with weary tears in her eyes.

'Humble as my boat is,' he had told her with a ravishing smile, 'it would be an honour.'

Humble was one word for his boat when they found it. Very small would have been another way of putting it. In a harbour bursting with some of the world's most technologic-ally advanced, expensive, oversized and glossy yachts, Elvis's offering was no more than a coracle, a wooden shell with an engine attached. But the Englishwoman was beyond arguing.

Having arrived on the island of Antigua straight from the London plane that afternoon, she was flagging a little by now.

'Lovely,' was all she murmured as she climbed down into the craft, which rocked to and fro rather unsteadily.

Out on the open sea, the engine was chugging along happily as the girl closed her eyes against the blissful warmth of the sun, so different from the grey skies of London she had left that morning.

'Lady,' whistled Elvis. She opened her eyes, blinking them against the glare. 'I tink you better put this on.' He threw over an old straw hat. 'And you should take yo' boots off too,' he added.

'Good idea,' said the girl gratefully. She winkled her feet out of her boots, took off her socks and wriggled her toes. Slipping off her suit jacket, she rolled up the sleeves of her pale pink shirt and leaned back in the boat, giving an enormous, involuntary sigh of relief.

'Where you staying?' asked Elvis, smiling at the figure before him, so different already from the uptight Englishwoman he'd encountered on the dock.

'I'm not,' said the girl. 'I'm going back to London tonight.'

'Whoa!' Elvis whistled between his teeth. 'Dat's what I call a schedule. You never heard of de telephone?'

'There's something I have to say face to face,' she replied.

'Must be mighty important news you got to tell,' said Elvis. 'What's your name?'

'Fleur,' said the girl. 'Fleur Bonner.'

'Well, Flo,' said Elvis, 'I hope we find dis boat you looking for and I hope when we do, it all seem worth it.'

'Thanks,' said Fleur. 'Elvis – you are a star.'

'Ain't nobody like the King,' said Elvis seriously.

Rocked by the soothing motion of the boat and warmed

by the gentle heat of the sun, Fleur dozed off, the slatted wooden bench feeling very comfortable after eight hours in an airline seat. So far, it was fair to say, she was having a most unusual Monday. At first, there had been absolutely no indication that this particular January day would be any different from any other. It had started quite normally, with Fleur lying prone under her duvet and pressing the snooze button on her alarm clock time and time again in order to avoid the dread moment when the week began in earnest. When eventually she could put it off no longer, she hauled herself out of bed, wincing at the temperature in her bedroom where it was so cold that frost patterns bloomed on the inside of the window and her breath vaporised in front of her face. As ever on freezing mornings, she made a mental note to get the central heating checked, something she had been meaning – but forgetting – to do for ages. Before Christmas, the weather had been spookily mild, as though the seasons were no longer sure in which order they went, and so the feeble efforts of the radiators in Fleur's rented flat had caused her no discomfort. As soon as the New Year had turned, however, the delayed winter had set in with a vengeance made more terrible by its late arrival. Overnight, blankets of furry white frost had settled over London, coating the trees and cars and roads with its harsh, glittery magic.

Cursing, Fleur had run to the bathroom, where, teeth chattering, she ran steaming hot water into the bath. 'I want to go somewhere warm,' she said out loud. She had noticed that over the past few months she had started talking to herself. This new habit worried her – it sounded like the sort of thing mad old spinsters did. She supposed she could get a cat and talk to it instead but she had a rash of single female friends of her age – that is to say, in their early thirties – who had just acquired cats for company. Generally these women announced that they had given up on love and would be living happily with Moggy for the rest of their lives but Fleur always felt rather suspicious of their real motives. As it was well known that you always found love when you stopped looking for it, Fleur thought the cat-manoeuvre might well be a decoy, designed to bring on Cupid's arrow by feigning disinterest. 'I wish I was somewhere sunny,' said Fleur to herself, figuring it was too cold to worry about whether she was insane or not. 'Somewhere the sea is really blue.' Outside the frosted window of her bathroom, the morning sky was still dark and faint splatting noises against the glass announced that sleet was spitting down from the heavens above.

Throughout the thirty-something years of her life, Fleur had often made wishes, sometimes with the full fervour of childish passion, at others with the whimsical inattention of an adult. She often wished to be thinner, always wished to be taller. When she was younger she had frequently wished her real father would reappear in her life and take some notice of her; now that she was older and he had, she found herself wishing he would go away again. But she had never actually expected any of her wishes to be granted. So when her desire to go somewhere the sun was shining came true later that very same day, even the rather pragmatic Miss Bonner was taken aback and wondered if there was such a thing as a pattern to existence after all.

'Fleur, my darling beautiful lovely Fleur!' her boss, Brinley St John Boulden, exclaimed joyfully as she appeared at the top of the stairs which led to the office. Fleur worked in an art gallery and antique shop which nestled in a tiny and easily missed street behind the swish and noise of Piccadilly Circus. 'You wouldn't know it was there if you didn't know it was there,' Fleur's boss, known to all and sundry as Brin, liked to say to people. The only reason Brin could get away with having such an obscure and yet expensive location for his gallery was because plenty of people knew exactly where Boulden's was as it had been in the same place for several hundred years. Founded by Brin's great-grandfather, Boulden's was certainly not the largest, the best known or even the most highly respected gallery and antique shop in London. But it had a certain cachet about it which appealed to people with old money, who saw Boulden's as a bastion of tradition and gentlemanly values, whereas to the nouveaux riches it represented the class into which they would very much like to buy. And in Brinley Boulden these happy recipients of recent fortune found absolutely the sort of knowledgeable and understanding person they needed to guide them through the tricky business of kitting out a newly acquired house in a way which hid their dearth of origins under a welter of expensive objets d'art. Brinley, in fact, formed a very handy middleman between old and new money as his childhood chums, mostly the inheritors of vast country estates, were only too glad to use him as a discreet conduit for selling off items they could no longer afford to insure, had never liked or would simply prefer to exchange for their monetary value than hang on the wall. Among these friends, Brin was fondly known as the 'Cash Converter', as you could pop in with a Dresden shepherdess from the Long Gallery and come out with several thousand in used notes in your pocket, most handy in these unforgiving, modern and highly taxed times.

'Fleur!' repeated Brinley, looking absolutely delighted to see her. His face lit up with a sort of radiance, as though the sight of a bedraggled employee, and one not in a particularly good mood either, had just made his life complete. But Brin always seemed overcome with joy to see Fleur – it had been one of the great charms of working for him. Fleur had never met anyone who seemed as thrilled by her mere presence as Brinley. Just lately, though, she had started to notice that Brin's rapturous welcome was not reserved for her alone. In fact, she was beginning to see that Brin put on his dreamy 'ravi de joie' look for anyone who walked through his doors. At first, she had found it endearing that Brin would treat the girl who came with the sandwiches to the same full-on beaming charm that she received, but now that she had been at Boulden's for some months she was starting to wonder if the old man wasn't just the tiniest bit of a fraud.

Taking the job at Boulden's hadn't been a universally popular decision. 'Over-qualified and underpaid,' Fleur's friend Matthew had said when she sat sipping green tea in his beautiful bijou gallery in Knightsbridge. 'Lovely as it is to have you back in London,' he continued, his gentle eyes resting on Fleur's face, 'I can't agree that taking a job working for a . . . man' – the length of the pause Matthew left before saying the word 'man' indicated he had thought of various alternative ways to describe Fleur's new boss before settling on the nondescript noun he eventually chose – 'such as Brinley Boulden is a good idea.'

'Brin's an old dear,' protested Fleur, who at this stage had only met him once. 'Anyway, it's not so much a job as a paid holding pattern until I decide what to do next.'

'You could have aimed higher,' said Matthew calmly, his long fingers wound round the crackled glaze of his eggshell-thin teacup. A man whose exquisite taste and razor-sharp eye had allowed him to build up a business selling rare and gorgeous antiques to wealthy but refined clients, he had transformed his gallery into a haven of calm and serenity. 'You were deputy head of an important American museum.'

'Until they sacked me,' Fleur reminded him. Matt grimaced.

'They didn't sack you,' he said firmly. 'You got caught in a coup d'état – half the trustees were forced to resign as well. It was a bad business but hardly your fault. Anyway, that's still no reason for you to be slumming it now you're back.'

'Oh, Matt,' sighed Fleur. 'Don't you understand? I loved that place – I mean I really loved it. I gave everything I had to that museum and look what happened. It broke my heart,' she added sadly. 'And I don't want to go through that again. For a bit, I just want a job where I don't have to get too involved. Someone told me Brin had a vacancy, I went to see him and he hired me on the spot.'

'That's hardly surprising,' said Matt, rather dryly. 'You'll be the best thing that's ever happened to Boulden's. Anyway, why didn't you ask me for a job?'

'I didn't know you were looking,' said Fleur.

'I'm not,' replied Matthew. 'But I would have made an exception for you. Come and work for me, Fleur.'

'But I've taken the job at Boulden's now,' said Fleur. 'I can't let Brin down – I promised him.'

'Far too honourable,' said Matt, seeing defeat in the obstinate set of her oval face. 'You can stay there six months at the most. After that, I'm coming to get you.'

'What are you going to do?' Fleur smiled.

'Make you work for me. Unless, of course, you've found something better by then.'

Fleur had been at Boulden's for three months now and it would be fair to say that during that time no two weeks had been the same. Never having worked on the commercial side of the art world, being a museum curator by trade, she had much to learn. During her various museum jobs, for example, she had never had to find a roomful of antique Chinese brocade wallpaper and ship it to New York so it could play host to a dinner party. She had never sold a walnut table to a pop star, a set of glum family portraits to some lottery winners or a Roman marble statue of Venus Bathing to a hotel in Dubai. The pace of life at Boulden's, so different from the rarefied, cultivated dignity of the life of a curator, was invigorating and it kept her mind off the unexpected transition she had undergone from being almost a somebody in New York to being suddenly a nobody in London. While Fleur was in no way connected to the debacle which lead to half the trustees of her museum walking out in disgust at the activities of the other half, she had made her loyalties far too clear to be allowed to stay. On that awful Friday when the newly revamped board told her they no longer required her services, she had known instantly that she wanted to go back home to England. Much as she had loved her time in New York, she knew she couldn't start again on foreign soil. As quickly as she could, she had packed up and left, arriving back in her native land with no plan and no destination. But being a resourceful girl, she soon rented a tiny flat in Battersea from a friend going overseas on business, set about reintroducing herself to London society – which had changed quite drastically in the five years she had been away – and found herself a job, even if her more august colleagues followed Matt's lead and turned their noses up at it. To Fleur, the job at Boulden's was a gift from the gods – it kept her busy when she might have brooded, she was still within the art world and could claim to be gaining useful experience, Brin paid her, she could leave at any time and there was no danger of her getting over-attached. Another huge bonus had been that Brinley had asked no awkward questions about why she left her previous job, thus sparing her the humiliation of relating a sacking incident in a manner which didn't sound deeply unflattering to herself. Fleur herself had interviewed people for jobs when they had been let go from their previous posts and had felt touched if embarrassed by their valiant attempts to justify a track record which contained a piece of nonsensical injustice. Little had she ever thought that one day she would be in the same position.

'My world would have come to an end if you hadn't arrived,' said Brinley in heartfelt tones, elaborating on the deliberate drama of his speech by raising his two hands to the heavens as well. Wearing a maroon velvet jacket over a crisp white shirt with a multi-coloured cravat tucked into the neckline, neatly hiding the fact that the once very handsome Brinley now had the loose throat of an elderly toad, Brin was the picture of risky Bohemianism, still seeming to revel in the fact that he was daring enough not to wear a tie. He clearly did not realise times had changed so much that currently it was the height of rebellion to be seen out in a suit and tie. In one hand, Brin held a coffee cup which Fleur knew well enough contained more whisky than it did caffeine, the other a dark-papered Sobranie cigarette.

'Yes, indeed,' said Fleur casually, taking off her stone-coloured raincoat, flecked with darker beige spots where freezing raindrops had landed on it. She wasn't deliberately snubbing Brinley – it was just that if she reacted to every fulsome compliment he threw her way, she would have no hours in the day left to do anything else. 'Where's Spook?'

'She returns anon,' said Brin, referring to their curiously named assistant, the only other permanent member of staff to share the cramped office above the shop where Fleur and Brinley worked. Fleur's office in the States had been immaculate, a vision in muted colours, tubular steel, matt leather and plate glass. At Boulden's, she made do with a repro Victorian desk with a creaky old computer perched on top, a piece of equipment which frequently went into furious sulks, refusing to acknowledge passwords, find documents or open spreadsheets. Rolls of yellowing fax paper lay about the office, decoratively sprinkled with ash from Brin's endless cigars, empty champagne bottles jostled for space with long forgotten polystyrene takeout cups of coffee, while lever arch files marked '1966' spilled their contents on the work surfaces. During her first week, Fleur had attempted to instil some order into the office, but finding it a task akin to pushing a boulder uphill had given up and adopted an air of Zen calm about her chaotic surroundings instead.

'Nice weekend, Brin?' Fleur asked, once she had arranged herself to her satisfaction in her corner of the office.

'Oh, dear girl!' said Brin, throwing his eyes to heaven and his bottom into an Edwardian mahogany armchair whose torn plum brocade upholstery was spewing forth padding. 'Dear girl,' he repeated, taking a sizeable swig from his coffee cup. Fleur swivelled round on the office chair she had insisted Brin buy her.

'Are you all right, Brin?' she asked, looking at him properly for the first time. 'You look rather pale.' His hands seemed to be shaking and his usually rosy face had taken on a pallid hue.

'Fleur, my darling,' he said slowly, 'I am not at all okay. I am an old fool and an idiot and I fear I have done something which may prove my undoing.'

'What is it?' said Fleur. His serious tone was very different from the usual light mockery with which Brin normally spoke.

He sighed deeply and, for added pathos, gave a large sniff.

'I'm ruined, Fleur,' he announced. 'Ruined! And I have no one to blame but myself.'

'Brinley!' exclaimed Fleur, who was starting to suspect that for once he was being genuine. 'What have you done?'

'Something terrible,' said Brin. 'Something awful, Fleur.'

'It can't be that bad,' said Fleur soothingly. 'Is there anything I can do to help?'

His watery blue eyes flickered upwards, taking in the Broomfield wall clock hanging opposite.

'Nine o'clock,' he said thoughtfully. 'You might just make it.'

'Make what?' said Fleur curiously. Brinley seemed to pull himself together.

'The plane,' he said in a more decisive tone of voice. 'You might just do it, if you leave now. Eleven fifteen it goes. Fleur, for the love of God tell me you won't say no to what I am about to ask you.'

'Yes,' said Fleur impulsively.

'Yes what?' said Brin.

'Yes, I won't say no,' said Fleur rashly. 'To whatever it is.' What the hell Monday, she thought to herself. It had to be more fun than cataloguing last week's invoices.

'Oh, Fleur, I worship you!' said Brinley, falling to the floor in front of her. He seized her hand and was kissing it passionately when a tall young woman with red hair walked in.

'Well, well, love's young dream,' she said.

'Spook!' said Brinley, jumping to his feet with surprising agility for a man of his age and build. 'Get on the phone and book Fleur a return ticket to Antigua, leaving on today's flight. No, stop, book her a taxi to the airport first, do the flight while she's on the road.'

'Yes boss!' Spook saluted. 'And Fleur, good thing you left your passport on your desk and I put it in the safe for you. Otherwise you'd be going nowhere.'

'When did I do that?' said Fleur in surprise. She thought she was the efficient person at Boulden's, not Spook.

'Last week, after you went to the bank,' said Spook. 'Aren't you cute in your photo?'

'Thank you, Spook,' interjected Brin gravely. 'Please get on the phone and stop chatting. I have urgent business I must discuss with dear Fleur.'

Dear Fleur was wondering what she had let herself in for – international disaster relief wasn't quite what she had been expecting.

'A sale has gone horribly wrong,' continued Brin. 'And you, Fleur Bonner, exquisite maiden that you are, may be the only person who can save it.'

'I didn't know we had a branch in the Caribbean,' said Fleur steadily.

'It was a *private* affair,' said Brinley, stressing the word private. 'It really had nothing to do with Boulden's. I just brokered the sale – it was a favour for an old friend in Monaco.'

'I see,' said Fleur. Many of Brinley friends seemed to operate on the Mustique–Monte Carlo axis, happy to go anywhere the gin flowed, the sun shone and the taxman held no sway. 'What did this sale consist of?'

'Well, it was a Monet,' said Brin, not looking Fleur in the eye.

'A Monet!' Fleur nearly screamed the word. 'Brin, what did you think you were doing?'

'Never mind that,' said Brinley, who was now standing by the office window, twitching back the blind to see if Fleur's taxi was in the street. 'Look, here's your cab. Come on, come on, we don't have time to waste.' He ushered her down the stairs.

'Brin, I still don't know what you're expecting me to do,' said Fleur as Brinley hurried her onward.

'It's very simple,' said Brin airily. 'When you get to Antigua, you'll find his boat – it's called *The Dalai Lama* – at the English Harbour. Just hop on board, tell him there's been a mistake and that we'll pay any money he likes as long as we get the painting back. Unharmed.'

'Why would he have harmed it?' said Fleur as Brin propelled her through the shop door on to the pavement.

'Oh! Didn't I say?' Brinley struck his forehead with his hand. 'Dearest Fleur, that's the reason we need the painting back. Apparently, he wants to cut it down to have a screen to cover his television made out of it. If this gets out – the disgrace! No one will ever do business with me again if I'm the man who let a Monet get cut in half. I'd be ruined – for ever!' He opened the cab door and, with the practice of many years of sending females yonder, adeptly loaded Fleur into the back. 'And, er, so would the Monet,' he added as an afterthought.

'What's his name?' said Fleur. 'The man who bought the painting?'

'Er,' said Brin, looking confused. 'Ritz-ee, I think. But that could be Ditz-ee. I'm not sure. You'll just have to ask around. He's a pop star, someone will know.' He slammed the door shut. 'Goodbye, Fleur. God speed!' He waved cheerily as the taxi pulled away from the kerb.

Settling back against the cushions, Fleur reflected that her time at Boulden's was meant to be a quiet opportunity for her to get her life into perspective. As she was headed for an airport with just a handbag as luggage, preparing to make a twenty-four-hour round trip to the Caribbean, she would have to conclude that her plan for a peaceful life was not yet coming to pass.

'Aha!' said Elvis triumphantly as his boat turned the corner into a bay where perfectly white sands received the constant

14

adulation of a warm turquoise sea. Some distance from the beach lay a huge gleaming yacht, the roof bristling with antennae, the decks strewn with brown bodies lapping up the end of the day's sun. 'Dat's him.' He cheerfully steered his tiny little dot of boat straight towards the menacingly large ocean craft whose name, *The Dalai Lama*, was picked out in black italic letters on the stern.

'Oh no,' said Fleur weakly. Until this point, the whole day had been such an absurd scramble, she had had no time to wonder what she would actually say, if and when she found her target. Brinley hadn't exactly given her a whole heap of clues as to how to proceed.

'Well,' said Elvis. 'You're here now.'

'Too right, Elvis,' said Fleur, gathering her courage. 'I just better get on with it.'

Fleur had little experience of nautical protocol so she wasn't entirely sure of the right way to board a ship as an uninvited and unexpected guest. The bemused faces that peered down at her from the larger boat seemed no clearer either.

'Good afternoon.' Fleur's clear voice drifted upwards on the evening breeze. She felt quite ridiculous, standing up in Elvis's boat, wearing rolled-up suit trousers and an office shirt. But she pressed gamely on. 'I have come to see Mr Ritz-ee.' Fleur had found his name thanks to a quick perusal of the CDs on offer at Heathrow. Most of Ritz-ee's hit songs seemed to revolve around themes of severe alienation, misery, inner city crime and deprivation, none of which Fleur felt Ritz-ee himself would be suffering from right now.

The beautiful, smooth faces peering over the edge of the boat twittered to one another. One lithe brown sprite in a scrap of a lilac bikini scampered away to return with a man who Fleur supposed must be the skipper.

'Who are you?' he asked, in a not unfriendly manner. Even

security personnel working in the Caribbean found it hard not to adopt a more relaxed, laid back tone.

'My name is Fleur Bonner and I have come from Boulden's art gallery in Piccadilly, London, United Kingdom,' said Fleur as Elvis murmured approvingly, 'You go, girl!' under his breath. The little boat rocked slightly. 'I have urgent business with Mr Ritz-ee concerning a painting he recently purchased with the help of Brinley Boulden, my boss.'

'Well, Miss Bonner,' said the skipper, laughing as he unfurled a rope ladder, 'in that case, I think we better let you come aboard.'

'Could I just use the, er, ladies?' Fleur asked the skipper, who had shown her into the mega-yacht's sitting room, an area of endless white sofas interrupted by tasteful dark wood furniture with no misguided design attempts to play on a faux nautical theme. At the back of the room hung a vast, sleek plasma screen television, but Fleur was relieved to see that, as yet, it had no cover made from a world famous painting, hocked by one of Brinley's less reputable mates.

'On the left, that way,' said the skipper, pointing. Following the direction of his rope-gnarled finger, Fleur found herself in a corridor where a strange high-pitched noise was floating about. She tried a few doors on the left as instructed but found herself first of all in the broom cupboard, then in someone's bedroom, before finally one swung open to reveal a marble bathroom.

'Thank God,' said Fleur, who was feeling quite desperate, dashing in, only to find she was not alone. Standing stark naked in front of the mirror, singing rather tunelessly into a hairbrush was a man Fleur semi-recognised from the photos on his CD covers at the airport.

'Hi,' said Fleur, meeting his eyes in the mirror.

'Well, hello yourself,' said Ritz-ee, turning round to face her. With the hand holding the hairbrush posed casually against his groin, he leaned back on the marble washbasin, his taut, perfectly sculpted body a mass of squiggly inked tattoos. A white boy who had made it big by sounding as if he was black, Ritz-ee had come a very long way from the crumbling, diseased concrete jungle of outer East London where he was born. His grey-blue dark-lashed eyes flicked up and down Fleur's body as though surprised to see a woman wearing clothes.

'Can I help?' he said calmly, as though this were an everyday occurrence.

'I was just looking . . .' for the toilet, Fleur was about to say when she was struck by a thought. In her experience of international rock stars – which was quite a bit greater than her appearance and lifestyle might suggest – it was extremely rare that you got a chance to talk to them alone. Usually they were surrounded by gaggles of other people, always very eager to behave as though they were promoting the star's interests by giving stupid advice. If she let Ritz-ee get dressed and meet her in the sitting room, she had no doubt that the scores of model girlfriends, lawyers, advisers and agents currently sunbathing their little tushes on deck would all want a say in the matter of the Monet. If she talked to him here, she had a chance of making her point uninterrupted. 'For you.' She finished the sentence. 'Fleur Bonner, assistant to Brinley Boulden, the man who sold you that painting.'

'I see,' Ritz raised a pierced eyebrow. 'And now you have found me.' He gave her a lazy smile. His self-confidence was supreme – the man who had rapped his way into millions was clearly not much beset with personal doubt.

'Yes,' said Fleur briskly. She longed to ask him to put on a towel but felt it better that she didn't. 'Mr Ritz-ee—'

'Ritz, please,' said the man himself. Casually, he lifted the hand holding the hairbrush and started to rearrange the locks on his head, his eyes never leaving Fleur's face as he did so.

'Ritz,' said Fleur coolly, ignoring his exposed pelvis. 'You have bought a Monet, a painting which is not only worth a considerable sum of money as an investment but also forms part of a great artistic heritage.'

'Ye-es,' said Ritz. 'Carry on.' Fleur noted that he had become used to giving orders.

'We've heard that you intend to reduce the size of the painting,' said Fleur bluntly. 'Which would be a great shame as it would significantly alter the composition of the piece.'

Ritz looked in no way abashed. 'What is a great shame, darlin',' he drawled, 'is that posh git Brinley sold me a painting twice the size he said it was. It's too big to fit on the boat.'

'That's still no reason to cut it in half,' said Fleur, parrying his thrust. She wasn't that surprised to hear a fundamental error on the part of Brinley and his chum lay at the heart of all this. 'And even less reason to make it into a television screen.'

Ritz gave a bark of laughter. 'You heard about that? Christ, I can't sneeze without someone the other side of the world making a comment.'

'What I would suggest you do,' said Fleur, not waiting to be asked, 'is this.' Something commanding in her tone made Ritz pay attention. 'Find a suitable home for the Monet – which shouldn't be waterborne anyway as the damage to the paintwork would be terrible. Why don't you lend it to a museum? That way the painting will be properly looked after in a manner which means it won't depreciate in value and you will have the bonus of appearing philanthropic. Then,' she continued crisply, 'look around – I can help you with this – for two smaller paintings, possibly pieces of contemporary art, which would fit the spaces you have available on your yacht.'

'What do you get out of this?' asked Ritz.

'I'm sorry?' said Fleur, momentarily thrown.

'A percentage?' hazarded Ritz. 'A cash bonus? What is it?'

'Well, nothing,' said Fleur in surprise. 'I'm just doing my job, I suppose. I don't think a four-hour holiday in Antigua counts as much of a perk.'

For the first time, Ritz-ee smiled. He nodded and rubbed his chin with his hand. And then he laughed to himself. Reaching out, he took a white towel and wrapped it round his thin, muscular hips.

'All right, Fleur,' he said at last. 'You win. The Monet goes to a museum, you find me two replacements. Anything else you want me to do, while you're at it?'

'Er, no, Ritz,' said Fleur. 'That was all. Thank you. Thank you so much.'

'A pleasure,' said Ritz-ee.

'I must be off,' said Fleur.

'Do drop in again sometime,' said Ritz politely.

'I will,' replied Fleur. 'Next time I'm passing.'

'It's like being visited by Wonder Woman,' said Ritz, turning back to his reflection in the mirror. 'Wonder Woman of the art world.' He resumed his singing to the mirror and Fleur slipped quietly out.

2

Fleur's winter break in Antigua, lasting as it did for just a few hours, gave her little time to enjoy the open skies, brilliant sunshine and air of contentment in the Caribbean, so different from post-Christmas London, languishing under a fog of over-spent credit cards and horribly expanded waistlines. As soon as she emerged from her bathroom interview with superstar rapper Ritz-ee, it was time for her to bid the world of indolent luxury goodbye and chug away with Elvis, patiently waiting in his inferior boat. While the skipper of *The Dalai Lama* tried to persuade her to stay a little longer, Fleur was eager to be on her way. Her flight left that night and she doubted very much that she had any leeway in her travel schedule. Scrambling down the rope ladder once more, she told Elvis that their mission had been a success, and they set off to motor round the north-west coast of the island to the airport, where Fleur boarded the night flight back to London.

While Brin had made every effort to ensure Fleur arrived as quickly as possible in Antigua, he was clearly less concerned with her return journey. Although she had travelled outwards in comfortable business class, she came back cattle, in the non-reclining seat at the back next to the toilet. It wasn't even a direct flight home – she detoured via Miami where she spent a few dark hours attempting to sleep in a waiting room before boarding a plane bound for England. Since an electrical storm broke as they were taxi-ing down the runway, take-off was delayed for hours. To amuse passengers while they sat on the plane waiting for the storm to pass, the stewardess switched on the in-flight entertainment, so Fleur was treated to a film about a gargantuan ecological disaster striking the east coast of America and wiping out anyone with the misfortune to be in an aeroplane when it struck.

It was already evening by the time Fleur straggled back to Battersea, where she lived in a red-brick block of apartments overlooking the tree-lined expanses of Battersea Park. The very small flat she was currently renting belonged to a friend of hers, recently posted abroad. Fleur had the sudden decision of his company to send him to Bombay to thank for the fact that she actually had somewhere to stay when she arrived back in London with a few heavy suitcases and not much else to her name. She could have gone home to live with her mother and stepfather, but she feared appearing like the failure adult child, unable to cope on her own, so despite the lure of family comfort she was determined to forge a new and independent life for herself in London.

The flat in Battersea was indisputably tiny but the size didn't bother her – it was considerably larger than her studio in New York, it was infinitely quieter and more peaceful and, for the moment, quite a lot cheaper. And, most important, it had become available just when she needed it. One of the surprises for Fleur when she came home from the States was to find how greatly her friends' domestic circumstances had changed. When she left, they were still at the flat-sharing stage, living in student squalor on executive budgets. An extra Fleur camped out on the sofa would not have disturbed any of those laid-back householders, who would have been happy to let her stay in return for a little washing up and food shopping, or simply as another person to take down to the pub.

But those messy, jolly days of communal habitation were largely over, the groups having subdivided into units of two who had mostly bought terraced houses in newly fashionable suburbs which they then did up to within an inch of their lives. Awash with stripped wooden floors, Heal's lampshades and stainless steel cookers, and tastefully decked out in shades of white, these were places where Fleur would be welcome for a weekend but no more.

So the flat in Battersea, like the job at Boulden's, seemed another lucky strike in a difficult world. On sunny mornings, Fleur sat on the wrought-iron balcony, drinking coffee and watching the leaves blow across the park, and reflected that despite the unwanted and unpleasant turn her life had taken it could be a hell of a lot worse, even though Boulden's would not have been her first choice of job, nor Battersea her ideal spot to live in London. A pretty but mixed area where relentless middle class rehabilitation over the past few years had laid a gloss of French polish over a difficult and poverty-stricken postcode, Battersea struck Fleur as an uneasy blend of upper middle class social aspirations with desperate sink poverty. All the useful shops selling bread and milk or hammers and nails had been replaced with boutiques flogging scented candles, estate agents and holistic healers. While on the surface the gentrification appeared complete once the pub on the corner was revamped to serve pan-fried foie gras rather than pickled eggs, it was only superficial. All the expensive bath oils and bottles of vintage Merlot in the world hadn't taken away the bleak housing estates behind the eagerly renovated apartment blocks and rows of Victorian terraced houses which clung to the edge of the park.

Normally, it was very quiet in Fleur's block, but this evening

the thump of music flowing down the stairs met the tired
traveller and her pounding head halfway up. As she struggled up the stairs, the music got louder and louder until her
head seemed to throb in time with the beat. She let herself
into her apartment, hoping to relax after the stresses of the
last two days. But the music was pouring through the ceiling
like a sewage flood, drenching her in its unwelcome effluent.
The song – if, Fleur thought crossly, that is what it could be
called – stopped and she had a brief moment of respite before
it started again.

By nature, she was really not a confrontational person but
this was too much even for her. She swigged down a glass of
water with two paracetamol, took off her suit jacket and set
off upstairs to the flat from where the party noise came.
Rapping smartly on the door, she prepared herself to speak
in her special frosty voice for dealing with difficult clients, but
when the door opened she found she herself completely
unprepared for what came next.

'F. Bonner!' he cried with joy. A tall man with café au lait
skin and very short black hair was beaming at her. 'You came!
I was just giving up hope!'

Fleur had seen this young man bounding in and out of her
building, sometimes in running gear, at other times in smart
but slightly eccentric suits. He seemed to have an endless
succession of different sports cars, as though he changed his
wheels every week. It had perplexed her that someone who
was presumably extremely wealthy, given how many cars he
owned, would live in one of the tiny flats at the top of the
building. The apartments got smaller and cheaper the higher
up you went – Fleur was on the fifth floor and the sports car
driver was on the sixth.

'Come in, come in!' he said. 'I'm so delighted you could
make it – I'm afraid some people have been here for a while

but I'm sure you can forgive them if they seem a bit weary. It's not quite in the training manual but I thought we could have a good social occasion and start work in earnest on Saturday. This probably isn't what you were expecting, is it?'

'Not at all,' said Fleur truthfully. She had dutifully followed him into his minuscule sitting room where a very eclectic assortment of people were standing around, clutching glasses of wine. In the centre of the room a large woman was holding court while smoking furiously, a circle of obedient listeners gathered around her. At the edge of the group, looking rather supercilious, stood another woman whom even through the dim lighting Fleur easily recognised as a type, namely the type that Brinley was so good at persuading to part with their money. With her beautifully cut hair, expensive casual clothes and long, perfectly manicured fingers, rings flashing with costly stones, she was just the sort of woman that Fleur had noticed browsing for art bargains, something lovely for around the £50,000 mark to hang in the dining room.

Dancing – if that was the word for the random selection of movements he was making – near to the group was a man who was quite simply the most breathtakingly malcoordinated person Fleur had ever seen. His limbs seem to move completely independently of each other with no thought for the overall picture. He lurched around, sending glasses and small pieces of furniture flying, only to give up once he cannoned into one of the other guests and spilt their drink.

'Come into the kitchen,' her host said, ushering her into the smallest cooking zone she had ever seen. If it hadn't been for the fact that it was entirely festooned with empty wine bottles, it looked as if it might once have been extremely tidy. He closed the door.

'Good, now I can hear you speak. So, what does the F. of F. Bonner stand for?'

'It's Fleur,' said Fleur.

'Oh, thank God,' he cried. 'I'm so glad it's not Felicity!'

'What's wrong with Felicity?'

'It's a bad, bad name for bad people,' he said mysteriously. 'I'd have been forced to blackball your membership of the Battersea Park New Runners' Marathon Club. As you are called Fleur, I shall grant you lifetime membership instead.'

'What?' said Fleur.

'The Runners' Club,' he repeated. 'I'm Ben, by the way. I put some leaflets through your door.'

'Oh yes,' said Fleur, catching on. 'The checklist.' For the past few weeks, her letterbox had been stuffed with brightly coloured bits of paper, which exhorted her to take the 'Lifestyle Checklist'. 'Do you lack purpose?' the first question had been, with a little printed box to tick for yes. 'Do you ever wonder what life's all about?' had been the next. 'Has Christmas left you fat, flabby and lethargic?' 'Do you long to do something magnificent?' At the bottom, it asked you to add up the yes ticks.

'What did you score?' said Ben.

'Ten out of ten,' said Fleur. When she had looked at the other side of the piece of paper to determine what her score meant, she had been rather taken aback to read: 'You are desperately in need of a challenging and motivating programme to take away your lacklustre and unenthused attitude towards being alive. How about running the London marathon this year? LET THE MARATHON CHANGE YOUR LIFE.' At the bottom of the leaflet, there had been some guff about a new training club, who could join, how to do so and whom to contact which, needless to say, Fleur didn't bother to read, having no intention of taking the checklist seriously.

'I'm so pleased you want to run the marathon,' said Ben.

'Run the marathon?' said Fleur in surprise. 'Do I?'

'Yes you do,' said Ben firmly. 'You scored ten out of ten on the checklist.'

'I was feeling very pessimistic that day,' explained Fleur. 'Normally, I'm much more cheerful. Anyway, I'm not at all athletic.'

'Nonsense, you're the perfect shape for running,' said Ben. 'Small and slender, gives you a great advantage when it comes to the marathon. It's going to be so exciting and you will get such a lot from the experience, both the training, the marathon and raising money for charity.'

'No, but really,' persisted Fleur, 'I just came up to ask you . . .'

'I'll ring your doorbell every morning for the training session,' said Ben, a wicked smile on his face. 'Whether you say yes or not. So I think you better join us, don't you, Fleur Bonner? I could be quite annoying otherwise.'

'Why me?' asked Fleur in confusion. She wasn't the person she would pick out from the crowd to nominate as Olympic athlete in waiting. At school, she had been the weedy kid, useless and unfit, the one left till very last to be picked for every team as her presence virtually guaranteed instant failure.

'You look like a nice person,' said Ben gravely. He leaned down and whispered in her ear. 'And I'm going to need an ally if I'm going to get this bunch through the marathon.'

He opened the door to the sitting room so they could see the collected odd bods within. He closed the door again and looked grave.

'Please help me. I put on the checklist leaflet that joiners should be fairly fit, be able to run five to eight miles already and have an interest in health in fitness. And look who turned up! They've drunk me out of house and home already and it's going to take days to air this place to get rid of all the smoke.'

'Why don't you just tell them they're not suitable?' asked Fleur, who was rather baffled by the situation. She couldn't imagine why this man would have such a pressing need to make very out of condition people imagine they could take on the biggest fitness challenge of all.

'That's just the problem,' said Ben. 'I made a promise and I need to keep it.' He winced. 'I pledged a hospice for sick children that I would raise money for them at the marathon. So they applied for places to run this year and I'm in charge of filling them and raising the money. So you see I don't feel I have much choice.'

'For children,' said Fleur pensively. 'I suppose that's rather different.' She reflected. 'Couldn't you just give them the money?'

'If I had it,' said Ben, 'I would give it to them straight away. But I don't, which is why I'm trying to raise it instead.' He was speaking slowly as though she was an idiot.

'But what about all those cars?' said Fleur.

'Oh,' said Ben, understanding. 'They're not mine, Fleur. I work in promotions for a car company – they're all part of the job, and sadly I can't just sell them and pass on the profit. Children, Fleur. With incurable diseases. And their families.'

Fleur looked Ben in the eye and prepared herself to say, politely but firmly, that she could not possibly run the marathon, however worthy the cause. She opened her mouth but something quite different came out.

'I'd love to,' she heard herself say. 'It's something I've always thought about doing.'

She closed her mouth once more, stunned by the lie she had just told. It was a supersize lie as well – to date, her only point of contact with the marathon had been watching it on television, wrapped in feelings of comfortable smugness that she would never submit herself to such torture.

'Hooray!' shouted Ben, jumping off the ground with both feet before landing and hugging Fleur. 'I knew you wouldn't let me down. Fabulous girl! Well done.'

'I . . . I . . .' said Fleur. What on earth was she doing? Why had she let her big mouth run away with her?

'You,' said Ben holding her by the shoulders and beaming into her face, 'have made my day, week, month, year! I love you, Fleur Bonner. You are awesome.'

His face was so open and honest, the nutmeg sprinkle of freckles across his nose, the barely there black curls on his head, the dazzling smile, that Fleur felt a little dizzy.

'What a hero,' he continued.

'Gosh,' said Fleur, who was rather overwhelmed. Museum curators rarely have the pleasure of hearing themselves described as heroic. 'What do I do now?'

'Nothing,' said Ben. 'Just enjoy the evening, come and meet the other runners, try not to die in a cloud of cigarette smoke in my living room, that kind of thing.'

'And it's for a good cause, right?' said Fleur nervously, unable to quite believe what she had just committed herself to.

'Absolutely,' said Ben. 'Every step you take, someone benefits. What could be better than that?'

'Not much,' agreed Fleur. 'Not much at all.'

'Excellent,' said Ben decisively. 'So, with no further ado, let me introduce you.' He flung the kitchen door open, pushed Fleur into the sitting room and announced, 'Ladies and gentlemen, meet Fleur, the newest and the last member of the Battersea Park New Runners' Marathon Club!'

3

'Hot news, Fleur!' exclaimed Spook, the flame-haired office assistant, as Fleur arrived late to work at Boulden's the day after the Runners' Club party. Fleur wasn't even remotely apologetic about getting in at eleven – after all, she worked so hard on some days that she liked to compensate by having a slow start on others. While this was a logical and quite reasonable working pattern to adopt, it was also seriously out of character for Fleur. In her previous job, she had worked ridiculously long hours, ploughing all her love, dedication and energy into the museum. Not that Fleur would accept it as true, but in many ways getting sacked had been the best thing that had ever happened to her. Before the sacking, she had been meticulous to a fault, punctual, extremely hard-working and rather obsessive in her quest for perfection and thus had neglected to get herself anything approaching a life. After the blow fell and Fleur realised that all her best efforts had not protected her from the vagaries of unkind fate, she loosened up considerably. Her need to be in control lessened, she relaxed, she became impulsive and light-hearted and gave vent to a side of her which had remained buried all these tight, rigid, formal years of hobnobbing with the aristocracy of the museum world. Having tried, in that world, so very hard to get everything right only to be so harshly rejected and

31

knocked back, Fleur was now resolved to enjoy herself a little more and worry a little less, a recipe for a happy life if ever there was one.

Spook was looking unusually starry-eyed today, evidently bursting with some piece of racy gossip which she would doubtless impart the minute she got a chance. As this was a daily occurrence, Fleur ignored her and started to unpack her briefcase. Spook immediately came and sat on the edge of her desk, crossing her very long legs, causing Fleur's computer to wobble angrily.

'Guess what?' she said excitedly.

'I'm trying, I'm trying, I'm trying,' said Fleur, not looking up. 'And oh no, I've failed, you're going to have tell me.'

'Go on,' said Spook, prodding her. 'Have a go.' Spook – real name Virginia – was like a posh, exuberant puppy – entertaining and cute but not always that helpful in an office context.

'Okay,' said Fleur, accepting that she would get little done until she did. '*Heat* magazine says you and Prince William are star-crossed lovers.'

'Oh, God, Fleur, you're so frivolous,' complained Spook. 'Guess again. But properly this time.'

'Well, I'm not playing if you're going to insult me,' said Fleur mildly.

'No, no, no,' said Spook quickly. 'Frivolous in a good way. Have another turn.'

'Oh, all right,' said Fleur. It was more fun than working, after all. 'Erm, let me think. I know! You've sold one of your titles.'

'If only!' sighed Spook in dramatic fashion. 'Who'd want them?'

'Plenty of people,' said Fleur. 'Just put an advert in *Loot* and they'll be queuing round the block. I'll run the auction for you, if you like.'

'Oh, cool,' said Spook enthusiastically. 'That's a great idea, genius girl.'

'Let me know how you get on,' said Fleur, hoping she had successfully diverted Spook on to pastures new.

'Ha!' said Spook. 'You don't get out of it that easily, young lady.'

'Young?' said Fleur, who at thirty-two was at least ten years older than Spook. 'Who are you, my maiden aunt?'

'I'm a person whose maturity is not measured by their tender youth,' replied Spook haughtily.

'I see,' said Fleur, who sometimes tried to be stern with Spook but usually failed entirely. 'So, Obi Wan Kenobi, what's cooking?'

'Ready?' said Spook.

'Couldn't be more so,' agreed Fleur.

'Okay,' said Spook, fixing Fleur with her enormous emerald eyes. 'Your. Dad. Called.'

'Is that it?' said Fleur in disbelief. 'Is that the hot news?'

'And. I. Spoke. To. Him,' said Spook, clearly in seventh heaven. 'And he called me darling!' She was ecstatic now.

'He calls most women darling,' said Fleur dryly. 'Saves him getting his wives mixed up.'

'Can I meet him?' said Spook, leaning forward so her mane of auburn curls tumbled round her face.

'Certainly not,' said Fleur. As Spook pouted, Fleur added, 'Trust me, Spook, it's you I'm thinking of.'

'Oh, well,' said Spook, twiddling her hair. She never held any sort of emotion for too long. 'What I can't believe,' she said reflectively, 'is that he's your father. Or rather that *you* are *his* daughter.'

'Neither can anyone else,' said Fleur, not even remotely offended. At least Spook was honest. It wasn't easy having a megastar for a dad and Fleur had grown all too used to the look of incredulity on people's faces when they found out her father was the grand old man of rock and roll. They would take in Fleur's neat, sensible outfits, her shoulder-length shiny hair, her air of competent self-containment, and feel somehow cheated. Where were the track marks on her arms? The semi-crazed expression, the stretch limo, the internet sex tapes, the avant-garde clothing, the hellraiser boyfriend? Could this really be the product of Jed Harris, sixties hippy, seventies disco maniac, eighties techo king, nineties crashing failure and noughties revivalist? Surely, bewildered people would think, looking at Fleur Bonner, we deserve more from the offspring of rock and roll than this rather ordinary-looking girl?

Of course, there were a bevy of other Harris progeny who fulfilled every criterion and more of the national expectations of rock kiddies, ranging from the beautiful but insane to the prolific and just mildly disturbed. It was a rare month that did not feature one or other of them somewhere in the news-papers or magazines, modelling clothing collections, opening shoe shops, attending parties with Hollywood stars or checking in to or out of rehab. But Fleur, who was modestly proud to be one of the few born – if not conceived – in wedlock, was never among their number.

Largely, this was due to the excellent influence of her mother, the delectable Rowena Bonner, who'd been a model and actress in the early seventies, a time when that job descrip-tion actually meant something. Rowena was endowed not only with the stunning good looks needed to get into a marriage with Jed Harris but also with enough good sense to get out of it quite smartly when she saw the direction that marriage was taking. A gentle creature whose interests lay more in the areas of homoeopathy, child rearing and gardening than in throwing televisions out of windows, all night parties with groupies and heroin, one day Rowena packed all her possessions into a rucksack, tucked baby Fleur under her arm and went home to live with her parents in St Albans. She divorced Jed by post and got on with giving her daughter the most normal, happy and stable upbringing she could. Along the way, she set up a successful organic skin care company, married her accountant and founded a home for unwanted pets as she said she knew far too well what it felt like to be just for Christmas and not for life.

If Rowena ever thought of Jed, it was with deep relief that he had let her go so easily. A life spent fighting to stay married to him, through the endless affairs, addictions, illegitimate children, broken friendships, hangers-on and tabloid photographers trying to take snaps of her bottom to see if she'd got cellulite yet would have been no life at all. Nothing – not the number one hits, the platinum albums, the first class travel, the honours from Buckingham Palace and certainly not the money, of which she had never asked nor been given a penny – could have made it better for Rowena. As it was, she had peace of mind, and that, she had decided, was the only thing really worth having.

'Was there a message?' Fleur asked her assistant, who she noted was humming 'Shoot Me To Heaven', one of Jed's greatest and most enduring hits.

'Just to tell you that He Called,' said Spook dreamily. 'Oh, and maybe he said something about lunch.'

'What do you mean "maybe"?' said Fleur. 'Either he did or he didn't.'

'Sorry, Fleur.' Spook looked abashed. 'It was just his voice, it was so delicious I couldn't really take in what he was saying.'

'Hmmph,' was all Fleur said in reply. Age might be withering her father in person but it clearly wasn't having any impact on his pulling power. More worryingly, the phone calls from Jed were becoming far more frequent. In the past, he had only got in touch when he was high, for an occasional long, rambling, barely comprehensible conversation. But these days the newly reformed Jed, a full-on Alcoholics and Narcotics Anonymous nazi, was becoming almost a telephone pest, something Fleur found distinctly unnerving. Having grown up without her father in person – during her childhood, a visit from Jed to the wholesome, quiet, organic household where Fleur lived was as likely as a shooting star falling all the way to earth – she had, inevitably, idolised him. Her ever-patient mother and stepfather had watched with saddened resignation as the teenage Fleur plastered posters of her father all over her bedroom. They had heard the young Fleur's desperate boasts that Jed was her father being received with scorn by other children, who clearly thought Fleur was a fantasist. 'If he's your dad,' they had taunted her, 'where is he?' There had even been the time Fleur had 'run away' to find Jed, only to be brought home, freezing cold and scared, by the police. But as Fleur grew up and her life priorities changed, Jed became less and less important to her until by the time she was at university she was able to wear, in fully ironic fashion, a trashy T-shirt with the words 'Jed Harris Is My Dad Too' on the front. The irony, of course, being that few people realised that the statement on her T-shirt, taken from a tabloid headline for a story about the multiple paternity suits levelled at Jed, was actually true in Fleur's case. When she moved to the States, she put him behind her for ever, so she thought. While Jed came to New York frequently, he didn't visit museums or have anything to do with Fleur's stuffy, highbrow coterie, just as she never hung out in the sorts of clubs or bars where she might have run into him. His world – the seamy, emotional, hyped-up, dramatic and messy lifestyle of a real rock and roll star – was light years away from the tightly controlled, graceful, elegant and subdued milieu in which Fleur moved. If she had become a librarian, she could hardly have moved further out of his orbit and into one of her own.

But now she was back in London to find not only had her father fashioned a very new lifestyle for himself but he was desperate for her to be part of it, something Fleur found most disconcerting. Lately, Jed's Alcoholics Anonymous sponsor, the person who oversaw the miraculous saving of Jed Harris from any manner of substance abuse, had been insisting that it was Jed's lack of a proper relationship with his firstborn which was standing like a road block on the path to recovery. This sponsor – whom Fleur had never met but her father invoked with such frequency and reverence that he might be a slightly lower version of Jesus Christ – was rapidly becoming the bane of Fleur's life. Were she to encounter the unfortunate fellow, she was quite determined to shove his serenity somewhere it probably hadn't been before.

'Fer-Ler-Her!' Spook's voice.

'Yup?' said Fleur.

'I just thought I'd let you know,' said Spook sweetly.

'What?' said Fleur.

'You were grinding your teeth. Oh, and Brin wants to see you. He's in the back office.'

'I've got some news too,' said Fleur casually, before she departed to find Brinley.

'Spill,' said Spook encouragingly.

'I'm running the London marathon.'

Spook didn't miss a beat. 'No you're not.'

'Yes I am,' said Fleur.

'Oh no you're not,' repeated Spook with the confidence of the pantomime chorus.

'I am!' said Fleur, knitting her brows crossly. This wasn't quite the reaction she had hoped for.

'Fleur, don't be silly,' said Spook patiently. 'You collapse in exhaustion if you stand up for too long. You need a rest after half an hour of filing.'

'I do not!' said Fleur. 'That is so untrue.'

'And you'll have to drink nasty sports drinks as well – the route won't be lined with people offering you caffe latte and a chocolate muffin, you know.'

'I used to live in New York, you know,' said Fleur, tossing back her hair.

'Fleur, residency of Manhattan does not automatically mean you are a fit person,' said Spook in chiding tones.

'I was a member of a gym,' said Fleur defiantly.

'Yeah, yeah, you went twice and paid the membership for five years, I know your sort,' said Spook. 'Anyway, you'll have to get up early for training and you know you hate that.'

'It's for a good cause,' said Fleur weakly.

'You'll rub your nipples raw, pee blood and won't be able to walk downstairs for weeks afterwards,' retorted her assistant.

Ben hadn't mentioned any of these side effects when extolling the virtues of improved fitness.

'Why can't you be like everyone else and just get a boyfriend?' said Spook. 'Actually, no, I'm remembering the egg poacher and all the trauma we lived through way back when . . .' Having seen Fleur through the break-up of one doomed relationship, Spook had no desire to encourage her to start another. 'Yes, Fleur,' she began again in a suddenly bright and positive voice. 'Running the marathon is an excellent idea. Why don't you do just that? I'll even sponsor you.'

'Thanks,' said Fleur dryly. 'Your support is greatly appreciated.'

4

The back office was a rather grand term for what was actually a kitchenette-cum-study, tacked on to the back of the shop. While the showroom which the customers saw was always immaculate – a vista of gleaming furniture, carefully hung paintings and cleverly arranged bits and bobs of antiquity – the back office was no more respectable than the chaos upstairs. A little room leading off the scruffy kitchen, where mugs with seventies floral patterns on them sat sadly waiting for the joyous day someone would actually wash them up, posed as Brin's private office. Here, among the assorted debris – steel-grey filing cabinets, leather-bound address books, a phrenologist's head, a seventeenth-century map of the world – sat Brinley, degenerately smoking a cigar as usual, sprinkling the ash wherever he so chose.

'Ah, Fleur!' said Brin, greeting her in his usual joyful manner. 'What news, my darling girl? Is culture saved from the onslaught of the barbarian horde?'

'It is,' confirmed Fleur. 'Although next time you sell a painting, I would suggest you check the dimensions very carefully.'

Brinley flashed her a rather piercing look. 'My dear,' he said in tones of muted outrage, 'I was not to know that someone would plan such an outlandish and terrible fate for an important and treasured art work.'

'Well, it's all fine now,' said Fleur. 'I've sorted everything out.' Ritz-ee's manager had called her that morning to confirm they would be lending the Monet to the National Gallery but Fleur must not divulge any details until the deal was firmly secured. Even Brinley mustn't be told, Ritz's manager had insisted. Fleur agreed without hesitation – she had, as Brinley had asked her, saved the painting from harm and she did not see that what happened next to the Monet was any of Brin's business.

'Good,' said Brin, who today was clad in a lavender pashmina, the fringed ends swooshed around his collar in what he clearly thought was a daring and provocative fashion. 'I'm so delighted you saved the day, Fleur. Thank God – you came to me like an angel from heaven,' he eulogised while Fleur felt mild boredom set in. She hoped he hadn't called her down to his office for hours of exaggerated praise – that really would be too tedious for words. 'The shame of it,' he continued, shaking his head sorrowfully. Brinley had the knack of discussing mistakes he had made himself as though they were a terrible blight caused by someone else. 'What the world would have said – it doesn't bear thinking about.'

Fortunately, Brin's musings were interrupted by the ringing of the shop buzzer. On the little closed circuit television screen used to admit clients, to her horror and disbelief, Fleur saw an altogether too familiar figure.

'Who's that?' she said to Brin, her voice sharp with sudden panic.

'It's Sean Duvall,' said Brin, pressing the button to let him in. 'He does some restoration jobs for us – I've asked him to work on my new acquisition.'

'Oh, shit,' said Fleur, who rarely swore. 'Shit, shit, shit.'

'Is there a problem?' said Brin curiously.

'No, not at all,' said Fleur in a strangulated voice.

'Are you sure?' said Brinley. They could both hear Sean's footsteps approaching through the shop.

'It's fine,' said Fleur quickly as Sean loped into the room.

'Hi, guys,' he said, taking off his woolly hat and gloves and dumping down his small rucksack, which was sprinkled with a light dusting of snow.

'Sean!' said Brin warmly. 'This is my newest member of staff, Fleur Bonner. A very distinguished lady, she comes to us all the way from the . . .'

'Fleur?' said Sean. 'Is it really you?' His brown eyes blinked several times as though he couldn't believe what he saw before him.

'Hello, Sean,' said Fleur, horribly aware that she was starting to blush. 'How are you?'

'But you went to the States,' said Sean, confusion spreading over his leonine face. He ran a hand through his mane of hair. 'You left.'

'I did,' agreed Fleur, trying to strike a light tone. 'But now I'm back.'

'But I thought you had this amazing job in New York,' continued Sean, wonderingly. 'And you would marry some rich art donor and live in a big apartment on Central Park and be one of those charity women in suits giving lunch parties . . . I'm sorry, I'm rambling.' He cut himself off. Sitting down on a rickety fold-up chair, Sean seemed to adopt the brace position so frequently displayed in unwatched airline safety videos.

'It didn't quite work out like that,' said Fleur, smarting. 'Instead, I'm sacked and single. And here.'

Brin took advantage of attention being focussed elsewhere to help himself to another slug of whisky from the filing cabinet.

'Well, well – Fleur,' said Sean, propping his head in his

hands, his elbows on his knees. 'It's been – how many years?'

'I take it you two know each other,' said Brin, breaking into the conversation.

'Yes,' said Sean, scrutinising Fleur's face. 'But I haven't seen Fleur . . . not for a while anyway . . .'

'No,' said Fleur uncomfortably, wishing she could think of something less monosyllabic to say. Her big mouth, so good at getting her into trouble, was being no use in helping her out of this somewhat embarrassing predicament. Hard as she tried to think of breezy, casual comments to cover her evident mortification, no one-liners suitable for dealing with ex-lovers who had just reappeared unexpectedly in a work context sprang to mind.

Before she left for New York, Fleur had worked at the National Portrait Gallery, where she had met Sean at a reception to celebrate the giving of a major portrait prize. A tall, lanky figure in a battered pinstripe suit, he had wandered over to where Fleur was primly discussing innovations in museum technology with one of the Great and Good and whispered in her ear, 'Let me take you away to a better world.' Fleur, distracted mid-flow from her monologue, was hard put to it not to burst out laughing, something which would have seriously disconcerted the humourless grandee she was addressing. Bringing her sales pitch to an end more swiftly than usual, she surprised that notable guest by ditching him rather promptly and taking a tour of the gallery with the mop-haired young man in the dreadful suit. It wasn't just the blue and black striped suit that was eye-catching – with it he wore a wildly clashing flowery shirt, ancient blond suede desert boots and heavy black-framed glasses. He was nothing like the sort of man Fleur normally went for, the tidy, super-clean, neatly trimmed and well-suited types with which she habitually consorted. But this man – an artist who had also trained as a restorer – was sweet and warm and funny and made her laugh and, as she discovered later that evening, possessed under the eccentric wrapping the most beautiful and agile body she had ever seen.

However, not long after Fleur and Sean met and instantly began their brief affair, Fleur was offered her job in New York and left almost immediately to begin her great new career in the States. Initially, Sean had tried to persuade her that leaving the country didn't necessarily mean their relationship had to come to an end. But Fleur was very full of her big plans and hopes for a glowing future in which Sean quickly came to see she had left no room for him. Very sadly and reluctantly, he realised he had to let her go. For Fleur, who had seen her liaison with Sean as nothing more than a light fancy anyway, it wasn't until quite a few years and bad relationships later that she understood what it was she had thrown away when she had so summarily ditched the nicest man she had ever met.

'I didn't think I'd ever see you again,' said Fleur. Sean's face was rather more creased than she remembered it, the lines of his generous smile now etched on his face when in repose, but the wide mouth, straight nose and patchy freckles were exactly the same as she remembered.

'And now here you are,' said Sean briskly, sitting up straight and suddenly busying himself by taking off his jacket, a sensible black padded affair, nothing like the purple velvet overcoat Fleur remembered as his winter wear of choice in years gone by. Under his jacket, Sean wore a neat pullover with no holes at the elbows, a shirt which had evidently been ironed, jeans and a pair of matching shoes.

'Let's get on, shall we?' said Brin, who felt the call of lunch approaching and was eager to hurry through a morning's work in order not to delay that enjoyable event.

'Yes, let's,' said Sean, who seemed to have recovered his equilibrium. Fleur said nothing. She didn't trust her own voice to speak.

'Now then,' said Brin, indicating a small piece of wood resting on top of his in-tray. 'I would like you both to take a look at this.' Dutifully, they both did, Fleur leaning forward to get a closer look, something she regretted as it brought her disconcertingly close to Sean, so close she could feel him breathing. She tried to focus all her attention on Brin's mystery object but her response to the physical proximity to Sean had become so acute, she thought he must be able to hear her heart, which had jumped suddenly on to overtime.

'Any ideas?' said Brinley. 'Come on, come on, my art geniuses! Surely you don't mean to tell me you don't know?' He sat back smugly, hands folded across his rotund stomach. 'Fleur?'

Fleur just shook her head. Usually, she would have come up with some waffle, designed to disguise her lack of knowledge. This morning, she couldn't even do that.

'Sean?' challenged Brinley.

'I would say,' said Sean slowly, tracing over the surface of the wood with his fingers, a movement which brought memories of those hands rushing back into Fleur's mind, causing her to erupt in a bright puce flush. 'Are you all right, Fleur?' Sean turned to her. 'You've gone very red.'

'I'm fine,' muttered Fleur, who was anything but.

'So, I would say,' Sean continued, 'that this is an icon, probably dates from the eighteenth century. I can't see enough to tell you who the saint is, but even so I'm going to hazard a guess it's not from Russia but maybe from Greece or the Balkans instead? I don't think it's particularly valuable on the open market although, possibly, it might be worth a lot to the right person or the right place.'

'Bravo!' Brin cheered. 'Sean, you are very good, may I say brilliant even? You are spot on. Marvellous, marvellous,' he enthused. 'Just what I thought myself,' he added, clearly delighted with this outcome.

Fleur, who was finding her own semi-silence quite oppressive by now, felt she had to make a mark on the conversation somehow.

'How did it get here?' she asked, for want of anything better to say.

'Yes, jolly good question,' said Brinley chummily, thus proving that one person's stupid query is another's intelligent probe. 'A man and his wife came into the gallery with something they wished to sell. Now, normally, as you know, I don't encourage this kind of transaction.' Brin looked very sanctimonious. 'It is far too easy to find oneself passing on goods with unsure provenance and I am always rigorous in ensuring we do not find ourselves in trouble.'

Fleur smiled faintly. Either Brinley was aware this was a downright lie, in which case he was indeed the old rogue some of Fleur's colleagues always said he was, or he didn't realise he was telling a patent untruth in which case he was drastically self-deluded.

'But this icon came with such a romantic story attached that I just couldn't refuse,' Brin went on mistily. He turned the icon over to reveal a note attached to the back of it. The writing was in faded ink, in an unfamiliar alphabet.

'What does it say?' asked Fleur, who was now determined not to let the situation get the better of her.

'The couple translated it for me,' replied Brinley. 'It says, "My father took this icon from the monastery for safe keeping when my family fled Serbia. We had only an hour to pack before we left our home for ever. My father ran to the monastery and took down the icon because the communists

were coming and he believed they would destroy it. My
father's last words were: 'Please take the icon home when the
communists have been defeated.'"'

'Wow!' said Sean, who seemed quite captivated by the tale.
'Who wrote the note?'

'The couple say the icon belonged to their great-aunt, who
emigrated to this country as a child in 1946,' said Brin. 'She
died recently, and when they were clearing out her belong-
ings they found this.'

'Couldn't they take it back themselves?' said Fleur, who
was finding the more she concentrated on the icon itself, the
easier it was becoming to revert to some kind of normality.
'I mean, now that the iron curtain no longer exists, surely
they could travel to Serbia and find out where the icon came
from?'

'I'm afraid their interest is not entirely without mercenary
content,' said Brin solemnly. 'I believe when they found the
icon, they thought they had stumbled on something which
would make them rich.'

'I don't suppose it did,' said Sean, tipping his chair backwards.

'No, I think they were disappointed with their valuation,'
said Brin. 'They argued for a while as to what to do but eventually they decided to sell it to me, even for the small sum I
offered.'

'Imagine,' mused Fleur. 'Saving an icon when you're fleeing
for your life.'

'Yeah, that's amazing,' said Sean. 'These days, people would
take their laptop.'

'Plenty of Russians arrived in Paris after the Revolution
with nothing but an icon in their suitcase,' remarked
Brinley. 'Which just shows how important they believed
their icons to be. To an orthodox believer, an icon is not

just a decorative painting, you know. It is imbued with spiritual and sacramental power. Just looking at an icon constitutes an act of worship.'

'It seems so sad,' said Fleur. 'Someone loved this icon enough to take it when they were running for their lives. And now their relatives are selling it off.'

'Don't be downcast, dear heart,' said Brinley gallantly. 'You haven't heard my plan yet.'

'What plan?' said Fleur.

'My plan to restore this icon to the monastery where it rightfully belongs,' said Brin. 'Wouldn't that be a wonderful thing to do? An act of charitable conservation? A return of rightful heritage?'

'It would be!' said Fleur, her smile breaking through what was nearly a trickle of tears, possibly brought on either by the poignant story of the icon or more probably caused by the nostalgic presence of a love she had lost through nothing more than her own fault. 'That would be such a great thing to do. Do you have any idea where it came from?'

'All the sellers could tell me is that the icon is of Saint Sava, the Serbian Orthodox national saint,' said Brinley. 'But these were second-generation immigrants with very little interest in their mother country and no grasp of family history.'

'What shall we do?' said Fleur, getting quite excited. 'Should we call the Art Loss Register, see if they have any clues?'

Brin gave her a rather shifty smile. Collaborating with the Art Loss Register, a body which was attempting to compile a database of all the art works that had mysteriously vanished into the ether, was not his favourite activity. While he had given fervent assurances to Art Loss when they had visited Boulden's that any suspicious paintings or works of art would be double-checked with them, it was unlikely he had ever upheld this promise. 'Ask no questions, tell no lies' would make a good motto for Brinley, were he ever to need one to illustrate a coat of arms.

The Art Loss Register was not so concerned with high profile items, like the recently stolen *Scream* by Munch or the Leonardo drawings pilfered from a Scottish castle, as very valuable or very famous works already had plenty of people looking for them. Their focus was on lesser known art works lost during world wars, periods of corrupt government or social chaos and upheaval which had allowed de facto looting to become commonplace. Ten years of near anarchy in Russia and her satellites meant that many valuable icons had disappeared from their rightful homes.

'Oh, Fleur, that won't be necessary,' said Brinley, attempting a merry chuckle. 'I have a plan already.' He gave a little cough to clear his throat. 'I contacted some dealers in Belgrade to see if they had any information, and . . .'

'How did you find them?' Fleur interrupted. This all sounded unusually efficient for Brinley.

'Via the internet, of course,' replied Brin. 'I am not a dinosaur, you know.'

'No, Brin,' said Sean. 'I'm sure you've made it past the ice age by now.'

'Thank you,' said Brin, misinterpreting Sean's comment as a compliment. 'And I have had results.' Sean raised his eyebrows. The corners of his wide mouth twitched. Looking at Fleur sideways, he gave her a sudden wink. So relieved was she by this first small show of friendship that she burst out laughing.

'Really, Fleur,' said Brinley rather crossly. 'You are being most peculiar today.'

'Er, must be jet lag,' said Fleur quickly.

'Been somewhere nice?' said Sean idly.

'Oh, just Antigua,' said Fleur. 'For half a day.'

'Now, Fleur,' chided Brin. 'Remember confidentiality rules.'

'Of course,' said Fleur, feeling the laughter bubble up inside her again. She stuffed it down by trying to concentrate on the icon once more, but the fact that Sean didn't seem to hate her was making her heart sing.

'Anyway,' said Brin firmly. They served bacon roly poly for lunch at his club on Wednesdays and if he didn't arrive early, he knew from bitter experience it would all be gone. 'I have found a dealer in Belgrade who is most interested in the icon – provided of course we undertake to restore it first.' Sean nodded. 'That's Sean's part of the job.'

'Do they know the monastery it came from?' asked Fleur, wondering what her part of the job would entail.

'Oh yes,' said Brinley. 'And if we get the icon to them in Belgrade, they will take it from there.'

'I see,' said Fleur, who could now hazard a good guess at what her involvement would be.

'As you did so brilliantly on your recent trip to the Caribbean,' continued Brin, 'I was very much hoping you would agree to transport the icon, once Sean has restored it, to Belgrade.'

'Couldn't we courier it?' said Fleur.

Brin pulled a face. 'Very little guarantee it would arrive,' he said dubiously. 'Serbia is only just out of sanctions and so we may have to collect a cash payment on delivery anyway.'

'Had you thought of going yourself?' said Sean innocently, his eyes very wide.

'Well of course, yes I had,' said Brin. 'But my doctor is very keen for me to avoid air travel at the moment. Until he's got the return cardiograph of my arrhythmic heartbeat, he does strongly advise against it. I can go, if you like, Fleur. I'm sure the possibility of my having a fatal heart attack en route is very slim.'

'When you put it like that, Brinley,' said Fleur, 'I can hardly say no.'

'Fantastic!' said Brin, beaming from ear to ear. 'There'll be just one more little job I need you to do while you're there.'

'Oh yes?' said Fleur. This sounded ominous.

'They've sent me these slides,' said Brin casually, handing three little transparencies to Fleur. 'These are some paintings the dealership in Belgrade would like to sell, via a London partner. I wonder if you would cast an eye over them while you're there.'

Fleur looked at the slides and handed them back. 'Don't be silly, Brin,' she said.

'I beg your pardon?' said Brinley haughtily.

'These paintings are not in Belgrade,' replied Fleur with total certainty.

'And how can you be so sure?'

'Brin, that looks like a Diego Rivera, a Seurat, and a Fantin Latour. As originals, they would be worth well over a million between them, if not more. Some little dealership in Belgrade does not have these works.'

Sean, who had taken the slides gently out of Brin's hand, gave a low whistle as he looked at them.

'Aha,' said Brin. 'Then who does?'

'I think we could find out quite easily,' said Fleur.

'All you will find out if you ask the Art Loss Register,' said Brin triumphantly, 'is that the current location of these paintings is unknown.'

'Really?' said Sean. 'But doesn't that mean they are in a private collection somewhere?'

'Exactly,' said Brin. 'But whose private collection?'

'Not one in a very poor former communist country,' said Fleur.

'You couldn't be more wrong!' said Brin. 'I forget sometimes how young you both are.' He smiled into the middle distance. 'However, I am sure you have heard of Marshal Tito, the great leader of Yugoslavia? Many, many years ago, when I was just a young art dealer, new to the business, my father told me of a rumour going around. Certain arts works were being bought in London, Paris, New York, and then vanishing from the international scene. Of course, it was all much less regulated back then. Anyway, it was whispered that the buyer of these paintings was none other than Tito building a private collection for himself.'

'How would he have had the money?' said Sean, looking puzzled.

'Oh, Tito, he was an old fox.' Brinley laughed. 'He was funded by both the USA and the USSR. He would have had plenty of hard currency. Anyway, the point is that none of those paintings have ever shown up again. Including the three you see on those slides. And yet when Tito died, the walls of his villa in the Adriatic – where visitors remember seeing some very valuable paintings on the walls – were empty.'

'But you don't know for sure that the paintings were bought for Tito, that they went to Yugoslavia or that they were ever hung in his villa?' said Fleur.

'Absolutely!' enthused Brin. 'It is one of the great mysteries of the art world. Did Tito have a collection, and if so, what happened to it? Imagine' – he leaned forward to draw them both in – 'that he did. And that it has lain buried these long years of war in the Balkans. And we at Boulden's uncover it. Now that would be something!'

'Can't argue with that,' said Sean, leaning back again.

'Are you with me?' said Brin. 'Are you willing to take part in this very great adventure?'

'Can't do any harm,' said Sean.

'I suppose not,' said Fleur. Perhaps there was something

about her planetary alignments which was causing her to get caught up in crazy schemes at the moment.

'Marvellous!' said Brin, checking his fob watch and seeing he just had time to be first in line in the lunch queue at the club if he hurried. 'Dear friends, I must fly! Do your best for the icon, Sean, and Fleur, buy a guidebook to Belgrade! Toodle-oo!' He danced out of the shop with the peculiar gait of an ample man oddly endowed with very small feet.

Sean turned his back on Fleur as he started packaging up the icon to take it away, wrapping it very gently in soft cloth to prevent flakes of gold paint from floating off the painting. Fleur stood up and waited foolishly for him to turn to her.

'I'll call you when it's ready,' he said, not looking round as he inserted the icon into a flat carrying case he had produced from his rucksack.

'Okay,' said Fleur, wondering if this was to be it. 'Do you believe this story of Tito's missing collection?' She tried to sound animated and chatty but failed miserably, coming across more like a cardboard Dalek.

'I really wouldn't know. I'm just a conservator,' said Sean evenly. 'You're the art expert, Fleur.'

Fleur winced. It looked as though he hadn't forgiven her after all.

'No need to wait, I can see myself out,' said Sean, still not facing her. 'I think you can trust me.'

'Of course,' said Fleur. 'Of course. I'll leave you to it.' But still she lingered. Sean finished wrapping the icon and put his jacket on.

'It's nice to see you again,' she said, desperate to engage him in some sort of dialogue before he left. 'You're looking very well.'

'You too,' said Sean politely. 'I hope it works out for you, now you're back.'

'Would you like to have dinner sometime?' The words came out in a rush.

Sean paused. 'We'd love to,' he said slowly.

'We?' Fleur couldn't stop herself from saying.

'My girlfriend,' said Sean. 'Bella. We're living together.'

'Oh,' said Fleur. That explained the tidy clothes. Her last scrap of hope vanished. 'Of course, I'm rather busy,' she blustered, 'as I'm doing the marathon this year.'

'Are you?' Sean sounded genuinely interested.

'I am,' confirmed Fleur proudly. At least she had got his attention.

'I did it last year,' said Sean casually. 'A great experience – I'm sure you'll get a lot from it.'

'Have you got any hot tips?' asked Fleur eagerly, spotting a brilliant ruse for staying in contact with him.

'Oh, yes,' said Sean, nodding.

'Perhaps we could have a drink and talk them through?' said Fleur, letting her mouth run away with her.

'I'll jot something down on e-mail and send it through,' said Sean, rather coldly.

'Oh, thanks,' muttered Fleur, feeling stupid and humiliated. 'That'd be really great.'

'Take care of yourself, Fleur,' said Sean.

'You too,' she said, feeling her heart shatter into smithereens, each as sharp and needling as a pointed icicle, while Sean turned and walked out of the door. As she stared at the empty space where he had been, she thought ruefully that you never know what you really feel until it is too late for that knowledge to be of any use to you.

5

Saturday was a schizophrenic day in the park. It started out empty and quiet, a peaceful, restful place until the hour of ten or eleven when the manic, hyperactive side of its personality broke through with full force. Small children who had been awake since six a.m. burst out of 4x4s, brought by their reluctant fathers who had been kicked out of bed by their wives and ordered to spend some quality time with their kids. In truth, there wasn't ever much quality parenting on display on a brisk Saturday morning in January – the dads were freezing, tired, hungry and wishing they were tucked up in a large, comfortable bed with some woman they'd never have to see again instead of trailing helplessly round a wet park after their tinies and their Tonka trucks. However, rather than bond with the other hapless males on duty, they preferred to put up a great show of interaction with their offspring whenever another beleagured dad hove into view, only to return to their inner musings on quite how their lives had turned out this way once the other parent – who might, if feeling very communicative, raise an eyebrow in greeting – was safely out of sight. At eight a.m., only the very henpecked were out already, as most of the weekend paters were still feigning sleep, even though the logical possibility of someone's being able to stay in the land of nod while battered about the head with Buzz Lightyear was quite slim.

The sun was trying to break through, in a weak watery fashion, intended more to reassure the inhabitants of the northern hemisphere that it hadn't died or gone away to light another solar system than to give them any fringe benefits of light or warmth.

'Bugger, it's cold,' said the man Fleur recognised as the ill-coordinated dancer from the inaugural party when she arrived to join the little group of runners who were hopping from foot to foot. 'Hello,' he went on as Fleur took her place in the circle next to him. 'I'm Peter. We didn't really meet the other night.' Over his running gear, which seemed to consist of an Aertex shirt, a pair of baggy khaki shorts and Green Flash Dunlop plimsolls, he sported a long dark winter coat. A lock of limp blond hair fell over his glasses and he shook his head to clear it away.

'Hi. I'm Fleur,' said Fleur, who was wearing a pair of saggy tracksuit bottoms, an antique pair of trainers and an old sweatshirt with the legend 'World Peace' emblazoned across the front.

'Not too ambitious, then,' remarked Peter.

'I'm sorry?' queried Fleur. Peter was smiling vaguely at her, blinking behind his thick spectacles.

'World Peace,' said Peter, indicating her sweatshirt. 'Just a modest goal.'

'Oh,' said Fleur, looking down at her chest. 'This is a left-over from when I was a student. Since then I've set my sights rather lower.'

'Ah, the death of idealism,' sighed Peter. 'However, as you're running the marathon, I would say you still have something of the dreamer about you.'

'Fantasist would be more accurate,' said Fleur, warming to this slightly strange individual.

'Not an athlete?' said Peter.

'Nope,' said Fleur. 'Think last person to be picked for the school teams – after the girl with only one leg – and that's me.'

'Ha!' Peter laughed. 'Then I'm in good company.'

'Coo-ee!' The large lady Fleur had seen at the drinks party waved to her. 'So nice to see you, Fleur.'

'Hi!' Fleur waved, having forgotten her name already.

'Roz,' said the large woman, pointing at herself. 'And that's Derek, Hamish, Jennifer, Sophie and Alice.' She motioned round the group, the last person being the woman with the pricey air Fleur had noticed at the party. Alice smiled tightly at Fleur and continued with her superior-looking stretching exercises. Unlike the others, who seemed to have come in whatever clothes might have been lying on the bedroom floor that morning, Alice was in top of the range exercise clothes, all tastefully coordinated with each other.

'Right!' said Ben. 'A few warm-up exercises and then we'll be off, see what you can do!' The group gave a mock groan. 'Yes, we do have to,' said Ben. 'Stretching is vital to warm up your muscles and prevent injury. Stretch up!'

'What do you do, Fleur?' said Peter as he raised his arms in the air.

'Stretch down!'

'I work for an antiques dealer,' said Fleur, her head hanging near her knees. 'I used to be a museum curator but now I work in a shop instead.'

'How interesting,' said Peter. 'I have some experience of the art world.'

'And calf stretch! Right side!'

'You do?' said Fleur. 'How come?'

'Left side!'

'I work in the criminal justice system,' replied Peter.

'Ham string stretch! Right!'

'Oh, dear,' said Fleur, laughing. 'We're not all fraudsters, you know.'

'Left!'

'Of course not!' said Peter, who was quite pink in the face already. 'It was just one case I worked on, concerning a very talented forger whose paintings turned up in the most unlikely situations.'

'Thigh stretch! Right.'

'Oh, I know who you mean!' exclaimed Fleur. 'The museum I worked for in the States had one of his – they were very cross about it. Furious, in fact – they wished you'd never uncovered it as a forgery.'

'No, I didn't make myself popular with that case,' agreed Peter. 'Mind you, I don't think I ever do.'

'Stop talking, you two,' ordered Ben. 'Let's try and concentrate, shall we?'

Peter looked rather startled, as though he wasn't used to being addressed in such a peremptory fashion.

'Now,' said Ben. 'I want you to set off round the outside track of the park. Take it at either a light jog or a brisk walk. This is not a competition – at least, not yet.' He smiled again and Fleur noted how his whole face lit up. He wasn't exactly what you would call good-looking but he exuded a sort of love of life which was definitely very appealing. 'If you are jogging and you feel you can't go on, slow to a walk, but try to make it all the way round and back here within' – he checked his watch – 'twenty minutes.'

Fleur didn't exactly imagine she was fit but she didn't think she was that unfit either – after all, she walked across Albert Bridge every morning to catch her bus to the office. She went up and down all those stairs to her flat, often carrying bags of shopping. Frequently, she found herself running when she was late for an appointment, and sometimes, when she could be bothered, she even attended a yoga class. She felt fairly confident that she would trot round the park at a respectable pace and be back well under the twenty-minute mark.

Roz, who was clearly under no such delusion, set off at a sustainable saunter with Peter traipsing languidly behind her. Even though they had only met for the briefest of times, Fleur still thought it typical of Alice that she ran in a neat, orderly fashion, moving in a manner that you just knew she would be able to keep up the whole circuit of the track.

Fleur herself set off at a racing speed, but to her horror she hadn't covered even the length of the lake when her lungs felt as if they might explode, her legs were exhausted and even her arms, which she hadn't thought would be playing any part in today's exercise, threatened to drop off from pure weariness. Ben loped up beside her.

'You started too fast,' he said. 'Walk until you get into the trees, then try a light jog for a minute only, then walk again, jog again. If you can keep it up all the way round, excellent, if not, just walk. We've got plenty of time to get you moving.'

'No we haven't,' panted Fleur. 'The marathon is in April.'

'Don't panic,' said Ben calmly. 'It's a big endeavour made up of small steps so if you keep putting one foot in front of the other, eventually you will reach your destination. Keep asking yourself, "Can I take one more step?"'

'Yes I can,' puffed Fleur.

'Louder – can I take one more step?'

'Yes I can,' shouted Fleur, sending the sparrows twittering in the trees above flying into the air in fright.

'Excellent,' said Ben. 'People assume the marathon is all about crossing the finishing line. It isn't – it's about the journey to the start. Enjoy it, Fleur. It's something special.' With that, he lengthened his stride and sprinted away.

Fleur wasn't quite the last person to make it back to the meeting point but she was shocked to see that even Peter was there before her. So, apparently, was Ben.

'Peter, you did go round the outside track, didn't you?' he was asking. Peter was looking very innocent indeed. With his schoolboy outfit and cherubic face under his mop of blond curls, there was a peculiar agelessness about him which made it impossible to guess how old he might be. Roz bustled up after Fleur, looking jolly if rather puffed.

'And I hope that wasn't you I saw having a cigarette in the bushes,' Ben said sternly to Roz.

'Me?' squeaked Roz. She was wearing a bum bag which contained a suspiciously rectangular package. 'Of course not. I'm trying . . .' she was interrupted by a fit of coughing, 'to give up.'

'Good,' said Ben. 'It is a stupid, expensive and nasty habit and you can't possibly think you can smoke and run the marathon.'

'Absolutely,' coughed Roz. 'That would be idiotic.'

'Right,' said Ben. 'I think we've established that we have serious work to do. I was going to suggest meeting three times a week but I'm going to up it to five. And those of you who are members of gyms, please go, do weights, do yoga, go swimming, get on your bikes. Those of you who are not,' he looked at Peter, Roz and Fleur who by chance were standing together, 'I suggest you join. And Peter, get a proper pair of running shoes.'

Peter looked down at his feet. 'But I've always found these very suitable,' he protested.

'For what?' said Ben, the disappointment of the morning clearly getting to him somewhat. 'Playing real tennis?'

'Well, yes,' said Peter in surprise. 'How did you know?'

'Just a guess,' said Ben grimly.

For the next half-hour, Ben put them through their paces as though they were new recruits to the army and he a sadistic PT instructor. The only one of the group who didn't hate him bitterly by the end was Alice, whose slender, flexible frame held more strength and stamina than the others put together. Just as Fleur was on the point of giving up entirely, Ben called time. And finally he smiled.

'That was great,' he said. 'No, really, it was. You all tried very hard and I feel proud of you.' The little group swelled slightly as their hearts expanded on hearing the unexpected praise.

'Remember, the marathon is a big undertaking,' he continued. 'The first marathon was run when a messenger from the battlefield at Marathon covered the twenty-six miles to Athens to bring news of victory. Sadly, he died once he'd given his message.'

'Oh, great,' said Peter. 'Run the marathon and perish.'

'The messenger didn't have people lining the route to give him Lucozade,' said Ben. 'So he probably suffered from chronic dehydration. As for you lot, drink plenty – of water, that is – eat well, get some rest and I'll see you on Monday.'

'So,' said Roz, lighting a cigarette the minute Ben's departing back was out of range, 'let's go rehydrate in the café.' With her non-smoking hand, she draped a bright African scarf round her neck. 'And you can tell me, Fleur, all about yourself.'

'Well, that won't be very entertaining for you,' warned Fleur, who had the feeling she and Roz were going to get along. 'I'm tremendously dull.'

'Somehow I know that to be a lie,' replied Roz, pretending to give Fleur a stern look.

'Maybe I'll dig up something interesting to say,' said Fleur as they tottered towards the cafeteria.

'I'm sure your life is more exciting than mine,' said Roz, stubbing a cigarette underfoot and immediately lighting up another. 'Sorry – it's the fresh air. Always makes me chain-smoke.'

'Really?' said Fleur, treading carefully now. It was easy for her to joke that her life was dull because she knew very well that by most people's standards it was nothing of the sort. However, it suddenly occurred to her that maybe Roz wasn't having her on and genuinely meant what she said. 'But your life has just become extremely exciting, now you're a marathon runner,' she added tactfully.

'That's the idea,' admitted Roz. 'I've suddenly found myself with rather a lot of time on my hands and I thought this would help fill it.'

Fleur didn't quite know what to say to this. With brand new acquaintances, it was always very hard to judge the right level of familiarity – too inquisitive and people backed off, too restrained and she risked being interpreted as cold. 'I'm sorry to hear that,' she said, hoping to strike middle ground with a non-committal comment.

Her companion smiled at her. 'Mother died before Christmas,' she said, still smiling although her eyes were looking rather bright, drops of salty water collecting on what were quite the longest eyelashes Fleur had ever seen, giving Roz the look of Ermintrude the cow. 'I'd been looking after her for years, poor dear,' she continued. 'I'm afraid it's left a terrible gap.'

'I'm so sorry,' repeated Fleur, feeling this was a rather inadequate response.

'So I thought I should get out and do something with myself,' said Roz, pushing the glass door of the café open. 'Do you know, when I took that Lifestyle Checklist, I scored ten out of ten?'

'So did I,' said Fleur. 'Cappuccino please,' she said to the waitress behind the counter.

'You wouldn't think it to look at you!' exclaimed Roz. 'You look as if you've got everything going for you.'

'Unfortunately, I'm starting to think everything has *gone* for me,' said Fleur, selecting a large piece of carrot cake. If she was going to do all this exercise, she might as well eat whatever she felt like. 'As in the past tense – I've had my chance and now it's all over.'

'Poof,' said Roz. 'Wait till you're my age, dear. Then you'll really know how that feels.'

Seated outside so Roz could smoke, they watched the nippy arctic breeze whisk gobbets of foam off their coffees and whirl them around to meet fragments of ash from her cigarette, whereupon they melded in mid-air like a grey snowstorm.

'Now, let's get to the interesting stuff,' said Roz, who clearly didn't believe in wasting time. 'Married? Boyfriend?'

'Neither,' said Fleur, sipping her very hot coffee.

'You're not,' said Roz, a look of horror crossing her face, 'divorced!' She said the last word in a showy stage whisper.

'No, just single,' affirmed Fleur.

'Thank God for that,' exclaimed Roz, laying one chubby hand on her large bosom. 'I'd have gone right off my pain au chocolat if you were.' Given the speed with which Roz was tucking in, Fleur doubted this was strictly true. 'Now, how can a lovely girl like you not have a nice man?'

'I don't know,' said Fleur. 'I suppose I just haven't met him yet.'

'Ah, waiting for The One,' said Roz approvingly. 'Good girl. Of course, you'll know when you find him, straight away. All this nonsense about being friends first, it never works. It has to be boom da da boom, the very first time you see him.'

'Are you married?' asked Fleur.

'Like you, I'm very choosy,' said Roz firmly. 'And I haven't met my Mr Right. But,' she said, deftly switching the focus back to Fleur, 'what I want to know, is are you looking?'

'I thought you didn't find love if you were looking for it,' said Fleur wistfully.

'Rot!' said Roz, who clearly had a fondness for antiquated sayings. 'How can you find something you're not looking for? Anyone nice at work?'

'One old codger and a very stunning young girl,' said Fleur. 'Oh, and an ex-boyfriend who doesn't like me very much.'

'Hardly ideal,' said Roz thoughtfully. 'Can't your friends introduce you to someone?'

'All the good ones have gone already,' said Fleur, who'd come back from the States countless times over the past five years to don a hat, drink too much fake champagne, dance badly to a mobile disco and stay in uncomfortable and over-priced bed and breakfasts up and down the country in order to bear witness to her friends' nuptial events. 'And the ones left over are not really the marrying type.' Fleur didn't neces-sarily mean they were gay, more than the single men of her acquaintance now in their thirties had espoused full time hedonism in a wholehearted and exuberant manner. Charming as these louche bachelors were, Fleur seriously doubted whether her Mr Right lay among their number, not least because when one of them did peel off to commit himself to a relationship, it was usually with somebody ten years younger.

All in all, it was a rather sensitive subject for Fleur. With a stunning disregard for how clichéd their behaviour was becoming, her married friends had sunk into all-absorbing domesticity, from which they occasionally reached out to their single friends in order to spread the word on marital joy.

'Met any nice men?' they would ask Fleur, their eyes ablaze with hope. They reminded Fleur of eager members of a cult, desperate to persuade other innocents to join them. Fleur thought darkly this was a very bad sign. In general, the human race was not prone to sharing good fortune, whereas misery, as is well known, loves company. People only begged you to join them if they were currently involved in something painful, exhausting and difficult, like, for example, running the marathon.

Since she had arrived back in England, Fleur had noticed that a third segment of her friends had taken off in a totally different direction, rejecting their handsomely paid citybound jobs for adventure in the far reaches of the world. With little or no training for such activities, they abandoned civilisation to ride bicycles across Africa, walk the Silk Road, canoe round the Pacific or cross the Antarctic in a biplane. No part of the globe was safe from the new breed of adventurer and their eccentric means of voyaging – from Kazakhstan to Patagonia, currently some privately educated professional with a degree was to be found drying their wet clothes over an open fire while eating reconstituted dried rations and either making notes for a book or taking video footage of themselves for a film. It was such an epidemic that Fleur, who had spent almost as many evenings at goodbye or welcome home parties for the frontier-busting friends as she had at weddings, felt quite left out. She never did anything particularly adventurous or testing and certainly never engaged in any activity which might make an interesting book afterwards and she minded this much more than she cared about not getting married. Running the marathon was a fairly pallid effort compared to climbing K2 backwards in a rubber chicken outfit but at least it would give her something to say at the next screening of *Travels in Kamchatka* or the book launch of *My Sudanese Diary*. With 26.2 miles under her belt, maybe she wouldn't feel such a dull wimp after all.

'I had a boyfriend,' said Fleur, referring to a short-lived romance she'd embarked on in her first couple of months in London. 'But he dumped me.'

'Did you see it coming?' asked Roz.

'No, but I should have,' admitted Fleur. 'When he gave me an egg poacher for Christmas.'

'An egg poacher!' said Roz. 'You should have dumped him!'

Fleur laughed. She suddenly felt better than she had done since the wretched egg poacher Christmas had cast a blight over her life.

'Did he give a reason?' said Roz.

'Apparently I'm co-dependent,' said Fleur. 'But as I don't know what that means, there's not much I can do about it.'

A polite cough interrupted them. Looking up, they saw Peter hopping from foot to foot.

'Hello,' he said, brushing his curls out of his eyes. 'I thought it was you two.' He smiled shyly. 'Sorry I had to leave early. It was a bit more than I can handle, on a Saturday morning.'

'Would you like to join us for a coffee?' said Fleur. By the faintly disinterested way in which Roz's eyes had flickered over Peter, she gathered her new friend had already decided that Peter did not ring the bell for her.

'Yes. Do,' said Roz, trying to hide her slight ire at having their girly chat disrupted.

'Oh, really?' said Peter, looking delighted. He signalled to the grumpy Albanian waiter who was posing as an Italian to bring him a cappuccino. 'Ahh, sunshine!' He closed his eyes under his heavy-framed glasses.

'Do you know anything about co-dependency, Peter?' Fleur asked.

'Absolutely,' he replied enthusiastically. 'All there is to know.'

'Well, go on,' said Fleur. 'What is it?'

'Basically,' said Peter, looking very serious, 'it means defining your self-worth by your ability to meet the needs of others. But,' he continued, 'it can also mean that someone is using psychobabble to insult you under the pretence of being caring. Like saying you've got issues – honestly, does anyone actually know what an issue is?'

'I certainly don't,' said Fleur.

'Quite,' said Peter. 'Someone at work told me she had issues with me the other day and when I asked her to define an issue, she told me I was being passive aggressive and stormed off. I was none the wiser.' He yawned, showing pointed white teeth and the pink tongue of good digestion.

'Late night?' said Roz, looking meaningfully at Fleur and then over to Peter. Fleur caught her meaning immediately and furrowed her brow as a silent 'No!'

'Most unadvisedly, yes,' said Peter, opening his light blue eyes very wide. 'Some friends of mine had a dinner party, with the aim, I fear, of introducing me to a female acquaintance of theirs.'

Roz perked up. 'You were set up?'

'Indeed,' said Peter. 'At two a.m. I was hiding in my hosts' bathroom in the hope that "my date" might leave before me. But no, they were determined I would see her home. It was all rather traumatic, but thankfully I had my marathon running as an excuse.' He looked at them very seriously for a moment before bursting out laughing.

'No Mrs Peter?' said Roz, warming to what was clearly her favourite theme.

'Such a lady does not exist,' he affirmed. 'A matter which is of much greater concern to my friends than to myself.'

'What do you do?' asked Fleur.

'I'm a barrister,' he said.

'What sort?' said Roz, narrowing her eyes.

'Criminal,' said Peter.

'Oh, good,' said Roz. 'I'm so glad you're not a family lawyer. I can't stand them.' She almost spat the last words.

'Dear lady,' said Peter, somewhat taken aback, 'what an extraordinary statement. Some of my best friends are family lawyers and I can assure you that, apart from a predilection to dinner parties, there is really nothing offensive about them.'

'All the misery they cause,' said Roz hotly. 'Destroying marriages, pitting couples against each other, breaking up families.' She paused. 'Oh, well. I expect they all have disastrous love lives,' she added hopefully.

Peter took off his glasses and polished them. 'Actually, some of the happiest marriages I know are among divorce professionals,' he said mildly. 'After all, they are under no illusions that marriage is not a business and a partnership. Rarely are they swept away in the false romance of a wedding, only to find out later that the elation withers as quickly as the flowers on the altar.'

Roz was looking so incensed that Fleur feared she might hit Peter, who appeared oblivious of the offence he had just caused. A tinkly sound broke the moment.

'Roz speaking,' the woman herself snapped into her mobile. 'Oh, dear.' She changed tone immediately. 'You better put me through . . . Hello, Rosalind Squires speaking.' She carried on in a warm tone, her eyes directed away from both Peter and Fleur. 'May I just say how very sorry I am . . . yes, I know, this is a very distressing time for you and your family . . . I do understand . . . hmmm . . . the register office closes at midday today but obviously . . . well, as superintendent registrar I do have it in my power to bend the rules just a little, as far as opening hours go . . . yes, if you can be there by twelve, I will meet you at the town hall and we can get the formalities sorted out. My sincere condolences.' She hung up.

'I've got to go to work,' she said sadly.

'On a Saturday?' said Fleur, misunderstanding.

Roz's eyes were brimming. 'I've got to register a death,' she said. 'And the family, they'll be . . .' She trailed off and wiped her eyes. Peter reached out a hand and clasped Roz's.

'Were you very close?' he said sympathetically.

'Oh, no,' said Roz. 'I've never met the deceased. It really is just part of the job, but however many deaths I register, it gets me every time.'

'Was it someone young?' said Fleur, who was rather perplexed.

'Eighty-nine,' said Roz simply. 'But the thing is, great age doesn't make as much difference as you'd think – it's still someone losing a parent or a grandparent or a husband. In a way, it's worse because that person has always been there and suddenly they're gone.'

Peter was still holding Roz's hand and gazing at her.

'Registering the death is just part of the paperwork,' said Roz. 'But often, it's the first time the family really understand that person is not coming back. Well, I better get a move on – I must nip home and put my suit on.' She retracted her hand from Peter's and started to gather her stuff. She reached for her wallet but Peter stopped her.

'Don't worry,' he said. 'You just go.' Roz smiled weakly at him, gave Fleur a peck on the cheek and chugged away, Peter's eyes following her. 'What a very . . .' He seemed lost in thought. 'What a very unusual sort of person.'

'Hmm,' said Fleur. 'It sounds a rather depressing sort of job, being a registrar of death.'

'Oh, no,' said Peter. 'She'll do births as well. And, erm, perform marriage ceremonies.' He watched Fleur as the penny dropped.

'Ah,' said Fleur. 'No wonder she's not keen on divorce.'

'Quite,' said Peter. 'Undoing all her hard work. Well, well, well.' He seemed to drift off into his private world.

'Peter,' Fleur said.

He started. 'I'm so sorry, my dear,' he said, coming to. 'I lost myself there for a second. Must be all that physical activity – bit of a shock to the system.'

'I don't want to abandon you,' said Fleur, 'but I think I should go home and have a hot bath.'

'You do that,' said Peter. 'I'm sure we will meet again.'

6

Peter's words were hardly prophetic – after all, Ben had given each of the members of the Runners' Club a photocopied training schedule which made it clear they would be spending a large chunk of their near futures together. Given that Ben had earmarked pretty much every morning and even a few evenings for the purposes of fitness improvement, the new runners found themselves relentlessly thrown into each other's company. Initially, athletic ability seemed to determine who became friends with whom. Those with speed at their heels such as Ben and the immaculately turned out, shiny-haired Alice tended to beat out a path round the park together, lost in conversation as their long limbs carried them effortlessly across the frozen ground, their breath emerging as puffs of white smoke in the freezing morning air. Roz, whose breath resembled smoke for quite a different reason, was more likely to be found lingering at the back of the group where, to her chagrin, Fleur also found her natural place to be. She was not delighted to discover she was the second slowest in the Runners' Club – even little Peter managed a slightly more rapid run than hers, lifting his feet in a peculiar, high-gaited action like a Viennese show pony pirouetting in the ring. Between the two leaders and the three stragglers at the back huffed along an indeterminate group of medium-rank runners: a tall, gangly accountant whom Fleur carefully avoided as he assumed an overbearing expertise on all matters concerning endurance sports that his physique did not support; a pair of cheerful Battersea new mothers attempting to lose the extra pounds from pregnancy who spent their runs bonding over hideous childbirth stories; and a wine merchant called Hamish whose pink eyes looked as if they might burst all their blood vessels from such exertion so early in the morning.

The consolation for Fleur for finding herself relegated to the also-ran position was having the affable and entertaining company of registrar Roz, a woman never lost for words even when she hardly had the breath left to get them out. Roz had a theory about the marathon – she had decided that people only ran it if they had some kind of burning inner issue to deal with. In her case, she told Fleur one day as the two of them dawdled across the bleak, windy grass in the park, discussing the direction their lives had taken, she had taken up running to fill the void left by the death of her mother. An only child, Roz had been left to care for her ageing mum after her father, a stolid and cheery vicar, had suffered a fatal accident involving a particularly tough bit of rock cake at the village fete one year. The shock of his death was terrible, made infinitely worse by the Church's insisting his widow vacate the vicarage immediately, to allow the new incumbents to take up residence. The rude and heartless fashion with which the religious body sent Roz's mother, an exemplary vicar's wife, packing, caused the young Roz to ditch her notions of working inside church walls and become a registrar instead. 'It was either that or become a white witch,' she had said. 'But registering seemed to offer a better defined career path.'

But a change of career from pulpit to register office wasn't the only knock-on effect of the tragedy which beset Roz's parents. Homeless, Roz's mother had moved to London to live with her daughter on a temporary basis, except that this short-term arrangement managed to extend itself until only the removal men from heaven succeeded in shifting the old lady out of Roz's life and into the next. As her mother had arrived at about the time when Roz might have expected to meet a man with whom to spend her life, Roz had found her romantic options rather curtailed. Most men were not keen on canoodling on the sofa at the end of a date when Mother might appear at any moment, looking for her tablets or her teeth. But Roz was philosophical about her single status and certainly didn't blame her mother for her spinsterhood. 'If it was meant to be, then whoever would have seen past the obstacles,' she said fiercely to Fleur when Fleur gently suggested that Roz's mother might have blighted her love life somewhat. 'Anyway, it would have to be someone excep-tional,' said Roz defiantly, 'for me to give up my liberty.'

'Of course,' said Fleur soothingly, not pointing out that the problem with exceptional people is that, by their very nature, there tend to be precious few of them.

According to Roz, Ben was the most straightforward when it came to underlying marathon motivations. Like Rabbit in *Winnie the Pooh*, he had an enormous network of friends and family, all of whom seemed to play an active part in his life. However, the quality of his friendship was clearly not damaged by the quantity in which he dispensed it – his whole marathon plan had come about as a response to a tragedy in the lives of some of his closer friends whose seriously ill daughter had spent time at the hospice. Raising money for the charity was Ben's way of showing them how much he cared. 'Added to that,' said Roz, who had quickly made the other runners' busi-ness her business, 'he actually enjoys physical exercise. Unlike the rest of us.'

While Roz had hardly reached even a basic standard of fitness, the fact that she could now speak and run at the same time was nevertheless a fairly dramatic improvement – during the first week of training, the other runners had been quite alarmed by her wheezing attacks after each short jog. But she had cut down enormously on her smoking – or so she claimed – and was already reaping a few of the benefits of improved fitness, even if her chances of finishing the marathon were still pretty remote. She was planning, she told Fleur, to run it in a giant furry rabbit costume. She had been inspired by the example of a man who did the marathon in an antique sub-aqua suit and finished five days after everyone else. 'After all,' she asked Fleur, 'how fast would anyone expect a giant rabbit to go?' Fleur, who didn't feel in any way qualified to answer this question, wisely stayed quiet on the subject.

Having summarily despatched the other runners' motiv-ations – the accountant, according to Roz, was a bore and had taken up running because no one would talk to him, the new mothers wanted to lose weight but would drop out quite soon when the going got tough and Hamish was going through a divorce – Roz moved on to Fleur. 'You've suddenly come to terms with the fact that you are thirty-two and you've dedi-cated your whole life to your career but that career has ground to a halt, leaving you empty-handed and alone,' she had pronounced as they ran along the river path one morning. 'You wish now that you hadn't sacrificed personal opportun-ity for career gain but you are also realising that you can't live in the past or dwell on your mistakes so have decided to move on. The marathon marks the divide between your two lives,' she said decisively.

'Yes, that's about the gist of it,' Fleur admitted. She hadn't realised that marathon training would have such a psychological angle to it. 'I can't really argue with any of that. But what about Peter?'

'Oh, well, Peter!' said Roz. 'I fear he is a lost cause.'

Roz wasn't the only runner to express faint despair at the prowess of the quick-witted but slow-moving barrister. Team leader Ben was clearly finding him somewhat exasperating too. Only that morning, Peter had shown up in a brand new pair of hightop trainers which flashed red lights in the soles when he ran. He claimed that when he bought them he had no idea they came with underfoot lighting, but Fleur didn't really believe him. His reaction to Ben's criticism of his new purchase betrayed a certain deep fondness for his footwear.

'You can't wear those,' Ben had objected.

'Oh yes I can,' said Peter haughtily. 'They may look like trainers to you, but to me they are the wings of Mercury.'

Ben sighed. 'Seriously, Peter,' he said. 'You can't run a marathon in those shoes. They've got air-cushioned soles, haven't they?'

'Indeed,' said Peter happily. 'They are absolutely top of the range.' It wasn't only his shoes that Peter had upgraded. Having passed his driving test three years before at the age of thirty-nine, Peter had been trundling around town in a Fiat Panda known as the Pram, thanks to its resemblance, both in appearance and speed, to an old-fashioned Silver Cross baby buggy. However, recently he had traded it in for a Mercedes SLK 200, a jump in car ownership for which his driving skills clearly weren't quite ready. 'I am always first off the lights,' he told them with glee, neglecting to mention that while this was true, he usually came to a shuddering halt about five seconds later when he stalled the car in the middle of the yellow box, causing instant traffic gridlock.

'Air-cushioned soles are no good for long-distance running,' said Ben patiently. 'When your foot hits the ground, it's bearing three to four times your body weight.' Roz winced at the thought and gazed at her feet with compassion. 'If your foot lands on an unstable surface bearing all that load, it will roll in too far and cause problems with your joints, possibly all the way up to your hip. So I suggest you get a pair with harder soles.'

Peter, who had been revelling in his new bouncing run, looked mutinous. 'All right, I'll wear my old Green Flash then,' he said petulantly.

'And I wish you'd asked me before you'd changed your car as well,' continued Ben. 'I could have advised you on something far more suitable. Cars are my job, you know.'

'Suitable,' said Peter crossly. 'All my life I've had people telling me to behave in a "suitable" or "appropriate" manner. I want to break free!' he continued, bouncing up and down in his springy shoes. 'I want to be daring and outrageous and magnificent instead!'

'Yo! Peter,' said Ben, giving up and laughing. 'Sorry I said anything, mate! You just carry on as you are.'

Alice had posed more of a problem for amateur psychologist and personal sleuth Roz. 'What's she running away from?' said Roz mysteriously, when Fleur had asked her to demonstrate how her marathon theory encapsulated Alice, the posh bird from the smart end of Battersea. 'That's what you have to ask yourself.'

'But surely her life is perfect?' said Fleur wistfully. It certainly seemed so from where Fleur was standing. 'She's beautiful, rich, has got kids, a nice house, and her husband adores her.'

'All that glitters, Fleur,' said Roz darkly. 'And if her marriage is so wonderful, why does she flirt so much with Ben?'

'I wish she wouldn't,' grumbled Fleur. 'Or I wish he'd see

through it.' Almost as annoying as finding Alice continually locked in merry, chatty conversation with the lovely Ben was the fact he seemed to enjoy it as much as she did.

'Men,' said Roz, in a resigned fashion.

In comparison, work at Boulden's seemed gentle, peaceful and nondescript. January was a quiet month for people in all trades, the world at large being spent-out and impoverished after the insanity of Christmas over-indulgence. During those weeks, Fleur had the sense she was just passing time in her life, marking out a period of her existence which afterwards would be totally unremarkable except for her membership of the Runners' Club. She wasn't the only person at Boulden's, however, who found the gloom of the winter after-lunch period difficult to quench.

'Thank your lucky stars you'll never know the tedium of being me,' said Spook one dark January afternoon, her copper-nut head laid sadly on her desk. Fleur, who had staggered through three weeks of marathon training, forcing herself out of her comfortable warm cocoon of a bed into the brisk snappy cold of the winter's morn, took a rather more energetic view of life.

'Don't be silly, Spook,' she said bracingly. 'There's nothing wrong with you. You just need a bit more self-esteem, that's all. Goodness, if I looked like you, I don't think I'd doubt myself for a second.'

'Easy to say,' said Spook gloomily. 'But you didn't spend your formative years as a twiglet in a red wig. It's not so good for morale.'

'Try adopting a more positive attitude,' said Fleur, sounding just a tiny bit smug. 'It's working very well for me.'

'You don't understand what it's like to be an idiot,' said Spook, speaking downwards into her desk top.

'We've been through this,' said Fleur patiently. 'You're not stupid. I just think you might be dyslexic. You can't spell but you're a brilliant creative thinker. I can't believe no one at your school picked that up.'

'Huh,' said Spook. 'That's because you've never been to my school or met any of my teachers. The torment, Fleur. Nuns, hockey, Scottish dancing, inhaling hair spray off a flannel for kicks. You can't imagine – you're so lucky to have gone to a state school.'

'Spooky-Spook,' said Fleur blithely, 'I think you're great. So there. And if you don't start looking more cheerful, I shall make you come out jogging with me.'

Spook lifted her head from her desk and gave Fleur a long look. 'Do you know,' she said at last, 'you are the first person who has ever said anything nice about my abilities?'

'Good thing I showed up,' said Fleur snappily. 'Now get on with some work.'

'I knew you had an ulterior motive,' grumbled Spook, but her eyes were shining where earlier they had been lacklustre pools of murky green.

The shop buzzer rang.

'Hello,' Spook said in sepulchural tones, especially designed to put off any customers. The shop, she and Fleur both agreed, was much easier to manage without customers messing it up, so when Brin was away they discouraged them as much as possible. 'Yup,' she continued. 'I'll send her down.'

'Someone for you,' she said to Fleur, replacing the handset.

'Someone with a name?' said Fleur. Her various assistants in the States had been very different from Spook in that they were all über-keen, sharp, highly qualified and immaculately dressed with the hungry, dangerous look of eager predators about them. Although they were extremely efficient, pleasant and helpful, Fleur knew full well that any one of them would have climbed over her dead body to take her job. Spook, on the other hand, was a quite different proposition. What she lacked in brute dedication to her job she certainly made up for in entertainment value.

'Alice,' said Spook decisively.

'Alice?' said Fleur. 'Alice in Wonderland? Alice Cooper? Any clues?'

'Nope,' said Spook. 'You're on your own, clue-wise. And before you say anything, if you want a better assistant, you should get Brinley to pay better wages. Honestly, you're lucky I even answer the phone on what I earn . . .'

'Yeah, yeah, yeah,' said Fleur, miming a mock violin.

'And don't give me your "When I was your age" speech,' warned Spook sternly. 'We know your historical knowledge is not helpful.'

'God, you're cheeky,' complained Fleur, wrapping her three-quarter-length cardigan about herself to ward off the cold, Brinley being rather mean about the central heating.

'And you're neglecting a customer,' reproved Spook. 'Go on, scram, get down there and sell, sell, sell!'

Once down in the shop itself, Fleur saw the back view of a tall slender woman, blunt-cut black hair, dark wool coat reaching down to mid-calf, smart grey trousers over beauti-fully polished boots. She could be any one of Brin's many female clients, some who came to buy but many of whom came to sell, often digging large and no longer needed engagement or eternity rings out of their Kelly bags. While Brin was not a jeweller, a discreet visit to him was a much easier way to unload jewels from a deceased marriage than taking a trip to the diamond enclave of Hatton Garden.

'Can I help you?' Fleur used her most professional-sounding voice.

'Fleur.' The woman turned round and gave her a half-smile.

'Alice?' said Fleur, coming closer to check. 'How . . . nice to see you. I hardly recognised you out of your track suit.'

'Should I have called first?' Alice seemed hesitant.

'No! Goodness, no!' said Fleur, surprise making her more effusive than usual. 'It's a shop, after all! You're quite free to come any time.'

'I wanted to ask your advice,' said Alice, taking off the very large pair of sunglasses she had perched on her head and toying with them with her beautifully manicured hands. 'Is there somewhere we could talk?'

'Talk away,' said Fleur, indicating the empty gallery with a sweep of her hand. 'My assistant's listening to her iPod and Brinley's gone to the south of France so I don't think they'll overhear.' Despite Brinley's protestations about the feeble state of his heart, he had seemingly travelled to Nice without its giving him cause for concern.

'I feel rather silly,' said Alice bashfully. 'Bothering you like this at work.'

'That's fine,' said Fleur, who had seen Alice every morning that week without exchanging a word with the other runner. 'Take a seat.' She indicated a balloon-backed chair into which Alice sank gracefully down. Then she just happened to glance up at the shop window, where a man was peering through the glass. 'Alice, look,' she said, suddenly grasping her visitor's arm. 'Do you recognise that man in the window? Quick.'

By the time Alice turned to look through the glass on to the street, where the lamplights were shedding their first yellowish gleam, the figure had gone. 'Fleur, there isn't anyone there,' she said, turning back to look intently at Fleur. 'Who did you think it was?'

'It looked like the man from the park,' said Fleur.

'What man?' said Alice.

'There's this guy – he's medium height, dark-haired – and he's there every morning when we're running,' said Fleur.

'Fleur, people do tend to go jogging in the morning,' said Alice sensibly.

'No, but I've seen him in other parts of London as well – like round here,' said Fleur.

'Perhaps he works in Piccadilly?' said Alice, still sounding very reasonable. 'Have any of the other runners noticed him?'

'Roz has – she's got a bit of a crush on him,' admitted Fleur. In fact, it had been Roz who had first pointed out the omnipresent runner.

'I think he fancies me,' she had whispered to Fleur, indicating the thick-set, heavy-eyed man who flashed a grin at them while overtaking on the track. 'He's always here and he's always smiling at me. What do you think I should do?'

'Say hello?' suggested Fleur. Nothing about the appearance of the middle-aged man put her in mind of romance so she could see no perils associated with a friendly greeting.

'I can't do that!' Roz sounded horrified. 'He'll know I'm interested.'

'Are you?' said Fleur in surprise. He looked too old and too unappealing to be an object of desire. But with a start, she realised he might only be five or ten years senior to herself. It wasn't a case of policemen looking younger, rather it was appropriately aged men looking older these days.

'No!' said Roz, the vehemence of her response indicating the contrary. 'Of course I'm not,' she added emphatically.

'Then don't bother,' said Fleur slyly, playing devil's advocate.

'But . . .' Roz floundered. 'It seems so rude, when he's so friendly.'

'Then just say hello, in a casual but friendly manner, and move on,' said Fleur gently. She'd got very fond of Roz during their short acquaintance. 'But don't make too big a deal of it, that's all.'

Fleur tore her gaze away from the empty shop window. Over the past week or so, she could have sworn she had seen that man everywhere – on the tube going home, in the streets in Piccadilly, in the park jogging in the morning. It must just be coincidence, she told herself. Or her imagination running away with her.

'How can I help you?' She gave Alice her full attention and realised, now that she was seeing her for the first time out of a track suit, what a true beauty Alice was. Her hair was so black, it was almost the dark blue of a midnight sky; her eyes were as soft and brown as a mink coat, and with her smooth skin and dusky pink cheeks she had the look of a Tahitian maiden from one of Gauguin's paintings. No wonder the men in the Runners' Club all danced about her like a pack of little fawns.

Alice produced a piece of paper from inside her handbag. 'I would really appreciate it if this could be in confidence,' she said timidly. 'I'd rather even Brinley didn't know and certainly not the other runners. I'm asking you as a friend.'

'Of course,' said Fleur, wondering when she and Alice had become friends, given that Alice spent all her time at training chatting up the men.

'I mean, I know you don't know me very well,' Alice saved herself by adding. 'We haven't had much chance to talk.' To Fleur's surprise, Alice suddenly looked very confused and rather vulnerable. 'Fleur, I need some help and I don't know where else to go.' She bit her lip and looked at the ground. 'I'm really sorry to barge in like this and start asking you favours but I overheard you talking about your work the other morning. I haven't got anyone else I can ask.' A lonely tear was threatening to break out from the confinement of her thick lashes.

'I'll help you if I can,' said Fleur, who felt much more inclined to do so now Alice had shown some signs of humanity. 'Let me see.' She took the crumpled paper from Alice and smoothed it out. 'It's a receipt,' she said. 'For a pair of paintings – it looks as if Brinley Boulden was the buyer.'

'That's right,' said Alice, not meeting her eye. 'Fleur, could you find out how much these paintings were sold for?'

Fleur felt herself to be in a somewhat awkward position. 'Alice,' she began gently, 'I can't really tell you something if it isn't in the public domain. If this was a private sale . . .' She trailed off. Alice was looking so distraught, she didn't like to go on.

'The paintings . . .' Alice whispered. 'They were all I had of my own and now they've gone too. I've got nothing, Fleur, nothing.'

'I don't understand,' said Fleur, who was rather taken aback by how different Alice seemed. Without her running gear on, she seemed like Samson shorn of his hair, weak, insecure and lacking in confidence, whereas the woman Fleur had seen morning after morning had been supercilious, snooty and aloof.

'I inherited those paintings from my grandfather,' Alice said slowly. 'He gave them to me, said they would be my insurance policy in case of a rainy day. Fleur, it's not raining for me now. It's pouring. And I don't even have the paintings.' Her voice rose hysterically and she clapped one hand over her mouth, as though to stop a sob from escaping.

'If you owned them,' said Fleur, who could see she had to handle this situation very delicately, 'how could someone else have sold them? Were they stolen?'

'Yes,' said Alice faintly. 'They were.'

'Then you must report them to the police,' said Fleur.

'I can't,' said Alice. 'That's the one thing I can't do. Please help me, Fleur. I just want to know how much they sold for and where they are now. I want to know they are safe – I loved those paintings,' she continued, unwittingly using the line of attack most guaranteed to melt Fleur's heart. 'They weren't just an insurance policy for me, they were my grandfather's legacy.'

'I'll see what I can do,' said Fleur, relenting. 'I'll help you as much as I can, Alice.' Even while she spoke, the thought flashed through her brain that Roz had been right – all was not well in Alice's supposed paradise.

'Don't say anything to Roz.' Alice seemed to read her thoughts. 'Please.' Before Fleur could say anything more, Alice stood up briskly. 'Thank you,' was all she said as she strode to the door.

'You don't have to be . . .' Spook was singing along to her iPod when Fleur went up to the office, Alice's receipt in hand.

'Move, I want your computer,' said Fleur, rudely pulling out one of Spook's ear pieces.

'Fleurski!' said Spook in delight, as though they hadn't met for ages. It must be an upper class thing, thought Fleur, this complete lack of short term memory which led both Brin and Spook to behave like goldfish in a bowl, constantly acting as though she were some kind of beloved long-lost acquaintance who had shown up totally out of the blue when in fact they had seen her about five minutes previously.

'Icon's ready,' Spook continued as Fleur leaned across her to type a search term into her computer, the only one in the office connected to the internet. 'So you can get a wriggle on to Belgrade. Although Sean wants to have a word with you before you go.'

'Does he indeed?' said Fleur. She didn't relish the thought. She typed in a password, followed by the code on the receipt. 'Can you call him and ask what it's about?'

'But Fleur, he's quite dishy,' protested Spook. 'Don't you think you should find out in person?'

'Spook,' said Fleur in the warning voice she used to indicate that certain topics were off limits.

'Okay, I'll call him but don't be sad when I'm married to him not you,' retorted Spook.

'I don't think it'll be you either,' said Fleur, jotting down some details from the screen. 'He's got a long-term girlfriend.'

'Boo!' said Spook. 'We *so* don't like her.'

'Sadly, I suspect she *so* doesn't care,' murmured Fleur.

Fleur had hardly had time to reflect on the nature of her findings on the curious matter of Alice's paintings before the shop buzzer went again. When she looked at the television screen attached to the entry mechanism, there appeared to be no one at the front door.

'Kids,' said Spook dismissively.

The buzzer went once more, but it seemed as though the invisible man must be pushing it. It rang three times in quick succession and then stopped before it rang for the fourth and longest time.

'I'm going down,' said Fleur. 'Spook, keep an eye on the CCTV and if you see anything odd, call the police immediately.' She felt strangely nervous as she picked her way through the shop. It would be most unusual for an antiques shop to be robbed in broad daylight, not least because most of the valuable items would need a lorry to take them away which rather precluded the 'smash and grab' approach to burglary. But crime in all forms was definitely on the rise in the art world and who was to say what new variant on a theme some resourceful thieves might have dreamt up? After all, Munch's *Scream* had recently been lifted from a museum in Norway while the security guards were having a tea break, a miniature Fabergé egg had left the Hermitage in the stomach lining of a brave female jewel thief and a small gallery in the Netherlands had lost all their valuable paintings when some fake picture conservators had taken them for cleaning, and, of course, never brought them back. The thought of these crimes, coupled with the man Fleur was sure she had seen hanging around, made her feel quite twitchy as she reached the glass door.

The shop bell sounded once more, yet even standing so close, Fleur could see no one. She opened the door and looked out on to the street, which seemed empty, the purple light of a London evening falling on to the dead end of the afternoon. There was clearly no one there. Fleur even stepped out on to the street to prove to herself that it must be some malfunction of the intercom rather than a mischief-making stalker.

'Aha!' Someone grabbed her from behind and Fleur screamed.

'Don't scream! It's only me! Fleur, it's me, Greta.' The panicked Fleur found herself wrapped into a hug made up of a multitude of different textures – velvet, fur, feathers and tweed all embraced her heartily.

'Fleur, it's Greta. There's no need to be afraid!' The apparition loosened the hug and held Fleur by the shoulders, standing back to take a look at her. With crimson lips, huge eyes outlined in heavy kohl, a tumble of ebony curls escaping from a pink top hat, a mink wrap over a man's tweed overcoat and a pair of wellington boots, Greta was really quite a sight.

'Look at you!' said Greta, rather incongruously, as beside her Fleur faded into total insignificance. 'Little Fleur, back in London again!'

'Greta?' said Fleur. The last time she had seen Greta, the

exotic artist had looked rather different – even if the eccentric chic was firmly in place, poor Greta had been grey, downtrodden, unhealthy and despairing. In the intervening years, however, Greta had been rescued from obscurity at exactly the point where she was just about to give up her art for ever and resign herself to the drudgery of an ordinary life. Fleur had been at least somewhat instrumental in what turned out to be Greta's meteoric rise to fame, as in New York she had put in a very good word for the then unknown artist with a major collector looking for more contemporary works. Where this collector went, money, public opinion, exhibitions and rapidly rising prices inevitably followed, and so Greta was quickly on her way to being discovered. She gave up her job as a police artist, something she had trained to do in a fit of hopelessness about ever breaking through in the art world, and breathed a sigh of relief that she would never have to lift a set of fingerprints, produce an artist's impression from confused eye witness accounts or render a court scene in pastel on paper ever again. And while the world of modern art offered no sure guarantees, Greta's enormous talent, commercial eye, appetite for hard work and bizarre personality made her almost perfectly suited to becoming a leading artiste du jour.

'Greta, you look amazing!' said Fleur. 'I love your hat.' The pink top hat was decorated with some scarlet feathers, stuck on at rakish angles. 'Come in and have a cup of tea.'

'Oh, no, thank you!' Greta widened her already huge eyes. 'My darling Fleur, I've come to take you away to a new and fabulous world of colour and energy and beauty, not sit in some dingy old shop with a cup of dishwater. I'm so excited to see you again!' she exclaimed effusively. Fleur was rather touched – many of her close friends had failed to react to her return to London with anything even approaching excitement.

'Oh, so you're back, are you?' they'd said in tones which meant either 'We knew it wouldn't last' or, worse, 'Much as we love you, we hoped your brilliant life in New York wouldn't work out because then we'd have been just too jealous.'

'You can't say success hasn't changed you.' Fleur smiled. The Greta of old that Fleur remembered was so impecunious, she had a habit of never refusing anything if it was free, even if it was a cup of dishwater tea. This selfsame habit meant that Greta had taken advantage of some very peculiar experiences, offered to her for no financial outlay. She had hitch-hiked all over Europe, partaken of an unusually wide variety of hallucinogenic substances, drunk many a strange brew and bedded down with persons of all shapes, sizes and sexes, all for free and all in the name of art.

'By way of a thank you,' said the new, successful and rich Greta. 'For what you did for me.'

'It was nothing,' said Fleur modestly, knowing that wasn't true. It was something and quite a big something too but she certainly hadn't done it in the hope of a reward. 'Anyway, I can't go far – I've got to close up the shop tonight.'

'Come,' said Greta loftily. 'Let us not talk of such mundane matters.' She grabbed Fleur by the arm and starting dragging her along the street. 'We shall have champagne and sweet-meats and recline on satin cushions while you tell me your traveller's tales.'

While the pub on the corner was able to furnish them with a bottle of half-decent champagne, Greta's request for sweet-meats was translated into a bag of Bombay Mix, and for satin cushions they had to make do with a rather ordinary set of table and chairs. But nothing felt that ordinary when Greta was present so the whole unscheduled outing held an aura of mystery and magic, not in any way impeded by the fact that it was taking place in Piccadilly and not Xanadu, the sort of place where one might reasonably expect a creature such as Greta to reside.

'How did you know where to find me?' asked Fleur, watching the bubbles drift carelessly through the primrose liquid in her glass.

'Sean told me,' replied Greta, lighting her pipe and puffing a cloud of aromatic smoke at Fleur. Sean and Greta had been art school contemporaries, both heroin-thin and pale-faced, with ripped clothes and cavernous, burning eyes. But whereas Sean had gone straight from art school to his lengthy course to train as a picture conservator, Greta had stuck it out in the brutal world of young conceptual art. When Sean met Fleur, he very quickly wanted to introduce her to Greta, still his best friend, to see whether she believed his instincts about Fleur were right. Fortunately, Greta had taken to Fleur straight away and even Fleur's defection to the United States hadn't changed the artist's opinion of the diminutive curator, made even higher by Fleur's helping hand in her sudden success. 'He said I'd find you at Boulden's.'

'Did he now?' Fleur sighed. 'He wasn't very friendly when I saw him.'

'Fleur, you did break his heart,' Greta reminded her, her black eyes glinting but not hard. 'Quite badly, as well.'

'His heart looks just fine now,' said Fleur, taking a swig of her drink.

'That's what worries me,' said Greta sharply. When she wasn't too busy being a mad artist, she could be refreshingly straight to the point. 'This girl – she's stifling him. He doesn't paint any more, he isn't any fun, he's all health obsessed and together. He probably spends his weekends at Homebase,' she finished in utter disgust.

'And he looks so tidy,' said Fleur.

'Fleur, he's becoming bourgeois,' said Greta impatiently,

using the worst insult she could think of. 'If this goes on, she'll have him retraining as an accountant. Did you know they've bought a house in Fulham?' Having been away from London for some time, Fleur was rather vague as to the exact lifestyle meaning of its different postcodes, but she gathered from Greta's tones that she did not approve. It was strange, reflected Fleur, that even free spirits such as Greta had their own system of social snobbery.

'You must do something,' declared Greta. 'You won't believe this Fleur, but Sean even ran the marathon! If that's not the activity of the socially diseased, then I don't know what is.'

Fleur made a mental note not to ask Greta to sponsor her. 'Really, running the marathon is not such a bad thing to do,' she was just saying when she was interrupted.

'. . . anyway, darlin', the thing is this . . .' A man had sat down at their table and just started talking to Fleur.

'Excuse me!' said Greta rather hoitily but the man just waved a hand at her and carried on talking. From the look of him, he seemed a very well kept sixty-year-old, his smoothly tanned skin pulled suspiciously tight round his eyes, his thick silver hair carefully dishevelled, his soft black leather trousers and fine black jumper swathing a small but wiry frame. 'You've got to ask yourself why? What is it that you're running from?' He signalled the barman. 'Cappuccino, decaff, soy, cheers mate. Anyway, when you think about it, what does your life lack? What are you trying to use this drink to replace? Is it love? Is it anger? Think about it, darling.'

'I'm not sure they do cappuccinos here,' said Fleur, who was rather stunned.

'Yeah, whatever,' said the man dismissively. 'I expect they'll try.' He was, of course, right, and only a few moments later the beaming bar man appeared holding an enormous frothy coffee. 'Thanks, mate.'

The bar man continued to hover, a huge smile plastered sycophantically across his face. 'It is you, isn't it?' he said. Nervously he held a biro in his hand, as though unsure whether to dare ask for an autograph.

'Yup,' said the man, snatching the pen out of the bar man's hand, writing something on a paper napkin and handing it to him. 'Now bugger off.'

'Of course, Sir Jed, of course!' The bar man seemed delighted, both with the napkin and with the command.

'Sorry about that, darling,' said the man. Greta was now staring at him open-mouthed.

'I've just realised who you are,' she said breathily.

'Then, darlin', I'd be glad if you'd let me know,' he replied. 'Cos I spent about thirty years and a million quid on bloody therapists tryin' to find out.'

Fleur remembered her manners. 'Greta, this is Jed,' she said, performing the most perfunctory of introductions. 'Jed, this is my friend Greta. She's an artist.'

'Can I paint you?' Greta was never one to hang back when it came to asking for what she wanted.

'Course you can, darlin',' replied Jed. 'If I can recognise meself, I might even buy it.'

'Anyway, Dad, what are you doing here?' said Fleur.

'Dad?' said Greta, looking from one to the other.

'Well, darlin', I tried you at work but you weren't there. Girl said I'd probably find you in the pub. As though that's where you always are by this time of day. Sent a cold shiver down my spine, that did.'

'Dad?' repeated Greta, as though in a daze. 'Jed is your dad?'

Fleur and Jed ignored her.

'We were just having a celebration,' explained Fleur.

'Yeah, darlin', but that's just the lies we tell ourselves,' said

Jed, seizing her hand. 'It always starts with just one little drink and you think you've got control but you don't. The drink's got you, Fleur. I know, Fleur. I was there. I know about denial and it ain't a river in Egypt.'

'That's a seriously bad joke,' said Fleur.

'Jed Harris is your father?' repeated Greta, who still looked as though someone had hit her about the head with a bag of wet sand.

'Dad, I do not have a drink problem,' said Fleur.

'Yeah, darlin'.' Jed breathed out heavily. 'That's what we all said. Oh, darlin', we all thought we were fine and the rest of the world was out of whack but it ain't the truth.'

'I can't believe you never told me!' said Greta, looking hurt.

'Look, Dad,' said Fleur, who was feeling quite annoyed by now. It was one thing to ignore someone for years and years on end but quite another to reappear and ruin their Thursday afternoon. 'Greta and I just popped out for a drink together because we haven't seen each other for years.' Jed was still shaking his head sorrowfully. 'It doesn't mean anything.'

'It means something to me,' put in Greta huffily.

'There, there, ducks,' said Jed soothingly. 'There's a better life for you – you don't need to numb the pain any more. We can sort this out and you will come to know a freedom and happiness beyond your wildest dreams. Happy, joyous and free – don't you want that, Fleur?'

'No!' said Fleur, her voice rising, unfortunately at the time when the song playing in the pub was just winding down to the end. 'What I meant is I AM NOT AN ALCOHOLIC!' A silence fell across the pub as everyone turned to stare at Fleur.

'I'm on my way to an AA meeting now,' said Jed softly. 'Come with me, Fleur. You'll be among friends. People who understand.'

Fleur groaned quietly.

'I'll come,' said Greta happily, draining her champagne glass.

'Fleur, I really want to help you,' said Jed, pleadingly. 'I really want to do something for you.'

'Well, this isn't it,' said Fleur, suddenly feeling years of frustration, anger and upset at her father's behaviour towards her burst out. 'You can't just waltz in and invent a problem for me so you can solve it. It doesn't work that way. You'll have to try a bit harder if you want to be part of my life. I'm sorry, Greta, but I have to go now. I've got work to do.' Gathering up her coat, Fleur flounced out of the door.

7

Now that the icon – which turned out, under the grime and dirt, to be a work of luminous sanctity, a radiant saint bathed in glowing heavenly light, the rapt expression on his face enough to move the most ungodly closer to belief – had been meticulously cleaned by Sean, preparations for Fleur's trip to Belgrade suddenly gathered speed, which was more than could be said for her running pace. Every morning, after Ben had insistently rung her doorbell, she dutifully staggered out to the park to trot round in an ever-lengthening circle. Sometimes she felt quite good about the prospect of running a marathon; on other mornings, rising panic would better describe her attitude to the forthcoming challenge.

'I can't believe I'm going to run twenty-six miles all in one go,' she said to Peter one nippy February morning.

'Twenty-six point two,' replied Peter, whose cherubic face was now ruddy and weather-beaten, a very different look from his paper-thin pallor on joining the club. 'The marathon was lengthened by three hundred and eighty-five yards so that Queen Victoria would have a good view of the finishing line from Windsor Castle.'

'It didn't occur to her to move?' asked Fleur.

'I quite like the imperial approach,' said Peter. 'Shows great certainty in oneself.'

'Lucozade?' said Fleur, offering Peter the bottle she held in her hand as they jogged along.

'No thank you,' said Peter, pulling a face. 'Did you know, at the first modern Olympics, the British marathon team were a total failure because they insisted on drinking champagne during the race?'

'Peter, do you ever go on TV quiz shows?' said Fleur. 'I bet you could win yourself some cash.'

Peter looked crestfallen. 'Oh, dear, am I a bore?' he said. 'Is that what you're trying to tell me?'

'Not at all,' said Fleur hurriedly. 'I meant it as a compliment. By the way, Peter, am I imagining it or has Alice disappeared?'

It was a week after Alice's visit to Boulden's and Fleur had still not had the chance to pass on what her research had uncovered for the simple reason that she hadn't seen Alice since that day.

'But her place seems to have been filled,' said Peter, nodding to where Roz was ambling along with the random jogger Fleur had been seeing all over London. The pair appeared deeply engrossed in conversation as their feet pounded the tarmac pathway beneath. Overhead, the trees were no longer the stark black skeletons they had been at the start of the training programme. Adorning the formerly empty, lifeless branches were dots of acid green, the signs that spring was on its way and that the winter of all their discontents was coming to an end. Brave yellow aconites and sleepy-headed white snowdrops were breaking through the frost-burnt ground and the air had lost the oppressive funereal chill of deep winter and taken on a light, airy brightness instead.

'Who is that man?' asked Fleur.

'Perhaps you should ask Roz,' said Peter rather forlornly. Until the mystery jogger arrived, Peter had often accompanied

Roz round the park as Fleur's new running pace meant she was covering ground rather more quickly than her friend these days. 'They seem to be getting on very well, don't you think?'

Ben loped up to join them.

'Ben, where's Alice?' asked Fleur. They'd been running for nearly an hour now and she didn't have the energy to go into long-winded explanations while on the hoof so she kept her sentences short.

'Don't know,' said Ben, looking perplexed. 'It's very odd – I've called several times but there's been no reply.'

'Can you give me her number?' said Fleur. 'I need to talk to her.'

'Certainly.' Ben looked surprised but pleased. 'I'm really glad you're getting to know Alice. She's a very nice woman.'

Peter gave a tiny snort. Alice had been very aloof with Peter, at first mistaking him for some kind of pensioned-off weirdo, and had defrosted by only a very few degrees when she found him instead to be a top-flight barrister. Her ideas of what an important lawyer should look like were clearly culled from television series where dashing actors played smooth sharp legal geniuses in crisp shirts with spray-on tans. To find that someone as small and scruffy as Peter was a big cheese in the profession seemed to knock her conviction that being successful was synonymous with being attractive and smartly dressed too. She hadn't been much friendlier with Roz although she had unbent enough to ascertain where Fleur worked and comment that she had once met her boss, Brinley Boulden. As for the few other peripatetic members of the Runners' Club, mostly they flew too low for her social radar to pick up, so they were left unchallenged by Alice's talk of house prices, school entry exams or curtain fabric. Apart from Ben, of course, for whom Alice turned on her full radiant and entrancing charm, a class act which had him borderline besotted before very long.

Feet pounding, three abreast, Ben, Fleur and Peter rounded a corner to find Roz alone, loitering under the spreading branches of a plane tree. Her cheeks were flushed and her brown eyes sparkled with naughty merriment.

'I have to dash,' she told them in tones of repressed excitement. 'I've got a very busy day at work today – six weddings! Can you believe it? Romance – it's not dead after all.'

She flashed Peter a challenging look. When they jogged together, the rotund registrar and the string bean barrister tended to indulge themselves in long arguments concerning the nature of love, Roz maintaining it was a semi-supernatural force which struck with no warning and caused untold delights and agony, while Peter was on the side of reason, rationale, tested compatibility and low expectations.

But this morning Peter didn't rise. 'I am glad to hear it,' he remarked politely, giving a little sigh as he looked at Roz's enflamed face.

'Well, I must fly!' said Roz, skipping away, but not before she had whispered in Fleur's ear, 'Call me later!'

When she got to work, Fleur tried faithfully to reach Roz by phone, but each time she called the receptionist told her Roz was busy, doubtless attending to one of her many weddings. In the end, Fleur left a message, saying she would call by the register office in the early evening. Situated on the King's Road, the Chelsea Town Hall where Roz worked was an old stone building on whose steps many a debonair soul had posed for their nuptial photos. Among their distinguished number was Fleur's own father, who had been married there at least three times. On the whole, Fleur thought this an improvement on the times he had got hitched while drunk in Vegas, naked in California or by mistake in Bristol.

Fleur arrived at the register office just as Roz was busy shepherding the last delirious couple of the day into the happy state of matrimony. As Fleur waited in Roz's office, where the walls were covered in flowery Thank You cards, she heard Roz congratulating them.

'Thank you so much,' the bridegroom was saying.

'It's been a pleasure,' Roz's warm voice said, ringing with sincerity. 'It's a wonderful privilege to unite two people so deeply in love. I wish you all the best.'

'It's been so special,' came the fluting tones of the bride, wobbling with joyful tears.

'Now, off you go,' ordered Roz. 'You've got some celebrating to do! And make sure any babies are registered with me – I'll want to do it personally.'

'How did you know?' The bride sounded a little concerned.

'You just run along and enjoy your wedding reception,' said Roz breezily. 'My very best wishes and congratulations.

'Phew, what a day!' she said, shutting the door to her office. 'I'm all wrung out.'

Despite her claims to exhaustion, Fleur had never seen Roz look better. Her sallow skin had an attractive flush, her brazil nut eyes were gleaming and she couldn't stop smiling, the sort of large, ridiculous grin which instantly signals that the wearer has just fallen in love. Although her nose was crooked, her face lopsided and her brown hair cut to lie flat like a skullcap on her head, and her cheeks were etched with the deep lines of years of smiling and smoking, her unusual appearance became more attractive with longer acquaintance. In her trademark wide-cut fine wool outfits in rich shades of umber, paprika or plum, chunky silver necklaces and baroque dangling earrings, Roz had a kind of highly individualised beauty which became all the more apparent from being initially hidden.

'Why so many weddings?' asked Fleur.

'It's the Christmas rush,' said Roz, opening the office window. 'Come February, the couples who got rather too jolly at Christmas and New Year suddenly find themselves expecting the patter of tiny feet so they all charge down to the register office to get hitched. Then in September, they give birth at the Chelsea and Westminster hospital and come back up the road to register the babies. It's very seasonal, my business.' She lit a cigarette and blew the smoke out of the window. 'Goodness, I need this.'

'I thought you had an acupuncture needle in your ear to stop you wanting a cigarette,' said Fleur.

'I did,' said Roz, a touch bashfully. 'But it hurt when I smoked so I took it out.'

'So what was the great excitement this morning?' asked Fleur. Roz threw her cigarette butt out into the street and flicked on the kettle.

'Well,' she said settling down for a gossip. 'You know that man – the one who's been smiling at me?'

'And stalking me,' Fleur reminded her. She had told Roz about the uncanny number of times she had run into him over the past few weeks.

'He's not stalking you, Fleur! How silly!' said Roz. 'He works in Piccadilly and lives in Battersea, that's why you've seen him. Anyway, he's asked me to go on a date with him!' Roz sat back, clearly expecting an effusive reaction.

'Peter's going to be so sad,' sighed Fleur. She'd noticed him looking with longing at Roz, as though he would love to ask her out but didn't quite dare.

'What's Peter got to do with it?' said Roz, who wasn't very happy with Fleur's response. 'Fleur, we're talking about Denny.'

'Is that really a name?' asked Fleur.

'It's short for something,' replied Roz.

'For what?' said Fleur, blowing on the cup of tea Roz handed her.

'Well, I don't know. We're not on full name terms yet,' said Roz huffily. 'Which is a nuisance because if I had his full name, I could look him up.'

'In what? Debretts?' said Fleur. She thought it was unlikely the enigmatic jogger was the lost heir to a great estate.

'No, on the database,' said Roz. 'I've got access to the National Database so I can double-check people's identities.'

'Do you normally look up people you've met?' asked Fleur, a thought forming in her mind.

'Er, sometimes,' said Roz airily. 'Biscuit?' She offered Fleur a plate of shortbread. 'Sorry we don't have fancy ones – budget won't allow it.'

'Have you ever looked me up?' asked Fleur.

'Oh, er, well,' Roz prevaricated. She tried to cause a distraction. 'Let me shut that window – it really isn't spring yet, is it?'

'Is that why you asked me when my birthday was?' Fleur persisted.

Roz was looking pained. 'I'm so sorry,' she said. 'Perhaps it's the job – it makes me terribly nosy. Are you cross?'

'No,' said Fleur. 'Just interested.'

'As you've mentioned it, I did want to ask you.' Roz glanced at Fleur to check she wasn't fuming and, finding her face mild and pleasant, continued, 'You see, there isn't anyone with your name and birthday. Were you born abroad?'

'No,' said Fleur. 'I've changed my name.' It was her turn to look abashed. 'And so would you if your parents had called you Astraea Xavia Tiphani Flower.'

'Is that you?' Roz was agog. 'I saw that entry. But the last name wasn't Bonner.'

'That's my mother's maiden name,' said Fleur. 'My father's name is Harris. Jed Harris.'

'Jed Harris?' said Roz in surprise. 'But I've married him.'

'Who hasn't?' said Fleur, a little glumly.

'No, I mean I've been the celebrant at some of his weddings,' said Roz. 'Goodness, he's been through so often, we joked he should have a frequent flyer's card.'

'Hey, well, that's my dad,' said Fleur lightly. He seemed to be cropping up with alarming regularity at the moment – she turned on the television and there he was, being interviewed on a breakfast news programme; go into a bar and they would doubtless be playing one of his hits; open a magazine and she'd see his face or, to cap it all, if he wasn't pestering her by phone, he'd appear randomly in person, as he had the other afternoon when she'd been with Greta. She was starting to feel that he was everywhere. She decided to move the conversation on. 'Tell me about your date with Denny.'

'Ooh!' Roz clapped her hands together and simpered a little, only too willing to be diverted on to this particular topic. 'Denny says the first time he saw me, he felt as though we'd met before even though he knew we hadn't.'

'That's lovely,' murmured Fleur, taking a gulp of her tea to fortify herself. She wanted to be happy for Roz, but she couldn't shake the feeling there was something odd about the man.

'Denny said he knew straight away he had to get to know me,' continued Roz, her eyes going misty. 'He said his destiny had led him to take up running after Christmas because that's when he saw me for the first time.'

'Hmm,' said Fleur cautiously. 'I have heard more romantic

sentiments than "Fate made me a jogger". Are you going to go out with him?'

'I'd *love* to,' said Roz. 'But I haven't been on a date for so long that I'm really scared I won't know what to do.'

'You'll be fine,' said Fleur, who felt exactly the same. The prospect of an actual date was quite terrifying. In the good old days, when you just got pissed and snogged someone, these things were quite straightforward. Now it all seemed so complicated and difficult. Everyone had so much baggage, was so scared of revealing their true selves, had so little time and yet such high expectations.

'I wanted to ask you . . .' Roz hesitated, 'and I know this is a lot to ask – whether you would come too.'

'What – on your date?' Fleur was staggered.

'I don't think I can go alone,' said Roz plaintively. 'I just can't. But if I don't go out with him, I might lose him altogether. He might be The One, Fleur. The One I've been waiting for.'

'Roz, how can I come on a date with you and Denny?' said Fleur. 'He'll find that so odd, I think you'd lose him anyway.'

'What-if-we-found-someone-who-could-come-too?' The words came out in a tumble.

'A double date?' said Fleur. 'That sounds . . .' She was about to say 'horrible' but she caught Roz's pleading expression. What if Denny really was heaven-sent to Roz? Didn't she at least deserve the chance of finding out? Not wanting to doom her new friend to a life of any more loneliness than she had already endured, Fleur relented. 'Okay,' she said. 'But provided the friend knows I'm not interested in him. I don't want to get into any situations.'

'Thank you!' Roz cried. 'Thank you so much! Will you kick me under the table if I talk too much or smoke too much or start getting drunk?'

'Yes, and I'll tell you if you've got spinach between your teeth too,' said Fleur. 'But I'm going away tomorrow – I've got to deliver an icon to a man in Belgrade, so you'll have to wait a few days.'

'You will be careful, won't you?' said Roz. 'I don't like to think of you flying off into the unknown with some priceless art work in your bag.'

'That's exactly what Peter said,' mused Fleur. 'But it's not priceless and I'm sure I'll be fine.'

'Check in with us while you're gone,' said Roz. 'So we know you're okay. Now, what shall we do on our date? Any good ideas?'

'I know!' said Fleur, perking up. 'I've been invited to the opening of an exhibition.' Greta's card had come in the post. Taking a date, even a fake one, would be a very good idea as no doubt Sean plus permanent other half would be present and going alone would make Fleur look a bit of a loser. 'Let's do that.'

'I like your style,' said Roz.

'It's a deal,' said Fleur. 'As long as you remember you owe me.'

'Pay you back in confetti,' said Roz. 'There's plenty of that round here.'

8

The inside of the Veliki Airlines plane smelt as though someone had vomited sweet lemonade over the beige brocade seats. A sloe-eyed hostess, her inky hair held in a smart chignon, put a tray of food in front of Fleur after they had rocketed upwards, presumably to regulation flying height although the plane had shot up so fast and so hard that Fleur would not have been surprised to see a few planets orbiting the bouncing wing. The pilot, a dashing soul who put her in mind of the sexy dark doctor from *ER*, seemed to be under the impression that Heathrow was a war zone from which he must airlift his passengers as quickly as possible, avoiding enemy fire by effecting a semi-vertical ascent. It must be the legacy of the war-torn Balkans, thought Fleur, although these days the pilot was probably right in assuming that any airport in the United Kingdom was a deeply dangerous place to be and one whence he needed to evacuate them post-haste. That she was flying to the relative safety of Belgrade, a city which only two years before had suffered a NATO bombardment that had ripped whole buildings into shards of twisted steel and concrete, seemed somewhat ironic.

Investigating her food tray, she found a sandwich whose desire to remain edible had clearly left it a few days previously, a mysterious pink square of wobbling jelly which

might – or might not – be ham, and the leg of a small creature, possibly feathered, roasted for her delectation. She looked
round at the other passengers. While it would be unkind to
judge a nation's cuisine on the quality of their airline fare –
although the French would probably argue that British
Airways could teach you everything you needed to know
about English food – this was spectacularly bad. It didn't bode
well for her prospects of eating decently while on her quick
trip. And yet, those of her fellow travellers who appeared to
be of Serbian origin were quite possibly the best-looking group
of people Fleur had ever laid eyes on. With their chocolate
eyes, thick black hair and olive skins, they exuded a sort of
restless vitality which no amount of vitamin pills could induce.
Perhaps, thought Fleur, the Serbs were the proof positive that
you are definitely not what you eat. Anyone who was the
physical manifestation of this kind of crap should be flabby,
pallid and lethargic, which was exactly how the non-Serbian
passengers, the sprinkling of northern Europeans and
Americans who had joined the fast plane to Belgrade, seemed.
She drank her over-sweetened apple juice instead, neatly
returning all other items to her food tray so it could be boxed
up and used again for the next passenger.

Getting through UK customs had entailed no little palaver
as there was nothing like travelling with a locked metal brief-
case containing a valuable icon to get officialdom drooling
with excitement. In her previous job, Fleur had never had to
actually travel with the art works in person. If her museum
lent, borrowed or bought, the items were delivered by a top
class firm of international couriers who took care of everything from insurance to paperwork to suitable travelling conditions for fragile paintings. But they did so at a price and Brinley
obviously felt that Fleur could do just as well with a return
ticket on a bargain basement airline with an incomparable

safety record, in that no other company dared operate international routes with such a very low degree of security.

It hadn't been easy for Fleur to work out quite what the procedure should be for travelling with an icon, but in part she had her own sense of pride to blame. She would have liked to ask Brinley but he was indulging himself in another of his mini-breaks away from the office, crucial he claimed for maintaining the 'supply' side of the business. Vendors were much harder to find than buyers, of whom there was always a limitless supply, so Brinley liked to trawl around the international cocktail party circuit, sniffing out whose declining fortunes might lead them to flog some of the furniture.

The person she should have asked for advice was Sean, but she baulked at the thought. All those years ago, when Sean had asked her not to take the job in the States but to stay in London with him while he finished his conservator's course, Fleur had unleashed a few snarky comments about their differing levels of ambition. The prospect of life in New York had rather turned Fleur's head, and while preparing for departure she had gone through a grandiose, uppity phase. She shuddered when she thought of what a toerag she had been, how unfeelingly and dismissively she had behaved towards poor Sean. She couldn't face asking for his help now and so all communication about the icon and its state of repair went through Spook, Fleur managing to avoid speaking to Sean directly. The harder he tried to contact Fleur in person, leaving messages at work or on her mobile, turning up at the shop, the more astutely she avoided him, even gaining a certain sense of perverse satisfaction in her success at hiding from him. She didn't want to reveal her professional ignorance to him and neither could she face the thought of his bringing her to account for her behaviour in the past.

But even so, the more persistently Sean tried to get in touch with her, the more a mounting excitement grew inside Fleur until she had persuaded herself that what he so urgently needed to tell her had nothing to do with the icon but was some personal matter instead. It couldn't be work-related, she told herself. He wouldn't make so much effort just to tell her something he could have passed on via Spook, so it must mean that what he wanted to say was for her ears only. In her mind, she built a whole elaborate fantasy involving Sean, his broken heart, his horrible new girlfriend whom he must be desperate to get away from and Fleur's sudden and unexpected reappearance in London. He wants me back, a little voice in her mind repeatedly whispered to her. Sean wants me back. He still loves me and everything is going to work out after all. Once she got back from Belgrade, she promised herself, she would give in and let him speak. For now, she relished the anticipation and the extra joy that the surprise discovery of lost love was bringing her.

Asking around her various art world friends for how best to transport an icon produced a variety of opinions ranging from 'Wrap it in a jumper and put it in your luggage. If anyone asks, you bought it on Portobello Market' to 'Are you mad? Get the professionals to take it.' Eventually Fleur decided honesty was the best policy and declared the icon at Customs, which led to so many complications in terms of endless paperwork that she nearly missed her plane. In the end, she had claimed that the lighting and humidity in the airport were adversely affecting the icon and that it must be locked into the case again to ensure its safety. This seemed to give the man from Customs and Excise the boot up the backside he needed as he swiftly completed his last form and sent Fleur on her way.

'Hi,' said the man in the airline seat next to Fleur. He had the fleshless hard face of a US president carved into the rock at Mount Rushmore. 'Not hungry?'

'I think I can wait,' said Fleur. 'I'm hoping my next meal will contain identifiable foodstuffs.'

Her companion laughed. 'You can eat very well in Belgrade,' he said. 'If you know where.'

'Do you know the city?' asked Fleur. She had searched for a guide book but found nothing, not even a mention in the Lonely Planet Eastern European guide. So far, her sole source of information was the official 'Tourist Belgrade' website. Spectacularly, for the national tourist board's only given information, it had contained no restaurant listings whatsoever but concentrated on how to get to – and from – Belgrade, something Fleur found rather ominous. It had categorised the methods of arrival with helpful tips such as 'By Car – Always. By Bus – Most Frequent. By River – Hardly.'

'Where are you staying?' he asked.

'I'm not sure,' said Fleur. 'I'm being met at the airport.'

'What are you doing in Belgrade?' said the American traveller, giving her a narrow-eyed sideways glance.

'Just some business,' said Fleur vaguely. When travelling for work, she never told casual passers-by her real mission.

'Okay,' said the man casually, seeming to lose interest. 'By the way, my name's Striker, Striker McCullum.'

'Fleur,' said Fleur. 'Fleur Bonner.' They shook hands awkwardly. She noticed he had unusually large hands.

'So, Striker,' she said, thinking what strange names American men tended to have. 'What takes you to Serbia?'

'I'm going on to Kosovo,' said Striker. 'I'm working for an NGO down there. It's pretty wild.'

'I'm sure,' said Fleur, hoping her neutral tone signalled her lack of interest in developing an in-flight relationship.

'Yup,' said the American traveller. 'There's all sorts going on in Kosovo.'

Fleur smiled politely and fished her copy of the airline magazine out of the seat pocket. Opening it, she flipped through the pages which extolled the glories of the Balkan region, illustrated with lurid, over-coloured photos of seaside towns, mountain ranges, and restaurants and night clubs packed with people sporting suspiciously outmoded hair-styles. Whenever she glanced up, she caught Striker's eye, but having no wish to re-engage in conversation with him she was forced to feign fascination with the glossy magazine until the plane began to shoot downwards out of the sky, by which time she had read the only article in English at least five times.

Fleur's small leather travelling bag was one of the first to arrive on the carousel so she set off speedily towards the double doors which separated the public area of the airport from the zone reserved for travellers. As the doors slid back, she was hit in the face by the stench of unwashed bodies, strong tobacco and diesel fuel. She walked through the doors with trepidation. There was a brief moment of calm as the waiting crowds looked in surprise at this tiny blonde woman, so different from the swarthy, jostling locals, but in an instant the crowd had closed in on her, with greasy men pulling her jacket and shouting 'Taxi!' 'Change money!' 'Hotel!' in her ear. Clutching her bag and her case closely to her, she tried to force her way through, but the pressure was coming from all sides. The smell was so dense and the air so stuffy, she thought she might faint, and then she heard a loud voice shouting 'Zadi!' and a long arm reached into the heaving crowd, pulling her back to safety.

'Zadi, zadi,' Striker was saying to the turbulent gangs of unwashed drivers, in a voice which invited no opposition, his large hands splayed in front of him in a menacing gesture.

The taxi men backed off quickly, muttering darkly about bossy Americans, trying to run everything.

'Are you okay?' Striker looked at Fleur, his hard face softened slightly, as though a little erosion had knocked some of the rigidity out of his rocky features. 'I shoulda warned you – that can be kinda hard core.'

Fleur took a few deep breaths. 'I'm fine,' she said, although her head was spinning somewhat.

'Is someone coming to collect you?' asked Striker, her new saviour.

'They should be,' said Fleur.

'What's the name?'

'Lazarevic.'

'Ima neki covijek ovde iz kancelarije Lazarevica?' he shouted. The slouching drivers, their hot eyes gazing at Fleur, shook their heads.

'Do you have their number?'

'Oh, shit,' said Fleur, realising how stupid she had been. Because she was travelling within the geographical limits of Europe – if not the political and economic ones – it hadn't occurred to her that arriving in Serbia would be all that different from a trip to Belgium or Greece. So while she had rigorously checked all the details pertaining to the icon, she had left Spook to make all her travel arrangements for her. Now she was standing in this airport, in this country which suddenly seemed as foreign to her as Timbuktu, with contact details locked firmly into a case she didn't want to open in public, no local currency and a mobile phone with no service, that didn't seem to have been such a good idea after all.

'Damn!' said Fleur, looking at the blank screen of her mobile.

'There's no mobile coverage at the airport.' Striker confirmed what she already knew.

'What am I going to do?' Fleur suddenly felt very far from home and very alone. She looked around her as though to seek for a clue but none presented itself. It was hardly a modern airport – instead of the ranks of neon-lit car hire kiosks, Starbucks coffee outlets and bookstalls which had colonised the places at which Fleur usually arrived, Belgrade airport had just a row of closed airline ticket offices, offering flights to obscure places such as Sofia, Tivat or Bucharest.

'I'm overnighting in Belgrade,' said Striker. 'Why don't you come to my hotel, we'll book you a room, and you can get yourself sorted out and start again tomorrow?'

Outside the airport, a dark foggy night showed little sign of life or civilisation. Loath as she was to take off into the unknown with this man, Fleur couldn't see quite what other option she had. 'Thank you,' she said, figuring she owed him a little more politeness than she had so far displayed.

'All those who travel,' said Striker enigmatically, 'are in the comfort of strangers. You need comfort and I'm definitely strange.'

It wasn't perhaps the most heart-warming sentiment Fleur had ever heard, although she felt she preferred it to the one about necessity making odd bedfellows. That was the last thing she and Striker were going to become.

'My ex-wife insisted I have a vasectomy,' Striker was saying to Fleur as they worked their way down their second bottle of Macedonian red wine in the Belgrade Hyatt hotel bar. So efficient had Striker been in booking Fleur a room when they had arrived here from the airport that he had paid for her fawn-coloured ensuite marble bathroom with over-air-conditioned double room before she had time to register what he was doing. She had protested that she was on business and should be paying for herself, but when she handed over her corporate credit card it was swiftly declined, leaving her in the embarrassing position of looking both foolish and ungrateful. Striker had just laughed and produced his Amex once more. 'The American government pays for me,' he said. 'So I think they can spare a little cash for you as well.'

'I thought you said you worked for an NGO,' said Fleur.

'Same thing.' Striker shrugged but he gave her another of his sideways looks.

'Of course, that was before she left me,' Striker continued, filling Fleur's glass once more. 'She was from Costa Rica,' he added as though this made everything clear.

'Couldn't she have had her tubes tied?' asked Fleur. It was one of the peculiarities about travelling that casual conversations with people who were ostensibly strangers could turn very personal very quickly.

'Too late now,' said Striker. 'So she's got both the kids and I'm left with nothing to offer.'

'I wouldn't say that,' said Fleur gallantly. 'After all, not every woman wants children these days.'

'Don't be so sure,' said Striker darkly. 'At least,' he cheered up a bit, 'I can't get anyone pregnant by mistake.'

Fleur hoped this wasn't an offer but as the bar was packed with fiendishly attractive women, many of whom she felt would be happy to not get pregnant by Striker, possibly for some degree of financial outlay, she felt quite safe, although she did wonder whether the American government paid for that too. He was quite handsome, she supposed, and definitely looking better after every glass of wine, except that she found men with too many muscles quite off-putting, especially as they clearly expected a high level of admiration for their bulges which Fleur was quite incapable of faking. A well-toned body was one thing but a physique like a string bag of Christmas nuts was quite another. Striker's bare arm, protruding from the rolled-up sleeve of his T-shirt, was the size and strength of one of her legs, although she was grateful that, unlike his rippled forearm, her veins had not yet popped out on to the surface of her skin.

'See that lot over there?' Striker motioned to a group of absurdly beautiful women, loitering around a set of grey-suited, thick-set men with flashing rings and angry eyes. Fleur had encountered one of the females in the ladies' loo, coming out of a cubicle with her dark glasses on. 'Don't spill their drinks.'

'Will I be swimming with the fishes if I do?' asked Fleur, who was leaning forward, her face cradled in her two hands, elbows perched on the edge of the small round table between her and Striker.

'Chewed to death by their pet piranhas, more likely,' said Striker.

'Do you work here by choice?' asked Fleur.

'I kinda like it,' said Striker. 'It's crazy, unpredictable, exciting. The Balkans are like a drug – you get addicted if you hang around here too long.'

'Not likely to happen to me,' said Fleur, who had rarely been anywhere she found less appealing.

'No,' agreed Striker. 'I think I can see that.'

'Anyway,' said Fleur, who suddenly felt very tired. 'I should go up to my room – I have a few calls I need to make.'

'Will you be okay?' asked Striker.

'I'm a bit wiped out,' she admitted. 'It's been a long day. Thank you.'

Striker inclined his head. 'It's been a pleasure,' he said gravely. 'You take care of yourself, now, Fleur Bonner.'

'Oh, I intend to,' said Fleur. 'Good night.'

Back in her 'everything in glorious beige' suite, Fleur settled herself on the bed with a list of calls to make. It was expensive, she knew, to use hotel phone lines, but without her mobile she didn't have much choice. She left a quick message for Spook at the office to tell her there had been some mix-up with the arrangements and that she was staying at the Hyatt, Belgrade; she phoned her mother to say she was fine and would be back soon; and then she had one more call she wanted to make before it was time to sleep.

The phone at the other end rang and rang. Eventually someone picked up.

'Hello?' said a rather woebegone voice.

'Alice? It's Fleur,' said Fleur, her tongue feeling rather thick, as though it had grown a little and was now too big to fit in her mouth.

'Oh!' Clearly this was a surprise.

'I said I'd call you about that receipt,' said Fleur, whose eyelids seemed to want to close of their own accord.

'Oh,' repeated Alice. 'The receipt.'

'Alice, thosh paintings,' said Fleur, having to enunciate very carefully. She must be much more drunk than she thought. 'Brin paid losh of money for them.'

'Oh, no,' Alice groaned.

'The seller . . .' Fleur struggled on, 'wash someone called Mikhail . . . Roscoff. D'you know him?'

'Yes, I do,' said Alice quietly. 'Fleur, you haven't mentioned me to Brinley, have you?'

'Of coursh not,' said Fleur, slurring her words. 'The paintings . . . they're in . . . in . . . our . . . warehoush.' Finally she got the word out.

'Are you all right?' said Alice's distant voice.

'Fine,' said Fleur. 'Alish . . .'

'Fleur.' Alice sounded sharper now. 'You don't sound very well. Can I call someone for you?'

'No . . . just tired . . . very tired . . . don' worry . . . bye.' Too tired to talk any further, Fleur hung up the phone and laid her heavy head back on the concrete pillows. A couple of minutes' snooze, she said to herself. Just a little rest, then she'd be fine.

9

Red wine usually gave Fleur a fitful, disturbed night's sleep, full of confused dreams and abrupt midnight awakenings. That night, however, was dark, black and completely unmemorable, Fleur sleeping incredibly deeply from the moment she dropped off to when she awoke. She opened her eyes, wincing a little at the sour taste in her mouth, and looked over to the bedside clock whose flashing red light announced it was 7.45 a.m. For a second, she had the feeling of extreme dislocation which comes with waking up in an unfamiliar place. She shut her eyes again as she pieced together the events of the night before – arriving in Belgrade to find no host to meet her, checking in with Striker, having a drink in the bar and then coming upstairs to her room where she had clearly fallen asleep fully dressed on the bed. She opened her eyes again and blinked a few times, relieved that nothing too awful had happened. Although she didn't remember drinking inordinate amounts, certainly not in the sort of quantity that would make her pass out, Fleur concluded that exhaustion after a long and stressful day had got the better of her. Deciding there was nothing more to it than that, she heaved herself off the bed and went to the bathroom, accidentally tipping the metal carrying case with the icon off the end of the bed as she did so. It split open as it hit the floor, the icon in its neat bubble wrap emerging as the case divided itself into two halves. Tutting to herself, Fleur picked the case up carefully and rearranged the icon before closing the lid. If she found it odd that such a slight blow should cause a secure lock to spring open, she gave it little thought in her rather drowsy morning state.

Yawning in the bathroom, she checked her reflection and gave herself a low five out of ten – altogether not great but definitely holding the possibility of looking up by later in the day. A steaming shower of metallic-smelling water restored her spirits quite nicely and within half an hour of waking she was lacing her up her trainers and ready to have a run around the streets of Belgrade. As she now had one bar of service on her mobile phone, she sent a quick text message to Roz: 'Running around Belgrade! Beat that! Fx' Then she strolled casually down to the lobby, through the revolving doors and out into the gently falling snow.

'Nice work Ms Bonner,' Roz texted back when she picked up the message only a little later that morning as she walked through the park to meet the others for her early morning run. 'You go girl! Rx' It was a soft, sunny morning in London, very different from the grey glowering atmosphere in Belgrade where Fleur was pounding along the slushy streets. It was not cold enough in Serbia for the snow to settle, only for it to land and create a sludge along the pavements which squidged underfoot as Fleur's white trainers rapidly turned a nasty shade of brown. A tram sliced through the traffic on the busy dual carriageway leading from Fleur's hotel, sending a wave of coffee-coloured foam over Fleur herself, drenching the lone runner as the densely packed passengers in the tram looked on apathetically. She had decided to run towards what looked like the centre, past rows and rows of identical tower blocks, each balcony fringed with a line of colourful laundry, attempting to dry in the thick damp air. She passed a bunch of kids tormenting a dog which howled ominously as Fleur ran past, making the mistake of putting one foot into the roadway to avoid the rabid canine as she went. Immediately, an insane hooting erupted behind her and she jumped back on to the narrow pathway just in time to avoid being mown down by a long black shiny car with pale blue net curtains in every window.

And yet despite the hostile, open-mouthed stares, the catcalls of derision or the looks of plain amusement, Fleur settled into a rolling jog, hopping over the broken, twisted pavements, skipping round the open manhole covers and dancing across the great lakes of caramel-coloured sludge lying between pavement and road. On and on she ran, over a bridge crossing the river Danube which lay beneath as flat and wide as a plate, up a hill towards a dome-like structure, sitting squatly in a frosty park, the ground melting away under the rhythmic pounding of her feet. As she scaled the hill leading to central Belgrade, passing huge posters with air-brushed photographs of candidates for the forthcoming presidential elections smiling menacingly down at her, she felt free, her limbs seemingly moving independently of any thought process, her speed steady, her heart rate stable. She felt as if she could run for ever, which was just as well as at the top of the hill she had to turn round and run back the way she came, huffing a little now with the exertion of what had turned out to be her longest outing yet. Her pace picked up as she skedaddled downhill, laughing as she caught the bemused expressions of drivers caught in the stationary traffic, a very high proportion of whom appeared to be picking their noses. Handsome traffic police stood in the midst of the non-moving barricade of vehicles, pointlessly milling their white-gloved arms and blowing whistles in staccato harmony with each other. Columns of black smoke rose from distant factories as a horse and cart clopped past on a side road, while all the time the wide river continued its journey beneath the bridges of Belgrade, flowing from Vienna in the west to the Black Sea in the east.

Along the north edge of Battersea Park, the River Thames – browner, faster, choppier and more congested than its distant cousin the Danube – was hurrying tugboats and barges out seawards. On the riverside steps of the Peace Pagoda, Peter was waiting for the other runners to appear, filling in the time until they arrived by executing a few t'ai chi poses, his latest hobby, adopting a series of graceful, dance-like postures while gazing as if rapt with wonder at the washed blue sky where fluffy white clouds scurried busily along. On the ground, spikes of bulbs emerged from the London earth, ready to erupt into colourful blooms the minute they were sure that winter had really gone.

'Good morning, good morning, good morning!' trilled Roz as she skipped up. Roz felt very empowered that morning. Breathing in deeply, she exhaled with a whooshing noise. 'Oh, how fresh the air is!' she exclaimed happily. 'I can smell the scent of spring on the breeze.'

'So the giving up smoking day went well?' Peter stopped his t'ai chi sequence and smiled at her.

'It was amazing,' enthused Roz. 'They deconstructed the myth of smoking for you.'

'Which myth would that be?' said Peter, reprising his movements. 'The one about spending lots of money on something that will eventually kill you? This one's called Open the Lotus Flower, by the way.'

'Yes, yes.' Roz waved her hand impatiently. 'All that, of course. But mostly, it was about fear – we smoke cigarettes to mask the fear we feel in different situations, but actually, smoking doesn't take away your negative feelings, it increases them.'

'I see,' murmured Peter. 'What about this one – Capture the Mountain Tiger.' He waved his arms around while kneeling on the ground.

'And,' Roz carried on, clearly a zealous new convert, 'how we fear giving up, not because we are afraid of life without cigarettes but because we are terrified of failure.'

'Remarkable,' said Peter. 'I take it you haven't smoked since.'

'Peace, people,' said Ben, arriving on his mountain bike and giving them the two-fingered sign of harmony.

'Ben, Ben,' said Roz excitedly. 'I went on the Stop Smoking course and it was brilliant.'

'Good.' Ben was looking rather tired, his usually sparkling eyes boasting a pair of bags. 'Well done, Rosalind. Welcome to the rest of your life.' He locked his bike to the railings.

'Thank you so much for booking me on it,' Roz prattled on.

'No problem,' said Ben wearily. 'It was really nothing. Now come on, let's get a move on.'

'But surely we're not all here,' said Peter, performing the Lotus Flower manoeuvre once more.

'Fleur's away,' said Ben. 'And this – us – is all we have left.' He gave the most almighty sigh. Roz and Peter exchanged glances. Peter raised his eyebrows at Roz who shook her head and pointed at Peter. In turn, Peter grimaced and indicated Roz herself.

'Oh, all right,' she hissed. 'Ben,' she said in her normal voice. 'Where's everyone gone?'

'That's a good question,' said Ben sadly. 'We've had a sudden rash of drop-outs. Tell me, you two,' he looked at

121

them seriously, 'is it me? Am I really horrible? Is that why no one's turning up to training?'

'Nooo!' said Roz quickly. 'Of course it's not!' She felt quite upset that Ben could even think that.

'You mustn't take it personally. People are not given to being very realistic about their capabilities,' explained Peter, executing a complicated sequence, which those in the know might recognise as the Waterfall.

Roz and Ben smiled at each other. If asked to pick which member of the Runners' Club approached their natural capabilities with the least dose of realism, they would both unhesitatingly have nominated Peter.

'He's right,' said Roz. 'Everyone loves the idea of running a marathon but not many people actually like it in practice.'

'So it wasn't anything I said?' Ben looked uncharacteristically nervous.

'No,' said Peter. 'You called me a malcoordinated tortoise last week and I'm still here.'

'Please tell me you guys aren't going to back out?' Ben pleaded. Roz took a deep breath. She had been on the point of quitting several times and only a few days back had made a mental note that if it didn't get any easier for her in the next couple of weeks she would definitely jack it in.

'No,' she said. 'We're not, are we, Peter?' she added fiercely. 'And Fleur will see it through – I had a text from her this morning. She's on a work trip to Belgrade and she's gone out running.'

'She has?' Ben's face lit up. 'But that's brilliant!'

'What about Alice?' said Roz. 'She didn't strike me as a quitter.'

'Well,' said, Ben looking perplexed, 'that's the one I understand the least. I had a message from her late last night, saying she wouldn't be coming back to training and that she was giving up the marathon.'

'Did she say why?' asked Peter.

'It was a weird message,' said Ben. 'I couldn't make out what she was saying although she did mention Fleur. I was a bit worried, though. She didn't sound too good. Shall we have a warm-up lap?' Obediently, the much-depleted Club moved away from the Peace Pagoda.

'I was wondering,' said Ben casually as they jogged forward along the river path, 'whether you might consider going round to see her, Roz?'

'Me?' squeaked Roz. 'I don't think so – we're hardly friends.'

'She speaks very highly of you,' said Ben in cajoling tones.

'She does not!' said Roz hotly. 'She doesn't take any notice of me!'

'Let's just imagine for a second,' said Ben as they ran gently onwards, 'that you're not the busy, successful, debonair and devoted London professional we know and love you to be.'

'Ye-es,' said Roz cautiously.

'But you're a stay at home mum instead,' continued Ben. 'You've lost your confidence a bit after all those years of looking after the kids, you're beautiful but you think people see you as some kind of rich man's trophy wife and you haven't worked for so long that you feel like an alien in the adult world. Especially when you meet a group of smart, sassy individuals with an opinion on everything under the sun.'

'Who are they?' asked Peter, who was trailing behind a little.

'That's us,' said Roz, with a touch of pride.

'Can't you see how intimidating that might be?' asked Ben.

'Well,' said Roz, who was only half persuaded. 'No one *made* her flirt with the men.'

'That's a self-protection mechanism,' said Ben. 'Like a reflex reaction.'

'Aha,' said Roz triumphantly. 'If you understand her so well, why don't you go and see her?'

'Because it would be really nice for all of us if we bonded as a group,' said Ben gently. 'And this would be a good opportunity for Alice to realise you are not as terrifying as you seem.'

'Am I terrifying?' Roz turned to Peter in outrage.

'Tremendously,' he agreed, but seeing the look on Roz's face he realised he had made an error. 'Not,' he added quickly.

'And if I was having a hard time, you're exactly the sort of person I would love to see,' said Ben firmly. 'Someone warm and lovely and caring.'

'And terrifying,' muttered Roz crossly under her breath.

'I wonder why she mentioned Fleur,' said Peter.

'Oh, I'll ask her this evening, shall I?' said Roz resignedly. 'When I go round.'

'Hurray!' Ben leapt off the ground with both feet. 'Thank you, my lovely! I'll give you her address.'

'Not promising results,' said Roz.

'You don't need to,' said Ben. 'You are brilliant! Hey, Roz,' he added as an afterthought. 'Where's your gentleman friend this morning?'

'Oh, he's got some work thing,' said Roz, blushing a little while Peter pouted. 'But I'm sure I'll see him soon.'

'Meess Bonner?' said a voice. The phone had been ringing when Fleur got back to her hotel room, after a short altercation with the doorman who flatly refused to believe the somewhat mud-splattered Fleur could possibly be a hotel guest. He was also flabbergasted by the fact that Fleur seemed to have been out without any form of documentary identification about her person. Fleur had been in mid-argument when a limo, the insides so securely reinforced that the door was a foot thick when opened, slid into the parking space in front of the hotel, and she suddenly understood she had been rather rash. Running around a very foreign city without a map, a mobile phone or any cash had perhaps not been the safest of activities but she was back now so she tended to think all was well that ended well.

'Yes,' said Fleur into the telephone receiver. She wasn't aware that anyone other than that peculiar man Striker knew where she was.

'Theess is Zoran Lazarevic,' said the voice, a rich baritone with resonant and rolling Rs. 'I am welcoming you to Beograd.' He used the local name for the capital of Serbia and Montenegro, the country fashioned from the leftover scraps of Tito's great vision of Yugoslavia.

'Why, thank you,' said Fleur, who was in a rather upbeat mood after her run.

'We are glad you are here,' continued the voice of Zoran. 'Please be in the lobby of your hotel in five minutes. My driver will collect you.'

'How did you know to find me at the Hyatt?' demanded Fleur. The first thing on her list to do that morning was to contact Zoran and tell him she was here.

'Your secretary,' said the clipped voice. 'She called me this morning to say you arrived at the Hyatt last night. She tells me you had a last minute change of plan.'

'She did?' Fond of Spook as Fleur was, she had been cursing her young assistant quite profusely ever since she had arrived in Belgrade and found no one to meet her. Usually Fleur was very tolerant of Spook's dyslexia, which often caused her to misread numbers or make simple mistakes which she couldn't spot however hard she double-checked. But this time Fleur had been feeling less than charitable – she had no doubt that all her travel problems had arisen owing to Spook's giving out the wrong arrival information, thus leaving her stranded and at the mercy of random lunatics such as Striker, the strange man from the plane. However, she must have rectified the problem so Fleur made a mental note to forgive her. 'I'm glad we all know where we are now,' she said.

'Exactly,' said Zoran, his voice faint and tinny on the crackling line. 'I had understood you were to arrive today but no matter. You are here now.'

'So I am,' said Fleur. 'Let's get to business, Zoran,' she said smartly, the seventies-style hotel room, old-fashioned telephone, strange exoticism of her location and name of her new acquaintance conspiring to make her feel as though she was in a Bond movie.

'I look forward to meeting you,' said Zoran, and hung up.

'So, you from London,' said Zoran's driver, his blond brush of hair and reflective sunglasses giving him the look of a Hollywood film star on hard times. Fleur just nodded. The Mercedes in which she was travelling was moving so fast she thought she would be sick if she opened her mouth. Thick clouds formed across the dual carriageway around them, rising in grey plumes of diesel smoke and dirt into the murky sky. As they drove up an avenue which once must have been an impressive, mittel-European boulevard of stone-clad houses, she could see where whole frontages had been ripped off by the fire flashes rained down from the skies in the recent NATO bombardment, the inner floors and stairwells now spilling out of the wrecked buildings as though making a bid for freedom. Steel girders poked out of the sides of the bombed houses like whale bones from an underwired bra, cut free from their casing. In western Europe such places would have been colonised, either by squatters or by developers, keen to take over such central city sites and cover them in cranes, placards and hard-hatted workers. But here they just sat, crumbling slowly into decline, a monument to repression by the unjust West and their heavy-handed manner of settling international disputes. A reminder that outsiders could not be trusted and that Serbia, proud, defiant Serbia, stood alone against a cruel world.

The car screeched to a halt. 'We are here,' said the driver needlessly. Fleur, who had been thrown forward against the headrest of the seat in front of her when the car stopped, sat back and tried to compose herself after her helter-skelter ride. As her driver made no move, she opened the car door and scrambled out, holding the metal case containing the icon to her chest. They appeared to be at a crossroads with various small tree-lined streets leading off it. A bus, packed with all shapes and sizes of dark-haired passengers, rumbled past, spewing yet more roadside effluent over Fleur as it groaned its way up the hill. She tapped on the window.

'Where do I go?' she asked. The driver sighed and pointed.

'In there,' he said, gesturing to a large house on the junction of two of the roads.

The house was like a deranged interpretation of a Disney castle. It had crazed turrets which lurched round the roof at strange angles, a marble porch and windows made of the same reflective blue glass as her driver's shades. Looking around, she could see various cars parked across the pavements, inside which lurked laconic figures like her own driver, seemingly waiting for a order from within. She knocked on the door, which swung back to reveal a shaven-headed man in an eighties-style grey leather jacket.

'Hello,' said Fleur as he stared at her, tapping the ash from his cigarette insolently on the ground near her shoe. 'My name is Fleur Bonner, from Boulden's art gallery in London.'

The man continued to stare.

'I have an appointment with Zoran Lazarevic,' she carried on bravely. In her coat pocket, she crossed her fingers for good luck.

The man muttered into a two-way radio, held in a paw so enormous it made the receiver seem the size of a match box.

'Come in.' He ushered her into the dark lobby, where it was a few seconds before Fleur's eyes adjusted to the gloom. 'Give me your case.'

'I can't do that,' said Fleur, defiantly clutching the brief-case to her body. 'I can only hand this over to Mr Lazarevic himself.'

The gorilla looked at her impassively. Behind him, Fleur could now see a metal detector. 'You must walk through,' the guard said, 'before you can see Mr Lazarevic.' The atmosphere in the lobby was dense and sinister, redolent of unpleasant happenings and brutal commands.

'Then,' Fleur raised her chin a little, 'you must tell Mr Lazarevic to come down here and meet me himself.'

'Oy!' The giant laughed nastily. 'You want to tell Mr Lazarevic what to do?' He raised his hand menacingly.

'Yes I do!' said Fleur haughtily. She wasn't going to be cowed by a bully, even if he was twice her size and probably had a gun and a long history of violence. 'Either Mr Lazarevic comes down to meet me here or I shall leave and take his delivery with me. I don't think he'd be very pleased if I did that, do you?'

The man looked at her, doubtfully this time. He wasn't used to being spoken to like this by a woman – at least, he was, but only by his feared and redoubtable mother, a terrifying apparition at four foot two and twenty stone. Suddenly Fleur was reminding him quite powerfully of his mama, something he found confusing enough to make him put down his radio and pick up the phone.

'Someone will come down,' he told Fleur. 'Wait there.' He gestured to a corner of the lobby. A few men strode in from outside and started back-slapping greetings. They lit up cigarettes, filling the already stale air with clouds of blue smoke as they chattered, the bumps under their jackets leaving Fleur in no doubt that they carried guns.

Suddenly a hush fell across the lobby. A small man had appeared on the other side of the metal detector – he was slim and dark and wore a black suit which, unlike the shiny grey double-breasted efforts Fleur had seen last night and this morning, looked of high quality and good cut. He nodded curtly at Fleur and spoke in lowered tones to the guard. The accumulated hangers-on in the lobby had fallen into respectful silence, even their cigarette smoke evaporating into thin air as though chased away by the presence of this man.

'Meess Bonner.' The man was calling to her. The guard ushered her round the metal detector. 'Zoran Lazarevic.' He smiled briefly and shook her hand. 'Please, come this way.'

Zoran's office was at the very top of the building with a view out over the curving river of Belgrade.

'You see,' said Zoran, leading Fleur to the plate glass window. 'From here you can see the Danube – it is one of the great rivers of Europe. That way is Vienna, the other Istanbul. And we are caught in the middle of east and west, Serbia, the blessed and the cursed.' He gave her a mournful smile. 'Everyone needs an enemy, Meess Bonner. It is part of the fundamental make-up of human beings. The Americans have Iraq, al-Qaeda, the faceless terror of Islam. Here, in the Balkans, it is the Serbs. We are the bad guys. Everything must be our fault.'

'Surely not,' murmured Fleur.

'Surely yes, Meess Bonner,' contradicted Zoran, handing

her a cup of pitch black coffee, his warm dry hand lingering against hers. 'Sanctions, bombs, persecution, exodus. All against the Serbs, never against those who threaten our people, kill them, take our land and live off the fat of it. And yet when we defend ourselves, we become evil.'

'You speak very good English,' said Fleur.

'Thank you.' Zoran inclined his head gracefully. 'Would you like to sit down?'

Fleur sank into a low armchair clad in biscuit-coloured leather, the sort originally fashionable in the 1970s whose design had recently made a huge comeback with owners of loft-style apartments paying through the nose for replicas from furniture stores or originals off eBay.

'Parlez vous français?' Zoran asked.

'Er, non, not really,' said Fleur.

'Shame,' said Zoran idly. 'The French are very popular here.'

'Mr Lazarevic,' said Fleur, 'what exactly is your business? I was under the impression I was coming to a gallery or a dealer.'

'Ah, Meess Bonner,' he sighed. 'In Serbia, nothing is that simple. Yes, it would be lovely to have a shop front, maybe on the Avenue Foch in Paris. But here in Beograd, I have to be a little more careful, a bit more discreet.' He smiled at her again, his dark eyes creasing over his high slanted cheekbones. A smattering of grey touched the black hair at his temples. 'And so, to business.' He held up his coffee cup and clinked it against Fleur's. 'Perhaps now you will show me the fruits of your labours, so to speak.'

Fleur opened the case and revealed the icon. Zoran's narrow eyes examined it, raking over the picture. He took the icon in both hands, kissed it and then put it down reverently, before making the sign of the cross three times.

'That is excellent,' he conceded eventually, switching the

intensity of his gaze to Fleur herself. 'Saint Sava at Zvornik. May I offer you a little slivovitz to celebrate?' He poured a half-inch of lethal, clear fluid into two crystal shot glasses. 'Your health!' He raised his glass to hers and they both swallowed in unison. The fiery water burned straight down to Fleur's toes, producing a moment of pure ecstasy.

'I'm so glad you are happy with the icon,' said Fleur. 'Did you know about the note that came with it?'

'The last wishes of the dying man?' said Zoran. 'Of course. That is what caught my interest in the first place. So much of our national heritage has been destroyed or stolen. It is a personal challenge to restore the icon to its rightful home. You know of Saint Sava?'

Fleur just nodded. She didn't like to think what the penalty for saying no might be.

'He is our national saint,' said Zoran. 'And you have brought him home, to Serbia where he belongs. You understand, of course, that an icon is much more than just a picture? Our icons have great spiritual power.'

'Will you let us know when you the find the monastery?'

'Indeed,' said Zoran. 'Once the icon is back where it belongs, there will be rejoicing among many.'

'Do you think the man who took the icon, all those years ago, was a thief?' said Fleur, who was still fascinated by the icon's emotional history.

'No, no.' Zoran tutted. 'I expect he was a true patriot who wished to save Saint Sava for the great day when Serbia the beautiful would rise once again.' The smile he gave her failed to reach his eyes, which remained watchful, alert and very very cold.

From the Lazarevic mansion, she'd been chauffeured to the deposit room of a private bank where she had been shown, as promised, the three paintings, kept in the airless, lightless confines of a top security vault. That they were originals, she had little doubt – they had the effortless touch of the work of masters, so different from even the most sophisticated attempts of a forger. Even in the stark light of the sealed room, she could see the loving care with which the layers of paint had been applied. Of their provenance, she felt less convinced, but Zoran had produced all the relevant paperwork and Brinley's instructions could not have been clearer – 'Just get the paintings shipped to Zurich and we can sort anything else out later.'

'You see,' Zoran murmured in her ear as they stood, silenced by the mute beauty of the paintings, 'even though the sanctions are lifted, it is difficult for me to arrange the appropriate level of international interest in such paintings. Such fine works of art deserve the best treatment, no?'

Fleur nodded abstractly, her mind whirling.

'This is why I need a partner in London,' continued Zoran, his breath touching the back of her neck. 'I want these paintings to go to a good home – if I auction them in Beograd, who knows? Maybe they will be bought by a Russian oil baron or a Hungarian pig farmer. There is plenty of money here but where is the love? The world will never see them again.'

'Is that why you want Brinley to act for you?' said Fleur.

'Exactly,' said Zoran, his black eyes glinting with dark fire. 'Also, we owe you a favour – you have brought us our saint, we must give you something you want in return. It is so in our culture,' he added. 'We always repay a favour.'

Fleur shuddered to think what the opposite of that statement might be.

'Where have these paintings been?' she asked, thinking of Brinley's fanciful hopes of a stash of masterpieces, lost during the years of communism and war in the Balkans.

'They are part of a great collection kept safely hidden during these past years,' said Zoran, much to Fleur's surprise. Was it possible Brinley had been on the right track after all? 'We cannot reveal too much at this early stage but I would urge you to believe me when I say these paintings are just a sample. There are far more where they came from.'

Even though she was fully aware it was a somewhat cartoon-like reaction, Fleur gasped. Discovering a lost collection of beautiful, treasured, valuable paintings would be such an extraordinary coup, entirely wiping out the stain of Fleur's past career failure. It would give her kudos and value and who knows? Perhaps even a mention in the history books. It wasn't quite discovering Tutankhamun's tomb but in modern terms it wouldn't be that far behind. If, of course, the paintings were genuine.

'Much has happened in Serbia.' Zoran was whispering in her ear again. 'The miracle is that these paintings have come through unharmed.'

'Indeed.' Fleur nodded thoughtfully. When the paintings got to London, the verification work could take place which would determine their real origin and worth. Even though she felt fairly sure Zoram Lazarevic was not a straight or trustworthy man, the way he talked about the paintings – his genuine, unforced enthusiasm, the way his eyes lingered lovingly on the works, his desire to find them a home where they would be cherished and appreciated – played straight to Fleur's heart. She had held serious reservations about the wisdom of doing business with such a man – it was one thing to sell him an icon, quite another to become partners in the sale of lost art works. But a combination of her excitement at the sight of these ravishing paintings and the very close physical presence of Zoran Lazarevic, whose warm, sinewy body smelt as dry and resinous as the floor of a pine wood in high summer, melted away the better part of Fleur's judgement. She was intrigued by him – on the surface he seemed cold and watchful, but under that façade she thought she glimpsed the signs of something else, as though behind the icy veneer danced the flames of real passion. Or maybe, she thought ruefully, it was just the plum brandy talking. The over-romanticisation of random stray men was, she well knew, the curse of the single thirty-something woman, always far too keen to read the signs of destiny into the most ordinary of encounters. And to attribute to quite banal persons a depth and desire that they patently lacked. She sighed and shook herself a little to try to restore some trace of objectivity to her clouded brain.

'Do we have a deal?' Zoran was holding out his hand.

Even though warning bells were ringing in the far reaches of her mind, Fleur could not resist the opportunity before her. 'We do,' she said, firmly shaking on her word.

'Excellent,' said Zoran gravely. 'As the Russians say, "Go to the devil." That is how they say "good luck".'

Lovely, thought Fleur. Just lovely. But she smiled nevertheless and said nothing.

10

Some say the devil is in the detail which when it came to Peter and his newly acquired Mercedes was nearly true, as Roz was to find out that very evening. While Fleur supped with the luciferous Zoran in darkest Belgrade, two other members of the Runners' Club, that innocent institution which was spawning all manner of unexpected activity, had a mission of their own to complete. Hearing Roz that morning reluctantly volunteer to visit Alice, Peter had endeared himself greatly to their leader in a tracksuit, Ben, by instantly offering her a lift to Alice's house. Roz had accepted quite gratefully and only when she was actually incarcerated inside Peter's automobile with his erratic driving style, complete lack of road sense and mysterious malevolent third party presence did she have occasion to reflect that the devil is not so much in the detail as in the dashboard.

The first sign of trouble had been Peter calling from his mobile to say he was outside in the car.

'Come in and have a drink,' said Roz hospitably.

'I can't,' said Peter. 'I can't park the car.' When she looked out of her bedroom window, Roz saw that a long silver car was occupying the whole of the small street below, not letting anyone past in either direction. Unsurprisingly, a great hooting had arisen from all the other drivers, blocked from going about their usual business by the invading Mercedes.

Roz lived in a tiny cottage in a grid of small streets at the bottom of the steep hill which led up to the shops and bars of central Battersea. Originally built in the nineteenth century for the railway workers, these rows of terraced houses, as picturesque and miniature as dolls' houses, had largely been bought up and refurbished by urban professionals who didn't mind living in such cramped accommodation. Roz's house was a particularly pretty example of such a place, with sprigged cotton curtains at the windows, a neat front garden and a glossily painted dark green front door with a shiny brass figure proclaiming this to be number 6. As Peter sat in his silver sports vehicle, admiring the attractive little house with its glowing golden windows, he had a sudden desire to abandon his ridiculous car in the middle of the road, ring the bell and ask the owner if it would be all right for him to come in and stay, perhaps for ever.

'Peter, you are such a nuisance!' Roz got in the passenger seat and slammed the door behind her.

'I am?' He turned doleful eyes on her. He wanted to be her rescuer, her hero and her idol, not some pest she'd like to be rid of.

'The Residents' Association is terribly fierce around here,' she said. 'They'll have me up before the committee for causing a disturbance. Honestly, it's like living under a repressive regime round here – put the wrong dustbin out on the wrong day and you can be court-martialled.'

'I'm so sorry,' said Peter stiffly.

'No, no,' said Roz hurriedly, hearing the hurt in his voice. She was still rather mortified by Ben's telling her she was terrifying. 'It's very kind of you to collect me. I've tried to contact Fleur to ask her if she has any idea what Alice is so upset about,' she went on, making conversation as the car lurched down a long straight street, 'but I haven't got through to her. Perhaps her mobile isn't working. Oh, turn left at the end here.'

'Turn right,' a bossy voice suddenly shouted from the dashboard as Peter turned left. 'You have turned the wrong way! Stop now!'

'What on earth is that?' said Roz, who'd jumped out of her skin when the disembodied voice spoke.

'Satellite navigation,' said Peter grimly. 'It's the bane of my life. It's like living with an automated tyrant.'

'You are going the wrong way!' The voice was getting hysterical. 'You must turn round immediately and go back to the last roundabout where you take the third right.'

'Shut up!' Peter shouted back.

'Go back,' ordered the voice, 'and proceed to the traffic lights where you will turn left.'

'Be quiet! Piss off!' shouted Peter, leaning towards the sat nav gadget. 'I hate you!' He struck the dashboard quite hard with his hand.

'Peter! Red light!' shrieked Roz.

Peter slammed his foot on the brake and they squealed to a halt at the traffic lights.

'You are going the wrong way,' said the voice nastily, with a definite hint of triumph.

'Bloody thing,' groaned Peter. 'I've tried ignoring it in the hope it would get the hump and shut up. But it's obviously very thick-skinned and refuses to take the hint. There's nothing for it – I'm going to have to sell the car.'

'Have you tried turning it off?' asked Roz.

'I don't know how,' admitted Peter.

'Did you look at the instructions?' queried Roz, who was fiddling with the gadget.

'No, I just threw them in the bin,' said Peter.

'Green light, you can go,' said Roz, who was starting to

feel like a driving instructor albeit one without the comforting safety of an emergency brake. 'Best to start in first gear, I always find. Save third for when you've got a bit of speed up.' She carried on twiddling with the knobs on Peter's dashboard, which was only marginally less complex than that of a jumbo jet. 'Well, no wonder,' she said.

'What?' said Peter.

'You haven't reset the city,' said Roz patiently. 'So it's still on the manufacturer's default.'

'Where does it think we are?' said Peter in astonishment.

'Dresden,' said Roz.

'You'd think it would be speaking German, just to give me a clue,' complained Peter.

'It can do that too,' said Roz.

'Links an der ampel,' added the sat nav helpfully.

'It's off now,' said Roz.

'Thank you,' said Peter humbly. 'I cannot tell you what a difference that will make to my life.'

'Was this car really a good idea?' asked Roz as they careered rather wildly round a long corner, for which Peter neither slowed down nor changed gear.

'No, but neither is running the marathon,' replied Peter blithely. 'Sometimes you just have to take a chance. Now, I believe we have arrived.' He brought the car to an abrupt halt. 'You did say number twenty, did you not?' The houses had got progressively larger the further west they had travelled, and the area they were now in was one where cabinet ministers and captains of industry housed their families in graceful, spacious and eye-wateringly expensive detached houses.

Roz rummaged in her handbag for the scrap of paper on which Ben had written Alice's address. As she searched through the contents of her bag, a small gold and white packet fell on to the car floor. She tried to snatch it up but Peter had already noticed. 'Smoking Kills' read the stark black and white letters on the front of the packet now lying face upwards in the footwell.

'Do you think I'm pathetic?' asked Roz, her face unusually vulnerable in the lamplight.

'On the contrary,' said Peter gallantly. 'I think you are magnetic and much to be admired. Now, let us proceed. Shall you go alone and call me if you need back-up?'

Alice's house was eerily quiet, the lonesome ticking of the clock the only sound that disturbed the empty silence. A round-faced au pair had let Roz in and pointed, with a look of total disdain, down the hall before heading up the darkened stairs. Roz tiptoed along the lushly carpeted hallway. She had visited the recently bereaved too many times not to recognise the telltale signs that this was a house of grief. It had that abandoned quality which signified that someone was no longer there: an absence of presence which would never be replaced. Tentatively, she tapped at a white door, and receiving no reply slowly opened it and walked into what turned out to be a large, expansive kitchen, decorated in duck-egg blue and dominated by an enormous dark blue Aga. The stone-flagged floor, wooden furniture and hanging rows of shiny pans would not have looked out of place in rural France, although in Battersea the note they struck was more designer shabby chic than farmhouse utilitarian.

Slumped over the imported kitchen table, carefully scrubbed to create a veneer of age and wear, was a figure clad in a tracksuit Roz recognised from the marathon training, although not in quite the condition she had ever seen it before. Like the table, it seemed to have been deliberately distressed, the pale blue velveteen spattered with a pattern of stains and marks, its edges covered with grey grime. Next to the weary head, laid flat on the table, stood a bottle, its level of yellow liquid perilously low. But this was not the most surprising aspect of the tableau. What was more astonishing was that the whole room was submerged in a mass of crumpled paper. Covering the table, the chairs, the work surfaces, the floor and any other available space, a blizzard of envelopes, bank statements, letters, account details and receipts appeared to have blown through the kitchen, depositing its white load all over the interior. It was an extraordinary sight, Alice's bowed head in the midst of piles of fluttering stationery, as though she was the paper equivalent of the Snow Queen, sleeping peacefully in her kingdom of parchment.

The first thought in Roz's head was 'Peter'. She ran back out to the car where she had left him with orders to wait until called, and tapped urgently on the window. 'I need your help,' she mouthed.

'What have you found?' he said, hurrying behind her into the house.

'I have no idea,' said Roz simply, ushering him through the kitchen door.

Peter sat beside Alice and gently shook her shoulder while with his other hand he took her pulse. 'Alice,' he said in a voice Roz had never heard him use, a firm but kind voice packed full of authority, the sort of voice whose instructions you instinctively wanted to obey. 'Alice, wake up.'

'Should I call an ambulance?' said Roz.

Peter looked up. 'Ask that girl to come down,' he said. 'We need to know how long Alice has been like this. And check the children are okay. And Roz.' She turned at the door. 'Keep an eye out for any bottles of tablets.'

Alice groaned.

140

'Alice, it's Peter,' he said very clearly. 'Can you hear me? Nod for yes.'

She nodded, her head swaying on her neck like an overblown poppy flower, barely supported by a fragile stalk.

'Have you taken any pills? Shake for no.'

Obediently, she shook her head.

'Have you drunk more than this bottle?' He indicated the nearly empty bottle of wine on the table.

Alice shook her head again.

The au pair entered the room and stood with her arms folded, glaring at Peter. Roz followed her in. 'Both children are safely asleep in bed,' she said, pursing her lips.

'How long has Alice been like this?' Peter shot the question at Alice's au pair like a pellet from an air gun.

The girl shrugged and pulled a face, indicating that she neither knew nor cared.

'Why didn't you call someone?' said Roz, her face like thunder. 'She's in a terrible state.'

'Is not au pair's job,' replied the girl sullenly.

'Just get out,' said Peter, who was clearly incensed.

'I leave,' said the au pair. 'I go home.'

'Fine,' said Peter.

Roz tried to intervene. 'Peter, you can't sack Alice's au pair – what if she needs the childcare?'

'I'll be her bloody au pair then,' snapped Peter. 'I'll give up the law and take up child rearing. We can't let Alice live like this.'

Roz looked sharply from Peter to Alice. It had never occurred to her that Peter might be on the list of Alice's endless male fans – she had rather regarded Peter as her own personal friend, although until that moment she had been unaware that she felt quite proprietorial about him.

Alice opened her eyes, which were no more than two glints

in a swollen, purple face. 'I tried to fight,' she whispered. 'But I couldn't go on.'

'Alice, you can go on,' said Peter firmly. 'That's what we're here to help you do. But I need to know if you've taken any medication or drugs this evening, anything which might react badly with the alcohol.'

She shook her head, ratty strings of black hair swinging about her face. 'No, jus' bit drunk,' she said.

'Good,' said Peter. 'Roz will run you a bath and I'll get to work down here.'

Getting Alice up the stairs wasn't easy. Even though she was as slender as a reed, her inert weight was still quite significant. Roz, whose build was much heftier, still buckled a bit as she half carried the younger woman up to the first floor, a manoeuvre not assisted by the au pair's simultaneously stomping downstairs, in a foul mood, toting a hefty rucksack.

Once she got Alice into the bathroom, Roz parked her on the wooden toilet seat while she ran hot water into the lion's foot roll-top bath, a luscious antique that Brinley Boulden himself would have been proud to sell. Rifling through the airing cupboard, she located a towel so large and fluffy that she felt obliged to admire its über-towel status for just a second. Burying her nose in it she caught the faint fragrance of lavender.

'You do live in some luxury,' she remarked idly.

'Did,' said Alice, resting her head against the cistern.

'Bath's ready,' said Roz. Having spent many years nursing her frail mother, she had no compunction in stripping off Alice's filthy tracksuit and pushing her into the warm, foaming water, which she had sprinkled with geranium and rose oil.

Alice lay back in the bath, fat tears sneaking down her pale cheeks.

'Don't cry,' said Roz. 'We're going to sort everything out.'

'I don't think that's possible,' said Alice bleakly.

'Now you listen to me,' said Roz sternly. 'There is always a way forward, however bad it looks at the time. Whatever has gone wrong can be fixed. You just need a little help.'

'But that's just it,' said Alice, sinking into the water. 'No one is going to help me. I don't have any friends, not real ones, I've lost contact with my family and my husband . . .'

Roz nodded. She had suspected that an errant spouse might lie at the root of all this. 'You have got some friends,' she said evenly. 'You've got me and Peter and Fleur and Ben likes you very much.'

'Really?' Alice opened her eyes and looked straight at Roz for the first time. 'You mean you don't hate me?'

'Why would I hate you?' said Roz, sitting down rather heavily on the mahogany toilet seat which gave a minuscule squeak of pain when hit by Roz's full weight. She hadn't been that keen on Alice but it had never occurred to her to take strongly against her.

'People do,' said Alice. 'Men like me if I flirt with them so that's what I do. Otherwise no one would talk to me.'

'Oh, dear,' sighed Roz. 'How silly we all are.'

By the time Roz walked Alice back into the kitchen, she was clean, warm, dry and semi-sober, and while this had not in itself performed any miracles, it was evidently preferable to being a smelly drunk in dirty clothing. A jug of milk sat cosily on the table with three mugs, while by the sink Peter was warming the pot. The mass of paperwork had been collated into neat piles which Peter had laid side by side on the long kitchen table.

'Peter!' exclaimed Roz. 'You are so efficient!'

'Your surprise is not altogether flattering,' he murmured.

'I just didn't expect it,' said Roz, thinking of his battered trainers, his crazy driving, his antiquated speech patterns and bookish manner. 'I thought you'd be a "lost in the library" type, you know, incapable of opening an envelope without cutting yourself.'

'Dear, dear,' said Peter, looking amused. 'Clearly I must upgrade my image. Like your good self, I am a servant of the Crown, and a modicum of proficiency with paperwork does rather go with the job. Tea?'

It took several refills of the teapot to get any sense out of Alice, who kept starting half-sentences and trailing off.

'I knew, I just knew it!' she cried several times before relapsing into mad staring mode. 'If I tried to talk to anyone about the situation I was in,' she burst out suddenly, the brittle fury of her tone making Peter and Roz jump, especially as the exclamation followed nearly five minutes of vacant gazing, 'they thought I was mad. And that I was imagining it! But I wasn't, I knew, I wasn't . . . but no one would believe me.'

'What did you know?' asked Peter patiently.

'That,' Alice's head was hanging so low between her thin shoulder blades, it was touching the table, 'we were living a lie.'

Peter nodded, as though he wasn't particularly surprised to hear this, but it made little sense to Roz.

'Excuse me for being blunt,' said Peter, 'but this isn't the moment for niceties. You have financial problems.'

'Not just problems,' shuddered Alice.

The tale she unfolded before them was not pretty. Alice's husband, Mikhail, was a swashbuckling venture capitalist who lately, it seemed, had buckled his swash rather too often. Having invested heavily in a number of new bio-tech companies, promising wonder drugs to treat everything from AIDS to cancer, he had seen a run of terrible bad luck wipe out all his investments. Lawsuits, bungled clinical trials, failure to get drugs approved and bad publicity coupled with a back-sliding economy had forced Mikhail to take ever greater risks in order to try to stay afloat. Of course, Alice hadn't known any of the facts at the time – all she had known was that Mikhail was at work all hours and was in a towering rage on the rare occasions he did come home, but that was enough to give her the suspicion that their lavish lifestyle was foundering. It had all erupted at Christmas, with Mikhail losing his temper on Boxing Day, claiming that Alice was bankrupting him and that he couldn't go on living with her. He had stormed out and Alice hadn't seen him since.

'Do you have any idea where he is?' asked Roz.

'No,' said Alice. 'I reported him missing to the police but they got through to him on his mobile and he told them I was just being hysterical and that he was abroad, working.'

'Doesn't he want to see his children?' said Roz in bewilderment. Tucked in bed upstairs were two of the most beautiful kids she had ever seen.

'Child,' said Alice. 'My eldest is from my first marriage. Mikhail said we were a pair of parasites and that we were bleeding him dry. He said we'd ruined him.' The sobbing started again. 'But that's not true! He asked us to come and live with him – he said he would take care of us.'

'I doubt very much that you are the root of the problem,' said Peter gravely. 'From what I can see, your husband's financial troubles are far more complex than that.' He laid his hand on one pile of paper, on top of which was a large red-top notice from the bailiffs. 'I will need to go through these carefully but it seems to me you are in danger of losing your house as the mortgage repayments are in arrears. Do you have any money of your own?'

'No,' said Alice. 'All I had was two paintings – they were

quite valuable. Mikhail told me he was having them cleaned for me for Christmas but . . .' She took a deep breath. 'I found a receipt in the desk drawer which Fleur looked at for me. She phoned me last night to say the paintings have been sold.'

'By your husband?' said Roz. Alice nodded mutely. 'And he's pocketed the cash? The shit!' Roz exhaled noisily.

'When I first met him,' said Alice slowly, 'I was very attracted to his confidence – he seemed like a man who would keep us safe. It was only later I realised he wasn't confident – he was ruthless. After Fleur called me last night, I started going through all the paperwork and I found bill after unpaid bill. The house is completely remortgaged, the school fees haven't been paid, the bank accounts are overdrawn and the credit cards are at the limit.'

'And Mikhail is nowhere to be seen.'

'And,' said Alice, 'as if that wasn't bad enough, he's taken his name off everything and left all the debts in my name alone. He asked me to sign some papers a while back – said it was for our life insurance. But it wasn't. I'm liable. For everything.'

'We have to find Mikhail,' said Roz.

'He . . . he doesn't have a UK passport,' said Alice. 'He's a Swiss national. I don't think he'll be easy to trace.'

'Well, well, well,' said Peter. 'And with him denying he is a missing person, he's left you very few options. What a complete and utter cad. I'm always astonished,' he said thoughtfully, 'how the dregs of humanity end up with such lovely wives.'

'I'll boil the kettle,' said Roz, more for the want of something to do than the desire to have another cup of tea. She passed the radio and without thinking flicked the on button. Pouring out of the speaker came the mellifluous tones of a beautiful male voice, singing a lovelorn ballad.

'Oh, it's Jed Harris!' said Roz in excitement. 'You'll never guess what, but he's . . .' She stopped abruptly. Fleur had made her promise not to tell anyone.

'He's what?' asked Peter.

'He's a really good singer,' concluded Roz lamely. 'And I really like him.'

'I'll remember that when Christmas comes,' said Peter, giving her a curious look.

'There is one more thing,' said Alice, once her Emma Bridgewater hand-painted mug had been refilled with loose-leaf organic tea. 'Mikhail left a message for me after I called the police. He said I mustn't tell anyone he had gone and I must carry on acting as normal. Or he would snatch our daughter Lali and I'd never see her again.'

'Oh, good, so he's a bully as well,' said Peter. He smoothed a piece of paper, took a pen from inside his jacket pocket and started writing. 'I'm going to put you in touch with a colleague of mine who can help you. Call him tomorrow afternoon, after I've had a chance to have a word.'

'Alice, can I ask you something?' said Roz reflectively.

'Be my guest,' replied Alice.

'In the middle of all this, what on earth made you think it was a sensible time to try and run the marathon?'

Alice groaned. 'It sounds stupid, doesn't it? But I got that Lifestyle Checklist through my door and it just said something to me. I thought it might at least take my mind off all my troubles and help me stay sane, for the children's sake. But I've backed out now.'

Peter passed over the piece of paper. 'Pain is temporary, quitting is for ever,' he said wisely, quoting from his new favourite book by superhero, cancer survivor and seven times Tour de France winner Lance Armstrong. 'Now that we are your main support group, I think you should carry on.'

'You've got this far,' said Roz. 'And we'll be there for you.'

'Absolutely,' said Peter in heartfelt tones. 'Please come back, Alice – only you stand between us and death by fitness at the hands of the merciless Ben.'

Alice smiled in a watery fashion. 'I'm not sure he'll make any concessions for me,' she said.

'Oh, I think if you ask him nicely, he might,' said Peter. 'If not we can always stage a mutiny.'

Roz produced a large hankerchief and wiped Alice's face, still pretty even under the swollen, exhausted mass of puffy skin. A little light showed in her soft brown eyes. 'Would you like me to stay?' she offered tentatively.

Alice shook her head. 'I can cope,' she said. 'If I can't get up and get two children to school, what sort of mother would I be?'

'A tired one,' said Peter. 'I think you should let Roz stay. I'm sure she is excellent with children. You might find a helping hand is just the thing.'

'I'm afraid my only experience of children is writing babies' names on a form,' said Roz, now looking a little worried that her kind offer was about to be accepted.

'Perfect,' said Peter. 'Doubtless your whole skill set will come into use somehow. Now, let us take Alice upstairs.'

Having put Alice to bed in the vast, hand-carved cherrywood king size which made her look like a lost small child, the travelling heartbreak first-aiders stole down to the front door.

'Why is your jacket rattling?' whispered Roz.

Peter withdrew several brown bottles from his various pockets. 'I took the precaution of removing these from upstairs,' he said seriously. 'Just in case.' He held out bottles of temazepam, aspirin and Valium.

'You're a lot nicer than you let on,' said Roz.

'It's a good thing it's that way round,' said Peter. 'Because usually I find the opposite to be true of most people.'

'It's not going to be easy for her, is it?' said Roz as Peter opened the front door to leave.

'No, it will be hell,' he said succinctly, lingering in the door-frame. 'But one day she'll wake up and realise she has come through it. Although she will need a lot of help to get to that point.'

'I must say, this wasn't quite what I had in mind when I volunteered to run the marathon,' said Roz thoughtfully.

'Me neither,' said Peter. 'And I have a strange feeling that we're going to go through much more before we cross the finishing line.'

'That's if we get that far,' said Roz.

'Oh, we will,' said Peter. 'We are doomed to see this to the very end. Good night, dear lady. And well done.'

11

A sign on the edge of the motorway said 'Goodbye from Beograd! We hope to see you again soon!'

'Not bloody likely,' Fleur muttered to herself as her taxi weaved through the three-lane traffic towards the airport. She had never seen such smog – the grey air hung heavily across the motorway, giving the impression that the atmosphere was so polluted cars had to punch their way through it. Zoran had tried to persuade her to stay another night, had promised an evening out in the city now becoming known, thanks to its air of liberation and decadence, as the new Prague. But Fleur had declined. Zoran was just too dangerous. She had hedonistic friends about whom she joked you were lucky to find yourself still alive after a night out with them. But with Zoran, she suspected that might literally be true. The least bad result of an evening in his company would doubtless be sleeping with him – he had the effortless magnetic sexual pull of a voracious and successful predator. While a casual encounter on a short business trip would have had its attractions, Fleur was still rather knocked off course by the Striker affair and so wanted nothing more than a swift conclusion to her errand followed by a speedy return home. That morning, when she had asked to leave a message for Striker McCullum at the reception desk of her hotel, she had been told that no one of that name had stayed there the night before. She had tried to describe him to the receptionist but the young man had been uninterested in her tale and moved away. As Fleur turned to leave the desk, she thought she heard the British woman behind her in the queue murmur something in her ear.

'What did you say?' Fleur asked the woman, who was now studying a copy of *The Times*. With her rotund figure clad in a tweed jacket and skirt, a double row of pearls at her throat, she was a classic expatriate British woman who most certainly drank a cup of tea on the dot of five each afternoon, had a gin and tonic at six, always stood up when she heard the National Anthem and never forgot to celebrate the Queen's birthday, all small affectations which those who actually lived on the sceptred isle felt no need to maintain.

'I didn't say anything,' said the woman, her voice matching her appearance perfectly in that it was antiquated, overdone and not particularly pleasant.

'Yes you did,' persisted Fleur. 'I heard as I turned round.'

The woman raised her gimlet eyes to Fleur. 'Maybe,' she enunciated. 'You. Should. Be. A. Little. More. Careful.'

'I thought that was what you said.' Fleur moved closer to her. 'Who are you?'

'Thelma Lovegood,' said the woman, checking her watch. 'British Embassy. Oh, is that the time? I must fly.'

'Why are you telling me to be more careful?' asked Fleur.

'Dear, dear,' said Thelma. 'Nice to meet you, Fleur. Having *heard* so much about you.' She put a peculiar emphasis on the word 'heard'. But before Fleur could say anything else, Thelma, the stoutly named representative of Fleur's crown and country, moved away with a swiftness which belied her portly frame. When Fleur ran after her, she found no sign of the diminutive diplomat who had, seemingly, evaporated into thin air. It was all very disconcerting and left Fleur wondering if she had imagined the brief sequence of events. However, the phrase 'be more careful' remained in her mind and had the useful effect of guarding her from potential liaisons with Balkan art dealers, however handsome they might be. Business, she decided, was business and should not be mixed with that dangerous and elusive elixir, pleasure.

Before leaving Belgrade, Fleur had tried very hard not to give Zoran a definitive valuation for his paintings, but he had refused to part with them without a written receipt, specifying their potential market value. So excited was Fleur at the cache of treasures she felt on the verge of unearthing that she relented and gave him a conservative estimate of £1 million, a figure by which he seemed strangely delighted.

As Fleur boarded the plane, the paintings, or so she hoped, were being loaded on to a lorry for the first part of the journey to London. The Lazarevic Foundation, as Zoran's business was grandly known, would truck them as far as Zurich where they would change containers before heading for London to be stored safely in Boulden's warehouse which lived in a strange and forgotten hinterland between the Eurostar train tracks and the south bank of the river. Fleur herself was heading home to Battersea, to store herself safely in her own bed for the night, the very thought of which made her sigh with longing for the crisp white sheets and feather pillows. Only a few hours, she thought to herself as she tried and failed to get comfortable in a seat which seemed to have been specifically constructed in order to fit no human physical frame. Being small, Fleur found the seat bent in all the wrong places for the length of her back, but her next door neighbour, who was definitely of average height, seemed no better suited to the strange curves of the regulation airline seat. As she was nearing her journey's end, or so she thought, she suffered the discomfort in silence, although realistically there was little she could have done about it.

When she disembarked at Heathrow, she hoped for a quick rush through the formalities and into the first available taxi back home, expenses charged to one Mr Brinley Boulden. But she reckoned without the formidable powers of Customs and Excise and their considerable interest in quite why she should be appearing with a case full of hard currency from Belgrade. It was three a.m. before they finally let her go, having at length decided that the fifteenth rendition of her story, exactly the same as all the others, must be the truth. It had been a day not so much long as desperately over-extended and Fleur felt exhausted, but even her dog tiredness was tinged with a great feeling of exultation. While it had never been an aim she had consciously expressed, there was still some small, buried part of her which yearned towards the brilliant, brightly lit, exultant fabulousness of her father's perceived existence, a life where everyone knew your name and constantly told you how special and different you were, where you were seen to have made a mark on the world. Discovering a lost art collection might be small fry compared to selling countless millions of records as a global superstar, but for Fleur it would be enough to validate her existence and give her back her pride.

When she got into her flat, the message light on her answering machine was flashing. She pressed play. 'Fleur . . .' Her father's voice floated out of the machine. 'We need to connect, baby. Look, I'm really sorry I fucked up again. I know I got it wrong – I just panicked when that girl said you'd gone to the pub in the middle of the afternoon, thought maybe you were turning out like your ole man after all. Fleur, I'm on tour now and I was reading my daily meditation . . . hang on . . . it's here somewhere . . . oh, where the bleeding hell has that book gone . . . have you taken it? Have you? Fucking bring it back now, you moron – yeah, that's the one, *Serenity and Peace for Every Day* . . . yeah, get me page thirty-six . . .' Fleur leaned against the wall and slowly slid down it until she was sitting on the hallway floor. 'Right, Fleur,' continued her father's recorded voice. 'Here it is. Ah-hm.' He cleared his throat and started again in a pious voice. 'To ache with our own forgiveness . . . no, no, NO!' Jed exploded telephonically. 'This isn't the right book, yer fuckwit. Oh, Christ, well, I'll tell you in my own words. I'm just trying to get through to you, baby, but you're putting up barriers, Fleur.' Fleur closed her eyes and waited for the machine to run out of tape to record. 'And I can tell you that I now know fear is at the root. I gotta make you see that I love you and that it doesn't matter to me if you just wanna spend the rest of your life working in a shop. That's okay, Fleur. Not everyone has to rock the world. You don't have to be like me. So if that's what this is all about, you've gotta let go, babe. You're special to me, Fleur, and that's enough. You are enough. I want you to repeat after me I Am Enough . . .' Mercifully, the message got cut off.

'I am enough,' echoed Fleur weakly as she sat in a heap on the floor. 'I am enough . . . but I'm not,' she continued, staring vacantly into space. 'That's the whole point. I am not enough.'

12

Over the following two weeks, Ben could have been forgiven for becoming disheartened with his motley crew of runners. None of them gave the impression of being hardened endurance athletes and one of them – Alice – seemed remarkably less fit than she had been when the training started. A suspiciously minty haze hung perpetually around Roz, indicating that her abstinence from cigarettes was less than total. Fleur seemed to be in a world of her own while Peter appeared increasingly bleary-eyed each morning. 'Heavy workload,' was all he would say.

'OK, time for a pep talk,' said Ben one morning when he could see spirits were flagging. 'We now have six weeks until the marathon, the last two of which we can discount for training purposes.'

'We can?' said Peter in surprise. 'Why?'

'Did you read any of the information I gave you?' demanded Ben.

'Er, no,' admitted Peter. 'But I meant to,' he added encouragingly.

'Did anybody?'

The group shuffled their feet and looked embarrassed.

'During the last two weeks,' said Ben patiently, 'we taper our training, meaning that we do one last long run a couple of weeks before, after which it is just short runs and rest. So we have rather a lot of work to do to get to the point where we can relax our schedule, as if we slowed down now we'd be standing still. Fleur, hello? Are you listening?'

'Oh, yes, absolutely,' said Fleur, who clearly hadn't been. 'Tapering,' she said firmly with no idea what that involved.

'We are going to run the greatest race on earth,' continued Ben. 'The marathon. An awesome race, a fabulous day and a magnificent event. But I want us to be ready. There is no bluffing with the marathon. If you haven't done the training, the marathon will find you out. And in some cases, that won't be hard.' He gave Roz a stern look and she blushed.

'It's my asthma,' she said feebly. 'It's making my chest very tight.'

'Asthma my arse,' muttered Ben.

Alice piped up. 'Are we allowed to walk if we can't run?' Ben looked struck to the heart that his protégée and best runner should ask such a question.

'Alice!' he exclaimed. 'You won't need to! You'll run all the way – it will be a breeze. Now come on, no more idle talk. Let's get running.' With that, he led the way, loping forward as the weary band trotted obediently behind him.

'What's up?' Roz caught up with Fleur, who was running at a very reduced pace.

'Nothing,' sighed Fleur.

'Something is,' said the toothpaste-fresh Roz.

'It's really not anything,' said Fleur.

'Tell Roz,' said the lady of that name. 'Is it about this evening?' That very night, they were to attend the opening of Greta's exhibition at the Tate Modern, a star-studded event which promised to be one of the major parties of the season.

'No, no,' said Fleur quickly. As the party was also to be Roz's first date with the mysterious Denny, on whom Fleur had guessed Roz was pinning a totally unreasonable amount of expectation, she didn't want Roz to know how nervous she was about it. Roz, she figured, had enough to think about without worrying about Fleur. Since she had returned from Belgrade, thrilled at the thought of meeting up with Sean once more, she had heard not a word from him. The days had ticked past with agonising slowness, with Fleur leaping to answer the phone each time it rang only to find to her chagrin it was never him. He did call once – irritatingly when she was out of the office – but Spook said he had just wanted to know she was safely home and there was no need to ring back. Nevertheless, Fleur did call but his mobile went straight to answerphone and she left a message which he never returned. In desperation, Fleur had done something her not-so-tender years should have told her was a very bad idea. She turned to that fickle friend, e-mail, to make her feelings clear, thus wrongly utilising a medium perfect for jokes, party invitations and work correspondence as a conduit for her deepest emotions. Like all those before her who have laid their heads on the keyboard muttering 'Oh, shit, shit, shit' as they realise an unfortunate and misjudged message has just shot off into cyberspace, Fleur soon learnt that getting trigger-happy with the 'send' button never leads to good news in return.

'Dear Sean,' she had typed out one afternoon when she was suffering from that combination of boredom and stress peculiar to office workers who don't cherish their jobs, 'seeing you again in London was a great surprise. I'm sorry that I didn't stay in touch when I went to the States but I thought of you often during the years we spent apart. I want to know if there is any way I can make up to you the hurt I caused you by my behaviour in the past. I deeply regret what happened and wonder if we could start again? With love, Fleur xx' With a mixture of bravado and pure foolishness, she hit send. The reply was almost instant. 'Fleur,' she read with a sinking heart, 'my life has moved on now and the past is exactly that – the past. I don't wish to revisit it and while I am happy to see you again, there are no circumstances in which I would consider restarting our relationship. Best wishes, Sean.' A chill had flowed through Fleur's veins. In declaring herself, she had sacrificed her dignity, and what for? So he would have the opportunity to reject her, without – and this was the bit that really grated – even the courtesy to finish his message with the usual 'Lots of love'. Just a paltry 'Best wishes', the same formula he doubtless employed when writing to his accountant. Clearly, she was nothing more than a work contact to him, someone he had to humour for business reasons but who held no personal interest for him or place in his affections. Even days later, she still felt deeply mortified and ashamed. Worse, she knew for a fact that Sean would be at Greta's party, as the artist had phoned her to tell her he was coming. Greta, who had taken one of her famous dislikes to Sean's girlfriend, had chuntered over the fact that he insisted on bringing Bella, saying cattily that Bella probably didn't let him out of Fulham without her. Never mind, the artist had added cheerfully, I'm sure he won't hang around with boring Bella for much longer now that you are back. However much she wanted to believe Greta, Fleur was starting to admit to herself that all the evidence pointed to the contrary.

'I wanted to do something to thank you for organising this evening,' said Roz, seeing she was to get no more conversation out of Fleur. 'So I wondered if you'd like to go speed dating. You know, cheer you up a bit.'

'Do what?' said Fleur.

'You have a three-minute date with everyone in the room,' said Roz. 'So you'd meet lots of lovely men. There's one called Sugar Daddy who I thought sounded promising.'

Fleur felt mortified. Now that Roz clearly imagined herself waltzing up the aisle with Denny, doubtless to throw the bouquet with Fleur as the target, it was obviously Fleur who had been handed the mantle of spinster of the parish.

'Do you know what a Sugar Daddy is?' she asked, quite crossly. 'It's code for a rich man wanting a bit on the side.'

'Oh, dear,' said Roz in disgust. 'I must have been thinking of sugar mice – I've always had a soft spot for them.'

'And speed dating is for losers,' snapped Fleur, who wasn't feeling quite her usual self.

'I hope you will do nothing so rash.' Peter had joined them. He wasn't looking his best either, although to be fair his best was never that good. He was red in the face, his blond curls sticking out at all sorts of unlikely angles, his face set in an expression which was far less than friendly.

'Why shouldn't Fleur go speed dating if she wants to?' retorted Roz. A certain froideur had settled over the former friendship between her and Peter, a development which the astute could have pinpointed to the day Fleur had asked Peter to accompany her on the double date mission. Peter had at first been quite enthusiastic until he had realised it was not Roz he would be escorting, as he had first thought, but Fleur. He had not been pleased to hear Roz was considering a date with a man she knew so little about and had agreed more to keep an eye on the proceedings than in the hope of an enjoyable evening.

'But I don't want . . .' Fleur tried to interject but Roz was having none of it.

'What's wrong with speed dating?' repeated Roz, her voice hardening.

'What is wrong with it?' In contrast, Peter's voice had risen into the falsetto range. 'When we find Fleur under the floorboards because she's met some psychopath at a speed dating evening, do you think you'll still be saying that?'

'Oh, for heaven's sake,' said Roz, lumbering onwards. 'She's going to meet a charming gentleman who will make her happy.'

'Aha, well, charm is an important part of the psychological make-up of a psychopath,' said Peter triumphantly. 'And speed dating would be the perfect vehicle for a serial killer looking for his next victim – no need to give your real identity, phone number, address. You'd be amazed, Fleur, by the number of murderers I've met who could pass for ordinary, no, even attractive members of society. They don't come with "I kill for a hobby" tattooed on their foreheads, you know. Roz, you may think it is acceptable to pick up people in the park in the name of love but I can assure you that most right-thinking people do not.'

Now he had hit a raw nerve. 'You just have to put a dampener on everything, don't you?' Roz stopped running and rounded on Peter. 'You can't bear to see anyone having fun.'

'How dare you!' Peter was incensed in return.

'Not everything ends in a criminal court case, you know,' said Roz, lowering her voice a little as passers-by were starting to look interested in the argument, including a man with a small dog who had stopped stock still and was gazing open-mouthed at them.

'It's a more likely ending than the Mills and Boon style scenario you are foisting on poor Fleur,' flounced Peter.

'Poor Fleur acts of her own accord,' snapped Roz.

'No she doesn't,' said Peter. 'You're filling her little head . . .'

'Little?' interjected Fleur crossly.

'. . . with silly notions of love at first sight.' Peter ignored Fleur's interruption. 'Which is complete rot.'

'That is utter rubbish,' shouted Roz, forgetting to care about the passers-by. 'Fleur is capable of making up her own mind – she is an adult, you know.'

Fleur suddenly felt very grateful that her parents had divorced at such an early age and with so little fuss. This must be what it felt like to be a pawn between two warring adults.

'Fine,' said Peter in high dudgeon. He took in a sharp breath and started to run again, pausing only briefly by the spectator with the hound. 'And I hate your dog,' he spat at the bemused bystander, who looked down at his innocent mutt before the pair of them slouched away in a saddened and dejected manner.

'Typical Peter,' said Roz, looking after him in amazement. 'He can even ruin an innocent animal's day.'

Ben jogged up. 'Ladies, I've lapped you – oh.' He looked at their faces. 'Don't look so worried, girls. I'll get you through it.' He peered into the bushes ahead of them. 'My goodness, is that Peter I see moving at speed?'

'We've just a bit of a set-to with him,' admitted Fleur.

'Wow! Well, if you could do that every morning, he might stand a chance of actually making the marathon.'

Behind him hovered Alice, who was road-testing a shy smile. Ever since the members of the Runners' Club had played such a fundamental role when her life was teetering on the verge of complete collapse, she had relaxed into a much nicer person. She no longer flirted like crazy with the men while ignoring the girls but made an effort to join in with the crew.

'Peter's got a good heart,' she said, rather timidly. With his assistance, she was just starting to unpick the financial nightmare her errant husband had dumped upon her.

'But a rather unfortunate manner,' said Roz, rather hoitily.

'Oh, great,' said Fleur. 'What's he going to be like this evening?'

'We'll be there with you,' said Alice, who had been touchingly thrilled when Fleur had suggested one morning that she might like to come too, Greta being a soft touch when it came to doling out invites.

'You can bring someone,' Fleur had said.

'But I don't know anyone who'd want to come with me.' Alice had suddenly looked panicked.

'Oh, nonsense,' Fleur had replied. 'You must have scores of eligible men up your little sleeve.'

'I don't,' Alice had protested. 'I only know Mikhail's friends and I certainly don't want to go out with any of them.'

'How about asking Ben?' Roz had put in slyly. His interest in Alice had not escaped her eagle eye for a budding romance.

'He wouldn't want to come with me.' Alice blushed.

'Try him,' Roz had said. 'Perhaps you'd be surprised.'

Fleur finished her stretching exercises, which she only ever bothered to do if Ben was watching, and put on her waterproof jacket.

'See you all this evening,' she said. 'And let's hope Peter's cheered up.'

'I'm sure he will,' said Alice soothingly. 'After all, what's the worst that can happen?'

'Oh, I suppose so,' said Fleur glumly. 'The good thing about getting up early is you can get the bad bit of the day out of the way at the beginning.'

13

Unfortunately, life being what it is, Fleur's day was in fact to get inexorably worse with little promise of the sort of silver lining to the cloud which renders earthly existence bearable. Having spent the whole of the previous evening trying on and discarding outfits to wear to Greta's exhibition, she had finally settled on a demure wrap dress which revealed a serious hint of cleavage, giving, she felt, the right 'sexy but unavailable' signals to the party at large. For once, she had had the fore-thought to lay out clean underwear and unladdered tights on her bed, meaning all she had to do was come home, shower, step into her glamorous attire and sweep along to the Tate to dazzle all and sundry. However, the winding ways of fate were to refuse her the opportunity to benefit from her prescience, leaving her no option but to arrive without the protective armour of smart clothes, high-heeled shoes and neat evening bag. Instead, she had to make do with her down-at-heel boots, an old suit and the large carry-all she hoisted around all day, not quite the dashing and together image she had wished to portray for the evening.

To thank for the diversion was a late afternoon call from the warehouse where Brinley stored his art works, asking her to come by before the end of the day. Ken, the avuncular security guard and warehouse manager, was most insistent that she check the contents of a new delivery before he logged it on the system and stored the crate away. Reluctantly, Fleur agreed – in theory, warehouse cataloguing was Brinley's job, but as he was still touring the south of France ('Such a bore, darlings, you can't imagine!' he had trilled down the phone when he'd called earlier) it fell to Fleur, yet again, to pick up the slack for him. While Brinley persisted in maintaining a casual attitude towards stock-taking, he was these days pretty much alone. Ever since a warehouse in East London had mysteriously caught fire, burning hundreds of millions of pounds' worth of art works, insurance regulations for storage had tightened severely, one knock-on effect being that deliveries now had to be checked by two people before they could be entered as present.

When she arrived at the warehouse, Ken was eating a bag of doughnuts in flagrant denial of the Atkins diet on which his wife had placed him.

'Bless you for coming,' said Kenneth, a jovial sort who clearly enjoyed bucking his spousal directives. 'Shift changes in half an hour but I can't knock off until I got everything penned in. Got a new guard starting this evening so I can't ask him to look through the crates.'

'Let's see what you've got for me,' said Fleur, trying to smile. It wasn't Kenneth's fault her life was a bit of a mess.

'It's this one,' said Ken, tipping the sugar from the doughnut bag into his grateful mouth. 'Comes from Switzerland.' A wooden crate sat on the floor in his office.

'Don't they all?' said Fleur. 'What's the country of origin?'

'Let me check, poppet,' said Ken. 'Here we are – oh yes, I remember now. It's from Belgrade – don't usually get stuff from there, do we now? Can you take a look?'

'Open her up,' said Fleur. 'Of course, I'll need Sean to take some samples as well.' She winced a little as she said his name.

'All right doll, I'll try and keep 'em safe till next week,' said Ken, winking at her as he levered open the crate. Carefully, he unpacked three paintings, the ones Fleur had last seen in the vault in Belgrade.

'Look all right to you?' said Ken. Fleur was checking her watch and doing some swift mental calculations which all added up to the fact that she wouldn't now have time to go home, change and get to the Tate in time to meet Roz and the two men at six p.m. She daren't leave Roz and the innocent Denny alone with Peter in his current mood, fearing he would instantly wreck the beginning of their romantic moment. She doubted even Alice and Ben would be lucky talismans enough to ward off a bad spell cast by Peter in one of his blacker moments.

'Erm.' Fleur glanced at the paintings. The first two looked perfect but something about the third one, the Diego Rivera, wasn't quite right. As in her hurry to get to the warehouse she hadn't thought to bring any images to check the paintings against, she only had her memory to rely on. Her whole trip to Belgrade having been so peculiar, she felt there was a possibility it was her own mind that was playing tricks rather than the painting. She decided to come back and have a proper look the next day when she wasn't in such a rush, bringing something to check the painting against with her.

'Right, I'll be off,' she said, feeling slightly guilty about her dereliction of duty. 'By the way, Ken,' she added as she turned to go. 'Did Brinley put in a couple of paintings a few months back, one called *To the Sea*, the other *Still Life with Peaches*?' These were Alice's pictures, the ones her husband had sold to Brinley without her knowledge.

'Rings a bell,' said Ken. He opened the log book and flicked through. 'Yes, here we are – brought them in just before Christmas.'

167

'Nice,' said Fleur, thinking that poor Alice really had snagged the all-time rat of the century in Mikhail. 'Can I see them?'

'Well, ducks.' Ken scratched his head and looked doubtful. 'Thing is, I didn't sign them in so it might take me a while to find out where they're stashed.'

'Okay,' Fleur sighed. 'I'll do it another time. Better go for now.'

'Somewhere nice?' said Ken.

'Nope,' said Fleur. 'A party.'

Roz and Peter were waiting for her in the lobby of Tate Modern when Fleur hurried in, Peter with a somewhat strained look about him and Roz clearly in a fit of nerves but trying not to show it. To keep her fluttering heart at bay, she was twittering away to Peter who was replying monosyllabically.

'Alice and Ben have gone in.' Roz was wearing a somewhat inadvisably girly pink flower clip in her short hair. She had evidently made a huge effort but it wasn't necessarily a successful one – Fleur thought she looked better when she dressed as herself. The linen shift she was wearing did her figure no favours and her feet looked awkward in very high heels. Fleur's heart sank a little and she was reminded that mixing your different worlds together is not always such a good idea. Streaming past them were legions of the beautiful and the chic, like a roll-call of London's most desirable residents, all headed to the exhibition hall to flirt, drink, charm and ignore Greta's paintings.

'Fleur!' A ravishing girl with waist-length blonde hair, perfectly round eyes and the complexion of a china doll, her lean frame wound about with layers of aqua-blue chiffon, stopped and blinked in amazement. 'I thought it was you,' she chirped in a fluty voice. Embarrassingly, she had the same flower hair clip as Roz in her tumbled locks, only on this maenad it looked perfect.

'Tibby,' said Fleur, brightening a little. Tibby – or Tiberia to give her her full name – was Fleur's nineteen-year-old half-sister, who was currently lighting up the town as the newest It Girl, model, actress and singer. 'You look beautiful,' said Fleur, acutely conscious of what a mess she must seem.

'So do you,' said Tib stoutly. They had only met a few times in their lives but Fleur had always found her the most appealing of her many half-siblings. Like Fleur, Tib had grown up in isolation from the Jed Harris mega-machine, only emerging quite recently from an island in the north of Scotland. Tib's mother had been one of Jed's backing singers and Tiberia had been conceived after a concert in Rome, but Jed's refusal to leave his then wife and marry Tib's mother had turned her very bitter. She had decamped to the islands where she found love with a crofter and declined to ever sing another note again.

'Watch it, though,' said Tib, lowering her voice. 'The she-devil's here as well.' The she-devil was Tib's nickname for one of their other half-sisters, a poisonous woman who resented Fleur horribly for being Jed's firstborn (she was number two) and hated Tibby on the grounds that everyone else loved her. 'Funny really,' continued Tib in deliciously bitchy mode. She certainly wasn't as angelic as she looked. 'I didn't think she was allowed out by herself but I felt the nasty sensation of two little demon eyes boring into my back and I knew straight away whose bad karma was coming to the party.'

'Is she really that bad?' said Fleur.

'No, she's worse,' said Tib airily. 'She tried to get *Vogue* to cancel me for a model shoot but fortunately she doesn't have half the pulling power she imagines. Anyway, must fly.' A much older man with the distinct aura of pampered prosperity was waiting patiently for her. 'See you later.' Tib planted a lip-gloss-sticky kiss on her sister's cheek and was gone.

When Fleur looked round for her two guests, she saw that Roz's date had at last put in an appearance, much to Roz's evident relief. He was standing very close to Roz and whispering something in her ear while seemingly handing her a small present. Whatever he was saying was having a magical effect on Roz, who looked utterly entranced.

'Shall we go in?' Fleur grabbed Peter by the arm and started to move him along.

'Fleur!' Roz called from behind. 'This Is Denny!' She even introduced him in capital letters.

'How do you do?' said Fleur politely, offering a hand which Denny took in both of his and kissed, something which made Fleur squirm.

'I am delighted,' he said gravely. Fleur had seen Denny plenty of times before, either while running in the park or the occasions she had crossed his path in Piccadilly, but she had never had a chance to view him from close up before. He wasn't a bad-looking man, she supposed, if you liked that thick-set, broad-nosed type. He was well dressed in a dark suit and white shirt open at the collar to show a little nest of black chest hair escaping upwards. Even so, Fleur found herself disturbed by his eyes, which were so overshadowed by heavy, hooded lids that it was almost impossible to see them.

'May I take your coats?' asked Denny. 'I will check them in for you.' There was something over-formal about his enunciation as well, as though he was trying too hard to articulate the words.

'Thank you.' Fleur handed him her overcoat but kept hold of her large bag. She noticed he was holding Roz's coat and handbag which gave him an oddly effeminate look.

'I will meet you inside,' said Denny, smiling at Roz as though she was the only person in the entrance hall.

Even Peter forgot the snide comment about Denny he had intended to whisper to Fleur as they entered the vast exhibition hall at the Tate, which was possibly the only space in London big enough to house Greta's enormous paintings. Fleur did wonder as she looked at the canvases, which reached from the floor to the ceiling thirty feet above, who on earth could buy one of Greta's works to hang in their own home. You would need to live in a deserted power station just to have the wall space. But once you saw Greta's paintings – with their energy, vibrancy, colour and sheer, inescapable love of life bursting out of every brush stroke – you never wanted to live without them. The crowds, usually so blasé at such events, were staring open-mouthed into the cavernous spaces above, the paintings dwarfing the spectators to such an extent that they seemed no more significant than an invasion of ants.

'Rather clichéd, don't you think?' said a voice in her ear. Fleur whipped round to find herself face to face with Tibby's she-devil, which was incredibly unfortunate as the unflattering nickname had wiped her real name clean out of Fleur's mind. With her delicate, sharp features, pointed face and fine bones, she reminded Fleur of an ancient Egyptian cat god.

'Aren't you going to introduce me?' The she-devil indicated Peter, who was loitering.

'Yes!' said Fleur, racking her brain. She knew how dreadful it would look to have forgotten the name of her own sister but then they weren't exactly a normal family and she hardly ever saw most of her closest blood relatives. 'Peter!' She tried to send him a psychic message to implore him to ask the she-devil her name. 'This is . . . my sister,' she finished bravely.

'I'm sorry, I didn't catch your name.' He leaned in and

smiled pleasantly. Fleur silently thanked him from the bottom of her heart and forgave him his bad temper earlier.

'It's Ursula,' said the she-devil. Of course! thought Fleur. How could she have forgotten that? 'Fleur's *half*-sister,' Ursula added with heavy emphasis on the 'half'.

'So what do you do, Ursula?' said Peter while Fleur felt deep gratitude to him for avoiding the obviously contentious topic of family.

'I'm just finishing my second novel,' said Ursula, looking down her nose.

'How splendid,' said Peter politely. 'I do admire writers. What is it about, may I ask?'

'It's a tour through the tortured mind of a schizophrenic,' said Ursula. She was gazing intently at Peter. 'I've drawn heavily on my own experiences, especially with psychoactive drugs. It's a ground-breaking work.'

'Fascinating,' said Peter sincerely. 'And very brave.'

Ursula turned to Fleur. 'I hear you got the sack and now work in a shop?'

'Yes,' said Fleur rather tightly. 'That just about sums me up.'

'Fleur is running the marathon,' said Peter reprovingly. 'After which she will get her career back on track.'

'Yes, I heard about the marathon,' said Ursula, her hot little eyes raking over Fleur's figure. 'Really, I'd have thought you'd be thinner by now, Fleur. Runners are usually very lean.'

Fortunately Fleur was saved from having to reply by a flurry of Greta swooping down on them, clad in brilliant swirls of silk with her usual full complement of feathers, jewels, fur stoles and an immense painted Japanese fan.

'Darling!' said Greta, embracing Fleur. 'You're here. What do you think?'

'Brilliant,' said Fleur. 'Amazing, fabulous, awesome.'

'But perhaps a little derivative,' drawled Ursula who was under the mistaken impression that famous people would respect her for her blistering honesty.

'Jed – what a wonderful man!' said Greta, ignoring Ursula entirely. 'I love him, your father.'

'*My* father,' said Ursula, through gritted teeth. 'Mine.'

Greta looked annoyed. 'I'm talking to Fleur,' she said.

'He's my father too,' said Ursula, stamping her foot. 'And he loves me more than he loves Fleur. Or Tibby. Or any of the others.'

'Let me get you a drink,' said Peter kindly, taking Ursula firmly by the elbow and steering her away. 'I'm longing to hear more about your new novel.'

While Fleur was glad that Peter had diverted Ursula, a few minutes later she found herself in the awkward situation of being left alone at a very busy drinks party, Greta being in such hot demand that she was spirited away just moments after Peter left. Fleur tried to look as though she was totally absorbed in the paintings and wasn't in need of any company, but she knew this ruse was pretty transparent and that no one watching her would be in any doubt that she was standing in the middle of a party with no one to talk to. The hall was so crowded that she couldn't see any of her friends and the last thing she wanted to do was push through the chattering throngs with no hope of finding anyone. A moment later she was sorry she had regretted her solitude.

'Good evening, Fleur.' It was Sean, looking tidy, tall and heartbreakingly handsome. By his side was a woman who was obviously Bella, a soft, smiling, freckled person with a generous sweep of shiny chestnut hair. The pair of them radiated togetherness with the aura of a truly compatible and happy couple. Worse, despite Greta's rude remarks about her, Bella looked genuinely nice: the sort of person that Fleur would like to have as a friend, with the light of real goodness in her eyes. Even in the first instant of meeting her, Fleur knew she had to face the bitter truth that Bella wasn't a monster she could hate. If she had been someone like Ursula, a self-obsessed whining pariah, Fleur would have held out some hope that one day, with a lot of luck and persistence, she could persuade Sean to give her a second chance. But looking at Bella, Fleur finally knew that it was all over with Sean and had been for a very long time; that she had had her chance five years ago and thrown it away. The realisation hit her like a physical blow to the stomach and she suddenly felt as though all the air had been sucked out of her lungs.

'Are you okay?' Bella laid a cool freckled hand on her arm. 'You look a little flushed – I think we should get you out of the crowds. Come on, Sean, make a way through.'

14

The first person Fleur saw in the entrance hall, so empty compared to the madding crowds inside, was Denny, who was just standing there, alone, looking around as though he was waiting for someone. Of all the people she'd come to the party with, Denny would not have been her first choice as a saviour, but so utterly mortified was Fleur by the fact that Sean and Bella had just kindly helped her out of the crush as though she was some incapacitated elderly female relative that she found herself quite pleased to see him and greeted him in a far more friendly fashion than she would otherwise have done.

'Denny!' She waved him over.

'Feeling better?' Bella was looking at her with an expression of sweet concern while Sean hovered behind.

'Oh, fine,' said Fleur quickly, wishing the pair would just go away. 'You enjoy the party and I'll come back in a minute – just get my breath.'

Denny was all solicitous, oily smiles. 'Here, please sit.' He took her over to a bench.

'Are you sure?' said Bella, Sean staying silent. 'I don't want to leave you.'

'Denny will look after me,' said Fleur firmly. The man himself nodded his assurance that he would do exactly that. She was glad she had chosen to throw herself on his mercy when Sean and Bella did that couple communication thing whereby each knows what the other means without exchanging a word and turned in perfect synchronicity to head back into the exhibition.

'Where's Roz?' asked Fleur, leaning back against the cool wall and closing her eyes.

'I have lost her!' said Denny, shrugging his shoulders. 'I am waiting here in the hope that she will come out to find me.' Opening an eye to assess him, Fleur had to say it didn't look as if he really cared.

'I'll call her,' said Fleur, rummaging in her bag for her phone. She'd received a text message, and opened it.

'Fleur, come to the warehouse NOW!' it said. 'It is very urgent – do not delay.' She didn't recognise the number but she tried calling it anyway, only to get no reply.

'You need to go?' asked Denny, suddenly looking very concerned. 'Shall I get your coat?'

'Er, yes, I do,' said Fleur, dimly wondering how he knew that yet feeling too confused by the twists and turns of her day to worry about it. 'I'm so sorry – will you tell Roz that I had to leave? I . . .' She didn't have time to say much more as Denny was back with her coat. Swiftly, he put it round her shoulders, marched her to the exit, accosted a taxi and bundled her into it. Before she knew it, she was gone.

By night, the south bank of the river where Brinley's warehouse was situated was not a glamorous place to be. Even the trains, whose tracks criss-crossed the area like slash marks on a self-abuser's arm, had slunk back into their sheds for the evening, leaving the rails empty of traffic, the stations deserted and ghostly. Yellow lamplight shone through the purple haze settling over the concrete roadways, dual carriageways riddled with potholes, cracks and creeping blight, whose underpasses seeped with damp and darkness and whose edges crumbled into the litter-strewn wasteland they covered. Far more time had passed at the party than Fleur had realised and it was now quite late, too late to be wandering this desolate area alone. She wasn't too thrilled at the thought of braving the warehouse approach by herself but as her bad luck would have it, her cab driver was the morose, unhelpful sort who declined to ferry her right to the door and refused her offer of waiting while she fulfilled her surprise duty.

'I'll leave you at the garage,' he said shortly, pulling into the nearby petrol station whose lights were a welcome beacon in the rank darkness of the surrounding area. When she tried to pay him, he rudely declared he didn't have change for her twenty-pound note and told her to go into the garage shop to get some. Fleur, who had been denied the chance of eating any supper that evening, bought a packet of pickled onion crisps and a bar of chocolate while she was there. She gave the driver his money and started the trek across the industrial wasteland towards Brinley's warehouse, feeding morsels of tasty synthetic e-numbers into her mouth as she went. To one side of her lay the vast expanse of the New Covent Garden markets, not yet sprung into life for the three a.m. kick-off. Old crates and abandoned vegetable boxes littered the road towards the warehouse, a couple of unwanted cabbages rolling about in the gutter like a pair of freshly guillotined heads. The fresh new stock of the day, trucked in from the fertile fields and farms of the English countryside, and its cheerful, early morning vendors with their bright shouts and cups of strong tea, were still hours from arriving. For now, the place was dead, stale and forgotten, with only vermin scurrying through the debris, seeking to feed on the rotting stalks of yesterday's produce.

As Fleur approached the warehouse, a thick, clogging smell

hit her nostrils, quite unlike the gentle scent of decay the discarded fruit and veg gave off. Underfoot, the pavement around Brinley's brick building was wet although it had not rained that evening, pools of oily liquid seeping in dark patches across the concrete. In the darkness, her feet skidded on a slippery puddle. Never having visited the warehouse so late at night, she was not aware that the outside light should have flicked on. She tried the door handle but it was firmly locked, no light emerging from inside the night-bound building. She rapped sharply on the door. 'Hello!' she called. 'Hello!' She didn't want to shout – she was suddenly aware she was alone in an area which might not be as empty as it seemed and anyone who lurked in this part of town at this time of day was not somebody she wanted to meet. She punched the security code into the pad on the warehouse door, which obliged her by swinging open.

Flicking on the lights in the narrow corridor, she went through to the office where only earlier that evening she and Ken had unwrapped the newly arrived paintings. She wasn't necessarily surprised to find the office empty with no one on duty – she wasn't totally au fait with Brinley's security arrangements although she knew enough to realise her entry would have been tracked by the internal CCTV camera linked to a centralised system which covered all the warehouses. But it did make her wonder quite why she had been summoned and who had sent that text message. She rummaged in her bag for her phone to check the number, but before she could find it, a piercing noise shattered the spooky silence, a frantic, urgent beeping sound whose frequency had been specially chosen to activate the mental panic button within the head of anyone who heard it. Grabbing her bag, Fleur ran into the hallway, where she tripped over a metal canister. The clogging, oleaginous stink she had noticed on her way in had got stronger, except now it was tinged with a dry, acrid fragrance, sublimated into blue plumes of curling smoke coming from the storage section of the warehouse. With no time to think, she picked up the canister and ran towards the door, wrenching it open and staggering out into the cool dark night. She ran backwards away from the door, her feet carrying her in a disjointed reverse sprint until she stumbled and fell, landing in a heap of shock and torn clothing, still clutching the only object apart from herself and her handbag she had managed to salvage from inside. A mist seemed to be settling over the warehouse, as though the river beyond had sent a miasma of fog to cloak the building in a grey shroud. But that was just an illusion – the smoke, Fleur could see, was spilling out of the warehouse itself, seeming to flow through the very bricks into the night air. From inside the building came a twisted, creaking screech followed by the noise of an explosion as part of the roof caved in, allowing a sudden shoot of iridescent amber flames to escape and reach for the sky. For a second, Fleur was rapt with the violent beauty of the scene before her, briefly admiring the vitality of the flames before she realised what the sight before her meant.

'Fire!' she screamed, pulling herself to her feet and trying to move. 'Fire!' she screamed again, but the breeze whisked her thin voice away. No answer came back from the silence other than the patter of rats running away from the blaze. Can under one arm, Fleur turned her bag upside down, hunting for her mobile phone, but it was gone. Frantically she searched her pockets but it was nowhere to be found. She turned to run for help but stopped when she saw the flashing blue lights of a fire engine roar up the slip road to the warehouse.

'Get back.' A firefighter rushed past Fleur. 'Get right back. Back to the road.'

'Wait,' Fleur called after the men as they set about dousing the fire, moving in harmony like a lethal synchronised ballet. She tottered backwards, feeling the awesome heat of the fire blasting towards her, the building now glowing like molten glass as bit after bit fell prey to the ravenous inferno.

'Get out of the area. We don't need spectators.' Another firefighter appeared from nowhere and ran past her.

'I'm not a spectator,' Fleur tried to say but he was gone. When she tried to move forward again, a burly man pushed her back quite forcefully.

'There's nothing for you to see,' he snapped at her. 'Go home.' He stomped angrily away in his fireman's seven-league boots, muttering about rubbernecking members of the public.

Fleur had started to trudge slowly back towards the main road when out of nowhere a man in firefighter uniform grabbed her quite roughly. 'What are you doing here?' he demanded, his face shadowed in the darkness.

'I . . .' said Fleur, who had just thrown the canister down on to the road.

'You were holding that.' He pointed with his boot at the can. 'I saw you.'

'I . . .' Fleur was feeling the after-effects of shock and her brain was not working quickly enough to keep up. 'I was in the warehouse. And I found this can. And I heard the fire alarm go off. So I ran out . . .'

A police car roared up, its beams of flashing blue light bouncing off the orange glow of the warehouse like a sinister but beautiful light and sound show. For Fleur, the next sequence of events happened as though she were experiencing an out-of-body experience – she felt as though she watched herself be bundled into the police car, her hands cuffed together without even a chain between the metal rings encircling her wrists. She saw the door of the panda car shut on her by a grim-faced man dressed in uniform, the car start and drive away from the fire. Like seeing herself on film, she observed her chalky face as she was walked up the steps of a police station and fingerprinted, then had her hands swabbed for forensic evidence, her clothes taken away and replaced by a white paper suit, her identity swapped for a number and her life changed for ever by a caution. As the detective intoned the words 'You do not have to say anything. But it may harm your defence if you do not mention when questioned something which you later rely on in court. Anything you do say may be given in evidence', Fleur heard only the noise of the shreds of her life collapsing with as final and as deadly a roar as the roof of the warehouse falling in on the precious paintings, destroying their beauty for ever with an act of senseless and incendiary violence.

15

'The main thing,' said Peter decisively, 'is to stay positive.'

'So it's bad news then,' said Fleur. She and Peter were sitting in the cells downstairs at Horseferry magistrates' court where Fleur had been brought that morning for her first appearance. It was a dingy, featureless little room where pallid light filtered through one small rectangular window set high in the wall. Not designed for ease and comfort, it offered neither of these amenities to the shocked interviewee and her newly appointed legal representative.

'Not great, I have to say,' admitted the blond barrister. 'But we are currently still in react mode and have not yet had time to strategise.'

'That sounds even worse,' said Fleur grimly.

They had let her make one phone call from Belgravia police station. It had been tough to know whom to choose as the lucky recipient, especially given how late – or rather early – it was by then. 'Hi, it's me, I'm in prison, they're wrongly charging me with arson and I think I need some help,' is not the most encouraging news to break to your near and dear. She couldn't bear to call Rowena, her sweet, gentle, adoring mother. It would break her heart, and in the first shock of her arrest, Fleur was still determined that this was all just some kind of mistaken identity crisis and she would be released later on that day. Jed was definitely out of the question and with the exception of Tibby, whose number she didn't have, she didn't trust any of her half-siblings. For a horrible moment, Fleur felt there was no one she could call – she could hardly phone any of her friends, at home with their small babies, to ask them to rescue her from the nick. Contacting anyone connected even remotely with work would set the rumour mill churning into overdrive and she wasn't going to risk humiliating herself in front of Sean yet again. As Greta never answered her phone, Fleur had a moment of utter bleakness when she felt alone, abandoned and totally unloved. And then she remembered Roz. With shaking hands, she dialled her number, and the sound of her warm voice on the phone was enough to cause Fleur to burst instantly into tears.

When Fleur's two minutes were up, Roz's immediate and instinctive reaction, caused by his calm and brilliant handling of Alice's problems, was to phone Peter. She relayed the extremely garbled version of the story that Fleur had sobbed down the phone to her and told him, among other things, where Fleur was currently languishing. Despite the extreme earliness of the hour, Peter had fortunately been awake already, lying in his bed and ruminating on how greatly his improved fitness had changed his attitude to getting up in the morning. He leapt up and immediately sprang into action, with the result that Fleur was most surprised to be visited not much later that morning at the police station by a serious-faced and very clean-looking young man called Andrew, who announced he was her solicitor and had been sent by her barrister, one Peter Greyson. Andrew politely but firmly told the police their interview was over until he had consulted with his client – the rather stunned Fleur Bonner who by now had no idea what was going on – and thus spared Fleur the problems arising from giving away any more than she already had to two granite-faced investigators, seemingly convinced they had a case for Arson with Intent to make against her.

Peter himself appeared a little later and he was a very different man from the red-faced runner she was used to encountering morning after morning. In his dark suit with his hair sleeked back he looked as dangerous as a snake poised to strike. But his eyes were still kind even if his demeanour was more polished and professional than the habitual bumbling manner to which Fleur was accustomed.

'Oh, Peter,' she said, her voice so wrenched with raw emotion it hurt just to hear her speak. 'I didn't burn down the warehouse, I simply didn't.'

'Of course you didn't,' said Peter dismissively. 'Absolute rubbish – I've already told them we'll be suing for harassment and wrongful arrest. That should scare them. I've never heard anything as idiotic in my life. I've spoken to Andrew and he's brought me up to speed with what's going on here. I'm so sorry I couldn't come earlier myself but you needed a solicitor not a barrister at that point.'

'Why do they think I did it?' asked Fleur, her ashen face and messy mop of hair putting Peter in mind of a Victorian waif.

'Ah, well,' said Peter, trying and largely succeeding in sounding brisk and breezy. 'At the moment, the one thing they don't have is a motive.'

'What do you mean, the "one thing"?' said Fleur in amazement. 'What do they have?'

Peter took a deep breath. 'Fleur, what happened last night?' he said. 'Take me through it step by step.'

'I was . . .' she faltered. 'I was at the party.'

'Exactly,' said Peter. 'Plenty of witnesses to that.'

'But I lost you all in the crowd and I suddenly felt rather

faint. So I went outside,' continued Fleur, as though in a dream, 'where Denny was waiting for Roz. I got a text message on my mobile saying I had to go to the warehouse immediately.'

'Who sent the text?' Peter looked up from his note-taking.

'I have no idea,' said Fleur.

Peter looked thoughtful. 'In which case, why did you respond?'

'I took it at face value,' said Fleur. 'I'm in charge while Brinley is abroad so I didn't think I should ignore it. And . . .' She tried hard to remember. 'Denny. He sort of shovelled me into a cab before I had time to think.'

'Well, when we check your phone, we'll find the text message and trace the sender,' said Peter briskly. 'Which will be a huge help. It will certainly show that someone lured you to the warehouse, possibly with malicious intent.'

'Peter, I haven't got the phone,' said Fleur, watching the reaction he tried to disguise. 'I must have lost it last night.'

'Ah,' said Peter slowly. 'That is a bit of a blow. Can you by any chance remember the number?'

Fleur shook her head.

'Right.' Peter seemed a little drained of confidence. 'You arrived at the warehouse by taxi. Do you know the driver's serial number?'

'No!' said Fleur. It never occurred to her to check such details.

'There is photographic evidence of you entering the petrol station around 11.03 p.m. – you were caught on their security camera,' continued Peter. 'There is also CCTV evidence from the central security unit of you entering the warehouse and going into the office. But it cuts out quite quickly – perhaps the heat damaged something and so it just shows you going in, not coming out.'

'I walked to the warehouse,' said Fleur. 'I used the security code to go in. I looked in the office but there was no one there and when the fire alarm went off I ran out.'

'What about the petrol canister?'

'What canister?' said Fleur, her face blank.

'The one the firefighter saw you throw on the ground outside the warehouse.'

'Oh, is that what it was? I tripped over it in the hallway so I picked it up and brought it outside with me.' Fleur's face was painfully innocent. 'I didn't know what it was so I sort of threw it away, to get rid of it.'

'Fleur,' said Peter, taking off his spectacles and polishing them on a handkerchief, 'do you understand that your actions, at this moment, are open to serious misinterpretation?'

'Not really,' said Fleur.

Peter took a deep breath. 'That you went to a party where numerous people who knew you could vouch for your presence, but once you had ensured you had been seen you stole away. You went down to the riverside where – for reasons yet unknown – you used your position as an employee to gain entrance to the warehouse, doused it in petrol, set light to it and were apprehended running away from the scene.'

The room swam around Fleur. 'That's not what the police think happened . . .' She trailed off. 'But they can't . . .'

'When the lab tests come back, they will show whether you had any incendiary matter on your hands,' said Peter quietly.

'Peter, why? Why would I do something like that? I've spent my whole career trying to protect works of art. Why would I suddenly want to destroy them?' Fleur leaned forward towards Peter, who she was glad to see did not flinch away. 'I know!' She sat bolt upright in excitement. 'Denny! He must have read the text message over my shoulder so he'll be able to tell the police that someone did tell me to go the warehouse.'

'Denny,' said Peter quietly. 'Yes. Of course, Fleur.' He wasn't sure he should tell her all he knew. He wasn't convinced she could cope with more. But Fleur, in the manner of people inextricably wrapped up in a life-shattering catastrophe, was developing that uncanny way of instinctively knowing worse was to follow.

'If you've got more bad news, you should tell me,' she said, her eyes raking his face.

'We don't know where Denny is,' admitted Peter. 'In fact, we're not sure we really know who he is either.'

Once Peter had put an emergency plan into place regarding Fleur, he had called Roz back. While the disaster of her date with Denny might seem almost unbearably trivial compared to the extraordinary events which had just befallen Fleur, Peter had a sixth sense about the man which told him he was trouble. Unwilling to let any detail of the night before the fire escape his attention, Peter had gently and kindly questioned Roz to see if he could find any clue in the peculiar behaviour of her mysterious escort.

For once, it had been nigh on impossible to get Roz to talk about her love life, usually her very favourite topic. Upset and concerned for Fleur, at first Roz batted away Peter's questions about Denny, saying it was irrelevant and pointless in the current situation. With some persistence, Peter managed to drag the sorry story out of her. One minute, it seemed, Denny had been all over Roz, the next he'd disappeared, bringing Roz's hopes of an end to her solitary life crashing to the ground. At first, when she couldn't find him, Roz thought he must have been taken ill or got lost so she waited while the party thinned out around her. Finally, when the caterers were clearing the smeared glasses and picking bits of canapé off the floor, she had to admit that Denny clearly was no longer there. She went home, hoping for some kind of explanation, but heard nothing.

'Why didn't she call him?' said Fleur. 'Why don't we call him and ask him what the hell he's playing at?'

'Because she doesn't have his number,' said Peter carefully.

Fleur groaned. 'I don't believe it,' she said.

'No address or last name either,' added Peter.

'How come?' said Fleur, who was flabbergasted. Roz's sudden bursts of complete naivety had always struck her as very innocent and rather sweet. Now they seemed more like life-threatening folly.

'It's this book she's been reading,' said Peter. Roz's new bible was a book on dating etiquette which decreed that women must never ever pursue men, call them, contact them or ask for a date. The theory was that if the man was worthy, he would do all the hard work. If he wasn't prepared to, then no woman should bother with him. So far, Roz had been really delighted by the results she had achieved by following this simple formula. Denny had persistently pursued her, without the need for Roz ever to exert herself. It had been bliss: no invented excuses to call, no pretexts for meeting up, no sitting staring at her mobile, wondering if she could risk sending him a text, as she didn't have a number to which to send it. The fact that she didn't have any contact details, not even a mobile number, had struck her as possibly a little strange, but the book was so insistent that she shouldn't need to do any of the work in a new relationship that she didn't push Denny for any details but let him take charge instead. When he called Roz, it came up on her mobile as 'private number' so she always knew it was him.

Peter had managed to hear Roz's confession without letting rip. 'I thought it was destiny,' she had said plaintively to him that morning. 'And if it was then it was meant to be and everything would work out. So I've been really stupid.' Roz burst into tears on the phone. She was too forlorn and abject for herself, too deeply worried and disturbed for Fleur, for Peter to hurt her any further. He kept the observation that if all women followed her dating guru to the letter, then the only men who would get dates would be psychos and stalkers, determined enough to carry on chasing a woman who had shown no discernible signs of interest, to himself.

'Perhaps we'll see Denny running in the park one morning?' said Fleur hopefully.

'Perhaps,' said Peter in a tone which signalled 'perhaps not'.

'What do you mean?' said Fleur, her blood running cold. 'Peter, you do believe I didn't burn down the warehouse, don't you?'

'Yes, I do,' said Peter with the utmost assurance. 'I wouldn't be here if I didn't, I can promise you that. I am in no need of the extra work, especially not with the marathon coming up . . .' He trailed off.

'But if you believe me,' said Fleur, 'then why don't the police?'

'They haven't seen you at seven a.m. five times a week for the last two months,' said Peter firmly. 'If you had any underlying criminal or psychotic tendencies, I would have noticed something by now. You couldn't possibly go through all the mental and physical pain of marathon training without letting another personality slip out, were you to have one. Even an MI5 operative couldn't have kept a legend going through that lot. No, Fleur, I know you – you're a fairly ordinary, decent, down to earth girl with very few surprises about you. So,' he continued in a more formal tone, 'Fleur, would you like me to represent you?'

'Absolutely,' said Fleur, who saw Peter as her only glint of hope.

'Strictly speaking, I am not supposed to take on cases where there may be a conflict of interest,' continued Peter. 'But in this instance, I am determined that I would not be professionally embarrassed and that our acquaintance is slight enough for me to waive the rules.'

'What does that mean?' said Fleur, who was having trouble keeping up.

'Nothing you need to worry about,' said Peter kindly. 'Now, our time is nearly over. Is there anything else I need to know?'

'Peter, there is one unusual thing about me,' said Fleur, swallowing hard.

'Yes, I know about that.' Peter waved a hand impatiently. 'Roz told me about your father this morning,' he continued. 'She was concerned about possible press involvement. Which was most sensible of her, given how distraught she was. Otherwise, not relevant for now.'

'You think?' Fleur was taken aback. She was so used to getting a dramatic reaction when she revealed her parentage that she was almost put out to find Peter didn't think it mattered. 'Really?'

'Really,' said Peter. 'We're talking about your innate personality here, who *you* are, not who your father is. If your father was Ronald Biggs, I would still say that you are probably one of the more straightforward characters I have come across.'

'Oh,' said Fleur. Despite everything, suddenly she realised she quite liked the astonished and admiring response she got when she laid claim to Jed.

'We will need to let him know where you are,' said Peter. 'We can't keep your parents in ignorance of what's happening.'

'I suppose so,' Fleur said reluctantly.

191

'You know,' said Peter gently, 'being an ordinary person with an extraordinary father isn't a crime.'

'That's just as well,' said Fleur bitterly. 'That would make two counts against me, none of which are my fault.'

A ray of sunshine braved the narrow window into the gloomy little room, landing on Peter's pale gold hair like a finger of light from the heavens above. There was no denying the reality of where they were.

'Peter, what else?' said Fleur in a small voice. Peter took one of her hands in his. He noted how the nails were already bitten down to the quick.

'Fleur,' he said, looking her straight in the eye, 'what I'm going to say next may strike you as very odd. I am going to advise you not to make a bail application.'

'What does that mean?' said Fleur in panic. 'Am I going to prison?'

'It's not necessarily a bad thing,' said Peter, trying to reassure her. 'Fleur, someone has tried to frame you for a very serious crime. What is more, they appear to have put quite some effort into it. In my opinion, for now you are safer inside than out.'

'But . . .' said Fleur.

'It's not going to be pleasant,' said Peter. 'But until we can find somewhere secure for you to go, you are, strangely enough, in the best place you could be. Just be careful and don't, for God's sake, tell anyone who your dad is.'

The tears that had been building up all morning leaked from the corners of Fleur's eyes.

'It's all going to be okay,' said Peter with much greater conviction than he felt. 'But you're going to have to trust me. And do as I say.' He stood up. 'I must go now, but I will be back very soon. Don't lose heart, Fleur. We'll have you out of here and crossing the finishing line in no time.'

16

The next morning dawned far brighter than the collective spirits of the much depleted Runners' Club. At the beginning, back in January, Ben could boast a reasonable selection of potential marathoners. But now that the chill winds of March were sweeping the treetops to and fro, most of those who had originally pledged their allegiance to the cause of charity and fitness had made their apologies – pressures of work, family and love being cited as covers for indolence, sloth and apathy. And with one of the remaining few producing the astonishing excuse that she'd gone to prison, the numbers were down to four.

'I can't believe it,' Roz exclaimed miserably. 'I just can't believe it.'

The others were still nose to the ground in push-up position, but Roz had sat up in horror at the tale Peter was telling. During that morning's warm-up, Peter had been explaining the events of the day before, how he had had an urgent call from Roz which had led him to visit Fleur and engage himself as head of her legal team. The bobbing body that was Peter said, 'Believe it. It's all happening.'

Roz was suffering from a mixed bag of hideous emotions. Denny had not been in touch and this morning showed no sign of him jogging around the park. Fleur, her friend, was

193

interned, facing some dire accusations. And Peter seemed convinced there was some link. Was it all her fault? Had her eagerness to find love led a good friend into terrible danger? For Roz, who had tried all her adult life to bring joy and solace to other people, this was a prospect so appalling, she wondered if she should just throw herself into the murky waters of the Thames and be done with it.

'But it's not your fault, Roz,' said Peter, who was still doing rapid push-ups when even Ben had ground to a halt. 'So stop thinking it is.'

Roz shivered. 'How did you know?'

'If I was looking at you,' Peter carried on with his exercises, 'I would say it's written all over your face. As it is, I can just feel that's what's going through your mind.'

Even through her sadness, Roz felt a tiny smile creep on to her face. A couple of days ago, she would not have thought that losing Peter's good opinion could matter to her one jot. But once she thought she had, she was unnerved by how incredibly painful she found it to consider that Peter might genuinely think very badly of her. When he extended the hand of friendship to her again, the hand she had swatted away quite brutally, she felt relief wash over her.

'It's all very peculiar,' said Alice, who had stood up and was stretching her hamstring.

'It is,' agreed Peter, who was still intent on his push-ups. Ben was counting them in a half amused, half horrified manner. 'But the most peculiar thing of all is that anyone should believe Fleur would burn down a warehouse.'

'Oh, absolutely,' said Alice vaguely.

'Arson is closely linked to revenge or financial gain,' puffed Peter. 'And I fail to see how Fleur fits either of those categories.'

'You don't think there could be something in Fleur's, ahem,

background,' said Alice delicately, 'that we don't know about?'

'No history of previous convictions,' said Peter, who had seen a copy of Fleur's Police National Computer check at the magistrates' court.

'A hundred – a hundred and one – a hundred and two,' said Ben. 'Mate, I think you should stop now – you've got steam coming out of your ears.' Roz was watching Peter with concern – he did seem unusually fired up this morning and she dreaded to think quite why he might suddenly seem so impassioned and alert. Was it possible that Peter was in love with Fleur and she had never noticed? The thought gave her a slightly queasy feeling which she didn't care to examine too closely.

'A hundred and three – a hundred and four,' said Ben, marvelling at Peter's prowess. 'And you are going to stop when you get to a hundred and ten or I will sit on you,' he warned.

'Some people pay a lot of money to be sat on,' puffed Peter. 'To a "squisher". It's a service, costs about two hundred pounds an hour.'

'Okay, too much information, Peter,' said Ben quickly. 'And that's a hundred and ten. Time to rest, old buddy,'

Peter sank to the ground where he lay face down, breathing heavily.

'These squishers,' said Ben, curiosity getting the better of him. 'Is that all they do, sit?'

'It is,' confirmed Peter, still lying with his nose in the mud. 'Men who like larger ladies enjoy the sensation, apparently.'

'Oh, tubby chasers,' said Ben knowingly. 'So you're one of them, are you, Pete?'

'You're so juvenile,' said Peter, sitting up with mud all over his face, including his spectacles. He took them off to polish them, revealing two white circles round his eyes where they had been. 'Size is completely irrelevant but yes, I must admit that I do find a fuller figure more attractive than the current fashion for stick thin.'

'Are you all right?' said Alice, turning to look Roz straight in the eye.

'Yes, of course. Why wouldn't I be?' blustered Roz.

'I thought you said something,' said Alice, who was gazing at her with concern.

'No, no,' said Roz, waving a hand around pointlessly. 'Not at all. Nothing. Not a word.'

'I see,' said Alice succinctly.

Roz blushed. Quite why Peter's admission of a preference for the larger woman should affect her, she didn't like to think. She put it down to intense confusion over the staggering events of the past few days.

'If there's anything on your mind,' said Alice rather accurately, 'you can talk to me, you know. I'd be so happy to listen. We're friends now, aren't we?'

Roz pulled herself together. 'We most certainly are,' she said. She'd become very fond of Alice since she'd come to realise that Alice's former snobbery had been nothing more than a cover for desperate unhappiness.

'Come on, you lot,' chided Ben, who was up and jogging from foot to foot. 'We've got work to do.'

'Um, guys,' said Roz rather faintly. 'Does anyone else feel rather heartless, carrying on training when Fleur's in prison?'

'I know what you're saying,' said Ben, who like the others had frozen at Roz's question. 'But no. As we all believe Fleur is innocent and will shortly be free, we would be foolish to abandon training. She's going to need us for support when she comes out so we should stick together. And training is what we do.'

'Can I just ask,' said Alice, 'do you think there is any danger to the rest of us?'

'Fair point,' said Peter as they set off at an easy pace for their warm-up run. 'But I don't think so. Whoever has targeted Fleur has not done so in order to nobble her for the London marathon – this is not an athletically motivated crime. However, for security purposes, I suggest we only discuss the matter during training sessions when it is nigh on impossible for anyone to overhear. And,' he gave Roz a mock stern look, 'from now on, we run with no one else.'

'I'm just trying to say,' Alice continued, 'that maybe we shouldn't be so quick to presume Fleur is innocent.'

'It is innocent until proved guilty,' ventured Ben.

'Actually it's more like guilty until you prove you're innocent these days,' said Peter. 'Especially when it comes to arson.'

'What do you mean?' said Roz.

'I mean that a new directive has just been issued, pointing out that eighty-four per cent of arson cases go unsolved and only two per cent of those brought to court result in criminal convictions. The powers that be are very keen that this should change.'

'Is that bad for Fleur? asked Roz.

'It means they are pushing for a conviction very quickly,' said Peter, 'because it will look good on the facts and figures sheet. This is exactly the sort of politically motivated shenanigans which makes my blood boil.'

'It all sounds rather far-fetched,' sniffed Alice. They were jogging along the river bank where the narrow boats floated calmly on the Thames, their jolly little window boxes and green and red paint shedding an alternative, gypsy glow on to the shingle beach.

'Given your experiences, I would have thought you'd know anything is possible,' said Peter mildly.

'I suppose you're right,' Alice reluctantly agreed.

'What do you think, Ben?' Peter asked.

'I think,' said Ben carefully, 'that Fleur tried help me by joining my marathon team when I'm sure she didn't want to and she certainly didn't have to. So I'm going to try and help her now. I don't know what I can do for her but I am very willing to give it a go.'

'That's the spirit!' cried Peter happily. 'Roz?'

'Absolutely!' said Roz fervently. The relief she felt that Peter was more professionally than personally intrigued by this case only added to her determination to pitch in for a friend in need.

'Alice?' said Peter.

'Oh, all right, yes,' said Alice, swayed, as Peter knew she would be, by Ben's reaction. 'But what are we going to do?'

'Aha,' said Peter mysteriously. 'What are we going to do. That, of course, is the big question.'

'Go on,' said Ben, who had slowed down to hear what Peter had to say. 'What are we going to do?'

'As I said, good question,' said the mercurial barrister. 'And one you should ask me tomorrow. Because today, frankly, I haven't the faintest idea.'

17

'I need to see you,' read the handwritten note delivered to Peter's chambers. 'Meet me at the Southfields Martenity Hospital at 4.30 this afternoon, room 23, name Bond. Bring flowers.' It was unsigned.

'Did you see who delivered this?' Peter asked the clerk who had brought the note to him.

'No, sir. It was just lying on the doormat,' replied his clerk.

'Thank you,' said Peter, absent-mindedly rereading the short missive. The writing was unmistakably feminine and had the large loops and confident swirls of a privately educated girl. The paper was thick and expensive. He rubbed it between his fingers thoughtfully. Could it be some kind of set-up? Surely there was little they could do to him in a maternity hospital, unless the nameless 'they' intended to drown him in a birthing pool or beat him to death with a breast pump. These were hardly the trademarks of a mafia style attack.

He looked at his watch, the watch his father had given him as a boy with the stern, Kiplingesque injunction to 'fill the unforgiving minute with sixty seconds' worth of toil'. His had not been an affectionate or loving childhood but a highly academic, hot-housed existence going from scholarship to scholarship with little time for idle moments or childish fun. It had never occurred to him, when young, to envy what he was missing as he rather snobbishly viewed others' amusements as puerile and contemptible. Only now was he beginning to see what a cold and isolated path he had taken through life and to long for some warmth and companionship to cheer his days.

However, his wish for someone to share his time with extended only to other adults. Babies and small children had featured not at all in his previous experience so it was with some trepidation that he set off for Southfields Maternity (which he assumed the writer of the anonymous note must have meant, despite their poor spelling), the private hospital where the rich or the well insured brought their offspring into the world. In some ways, Peter would have felt more confident en route for a gangland heist than he did in entering the cloistered sanctum of the new mother. Probably, he reassured himself, he would not actually have to see any babies and he certainly would not be required to assist in any birthing activity. All he could think was that a medical professional had in some way become involved in the aftermath of the warehouse fire and needed to see Peter at his or her place of work to bring some piece of evidence to his attention. At least, that was what he hoped.

Behind the reception desk of the Southfields hospital, a starched matronly figure was on the telephone.

'No, dear,' she was saying. 'That noise is quite normal . . .' The receiver in her hand shook with the squeaks coming from it. The nurse smiled apologetically at Peter. 'Baby's just trying to tell you she's hungry,' she continued in a calm voice, raising her eyebrows at Peter and shaking her head. 'No, I wouldn't wait until Nanny gets back, I'd feed her now . . . oh, you've never fed her. Oh . . . I see . . . what time is Nanny back? . . . ah, she's resigned, has she? What did she go and do a thing like that for? . . . you asked her to what . . . well, dear, cooking a dinner party for twenty-four isn't really in Nanny's job description . . . I'm sure you were paying her a lot of money but even so . . . have you ever changed a nappy . . . not done that either . . . hmm, well, I suggest you get yourself over here and we'll have a little lesson, shall we? Did you not come to the ones we offered at the hospital? . . . oh, you sent Nanny to those . . . I expect she knew some of what we had to teach already, what with her Norland qualifications and all . . . never mind, I'll see you right . . . yes, you'll be here soon, see you then.' She put the phone down and sighed.

'Motherhood doesn't come easily to some of my ladies,' she said confidentially to Peter. 'It's not quite the same as a double page spread in *Hello!*. Those are lovely flowers,' she added, indicating the bouquet Peter was nervously holding. In order to cover all eventualities, he had bought little pink roses interspersed with pale blue hydrangeas, set off with sprays of white mimosa. 'Who are you visiting?' The nurse had the green eyes and perfectly symmetrical face of a Botticelli angel.

'Erm, Bond,' he said.

'Of course, I should have guessed. Clever you with the flowers,' said the nurse. Peter just nodded, having no idea what she was talking about. 'Let's have a look on the list – name? And do you have some ID?'

'Peter, Peter Greyson.' He held out his driving licence for her to inspect.

'Here you are,' she said, putting a tick on the clipboard.

'Do all visitors have to be on the guest list?' he asked curiously.

'Oh yes,' said the nurse, leaning forward over the desk a little. 'We can't just let anyone in here, you know. Security is very tight – I'm not saying that any of the little babies is more precious than the others, mind you, but we do have some very famous mums here.'

The phone rang again. 'You go through,' said the nurse. 'Up the stairs, last door on the left.' As he walked away he could hear her answering the call. 'Hello, Southfields Maternity. Oh, hello, yes. Well, I would think in this weather that one cashmere blanket would be enough to keep baby warm . . .'

No noise emerged from the door of 23. Peter tapped tentatively and a quiet voice entreated him to come in. Inside, a woman lay sleeping in the bed, surrounded by so many flowers, it looked as though a wedding had taken place inside the small hospital room. In the corner, a leggy redhead sprawled in an armchair, idly flipping through a glossy magazine while drinking champagne from a tea cup. She looked up as Peter came in and put a finger to her lips.

'Shhh,' she said. 'They've just dropped off so we don't want to wake them.'

'They?' whispered Peter.

'Three babies and one tired mummy,' said the girl, pointing to the other side of the room where in a row of little celluloid cots slept three of the neatest, tiniest and most perfect mini-people Peter had ever seen.

'Triplets,' gasped Peter. He felt suddenly very moved by the sight of such vulnerable, tender young scraps of life, bundled up in their fluffy towelling Babygros, one white, one pink and one blue.

'IVF,' said the girl. 'It worked a bit too brilliantly.'

'It's a miracle,' breathed Peter reverently.

'It's quite a few miracles,' said the girl, smiling. 'My name's Spook, by the way.' She held out an elegant hand, adorned with purple nail varnish.

'Peter Greyson,' he said, taking her hand in his.

'I am – or I was – Fleur's assistant at Boulden's,' said the girl.

'Ahh, it becomes clear,' said Peter, who had quite forgotten for a moment why he was there.

'You're acting for Fleur, I believe,' said Spook.

'Indeed I am,' said Peter. 'Am I right in thinking you have some information for me?'

'Yes,' said Spook gravely. 'I think I do.' She handed him a piece of paper. Peter studied it intently.

'This appears to be a menu,' he ventured.

'Oh, sorry,' said Spook. 'Silly me! I've given you the wrong thing. Do you want something, by the way? The food here is really very good.' The Southfields in-house dining service offered a range of delights from organic sirloin steak in a peppercorn sauce to yellow tail tuna sashimi. 'I've got some champagne already if you'd like some.'

'No, really,' said Peter, taking the seat opposite her. 'I'm fine. Perhaps a cup of tea a little later. First things first – who is the lady in the bed?'

'My sister, poor lamb,' said Spook. 'But she's registered here under her married name.'

'Meaning?' said Peter, who was finding this a very strange interview.

'Well,' said Spook, speaking very quickly and very quietly, 'as you are defending Fleur and I work at Boulden's, I should be careful not to be seen with you. So I thought this was the ideal place to meet. If anyone's following you, they won't be allowed in but they'll think you're visiting a friend with a baby. That's why I said to bring flowers. As my sister's got a different surname from me, even if someone managed to get a list of patients – which would be quite difficult, by the way – no one will make the connection between Mrs Bond and Spook Dandy.'

'Probably unnecessary,' Peter was looking at Spook with something akin to respect. 'But very clever all the same.'

'Thank you,' said Spook. 'I thought so myself.'

'But if someone is watching me,' said Peter thoughtfully, 'might they not see you leave later on today?'

'No,' said Spook patiently. 'Because if they're following you, they'll have to leave when you leave or they'll lose you.'

'Of course,' said Peter humbly.

'But I'll go out by the back door anyway, just to be on the safe side,' said Spook as a concession.

'Might they not tail your sister, when she leaves with the babies?'

'If they follow her all the way to Ulan Bator, they'll be doing jolly well,' said Spook. 'Her husband's just been made British Ambassador to Mongolia.'

'Dear, dear,' commiserated Peter.

'I know,' said Spook. 'Apparently, it's a promotion.'

A mewling cry came from the baby in the white outfit.

'Oh, crap,' said Spook maternally. 'Eminem's waking up.'

'Is that his name?' said Peter in surprise.

'No,' said Spook. 'They've got real names but I've christened that one Eminem, Robbie's in the blue and the pink is Beyoncé. God, I hope he goes back to sleep.'

Sadly the infant king of rap had other ideas. Opening his tiny little mouth so wide it looked as though he might swallow his own head, he emitted a noise loud enough to put a low-flying supersonic aircraft to shame. Spook wasted no time – she whisked a bottle of milk out of a mug of warm water and Eminem out of his cot, inserted the teat between his rosebud lips and installed him in Peter's arms before the beleaguered barrister could whimper his protest.

'Remember to support the head,' said Spook sternly.

'But,' said Peter weakly, 'wouldn't it be better if you fed him?'

Spook gave him a look. 'Now,' she said. 'To business. Here.'

She found another piece of paper and waved it at Peter. 'I have a list of all the items Brinley – that's our boss, by the way – claims were in the warehouse when it burnt down. However.' She paused impressively. 'I happen to know for a fact that at least some of these paintings were *so* not there.'

Peter had been gazing down at the little bundle in his arms but he looked up sharply. 'How can you be sure?'

'Because,' replied Spook, 'some of the same paintings will be sold at a very private event in a few days' time.'

Peter whistled quietly. 'Spook, how come you know this?'

'Brinley thinks I'm thick,' said Spook blithely. 'So he doesn't imagine I'm capable of raiding his computer or double-checking information he gives me. He's asked me to contact a select few clients and invite them to a drinks party where he intends to sell some of the paintings that he'll also be claiming for on insurance.'

'So the warehouse was insured?'

'Very much so,' said Spook. 'With Lloyds.'

'That is very interesting,' said Peter. 'Spook, you don't believe Fleur burnt down the warehouse?'

'I didn't know what to think at first,' said Spook candidly. 'I love Fleur and I didn't *want* her to be guilty but it all looked so bad. But then I remembered she crashed her car a couple of months ago because she was trying not to hit a bumble bee. So I don't think she can have done it.'

'Interesting logic,' mused Peter. 'But good conclusion and I agree with you. Now, I take it Brinley has no idea you are consorting with the other side?'

'No,' said Spook. 'He thinks I'm far too stupid to be a double agent.'

'Make sure he keeps thinking that,' said Peter. 'In your opinion, did Brinley burn down the warehouse himself?'

Spook scrunched up her face and sighed. 'Somehow it's

not like him,' she said slowly. 'He's just too lazy. And too disorganised. It's completely in his nature to profit from someone else's misfortune but arson really isn't his style.'

'Good,' said Peter. 'Spook – can you get a couple of people added to the guest list for the auction?'

'That depends,' said Spook.

'On what?' said Peter.

'On whether they're the right sort of person.'

'What do they need to be?'

'Rich and dodgy,' said Spook. 'They've got to look the part and have the cash. Otherwise they'll be sniffed out in an instant.'

'Yup,' said Peter. 'Rich and dodgy I can supply.'

'Names?' said Spook.

'I'll get back to you,' said Peter. 'Can you find out if Brinley ever met someone called Mikhail Roscoff in person or whether they did their business remotely?'

'Of course,' said Spook. 'Is that who's coming?'

'No,' said Peter. 'But his wife might be. She's met Brinley before so he'll know she's the real thing. The person she brings as her husband, however, will be an impostor.'

'Fabulous!' said Spook. 'I love the word "impostor" – shame I can't spell it.'

A bat's squeak resounded from the baby in the pink 'gro.

'Oh, dear, Beyoncé wants to join in,' said Spook. 'Is Eminem done?'

Little Eminem's navy blue eyes had fluttered to a close behind the rapidly emptying milk bottle.

'Hand him over,' said Spook.

'Do I have to?' said Peter, who'd grown strangely fond of the smallest person he'd ever met.

'You do,' said Spook. 'I need to burp him.'

Hastily, Peter gave her the baby, whom she expertly hoisted

on to one shoulder. She began rubbing his minuscule spine until a satisfactory pocket of air was expelled from his windpipe.

'You better go,' said Spook. 'It gets a bit crazy in here when the band strikes up.'

'Just one thing,' said Peter. 'Why Spook? I mean, why are you called that?'

Spook blushed. 'When I was little, I wanted to be a detective,' she said. 'But everyone said I was too dumb and should work in an art gallery instead.'

'Maybe,' said Peter, 'you just got yourself a new career.'

'Do you think?' said Spook, her wide smile breaking out over her face.

'Let me know when you need a reference,' said Peter. 'I'll be happy to oblige.'

18

'Bonner.' The door to her cell was thrown back and one of the screws, with the sort of face you only got after at least thirty years of giving people nasty looks, was standing there, looking mean.

Fleur had just dropped off to sleep, no small achievement on the hard, thin foam mattress with only a single, scratchy blanket to pull around her. Much as she hated the daytimes with their tedious routine broken only by frightening and demoralising incidents – having her pony tail tweaked from behind by unfriendly hands or her bowl of porridge knocked off her tray, or being tripped up by someone who then said 'Sorry' in sarcastic tones of ultimate menace – the nights were worse. She'd been in prison now for a week but it felt like an eternity, the days that dragged themselves along endlessly with no promise of respite or a better tomorrow, the nights whose black minutes each stretched out to be a lifetime in themselves. She would lie, bleak, friendless, alone and in despair on her bunk bed, listening to the rhythmic snoring of the girl below, praying for the gentle oblivion of sleep to give her some peace and yet not wanting to drop off as it would hasten the beginning of the next hideous day.

Before her sudden and unexpected incarceration, Fleur had no idea how reliant she had become on the various methods of communication offered by the modern world. Without a computer to send e-mails, a mobile to text or make calls on or her landline to check for messages, she felt as though one of her limbs had been cut off. This feeling of appalling isolation got worse in the dark – from the tiny cell window positioned high up in the wall, she would gaze at the black sky, but even the sight of the stars on a clear night gave her no comfort. Previously, she had always found their presence reassuring, as though they were watching over her, but now they looked distant and unfriendly, devoid of spiritual meaning and nothing more than balls of flaming gas in galaxies so far away as to be irrelevant to life on earth.

A criminal – the words burnt on to her brain with a terrible ferocity. At first, her certainty that she was innocent had sustained her, but now she was starting to doubt even that. What if she had started the fire accidentally? Perhaps she had touched something with a faulty fuse, somehow igniting it? Or had she dropped a cigarette lighter or box of matches which had then burst into flames? As she didn't smoke, this was a ridiculous thought, but the problem with Fleur's type of incarceration – trapped in the cycle of destructive thoughts inside her own head with no voice of reason to break the vicious logic of her own assumptions – was that it fed itself just as the fire had on the dry contents of the warehouse. In her nightmares, time and time again the figures in the paintings came to life as they burnt to death, groaning, crying, screaming and begging Fleur to rescue them from their fate. They wept and pleaded with her to save them, they who had survived kings and queens, wars, plagues, disease, upheaval and tragedy, now to perish in some dark corner by a dirty river in the one place where they should have been safe.

Waking in a cold, clammy sweat, Fleur would lie panting with horror in her bunk bed, with few cheering thoughts with which to comfort herself. The past few days had contained nothing but one seismic shock after another. At their last meeting, Peter had told her he suspected Denny had deliberately targeted her, and that in befriending Roz his ulterior motive had been to get close to Fleur.

'Why did he use Roz?' Fleur had gasped. To hear that a friend of hers had had her emotions cruelly toyed with for such a reason was quite horrible. Peter, who had resisted the temptation to point out that he'd never like Denny in the first place, cursed the man again. On the one hand, Roz was still racked with guilt that she had brought Denny into Fleur's orbit, while on the other Fleur was now mortified that Roz had been humiliated because of her.

'I expect he realised she was a soft touch,' said Peter sadly. He hated to think of big-hearted Roz being taken for a ride. 'Probably knew you wouldn't give him the time of day.'

'I can't believe it,' said Fleur, her shoulders sagging.

'No, neither would the police at this stage,' said Peter. 'We need proof. But to get it, we have to tread carefully. We have to make whoever did this think their plan is working.'

'Why?' burst out Fleur. 'Why would anyone want me to go to prison?'

'Yes, that's interesting, isn't it?' said Peter, with the detached dispassion of the criminally aware. 'You'd think if someone had a strong grudge against you, they'd just kill you and be done with it. I wonder why they want you to be shut away?' He said it in the same tone of voice he might use to discuss the weather.

'I'm not sure interesting is the word I'd use,' said Fleur.

'I think that may be where the clue lies,' said Peter. 'It looks like a fairly specific form of revenge. But we still don't know for what.'

'I'm lost,' said Fleur simply. 'I really can't think.'

'Unless,' said Peter slowly, 'it's an eye for an eye – a fairly old-fashioned sentiment but one that's still quite common in various parts of the world, like eastern Europe for example.'

'Did you check out Zoran?' said Fleur.

'Yes, we did,' said Peter. 'Zoran Lazarevic himself has left Belgrade, no current contact details available. I spoke to his lawyer in Zurich, though, several times – he called me in high dudgeon, ranting about their burnt paintings. Apparently you gave them a receipt which included a valuation – that's the figure they're putting forward to the insurers.'

'They can't do that!' exclaimed Fleur. 'It's not a proper receipt. We never had a chance to verify the paintings. We've no idea whether they're worth that much.' She stood up and started pacing round the small room.

'Could they be forgeries?' asked Peter.

'Absolutely!' said Fleur. 'There's no real proof those paintings were originals.'

'And none that they weren't,' Peter reminded her.

'But that would be a motive, wouldn't it?' said Fleur, who was still rather excited by this chink of light in the gloom. 'And if someone else had a motive then the police would see it wasn't me, wouldn't they?' Her face was hopeful.

'Well, yes it would,' said Peter carefully. 'But we have no way of proving the paintings were fakes – according to the receipt you signed in Belgrade, they were valuable originals. So for you now to turn round and say you don't believe the paintings were real throws considerable doubt on your integrity. Until we have some proof, that would be quite a dangerous route for us to go down.'

Fleur's disappointment was so bitter she could taste it in her mouth. 'Did you have any luck with the British Embassy in Belgrade?'

'Very insular,' said Peter. 'They do have a staff member

called Thelma Lovegood but she sent a message saying she had no knowledge of you or your trip to Belgrade.'

'That's ridiculous!' said Fleur. 'I definitely met her. How about Striker McCullum?'

Peter shook his head. 'No one of that name appears to exist. Anywhere. Do you have any other salient details which might help us identify him?'

'He's infertile,' said Fleur. 'And his ex-wife is Costa Rican.'

'I see,' said Peter sceptically. 'Those sound like the hallmarks of an unnecessarily elaborate cover story to me. All in all, it does seem rather odd. I wonder if something else wasn't happening at the same time as you were there, of which we are not aware.'

Fleur was rather lost in all the negatives of Peter's last sentence. 'Could you say that again?' she asked.

'I think you've got caught up in something which no one wants us to know about,' said Peter more succinctly. 'The problem is going to be finding out the information which is deliberately being withheld.'

'Oh, is that all?' said Fleur wearily. She was fast losing hope that she would ever again know the simple joys of an unfettered life.

'Not really,' said Peter. 'Don't be downcast, dear girl, by what you hear next.'

The second great blow, which had winded Fleur even more than the mysterious activities of the man known as 'Denny', had been the turncoat attitude of Mr Brinley Boulden. Reappearing from the south of France with a cast-iron alibi for his own activities on the night of the warehouse fire, he had proceeded to stick the knife fair and squarely into Fleur instead. While Fleur had hardly expected him to come forward to save her, she certainly hadn't thought it would be Brinley who would seemingly seal the case against her by providing the police with a motive. In an interview with the detective in charge of the case, he made the shock claim that he had recently sacked Fleur for incompetence. With his bluff, cheery, upper-class demeanour, which portrayed him as an honest but perhaps not so clever sort of chap, he seemed all too plausible, especially when he revealed some information about Fleur which painted her in a less than flattering light.

'I had no idea when I hired her,' he had whispered confidentially, 'that she came fresh from a sacking in New York! I would never have taken her on if she hadn't deliberately concealed that fact from me. I'm afraid that's the sort of person we are dealing with.'

The policeman conducting the interview failed to warm to Brinley but he couldn't let his personal judgement interfere with hearing the wretched man's story. Fleur, Brinley revealed, had been asked to leave the museum she worked for in the States after a scandal had erupted, involving some serious mismanagement of the finances. In a twisted and manipulative way, what Brinley told the police was true – at least half the trustees had resigned in order to save their good names from being sucked into a sordid tale of embezzlement. Fearing more whistle-blowing, those trustees that remained quickly took action to sweep out anyone with loyalty to the former regime, Fleur being the first on the list. But by blending the two stories together, Brinley made it sound as though Fleur herself had been found guilty of serious misconduct and made to leave as a result when in fact she had been an innocent victim.

With his usual penchant for excess, Brinley couldn't resist taking it one notch further – in the description of Fleur he gave to the police, he painted her as erratic, difficult, prone to emotional outbursts, childish and manipulative. Every mistake that Brinley had made and Fleur had rectified he laid squarely at her door, even blaming her for selling a wrong-sized painting to an infamous rapper, an error he claimed to have set right himself.

When Peter related this sorry tale to Fleur, she felt as if someone had vacuumed out part of her soul, so painful was the revelation. That Brinley should just turn round and drop her into a foul mess was appalling. No matter how many times Peter assured her that Brin's comments about her were deliberately spiked to make her look dreadful, Fleur felt horrible, sick and used.

'I don't understand,' she said miserably to Peter. 'I thought Brinley liked me.'

'I expect he did,' said Peter. 'This isn't about personal feelings – he's got some background reason to say those things. We just need to find out what – but in the meantime, remember, losing heart will not win us the battle.'

Despite Peter's stirring words, Fleur continued to feel abject and bruised, especially in the middle of the night, when abruptly summoned to quit her bed and present herself for inspection. 'Bonner.' The screw's voice was scarcely less rasping than the screech of the heavy door. 'Get up.'

Fleur tried to sigh silently. The screws hated to hear their commands greeted with a despairing exhalation of breath. What would it be this time? Fleur had been on kitchen detail this morning so she fully expected to be told to scrub out all the pans again, wash the floor and wipe down the work surfaces once more. Her sympathy for Cinderella grew although at least that maiden was rescued by a handsome prince, something Fleur had given up hope for herself.

She tugged on a fleecy jumper over her pyjamas and slipped her feet into flip-flops against the freezing linoleum of the hard floor. Blearily, she followed the screw down the metal staircase, which rattled mournfully in the empty silence of the night-time prison. Usually heaving with sweaty, disgruntled femininity, for once the communal areas were abandoned as the flocks of jailbirds were neatly locked into their cages for the night.

'This way,' croaked the screw, taking Fleur to the partition door between the inmates' and the officers' areas. Using several keys, a computer swipe card and a punch-in code, the screw opened the door and led Fleur into an area which, while still neon-lit and institutional, had the fresh air of freedom rather than the stale breath of captivity about it.

Mindlessly, Fleur slopped along behind the neat clacking steps of the prison warder, too tired even to imagine why she might be taken on this strange midnight journey in her pyjamas. As they rounded another corner on the endless corridors, she saw a man waiting for them.

'Peter!' said Fleur, her face lighting up with joy. 'What . . . what's going on?'

'Fleur.' She saw him smile properly for the first time since her nightmare had begun. 'Come with me. I've got someone to see you.'

'Who?' said Fleur.

Peter held up a warning hand and indicated the waiting screw with his eyes. 'Just come with me,' he said. 'All will become clear.'

They approached one of the private interview rooms, outside which stood an enormous, burly giant whose size made everyone around him feel as though they had strayed into a world of the wrong proportions. The screw went to open the door but the giant motioned her back.

'Only these two go in,' he said.

The warden spluttered. 'I am a prison officer and this is an inmate under my charge,' she snapped. 'I will not told what to do by . . . whoever you might be.'

The giant gazed at her, totally unmoved. 'Just these two,' he repeated.

'Where do you think you are?' said the warden in disbelief. 'This is one of Her Majesty's Prisons.'

The door he was guarding opened and the Governor – by day a model of prim propriety and disapproval but now unusually flushed and somewhat excited – emerged, clutching what looked like a CD and a pen.

'Ma'am, this man,' declaimed the warden, pointing at the freakishly large guard, 'won't let me through.'

'Oh, well, never mind,' the Governor simpered girlishly, patting her steel-grey helmet of hair. Fleur had never seen this woman wearing quite so much make-up, although her lack of expertise in applying it had led to some peculiar results around the eye area where she had rashly applied two brilliant patches of glittery blue shadow. 'You can wait outside.'

'But . . .' The warden boggled. 'We don't leave prisoners unaccompanied in the interview room.'

'If I authorise a decision,' said the Governor sternly, 'I do not expect to be challenged. Bonner, you may go in.'

The interview room, once Fleur had got past the outsize bouncer, was dimly lit. At one end, with his back to her, stood a figure draped in a dark cloak and hood which reached right to the ground. At the sound of the door, the figure turned. Backlit by a flickering neon tube, he stood framed by greenish light as the hood fell away to reveal the trademark grey-blond hair, glittering silver eyes, curved nose and wicked smile that would be recognised the round globe over. As though to the beat of a backing group, to the cheers of hundreds of thousands of ecstatic fans and the opening strum of the guitar, he flung both his arms wide, a magnificent, expansive gesture which his insalubrious surroundings could do nothing to tarnish. Even in prison, Jed Harris just couldn't help being theatrical.

'Baby,' he cried, his voice breaking with emotion. 'Come 'ere an' give your ole man a hug.'

'Dad?' said Fleur, feeling hot tears tumble recklessly down her cheeks.

She ran forward to be swept into a tight embrace in the warm, soft folds of his cape. Burying her head in his shoulder, she felt his hand stroke the back of her head as he murmured, 'It's gonna to be okay, promise you, baby, I'm here now. I'm going to sort it.'

'Dad,' wept Fleur. 'Dad. I'm so sorry.'

'Shush,' said Jed. 'Don't be sorry, sweet'eart. 'S gonna to be okay.'

Fleur pulled away from him. 'I can't believe you're here,' she said, his face blurred by the mass of salt water clogging up her eyes.

'Wouldna have missed it for the world,' said Jed happily.

'But Dad, I'm in prison,' said Fleur miserably.

'Yeah, I'd noticed,' nodded Jed, who was beaming from ear to ear.

'I've made such a mess of everything,' sobbed Fleur. 'You must be so ashamed of me.'

'Ashamed?' cried Jed. 'Darlin', I'm bloody delighted! That's wot I said, soon as I found out.'

'What?' said Fleur. Her father had always been a bit strange but this reaction was off kilter even for him.

'Si' down,' said Jed, pulling out an orange plastic chair for her. She sank gratefully into it. 'Fleur,' said Jed passionately, 'this is the first time in yer life that I have ever been able to help you. You never needed me before – so when your mate called me in Singapore, I knew this was my Higher Power giving me the chance to get close to you. That's why I cancelled the tour.'

'You cancelled the tour?' Fleur was so shocked, she didn't even register the reference to Jed's Higher Power, something which in normal circumstances would have made her cringe. 'What about the fans?'

'Fuck 'em,' said Jed airily with a wave of his beringed hand, thus summarily dismissing the huge numbers of people who had begged, borrowed, stolen or queued all night to get tickets to see their idol on his world tour. 'Doesn't matter.'

'But who called you?' said Fleur. 'Mum's been trying to reach you but they wouldn't let her speak to you.'

'Ah,' said Jed looking shifty. 'Yeah, a bit of a misunderstanding. Got a tour rule: no calls from ex-birds – 'specially if I were once married to 'em – while we're on the road. Course, didn't akshully mean your ma but then I was 'ardly expecting her to get in touch after all these years to tell me you was in the clink.'

'It was Roz,' said Peter, who was hovering at the back of the room. 'Using her admirable persistence, she managed to persuade any number of assistants that she really did need to speak to your father.'

'That's right,' said Jed. 'Thing is, she used your real name – the message was tell Jed that Astraea Xavia Tiphani Flower is in trouble. That's how I knew she was for real, not some bleedin crank trying to give me what for down the blower. So there was I sitting in some fucking 'orrible poncy hotel in Singapore, trying to get a rise outta drinking Diet Coke, when this nice lady tells me you bin put away for arson. That's my girl, I thought, and got the first plane out of that hellhole. I gotta go back in a couple of days though or the press'll crucify me.'

'Officially, your father has twisted one of his vocal cords,' said Peter, who was grinning with excitement. Even he had been infected by the very palpable aura of magic which surrounded Jed Harris. 'So far, no one – apart from Roz, that is – has worked out the link between the two of you. Which is a good thing for now.'

'Yeah, I'm undercover,' said Jed, who was also showing signs of boyish glee. 'It's great being anonymous. Haven't had such a larf since I sank a houseboat in Kashmir in '69.'

Fleur felt doubtful that Jed's version of anonymity would pass muster with MI5 – a long black cape and huge security guard were not perhaps the definition of inconspicuous – but she had other things on her mind. 'I can't believe you came,' she repeated, feeling a wave of emotion break over her head.

'Oh, darlin',' said Jed, his old rocker's rasp moving down to a softer gear. 'I bin waiting for this moment for years.'

'But why?' Fleur burst out.

Jed ran a hand through his spiky hair. 'I know I was a crap dad to you, Fleur, but that wasn't 'cos I didn't care.' He sighed deeply. This was clearly a pre-prepared speech. 'I was a mess, Fleur, a real mess. A right selfish, shitty little bastard, but even so, I had a heart, and your mum broke it.'

'It wasn't Mum's fault,' said Fleur pleadingly.

'I know,' said Jed, suddenly looking weary. 'I know that. But it ain't easy living with an angel. Your mum was so frigging perfect that even when I was the most famous man on the planet, she could make me feel like the world's biggest loser. And then she left me. And took you with her.'

'You could have tried to find us,' Fleur got up the courage to say.

Jed looked at her for a minute, his grey eyes pensive and clear.

'Sir Jed.' Peter coughed discreetly. 'Would you like me to leave the room?'

'Nah.' Jed waved his hand. 'Don't open the door, mate, we don't know who might try and come in next.' He took off his black cloak and placed it over Fleur's shaking shoulders, and pulled up one of the uncomfortable seats. 'I did try to find you,' he said quietly. 'But by then it was too late.'

'Why too late?' demanded Fleur fiercely.

'When your mum left,' said Jed, 'at first I was relieved. It meant I could get on with being as fucked up as I liked without the angel of purity giving me disapproving looks. OK, I'm not proud of that,' he added quickly, seeing Fleur about to flare. He cupped her face in his hands and gently wiped away a few tears with his thumbs. 'But that's how it was. One day I was just coming off a bender in Brighton when I got in a cab and told him to take me to Hertfordshire, up to your place. I'd tried to push the pain away with drugs, drink and sex – sex, drugs and rock and roll, I s'pose.' He laughed to himself. 'Guess what, it didn't work. So I thort I'd take a trip to see you guys. You'd have been about three years old.'

'You came to Grandad's house?' said Fleur in disbelief. 'But no one ever told me.'

'They didn't know,' said Jed. 'I stood in the road and watched you playing in the garden, Fleur. There you were, sweet as a little flower, larfing and jumping about till you fell over and hurt yer knee. A man picked you up and comforted you. You stopped crying. And I thought, bleedin' Nora, my gel's got a new daddy.'

'You should have come in,' said Fleur.

'For wot?' said Jed. 'So your grandad could batter me to death with the garden fork? He was a fierce old boy, sweet-'eart, and he never liked me, not one little bit. He thought your mum deserved quality and some twatty little Essex boy with an ear for a good tune wasn't quite what he had in mind. Anyway, then your mum came out, looking beautiful, and the three of you sat in the garden together, for all the world the perfect little family.'

Fleur didn't trust herself to speak.

'I knew,' said Jed slowly, 'that all I had to do to wreck that pretty scene was to take a few steps forward. I could have wreaked havoc in all your lives, if I'd chosen to. There I was, alone, covered in booze and shit and piss and fag ash and God knows what else, jealous, bitter, wanting vengeance on the only woman I'd loved who'd had the nerve to leave me – me! Jed Harris, superstar!'

'But you didn't,' said Fleur, who was starting to understand.

'I didn't,' agreed Jed. 'I turned and I walked away which may be the only good thing I've ever done. I left you in peace, you and yer ma. Back then, I didn't know anything about "moving on" or "closure" or any of that other therapy shite. I just did what I thought was right – to give you the chance to grow up without me. You didn't need me, Fleur, not then. All I could have done was mess you up. But you need me now and here I am. I've come to make amends.'

'But . . .' Fleur started.

'I've always regretted it,' said Jed. 'I regretted it soon as I walked away. But I couldna let myself go back so I got the cabbie to take me to the nearest boozer. That was full of your grandad's ole mates from the Rotary so we went on to the next nearest – and the next – and the next. By the time we got back to London, I'd got thirty new best friends and a motorcade of taxis following.' He laughed. 'Took me days to get rid of 'em.'

A tap at the door interrupted Jed's tales of the past.

'Sir Jed, Fleur,' said Peter. 'I think we need to move to the present.'

Jed snapped his fingers. 'Okay, darlin', here's the deal.

Danny's checked out your man here and says he's hot stuff.' Danny was Jed's lawyer, a man who got so much business from his celebrity client that he no longer worked for anyone else. 'We fixed your bail and you are leaving tonight.'

Fleur gasped. The bail had been set at such an astronomically high figure she had had no hope of ever seeing daylight again. 'That's so much money,' she groaned.

'It's not real money,' said Jed smartly. 'Just a guarantee. Anyway, you in't cost me a penny so far. Nice change not to be paying for rehab.'

'Can I really leave?' she asked, looking to Peter for confirmation.

'Yes,' said Peter. 'As we speak, the Governor is just finishing off the paperwork and then you will be free – although obviously still under the conditions of bail.'

'I can go home?'

'Home is probably not the best place for you,' said Peter. 'We would like you to stay at your father's house until the trial. I understand he has excellent security arrangements.'

'Yeah,' said Jed. 'My staff have got such tight confidentiality contracts, I can string 'em up by the balls if they so much as tell anyone I've 'ad a cup of tea. So you'll be quite safe.'

'It won't be for long,' said Peter soothingly. 'But it is definitely the best place for you for now.'

'Can't I go to Mum's?' asked Fleur timidly. She was a bit overwhelmed by the recent chain of events and longed for some familiarity.

'Fleur, we think someone has tried to frame you for a very serious crime,' said Peter. 'We need you to be somewhere totally secure.'

'Woss your mum going to do, eh?' said Jed. 'Frighten them off with 'er tofu burgers?'

'All right,' said Fleur meekly, trying to ignore the thought that in swapping prison for Spaldings, Jed's country mansion, she was jumping out of the frying pan and into the fire.

Jed's blacked-out Mercedes pulled away from the prison with a superior muted roar. In the back, Fleur felt dizzy with the sensation of liberty, something she had never experienced before as she had always taken her freedom, that most basic of human rights, for granted.

'So how is Rowena?' Jed asked ultra-casually. 'Apart from her only daughter being shoved in the nick, I mean.'

'She's fine,' said Fleur cautiously.

'Oh, don't worry,' said Jed. 'I'm not going to try and win 'er back. I'm quite 'appy by meself for now, in't I, Barry?' He appealed to the security guard who was now chauffeuring the car.

Barry laughed, a rumbling noise like the warning signals of a small volcano. 'Don't listen to him,' he said, addressing Fleur in the back, his Caribbean accent like the sound of balmy evenings with nothing to do but smoke weed and watch the fireflies. 'He pretends to be a bad man. But he has a very good heart.'

'I'll say,' Peter chimed in from the front seat. 'I think Jed is a jolly good chap.'

'Oh, get lost,' said Jed in mock disgust. 'I don't believe it. My saintly daughter is a jail bird and now I'm a nice guy. What the fuck is going on?'

19

At exactly the required hour, Ben rang Alice's doorbell, brandishing a bunch of pale yellow roses.

'Bonsoir, madame,' he said, executing a low bow as she opened the door. He drew himself up to his full height and gave her the benefit of his wide, mischievous smile. Alice, who had never seen Ben in formal clothes, gasped slightly. He wore an impeccable dark charcoal wool suit with a crisp, faintly striped blue and white shirt.

'Wow!' she said, taking in the transformation from sweaty man in running gear and woolly hat to the urban tiger before her. 'You look fantastic.'

He laughed. 'Do I scrub up okay?' He leaned one arm on the door frame, his long body making a gentle S shape as he bent down to kiss her on the cheek. 'And you,' he said, 'look absolutely beautiful.'

Alice, in a deceptively simple black dress with high heels, exuded a soft radiance.

'I'm not going to be able to stop staring at you,' said Ben quietly.

'Don't overdo it,' said Alice, blushing slightly. 'We are meant to be married, after all. So really, you should ignore me all evening while flirting with other women.'

'I don't agree,' said Ben, handing her the flowers with a

flourish. 'Tonight, you are going to have an attentive and besotted husband by your side.'

'That would be a nice change,' she admitted, standing back to let Ben through the door. 'Will you come in for a minute? The children are longing to see you.' Ever since Ben had learned from Roz and Peter that Alice's perfect marriage was total fiction, he had started popping up at her house with the simple aim of making himself indispensable in her life. As Mikhail, Alice's renegade husband, had set such ridiculously low standards of spousal behaviour, it wasn't very hard for Ben to shine in comparison, integrating himself happily into her household where he took the kids out, put up shelves, lifted heavy shopping or changed light bulbs with cheerful aplomb. Despite the manner in which Alice had flirted with him when she first joined the Runners' Club, Ben knew enough to realise that under the glossy façade she was deeply insecure and that if he were to win her heart, he would need to do it gently and by degrees, building her trust in him until she could see how different he was from the men who had gone before. Like his theory of successful marathon running, he had decided to take small steps to conquer.

'Ben!' The boy skidded down the hallway towards him. 'I got a merit award at school today and I got a medal for football and I got a prize for cross country running.'

'Yo!' Ben raised his hand. 'Give me five! Nice work, Josh.' He ruffled the boy's hair affectionately but withdrew his hand quickly. 'Sorry, mate, didn't mean to mess up your style.' He refashioned Josh's hair. 'Using hair wax now, are we?'

'Oh, yes,' said Josh. 'Our teachers don't like it but I think it looks cool.'

'It certainly does,' said Ben seriously.

'Hello, Ben.' A dark-eyed small girl, who was an exact

replica of her mother, even down to the rather prim expression round the mouth, peered out from behind Alice's skirt.

'Hey! Lali!' said Ben, as though greeting his best friend. He squatted down to her level.

'Well,' said Lali sadly, 'I did my SATS exam today and I'm feeling quite stressed.' Lali was eight.

Ben took the little girl by the shoulders. 'You're going to be fine,' he told her.

'All right, kids,' said Alice. 'Time to be good without me.' Behind the children hovered their new babysitter, Roz.

'Can't Ben stay?' said Lali. 'We could watch *The Incredibles* and then he could sleep in my room.'

'So-rree,' called Roz. 'You'll have to make do with me.'

'That's okay,' said Josh generously. 'We don't mind. In your own way, you're not that bad.'

'Why, thanks,' said Roz, laughing. 'That's very reassuring.'

Brinley's auction, where the suddenly bespoused duo were headed, was to be held in a very discreet, very ancient private members' club where those who had gained entry could probably build a nuclear bomb inside, so high was the level of trust in the honour and integrity of anyone found worthy of being a member of such an august establishment. Brinley had been hosting a private clients' evening there for some years now, so ostensibly there was little that was remarkable about the event, except of course for the fact that at least one of the paintings was not so much hot as supposedly burnt to a veritable cinder and registered with the police as no longer available for purchase.

'Who are they?' Brinley hissed to Spook as he circulated the pre-auction drinks party.

'That's . . . let me see . . . that is . . . Mr and Mrs Roscoff, Mikhail and Alice,' replied Spook, who didn't actually need to look at the list on her clipboard to know who Brin was talking about but did so anyway, for appearance's sake.

'What on earth is Mikhail Roscoff doing here?' said Brin furiously. 'Bloody man's lost all his money, you idiot. I told you to invite people with disposable income, not washed-up bankrupts.'

'You put them on the list,' lied Spook calmly, her eyes this evening the colour of shelled pistachio nuts. 'See?' She showed him.

'I did?' Brinley stopped short. He had been drinking quite heavily lately, which at his age tended to lead to terrible memory lapses. Fortunately for the impostor and his wife, several small incidents had recently befallen Brinley which were sufficient to convince him this could well be his mistake. 'I better go and talk to them. What do I need to know?

'He's a major venture capitalist who's been on hard times,' said Spook. 'But he's on the up again. She does a lot for charity and you've met before.' She'd been well briefed by Peter. As Brinley ambled away to greet them, Spook allowed herself to breathe out gently.

The plan was hardly watertight. Through strategic probing, Spook had ascertained that Brinley had never actually met Mikhail Roscoff – all business had been conducted via Mikhail's office – although when discreetly questioned, Brin did have a vague memory of once encountering Alice. It had been this information, relayed to Peter Spook-style, that is as a verbal message entrusted to a young lawyer with a terrible crush on her (never write anything down, never use telecommunications being her new policy) that had given Peter his idea.

When Spook had told him of this auction, he had seen a great opportunity to recover a so-called 'burnt' painting as proof of underhand dealing. The very fact that Brin was selling off paintings which he had listed as lost in the fire must, Peter reasoned, shed doubt on the current findings of the investigation and might force the police to examine other ideas. It might also make them discount Brinley as a powerful witness against Fleur and make them question his assertion that he had sacked her, something Fleur strenuously denied. Currently, they seemed far too happy with the situation and were extremely unwilling to pursue other leads into the warehouse arson affair. A painting supposedly burnt to a cinder would be a useful piece of evidence, if they could get their hands on it.

'Why don't we get the police to raid Boulden's?' Alice had asked.

'It's too soon,' Peter had replied. 'We'd be showing our hand too early and it might prevent us from finding out more.'

'Like what?' said Alice.

'I don't know,' admitted Peter. 'Like Donald Rumsfeld, at the moment we don't know what we don't know. So softly softly catchee monkey.'

'Children?' Ben was saying to a statuesque blonde who'd clearly used some of her husband's insane wealth to rearrange her features, not entirely to good effect. 'Yes, we have children, two gorgeous ones.' He took a sip of champagne and tightened his grip round Alice's waist. A couple of other people standing in their little group nodded politely. 'Of course, I hardly ever see them. I have far more important things to do.'

'Vere do you vork?' said a Russian oil baron, his grasp of English not quite good enough to pick up on the oddities of Ben's conversation. In fact, he was finding Ben's attitude rather refreshing.

'Mikhail's in VC,' put in Alice quickly.

Ben smirked. 'Obviously, domestic matters are way beneath a man of my standing.'

'Yes, yes,' agreed the oil baron, rubbing his hands together. 'So true. These New Men – they make me sick! I would round them up with a pitchfork and drive them into the forest.'

'Absolutely!' agreed Ben enthusiastically. 'Just the ticket.'

Brinley smarmed over to join them. He wasn't delighted the Roscoffs were there but at least they were keeping Gregor Besaronovich occupied. Gregor was a bit of a wild card – his billionaire status gave him an instant entrée to London society, but it would be a few generations before the name Besaronovich became really respectable. While Gregor himself had great cunning, guts and determination, he lacked any form of social polish and his manners were tremendously brusque. Rumour had it that Svetlanka, the towering blonde with him, had hired a team of etiquette consultants to try to smooth off some of Gregor's rough edges. But Gregor would have none of it and had sent them and their tips on how to deal with multi-choice cutlery at the dining table packing.

'I haf bought a football team,' Gregor was saying in disgust. 'But they are bloody useless fools. I vent to vatch them and I tell you,' he was gesticulating with a huge cigar for emphasis, 'they stink. But,' his bald pate gleamed, 'one Russian comes to London and buys Chelsea and so now, if you are Russian in the West and you hav money, you must buy a football team. Har! Har!' He chomped on his cigar, his little dark eyes flicking swiftly over Alice and Ben. 'Ve are all fools, no?'

'I couldn't agree more,' said Ben coolly.

'Ve vill buy paintings ve don't like that ve von't look at. For vat?' said Gregor.

'Because we can,' said Ben. 'That's why.'

'Exactly!' said Gregor joyously, throwing his hands in the air. 'I like you. You vant new job, you come see Gregor.'

'Mikhail!' said Brinley. 'Alice!' He greeted them as though his whole life had been enhanced by the mere sight of them.

'Brinley.' Ben inclined his head. 'I am very pleased to make your acquaintance. Of course, you know Gregor Besaronovich.' Gregor was watching Ben very closely.

'Indeed,' said Brinley, rubbing his hands with faux jollity. 'Gregor. Such a pleasure. How are you?'

'I am,' said Gregor with impressive slowness, 'even richer than last time we met, Mr Boulden.'

'Super!' said Brin, who couldn't afford any social snobbery these days. 'You are a modern marvel, Gregor.'

'Yes,' Gregor agreed with him. 'I have commissioned a writer to do my autobiography. A tale of the peasant boy from Siberia who became one of the world's most powerful men. I think it will be very heartwarming.'

'I'm sure,' said Alice. 'What is the book called?'

'*My Soul*,' said Gregor simply.

'The auction will begin a few minutes,' said Brinley. 'Perhaps you would like to take your places – I hope you will find some trifle that appeals.'

Ben smiled. 'Oh, I have my eye on a few items,' he said smoothly.

'Excellent,' said Brinley. 'It is a great honour to have you both here – Mikhail and Gregor, two great financiers of our times. Although,' he turned to Ben, 'would you forgive me, Mikhail, but you are quite a bit younger than I expected.'

Alice flinched. Not only was Ben a good decade younger than Mikhail, but he also had the sort of fresh-faced joie de vivre that a man wedded to his office work simply could not possess.

Ben, however, was completely unfazed by Brinley's comment. 'Yes,' he said, smiling. 'Everyone says that.' He continued smiling at Brin but offered no further explanation.

'Talent,' said Gregor expansively, jumping into what was becoming a slightly awkward silence. 'This man has talent –

Gregor has a nose for these things. That is why he has risen so far so young, I can assure you, Mr Boulden. Gregor knows these things.'

'Of course,' said Brinley. If Besaronovich, who was notoriously shrewd, was satisfied, then so was he. He tweaked Ben's arm, moving him slightly to the side for a second. 'I am delighted that your business has seen such an upturn over the past three months,' he said, *sotto voce*. 'Perhaps you will buy back the painting you sold me?'

'I'm considering it,' he replied coolly before walking away to take his seat next to Alice.

Once his guests were seated in the rows of spindly-legged faux Louis Quatorze chairs, arranged for that purpose, Brinley took the floor, all beaming smiles and unctuous charm. But the flowing speech and beatific grins were a fast-cracking front. The past few weeks had been an ordeal for Brin. Before the fire, he had been planning to sell the gallery, all the stock and the warehouse and take a quiet, gin-fuelled retirement in Monaco. Now that he was knee-deep in a police investigation and an insurance claim, which would doubtless drag on for years before he saw a penny of compensation, he found himself in a most awkward position. He had debts everywhere and urgently needed some operational capital, which was why he had resorted to a little fraud of his very own. Selling pictures he had put in an insurance claim for was perhaps not his greatest 'get rich quick' scheme, but seen in the light of utter desperation it looked far more plausible than it might otherwise have done.

So wrapped up in his own dire predicament was Brinley that he had no room left in his withered heart to care about anyone else, including Fleur whom he had so unfairly pilloried. He had plenty of his own worries to be dealing with, and while he knew that his treatment of her had been dire, he had, he felt, been pushed into it. Scared for himself and his own future, he had thrown Fleur to the wolves in the hope of saving his own wrinkled skin.

'Well, this is a pleasure,' he said heartily to the collected roomful. 'My very favourite people, all together. What a very great treat.'

Gregor, who had sat himself next to Ben, muttered rather loudly, 'Get on vith it, you old fool.'

'Thank you all for coming,' continued Brin hurriedly, as if he had heard Gregor's *sotto voce* instructions. 'I am very honoured by your presence at my annual private sale, a service I provide to only' – he paused for a brief simper – 'my most exclusive and highly treasured clients.'

'Ha ha ha,' Gregor whispered right into Ben's ear. 'He means he has vorks he can't sell openly so he hopes to palm them off on us.'

'But surely you don't mean that Brinley might be selling items of dubious provenance?' whispered back Ben. Gregor, who clearly had no concept of personal space, was leaning against him to speak into his ear in such a manner that he was practically sitting on Ben's knee.

'Tsk, tsk,' he said. 'Why else do you think he has these little soirées?'

'Isn't it rather risky to buy something?' said Ben.

'Paf,' said Gregor. 'I just put them in a bank vault in Japan to vait for the day my empire collapses.'

'I see,' said Ben.

'All great fortunes come and go,' said Gregor. 'When I'm bankrupt and on the run, then I vill sell my art works to the next criminal billionaire.'

'That's a very forthright attitude,' said Ben.

Gregor winked at him. 'It is the secret of my success,' he said.

233

Alice, who had got stuck with Svetlanka, could only watch in trepidation – she wasn't close enough to hear what Gregor was saying to Ben and she had Svetlanka persistently prattling into her own ear, asking her for recommendations on everything from facial peels to household linen. Having spotted Alice as a perfect example of an English lady, Svetlanka was determined to wring as much information out of her as possible. Where should one buy towels in London? Who was the best hairdresser for highlights? Where should one's dog be shampooed? Which restaurant to suggest for a casual lunch/evening drinks/formal dinner/Sunday lunch? What was the correct form of address to use for a duchess? Several times during the evening, Svetlanka's habit of nodding her head as she listened to Alice's patient replies perverted the bidding quite dramatically, as each nod was taken as an indication to raise the price of an item. Brinley, of course, realised that Svetlanka had no idea she was inadvertently taking part in the auction, so wrapt was she in her conversation with Mrs Roscoff. While he found her very useful in jacking up the prices, he wasn't foolhardy enough to try to saddle her with any purchases. He feared Gregor's wrath far too greatly for that.

At last, lot 27 appeared, an innocent-looking painting, depicting a summer's afternoon where a small child in the foreground sat gazing out over the distant green and yellow hillscapes to a far away and only just visible indigo sea. The sky was a gentle sweep of violet, grey and white, the landscape and sky made up of lovingly arranged pinpoints of colour which blurred into each other to create a soft and undulating panorama. It was a beautiful piece of work and one which filled the room and the spectators with peace, calm and sunshine. It seemed impossible that a mere rectangle of canvas covered in dots of colour could create a totally new atmosphere within the room, but as soon as Brinley unveiled *To the Sea* a hushed silence fell and even Svetlanka broke off her queries as to what colour nail varnish was currently fashionable for toes. And yet *To the Sea* was not a major work. In the style of the more famous Impressionists, it came from the brush of a minor Dutch artist, somewhat despised for his ability to copy rather than innovate. *To the Sea* had yet to ascend to the pantheon of paintings known to the vast majority of the Western world as greetings card or poster fodder.

Alice gasped but turned it into a cough. As Spook had been unable to provide a full roll-call of exactly which paintings Brinley would decide to put on sale, they had had no warning that one of Alice's pictures would appear in the auction. All Ben and Alice had were a couple of lot numbers with instructions to buy at least one of them. 'That's my painting,' she hissed to Ben, who, looking at the tense set of her face, for the first time in his life passionately wished he was a very rich man. 'We must get it.' As luck would have it, lot 27 was on Peter's list.

Gregor chomped thoughtfully on his cigar while watching Ben from the corner of his eye. Gregor had thrown out a few half-hearted bids so far but Ben had not chanced any purchases yet. When planning the evening, Peter had suggested that Ben should join the bidding from the beginning, to make it clear he was a player and to disguise the fact that he was only genuinely interested in one or perhaps two lots. But Ben was not happy about this idea – horribly conscious that it wasn't his money he would be bidding with, he said he would only bid for the paintings they really wanted. As whatever they bought would be paid for ostensibly by Alice's credit card but in reality via a slush fund provided by Jed, Ben didn't feel he could take too many chances. It wasn't that Jed was mean, but he hadn't been totally thrilled by the idea of financing such a wacky scheme, especially when he realised he'd be buying a painting which he might never actually get to own.

Spook stood next to lot 27 on the makeshift stage at the front of the room, her face deliberately neutral as she mentally willed Alice and Ben to hold their nerve and buy this painting. *To the Sea* was clearly listed in Brinley's insurance records as burnt in the warehouse, whereas in fact it had been lodged inelegantly in a cupboard at Boulden's. It was the perfect piece of evidence for Peter as it would show beyond all doubt that Brinley had been indulging in some underhand double-dealing. Obviously, Brinley was taking a risk in offering his best clients an art work they might find hard to re-sell, but his thinking had deteriorated to the purely short term and he kept his mind on the money.

There was certainly plenty of that in the room before him, enough probably to refinance the debt of a few poverty-stricken third world nations. The weight of their collective wealth seemed to sit heavily on the assembled company, dragging the corners of their mouths, their jowls, their eyelids and their stomachs downwards towards the floor. It was such a business, being tremendously rich, that just occasionally an oligarch like Gregor would reflect that life had been much simpler in the days when all he had to do was earn the money rather than spend all his time, energy and passion on administering the sums he had already amassed. Being insanely moneyed was also far less fun than it sounded as the richer one got, the more people gathered around to try to take the money away. Being well aware of the impossible lure of his vast fortune, these days Gregor tended to orientate himself towards people he could see were genuine and unconcerned with financial gain, a very rare breed, one of whom he had been most taken aback to discover this evening in the form of venture capitalist extraordinaire, Mikhail Roscoff. So very unusual were such people that Gregor was quite prone to offering jobs to those who his ever-twitching nose told him could not be bought for any sum of money.

'Lot 27, reserve price £24,000,' said Brinley, opening the bidding with a very modest sum. Experience had taught him that sometimes it worked better to start low and lure in a few buyers intent on snapping up a bargain.

Casually flicking one finger up in the air, Ben signalled his bid. He felt Gregor's beady eye on him.

'Thank you, we have £24,000. Do I have £26,000?' He appealed to the room where a gentleman at the back nodded his head. 'Twenty-six – do I see twenty-eight? Thank you, the lady with the glasses and thirty, back to the gentleman in the middle. Thirty-four? Thank you, and over in the corner, I have thirty-eight.' Brinley was smooth, there was no doubt about that. He effortlessly kept the bidding going, raising the sums by which he increased the price just a little each time until each new bid brought jumps of tens of thousands. Despite the wealth of his audience, Brinley knew full well that these people still had to be brought gently into the trap, perhaps even more carefully than his more impecunious clients.

'Two hundred,' he said, pointing a stubby finger at Ben, who felt his stomach turn over. On the one hand, he felt a stirring sense of excitement that he should be gambling with so much money, on the other terrible guilt. It wasn't his money and yet there he was gambling like a high roller in Vegas with a credit limit of millions.

'Two-sixty,' said Brinley. 'Am I bid two-eighty?' The room was quiet, the enthusiasm having dimmed once the painting went over the 250,000 mark, mostly because a painting bought for anything more than quarter of a million would require an export licence, something the assembled buyers would be loath to have to acquire.

'Two-sixty,' said Brin, who was nevertheless delighted. As a cash sum, this would get a couple of his less pleasant creditors off his back, men who made Gregor Besaronovich look like Mother Teresa in comparison. 'Going, going . . .'

Ben was just about to breathe out a huge sigh of relief when, next to him, the fat Russian waved his cigar and said, 'Two-eighty.'

'You bastard,' Ben whistled under his breath. Any faint feelings of kinship he might have built up with this fellow promptly dissipated. Alice shot him a panicked look – she knew only too well they literally could not afford a bidding war with Gregor. Brinley was looking to Ben, who raised his chin defiantly and said, 'Three hundred.'

Gregor clapped him on the back. 'Excellent!' he hissed before bidding, 'Three-twenty.'

'Three-forty,' said Ben confidently. Gregor, he figured, must be some kind of psychopath, the sort of man who built up relationships with the express desire of destroying them at the first opportunity.

'Four hundred,' said Gregor challengingly. He nudged Ben and smiled encouragingly, which gave Ben the desire to punch him in his all-knowing face.

'Four-ten,' said Ben, trying to slow the bidding down.

'Four-fifty,' said Gregor.

'Four-fifty-two and a half,' said Ben.

'Five hundred,' said Gregor. By the smirk on Gregor's face, it looked as if he had read his opponent perfectly.

'Five hundred,' echoed Brin in tones of finality. 'Five hundred. Going . . .' He left a very long pause. Ben closed his eyes, not knowing what to do next. If they didn't buy the painting but allowed it to slip into Gregor's hands, it would probably never be seen again. And neither would Fleur, who would be spending the rest of days residing in prison. The painting that didn't burn in the warehouse fire was currently the only shred of evidence pointing to a different sequence of events from the one the police had seized on.

'Going,' said Brinley's voice slowly.

'Five-ten,' a woman's voice interrupted crisply. Ben opened his eyes again and saw Alice, with great poise, entering a bid.

Gregor looked across at her, gave her a polite half-bow from his seat and smiled.

'Gregor,' said Brinley. 'Do I hear five-twenty?'

Gregor shook his head slowly. He turned to Ben. 'I like your wife.'

'So do I.' Ben glared him down.

'Don't vorry.' Gregor tapped him on the knee. 'I haf just been testing you.'

'Five hundred and ten thousand pounds,' said Brinley, who couldn't believe his luck. 'Going, going, gone to Alice Roscoff.' The gavel come down with a hearty smack, earning the painting a new owner and Fleur Bonner the first very faint glimmer of hope that somehow, someday she would be free.

20

'Hi honey, I'm home,' said Jed, swaggering into the room. His proprietorial manner was quite forgivable. After all, he was master of all he surveyed, and should he choose to look round there was quite a lot to see once you added the up the eighteen-bedroom mansion with own cinema, billiards room and bar (now defunct), separate pool house with Jacuzzi and sauna, guest chalets in the rolling parkland surrounding the main house, ample garaging and, in the distance, a copy of a small eighteenth-century folly which Jed had taken a fancy to when visiting Mick Jagger's country house.

Fleur was curled up on one of his capacious sofas which was as comfortable and enveloping as an old-fashioned feather bed. Her time at Spaldings had passed much more peacefully than she had expected, the old mansion having undergone a major revamp in the years since she had last visited. So different was it from its legendary past that former friends who dropped in, expecting to receive a real rock and roll welcome, were utterly horrified to find the champagne fountain switched off, the bunny girls sent home, the cocaine mountains dissolved and the orgy room locked for ever. Instead, they found cohorts of very calm people, drifting about in a haze of their own benevolence, an eclectic assortment of the therapists, reflexologists, psychics and healers that Jed had accumulated to accessorise his new sober lifestyle. Fleur didn't mind these gently smiling inhabitants who were always on hand to offer a foot massage, a cup of herbal tea or some soothing platitudes about a universal masterplan which was hidden from our eyes and only revealed to us in stages as we needed to know. In her break from incarceration, Spaldings provided Fleur with a haven as far removed from the reality of her day to day existence as her time in the clink had been but in much more luxurious and beautiful surroundings. Jed's current lack of a significant other in his life also contributed to the harmony on display in his household. As he was intent on breaking his patterns of previous behaviour, it was very important, he told Fleur, that he didn't get into a relationship until he had truly healed his wounds from the past and learned to move on. Fleur, who had never known her father be single for longer than about five minutes, was favourably impressed. Jed had no gift for solitude whatsoever; in fact, he obviously needed to be constantly surrounded by other people to re-assure himself he was indeed alive. And yet he seemed to be making a real effort to change, to ignore the false plaudits the world constantly threw his way, and become a genuinely nicer man. Going to prison had been a huge surprise but rediscovering her father and finding she actually liked him was almost the greater one.

The only problem with Spaldings was that sometimes it got quite dull. Jed was frequently away, so to cope with the mild ennui which usually set in after her thirteenth cup of camomile tea Fleur started running again, using Spaldings park as her track. She had given up any real hope of taking part in the marathon – her preliminary hearing was sched-uled for two days before and Peter had warned her that it might well not produce a favourable result. There was a real possibility, he had told her, that she might find herself facing a full trial, which could in turn lead to some kind of sentence. Sometimes, Fleur lived in the hope that somehow this insane nightmare would come swiftly to an end and she would have her freedom restored. At other times, with grim resignation, she forced herself to face the worst case scenario. Just as Jed came in, she was picturing herself shuffling out of the prison gates in twenty years' time, with nowhere to go, no friends, no money and no hope.

'Oh, darling,' said Jed, who was considerably more perceptive these days than in the bad old times of complete physical and mental annhilation. 'You're not all right at all, are you?'

'Would you be?' Fleur raised a smudged face to him.

'Baby,' said Jed, rubbing his chin thoughtfully with one ringed hand, 'I've been through some big highs and lows in my life. And the one thing I can tell you without any doubt is that this too shall pass. But in the meantime,' he looked her over with his slanted tiger eyes, 'you and I are getting out of here.'

'But Dad,' breathed Fleur, 'Peter told me not to leave Spaldings.'

'Oh, fuck it,' said Jed, smiling. 'You're not in bloody prison yet. Come on, let's be quick before all the nutters decide to come too.' Usually whenever Jed made a move towards anything resembling a door, scores of the Spaldings people scrambled in his direction, abandoning their serenity in their eager desire to accompany their idol wheresoever he might choose to go. But at that moment the house was quiet, save for the muffled knocks and banging coming from the séance room where most of them were ensconced, busy receiving messages from their spirit guides. Even big Barry, Jed's Caribbean minder, was having a quick snooze. It was a once in a lifetime opportunity for the two to be alone together.

As Jed and Fleur roared out of the driveway in what Jed had picked as a nice inconspicuous little roadster, a baby blue Corvette with twin exhaust pipes which, admittedly, was less eye-catching than the white HumVee he had originally wanted to take for a spin, Fleur felt the dizzying sensation of freedom once more. Was this one of her last opportunities to enjoy liberty? Her next journey would be back to London to the courtroom where the next stage of her fate would be decided. If it went forward to a full trial where she was found guilty, she could find herself in an unmarked van, heading towards a women's prison.

Jed seemingly read her thoughts. 'Look, darling, these days it's private security firms wot ferries prisoners around. So I've got Barry to make some enquiries. Reckon we can spring you while you're in transit, if we have to.' Peter had repeatedly tried to impress on Jed that Fleur was in one of the few situations in the world out of which vast wealth alone could not buy her. But Jed just kept on trying to find a way.

'Do you really think I might go down?' asked Fleur.

'Nope,' said Jed. 'But did I think you might be framed for arson? Also no. So best to be prepared for all eventualities from now on in. But don't you worry,' he added. 'I've got it all under control.' At that moment, the Corvette let out a shriek of grinding pain and stopped so suddenly that the back end of the car was thrown forward, spinning the little vehicle and jamming the nose firmly into a hedge. Neither father nor daughter was hurt but the poor Corvette had taken a distinct hammering in the roadworthiness stakes.

'Oh, fuck,' said Jed, banging the steering wheel. 'Fucking hell, thought this bloody car had been serviced.'

'Dad, you've run out of petrol,' said Fleur, looking at the gauges. 'That's all.'

'Oh, bleeding Nora,' grumbled Jed. 'Oh, bloody typical.

The minute I want to actually use something which is actually mine, there's no effin' petrol. Sorry, darling. You got a phone?'

'No, Dad,' said Fleur. 'Mine was stolen – haven't you got one?'

'Nah,' said Jed sheepishly. 'Didn't think.' The truth was that Jed so rarely did anything for himself that it was a miracle that he could still put on his own trousers. He hadn't bothered to look at the petrol gauge because it simply didn't occur to him to do something so mundane.

The night was falling around them as the duo trudged along the country lane in search of some form of life. Fleur, in trainers, jeans and a jumper, was better clad than her father who, not being a very tall man, was wearing cowboy boots with heels, leather trousers and a yellow T-shirt with a picture of Dennis the Menace on the front.

'Cold, innit?' remarked Jed.

'Do you want my jumper?' asked Fleur kindly.

Jed gave a bark of laughter. 'If you were one of my "people"' – he sketched inverted commas in the air with his hands – 'I'd probably say, yeah, hand it over. But you're not.'

'I am one of your people in a sort of way,' said Fleur.

'I know you are, darlin',' said Jed. 'You're my VIP. Or should that be VID – Very Important Daughter.'

'That makes you my VID – my Very Important Dad,' said Fleur, her head down against the wind which was blowing along the narrow lane like a wind tunnel.

'I think that should be VCD,' said Jed. 'Very Crap Dad.'

'Noooo,' said Fleur, unconvincingly. 'What about GIACD?'

'What the fuck does that stand for?'

'Great In A Crisis Dad.'

'Har, har, better late than never you mean,' said Jed,

rubbing his bare arms to warm them up. 'Fleur, tell me, do you have any good memories of me, present situation apart?'

'Erm.' Fleur thought hard. She remembered the time when Jed developed a bizarre paranoia about spiders taking over the world and wanted to stopper all the bath drains at Spaldings to prevent them from coming to get him. She pictured the awful time when he been drunk in an interview with Michael Parkinson. She thought of all the times he simply hadn't been there throughout her life.

'Got one!' she said triumphantly.

'What is it?' said Jed, whose nose was turning a little blue.

'Years ago, I came to see you in concert,' said Fleur.

'When?' squeaked Jed. 'Did I know? Did you come back-stage?'

'No,' said Fleur. 'I was about sixteen. I bought a ticket and came by myself to see you at Wembley. You were . . .' She remembered the evening, her aching pride in the brilliance of Jed's performance, her heartbreak at being alone in the auditorium. 'Magnificent.'

'Fuck,' said Jed. 'So your best memory of me, your father, is standing in a crowd of thousands while I'm a dot on the stage. Is that it?'

'Well, yes,' said Fleur reluctantly. 'I suppose it is.'

'Marvellous,' said Jed crossly. 'I'm such a dickhead, I don't believe it myself sometimes.'

'You're not that bad,' said Fleur encouragingly. 'You haven't even mentioned your sponsor once since I've been here.'

'Yeah, well,' said Jed. 'I saw him. In Tesco's, buying a crate of red wine.'

'Perhaps it was for someone else?' suggested Fleur. She felt sorry she'd dissed the poor sponsor now that he had shown signs of human weakness.

'No, baby, he was drunk,' Jed sighed. 'Can't trust anyone these days.'

'Hey, Dad,' said Fleur, a thought striking her. 'What were you doing in Tesco's?'

'I was buying some salad,' said Jed defensively. 'I'm trying to give meself back some power by learning to care for meself again.'

They came to a crossroads where for the first time in over an hour of walking, there were signs that human life still existed on planet earth. A pub, the sign swinging in the spring breeze, sat glowing with warmth and light, the door just ajar in an inviting and friendly fashion.

'Brilliant!' said Fleur. 'We can go in there and make a call.'

Jed had halted very suddenly. He looked like a frightened racehorse, refusing to leave the traps at the start of a race.

'Oh no, darling,' he said, backing away. 'I don't think so.'

'Come on,' said Fleur impatiently. 'If you stay out any longer, you'll get pneumonia. Let's go in.'

'Oh, baby,' said Jed. 'I'll wait for you outside.'

'No!' said Fleur, stamping her trainer-shod foot. 'It'll be ages before anyone gets here to pick us up – you've got to get out of the cold.'

'Last time I went into that pub,' said Jed quietly, 'I woke up a week later in Acapulco with a beard, a transvestite and one kidney.'

'That was then,' said Fleur firmly. 'This is now. I'll look after you.'

She marched him through the door into the grateful steamy heat of the crowded pub. Finding a corner seat, she pushed him into it, told him not to talk to anyone and went over to the bar to use the phone. On stage, a gruesome provincial band was just finishing their set to the great glee of the audience who'd been happily pelting them with any missile that came to hand.

'We're taking a break now,' said the leader of the band, a man for whom the term 'Dad-Rock' might have been coined. Even his ancient Iron Maiden T-shirt and leather trousers couldn't disguise the fact that he had a stable life, a nine to five job and a happy marriage. 'And if you're not nicer to us next time, we might not play your favourites!' He spoke in the voice of a man used to addressing small children.

'Oooh-err!' said the crowd.

'Gerroff!' someone yelled.

'Davey, you're shite!' shouted someone else.

'Stick to the day job,' crowed another inebriated punter. Obviously, they were loving it.

But when Fleur got back to the table where she had left her father, he was nowhere to be seen. A chill ran through her – what if she had just reversed years of therapy by bringing him in here? And if she had, what was she to do about it?

On the stage, a new singer had picked up the guitar and was tapping the microphone head. Feedback screeched through the amplifiers, shocking the rowdy crowd into a moment's silence.

'This song is for someone very special,' the man said, twanging a guitar string, 'who's here in the audience tonight. I wrote this for her many, many years ago.'

'You're crap!' a heckler shouted.

'What's he doing?' The outraged band stopped forcing their way to the bar and advanced on the stage to reclaim their instruments.

'Gerroff,' bellowed a pissed punter. 'Who do you think you are? Jed bloody Harris?' A crisp packet flew through the air. Jeers rose from the throng who loved to see a man humiliate himself by song. 'Rubbish, rubbish, you're rubbish,' bayed the enraged drinkers before even hearing him strike a note. As far as they were concerned, he was a dead man.

Unfazed by the negative crowd reaction, the singer played a few chords with practised calm. Then he sang, 'Flower . . . you're my flower . . . I've never seen anything as beautiful as you . . .' His voice poured into the microphone like molten silver, quieting the madding masses and playing to them the very sound of their own dreams. Fleur stood on a chair to see over the crowd but she didn't need to. She knew who was on stage. It was her dad.

'My pretty flower,' sang the legendary Jed Harris in his first pub concert in nearly thirty years. By now, the unruly pub-goers were singing along, picking up the chorus line to the simple ballad. Lighters waved in the air as they crooned, 'Flower . . . you're my flower . . .'

At the back of the pub, big Barry, who'd just arrived to take them home, wiped a tear from his eye. He was genuinely fond of Jed and had been a horrified witness to his decline. Watching him sing unaccompanied in a rundown pub in the middle of nowhere, Barry knew with certainty that the boss he loved, the man he admired and the friend he so cherished, was finally back from the infernal beyond.

'Thank you, ladies and gentleman,' said Jed, taking a half bow over rapturous cheers from the crowd. 'That one was for Fleur.'

21

Much later that same evening, in London, Roz and Peter were admiring their brand new painting, *To the Sea*, which was propped up on Peter's draining board.

'It's beautiful,' Roz sighed.

'Isn't it?' agreed Peter. They were in Peter's tiny apartment, tucked away inside the Inner Temple, the prestigious and exclusive home of some of Britain's best legal minds. Hidden behind the whirl and noise of Fleet Street, it was like going back through time to a secret Victorian garden where fountains tinkled their watery music in quiet quadrangles, illuminated by the yellow streams of light pouring from diamond-paned windows set in the old stone walls. The church inside the walled enclave was so very ancient that some said the crusaders themselves had set forth from this spot. In the crypt, stone figures slumbered on their graves, their chain mail carefully rendered in hard rock, small dogs lying faithfully at their feet. The walkways, paved with granite slabs which for centuries had born the footfall of the judiciary, never thronged with life. Within the gates, the atmosphere was always silent, dignified and yet strangely awake. This was no peaceful haven – it was the quiet but watchful home of those who set the laws by which the country ran, powerful yet still, alert and attentive.

Peter maintained a small flat in the Inner Temple, the cost of which he claimed was nearly less expensive than all the times he would have had to take a late night cab ride back to his real home in Battersea. It was a tidy, clean place, upon which Peter had made very little personal impact. He had invited Roz here to have a glass of wine, view the painting, and hear an update on the progress of the case. However, he had something of a personal nature to say first.

'Rosalind,' he began seriously. 'I am so sorry I was so rude to you. That morning – before it all began.'

Roz was rather taken aback. The fault so clearly lay with her that his apology caught her by surprise.

'No, Peter,' she said, her eyes welling up. 'I'm amazed you've ever spoken to me again, after the mess I got us into.'

'You didn't,' said Peter firmly. 'You were manipulated and misled. A cruel trick was played on you.' Denny, they now felt sure, had been instrumental in bringing about Fleur's downfall, although quite why he should have wanted to do so was still a mystery.

'I don't believe in love at first sight any more,' said Roz sadly.

'No?' said Peter, sounding rather disappointed. 'But what if someone fell in love with you the first time they saw you, rather than the other way round? Would you believe in it then?'

'Well, that won't happen,' said Roz, swigging her wine. 'You were right, Peter. Love isn't a crazy, swept-away, wonderful feeling. It's a cautious, careful, well thought out life move after all.'

'I'm rather sorry you think that,' said Peter. 'It wasn't at all what I meant.'

'No, you're definitely right,' continued Roz, not listening

to him. 'I'm going to stop this stupid pining and enjoy the life I have. I've been a fool, Peter. I just saw the wedding day, the dresses, the smiles, the adoration. I never thought about the reality. I'm over love,' she concluded defiantly. 'I shall never seek it again.'

'How sad,' said Peter in a faint, echoing voice. 'I never wanted you to change, you know.'

'So, to business,' said Roz briskly. 'Does this lovely painting get us anywhere?'

'It points us in the right direction,' said Peter slowly. 'It proves something dubious went on at Boulden's. By itself, it doesn't show that Fleur is innocent. But it will certainly give the prosecution something to chew on.'

'What about the money they spent on it?' Roz squeaked.

'We have a few days in hand,' said Peter. 'That girl Spook is a smart operator – she's got Brinley hanging on, waiting for the transaction to clear.'

'Peter,' said Roz, 'is this how you normally work?'

Peter closed his eyes. 'This is a most peculiar case. Usually, I build a picture in my mind, piece by piece, as though I am doing a jigsaw puzzle. In my head, as I fit it all together, each piece of the puzzle is totally clear to me, although I don't know what the full picture will look like until the end. This time, it's as though I can see the whole picture at once, but it's terribly faint and misty – I can't make out any individual details but I can actually see the big picture. I'm sorry – I can't explain it any better than that. It's only when I'm running that I think I come close to finding the answer. I took it up in the hope of finding some mental clarity although I wasn't expecting to need it quite so badly.'

'Well, finally,' exclaimed Roz. 'We've all been searching for the reason why you signed up for the Runners' Club.'

'And now you know,' said Peter.

'None of us will ever be the same again, will we?' said Roz. 'Do you mind if I smoke? The tension is getting to me.'

'Smoke away, dear lady, smoke away,' said Peter. 'The marathon has certainly had a dramatic impact,' he mused. 'I for one never imagined that taking up running would change my life for ever. Foolishly, I thought I was just getting fit.'

His phone rang. 'Hello,' said Peter cautiously. He didn't get many calls on his private line at the Inner Temple as it was a number he was very careful not to give out.

'Peter!' It was Fleur, back at Spaldings after her unscheduled trip to her dad's impromptu pub concert. She was almost screeching. 'Thank God I've found you – turn on the television! Turn it on now! BBC1 – the news.'

The TV set in Peter's rooms was clearly a relic of a bygone age. He twiddled the on-off knob and the apparatus began to hum.

'It's just warming up,' he told her down the phone.

'Warming up?' shouted Fleur. 'What the hell are you talking about?'

The black and white screen flickered to life.

'Got the picture now,' said Peter. 'What am I looking at?'

'That man!' yelled Fleur. 'The man on the screen. It's him – it's the man I met on the way to Belgrade – the man we couldn't trace. It's Striker McCullum – I know it is. You've got to find him, Peter. He's the key.'

22

In the final couple of weeks before the marathon, the Runners'
Club no longer met regularly as by this late stage in their
training, it was imperative that they rest in order to get their
strength up for the big day. After their last long run before
the marathon – the mammoth and exhausting twenty miles
round Richmond Park to the south of London – Ben told them
to take it easy and not to push themselves. It was too late to
make any real improvement in their timing – the only result
of frantic last minute training now would be injury and
exhaustion on the big day.

'It's not like an exam that you can cram for the night
before,' he told his wrung-out little group as they bathed in
the spring sunshine over Richmond. The rolling hills of the
park where deer paraded their impressive antlers could have
been somewhere many miles removed from the hustle of city
life if it weren't for the jet planes constantly swooping downwards in their approach to Heathrow. 'You've done the hard
work, you've done the training – time now to have a break.'

'Do you really think we're going to make it?' asked Peter,
who was mottled pink and white from the effort of the run.

'I do,' said Ben calmly. 'It's going to be a breeze. On the
day, the atmosphere is fantastic and it will carry you on much
further.'

'What happens if we hit the pain barrier?' asked Alice, whose hair was slicked back with sweat.

'You won't,' said Ben. 'The pain barrier affects people who haven't done the proper training, and you have. Now, time to go home and have a nice cold bath.'

For some weeks, Ben had been extolling the virtues of 'icing' – according to him, having a very cold plunge after running was just the thing to stop inflammation. Roz had tried it by default – she had run a bath without realising her boiler was switched off. When she got in, the temperature had given her such a shock, she had slipped and fallen into the icy water. She sprang out as quickly as she could. Paula Radcliffe, so said Ben, swore by it. Roz just swore.

'And eat carbohydrate,' said Ben. 'Lots and lots of lovely carbohydrate.'

'I'll bear that in mind,' said Peter, who was leaving for the airport the next morning. He had refused to tell the others what he was up to, saying he was possibly about to take the longest shot of his career but in the absence of any other alternatives he thought it worth a punt. 'Call it a hunch,' was all he would say as he got into his ridiculous car to drive home. 'And pray it's a lucky one.'

It had taken a mind totally cleared of alternative distractions to come up with the idea that had struck Peter one day when he was out jogging. Who on earth, he had been musing as his trainer-shod feet struck the pavement in relentless harmony, could help him track down the mysterious operative using the name Striker whom Fleur had encountered in the Balkans and now claimed to have identified via a headline-grabbing US documentary? He had been running alone that day, using his new-found love of jogging as a relief from the overload of work from which he currently suffered. Suddenly, like a cloudburst of light through his foggy brain, he knew exactly where to go next with his enquiries. Turning for home, he sprinted all the way back to his chambers where he booked himself a return ticket for The Hague, leaving a couple of days hence. When the day arrived, his stiffened legs from the twenty-mile run the previous morning were not too delighted to be cramped into airline conditions but he kept up the carb intake with a steady stream of muffins throughout the short flight, something which caused his fellow passengers to give him a few strange sideways looks. 'Marathon,' explained Peter through a mouthful of crumbs to the woman sitting next to him. 'Got to get the glycogen into my muscles.'

It was raining so hard as Peter walked through The Hague to the long white building which housed the International Criminal Tribunal for Yugoslavia that the water spouting from the fountains outside was scarcely distinguishable from the overload of precipitation pouring from the skies. Furling his black umbrella neatly on the steps, Peter entered the great sanctum of international justice, where a multilingual receptionist wearing an airline-style headset led him through the elaborate security procedure he needed to undergo before he could keep his appointment with the august and distinguished gentleman he hoped held at least some of the answers to his prayers.

Sir Geoffrey Palmer was still wearing his red judge's robes as he sat with Peter in a little room somewhere in the vast court building where thousands of public servants toiled endlessly to bring those responsible for genocide, ethnic cleansing and horrendous crimes against humanity during the Balkan wars to justice. Their struggle to find, indict and prosecute wanted war criminals had been going on for years, a frustrating, painful and impossibly slow process, wearing and dispiriting at times even for the highly dedicated law enforcement team assembled.

'Slice of lemon?' Sir Geoffrey offered Peter a plate with wafer thin slices of yellow citrus fruit on it.

'Thank you,' said Peter, popping one into his pale amber cup of Earl Grey.

'It's been a terrible struggle to get them to provide decent tea,' said Sir Geoffrey, veering off on a tangent. 'Of course, they just think I'm being all English and fogey when I complain about the stuff they serve, as though I'm some kind of anachronistic national throwback. I've taken to bringing my own bags to court with me and boiling the kettle myself. It seems to be the only way.' He sighed deeply. 'The others all drink coffee, you see. But apparently that's dire as well. You would think with a budget of over two hundred million pounds we could have a decent cup of something to keep us going, wouldn't you?'

'Yes, Judge,' murmured Peter.

'Oh, for heaven's sake, call me Geoffrey,' said the judge. 'We're not in court now and we've known each other long enough.'

'I'm delighted you remembered me,' said Peter politely.

'Peter, I could hardly forget you,' said Sir Geoffrey, smiling serenely from behind his thick spectacles. A small, benevolent chap, he had the wise air of an old Chinese mandarin, a man to whom advanced age had brought great knowledge and power of judgement rather than any loss of facility or perception. Behind the glass of his bifocals, his eyes sparkled with the bright alertness of one much younger. 'I've never known a young barrister cause such a rumpus,' he continued, sipping his hot, fragrant tea. 'I knew you'd go far – if you didn't annoy too many people, that was. I always enjoyed your appearances before me.'

'Yes, they were good, the old days, weren't they?' said Peter pleasantly. 'I admired you greatly as a judge on the circuit.' Getting in touch with Geoffrey – whom he had not seen since his days a young barrister when he had frequented the court over which Geoffrey presided – had been Peter's great brainwave. With Geoffrey now on the inside track at the body who must know more than anyone else about shady dealings and strange characters operating in and out of the Balkans, Peter had decided to consult the venerable judge to see if he could throw any light on the strange matter of the man who had called himself Striker McCullum and quite what he had really been up to in Belgrade. Geoffrey had readily agreed to see Peter but asked him to come in person to The Hague where he would make time between court sittings to talk to him.

'I was delighted when I read of your appointment to the ICTY,' continued Peter.

'Ah, yes, a great honour indeed,' said Geoffrey, looking rather inscrutable.

'How's it going?' said Peter.

'We've got the ex-president in the dock at the moment.' Geoffrey nodded slowly. 'Who has taken the unusual decision to defend himself from the numerous charges laid against him.

'Gracious,' murmured Peter. Their eyes met and they exchanged lawyer-style glances, conveying what they both thought of anyone foolish enough to dispense with legal representation.

'At the moment, he's taking us on a tour of history,' said Geoffrey, his eyes gleaming. 'Which, while fascinating in a way, is extremely lengthy. Some of my other colleagues believe he is trying to bore us into finding him innocent.'

'Well, that's an original approach,' said Peter. 'But I can see why you feel the need for a decent cup of tea.'

'Thank you, Peter,' said Geoffrey, snuffling with laughter like a very old vole. 'If only the catering manager of the ICTY thought as you do. The wretched woman is obsessed with getting us all on some GI diet when all I require is Twinings and some nice sandwiches. Anyway, you haven't come all this way to hear my erudite thoughts on refreshments. How can I help you, my very learned friend?'

'Geoffrey, can you tell me anything about a man called Martin Benvartis?' Peter got straight to the point.

'Benvartis?' Geoffrey's bushy eyebrows shot up. 'Well, well, he is rather the man of the moment. What's your interest in him?' Gone was the avuncular, cheery chat about tea and sandwiches. Peter wasn't surprised – he knew that was just a smokescreen for a rapier-sharp mind.

'A client of mine met him in Belgrade – operating under a different name, of course,' said Peter. This was not the time to beat about the bush. Sometimes, in discussion with other lawyers, he would use language so convoluted and arcane that only another barrister could possibly understand what he meant, and even then it would be a meaning wide open to various different interpretations. With Sir Geoffrey, he felt confident enough to be direct. 'Since then she has been framed for arson. I believe there is a connection to Martin Benvartis – or Striker McCullum, as he called himself on that occasion.'

Geoffrey looked pensive. 'I take it your client has identified Benvartis thanks to his participation in *that* documentary.'

Peter nodded his assent. *That* documentary was a piece of film causing an uproar on both sides of the Atlantic. It was the work of two renegade directors from Hollywood who'd abandoned light comedy in favour of making a film on the ways the right-wing US government had interfered in foreign countries across the globe. Fearless, stinging and intensely

critical, the duo had amassed material which included inter-
views with many former politicians, businessmen and dis-
affected military and intelligence types. The American
government had tried its very best to stop the two film-makers
from completing the project but to absolutely no avail. Time
and time again, the resourceful pair proved they had been
wasted on producing teen flicks when their real talent lay in
political exposé.

Realising they were failing to stop the documentary from
being made, the US powers that be decided to implement
what their leader called a 'damagisation limitless potential'
(understood by those who worked for him as a 'damage limi-
tation policy') by offering up their own candidate for interview, a man they trusted to present a reasoned and intelligent
argument for US intervention overseas. This chap, a high-level
CIA officer by the name of Marty Benvartis, duly presented
himself for interview only to find that the wily film-makers
managed to wrong-foot him into confessing he had once
played a part in perverting the course of what should have
been a free election in none other than the Balkans. For the
film-makers, this piece of footage was gold dust and it was
this excerpt which was shown on the BBC news when Fleur
just happened to be watching. The man she saw on the television identifying himself as Marty Benvartis was, of course,
none other than the person she had encountered in Belgrade
under the name of Striker McCullum.

'It's causing us no end of a headache,' said Geoffrey. 'This
business with Benvartis. And of course, the Americans are
just hopping mad. We can't get any sense out of them at all
at the moment.'

'Why should it affect the ICTY?' asked Peter.

'As you probably know from the newspapers, we recently
had a bit of a triumph,' replied Geoffrey. 'We've brought in

Sava Namanic – the most wanted man in the Balkans. You'll remember him – his nickname was The Killer. Ran death camps and purged whole areas,' said Geoffrey, his mouth puckering with distaste. 'So obviously, for us, this seemed a huge step forward.'

'I sense a "but",' said Peter.

'You do indeed,' agreed Geoffrey. 'It was Benvartis and the CIA who captured Namanic, which technically is not quite right. They should have informed the troops on the ground and got them to pick him up. The CIA didn't want to give away any of their own intelligence so they ran the whole operation themselves.'

'Surely the end justified the means?'

'We thought the same,' said Geoffrey. 'But now the problem is that Namanic – who has got God, by the way, gone all Old Testament and prophet-like – has a surprising number of supporters.'

'Incredible.' Peter whistled through his teeth. 'Mind you, criminals always exert a fascination that their poor victims lack.'

'Exactly,' nodded Geoffrey. 'Namanic's lawyers, of which he has plenty, are claiming that his method of capture breached his human rights – if you please – and that Benvartis, thanks to the information from the documentary, should also be indicted as a war criminal.'

'That's crazy,' said Peter.

'Welcome to the ICTY,' said Geoffrey. 'So we've put in a request that Benvartis appear before us as a witness and we're waiting to hear back.'

'When might that be?' asked Peter eagerly.

'Next year sometime,' said Geoffrey.

'Next year?' said Peter in horror. 'But I need to speak to him immediately.'

'You know how slowly the wheels of justice turn,' said Geoffrey.

'Not for my client they don't,' said Peter. 'They're turning frighteningly fast for her.'

'Currently, Benvartis is probably being taken to pieces and reprogrammed at CIA base camp,' said Geoffrey. 'So I doubt you'll be able to get to him.'

'Haven't they kicked him out?'

'They could hardly do that,' said Geoffrey. 'After all, I hear they made him take part in the documentary in the first place. And he probably knows many things they'd rather he kept quiet. But I doubt they'll let him take a turn in front of the cameras – or anyone else – again.'

'Bugger,' said Peter.

'Couldn't agree more,' said Geoffrey. 'Come in,' he said, hearing a tap on the door.

'Your honour, the court will resume in five minutes,' said an usher, poking his head round the door.

'Very good, thank you,' replied Geoffrey, waiting for the door to close again. 'I'm sorry not to be more help, Peter.'

'No, thank you for your time,' said Peter. 'And for seeing me at such short notice.'

'It's been a pleasure,' said Geoffrey. 'You're looking very well, by the way. Rather fit and healthy. Lost that peaky air you used to have.'

'Lots of fresh air,' said Peter. 'Works wonders.'

'Not much of that in this building,' said Geoffrey longingly. 'If I hear anything, I'll let you know.'

23

'And so,' Peter concluded gloomily to the giant furry rabbit sitting next to him, smoking a cigarette on a bench in Hyde Park at 5.30 a.m., 'I'm now facing the prospect of going into court on Friday with nothing but a painting of dubious origin and a half-baked tale of CIA involvement to try to get my client acquitted of arson. Not only will it make me a professional laughing stock; more importantly, I will have failed Fleur.'

In full confidence that he would have amassed enough evidence to prevent Fleur's case from going to a full trial – an ordeal Peter was very keen to spare her, knowing that the nature of the crime and the details of her background would turn her trial into a sensational circus – he had requested a special preliminary hearing, to be held that coming Friday, at which he would make an application to dismiss Fleur's case. The hearing was to be held in front of a judge and the prosecution and represented a chance for Peter to stop the machinery of justice from squashing Fleur any further. To succeed, Peter would need to prove beyond reasonable doubt that Fleur was not involved in the warehouse fire which, at this point, pretty much amounted to finding someone who was. Having made a lot of fuss in order to secure the hearing, including applying for leave to call evidence – not usual procedure at this stage for the defence – Peter was in the difficult position of having nothing of any import to say. 'And two days later, I'm running the marathon.' He looked close to tears.

'Surely there must be something else we can do,' said the giant furry rabbit in Roz's voice. Tenderly, the rabbit wiped Peter's face with one of its long, bunny ears. 'You're so wrapped up in this case,' it said. 'Do you always get this attached?'

'No,' said Peter, laying his head on the furry rabbit's shoulder. 'But I like Fleur and I know she's innocent. I believe in justice, Roz. And it hurts me to see injustice being done – it's like you, when a couple you've married get divorced. Just feels all wrong.'

'Have you got those fingerprints?' said the big bunny. 'Perhaps they might help?'

'That Greta woman is barking,' said Peter, muffling his voice in the comfort of the bunny's coat. 'Completely insane,' he continued, oblivious of the irony of calling someone else mad when he was having a conversation with an enormous rabbit. 'She keeps leaving messages to tell me she's done some detective work of her own and uncovered some very exciting new evidence, but when I call her back she never answers.'

'Oh, look. There goes the rhino!' said the rabbit, waving a paw as a rhinocerous lumbered past. 'And – I don't believe it! There's a carrot.'

'Quick, you should run after it,' said Peter, sitting up. 'After all, it is your primary food source.'

The carrot wheezed to a halt in front of the bench. 'How's it going?' it said to the rabbit.

'More difficult than I thought,' said the rabbit. 'And itchy.'

'I know,' said the carrot. 'Good thing someone told me to practise – otherwise, I'd have put my costume on for the first time for the marathon and that would have been a disaster.'

'I can't believe there are so many of us,' said the rabbit in a huff. 'I thought I was being original.'

It had been with great excitement that Roz had called Peter the night before. 'It's arrived!' she said with glee.

'What has?' said Peter.

'My costume for the marathon – you know, the furry rabbit one I ordered. The only thing is I think I should have a practice run.'

'Ben told us not to train,' warned Peter.

'Yes, but I must just have a go,' said Roz. 'Will you come with me? I don't think I can face going out in costume by myself.'

'We better go early,' said Peter. 'Or you might get arrested. Tell you what, shall we try Hyde Park for a change? Let's meet there at five tomorrow morning.' As it turned out, they weren't the only costumed runners who had had the same idea. During their early morning stint in the park they counted one rhino, one carrot, two pantomine horses, an elephant and three Mr Blobbys, staggering around Hyde Park as though an impromptu version of *It's A Knock Out* was being staged.

'Are you doing anything after the marathon?' said the carrot to the rabbit.

'Oh, I don't know,' said the bunny, sounding pleased. 'I don't have anything planned.'

'Actually,' Peter cut in, 'we are having a private conversation. So I'd appreciate it if you'd move along.'

'No need to be unfriendly,' said the carrot and – if a root vegetable could be said to move in such a manner – it flounced away.

'You were very rude,' said Roz to Peter as they got up from their bench.

'I just think you could aim higher,' said Peter simply. 'Now come along, bunny mine, let's get you some breakfast. Oh, hang on, my pocket is tingling.' He fished out his mobile. 'Strange number – well, I suppose these are strange times. Hello, Peter Greyson speaking.'

'Hello, Peter,' said a distant, tinny voice. 'Geoffrey here.'

'Geoffrey!' said Peter. 'Good Lord, isn't it a bit early for you?'

'I'm just out for my morning jog,' came the minuscule voice. 'But I thought I'd give you a quick call – I'm in a phone booth so I have to be quick.'

'What is it?' asked Peter, who had stuck one finger in the ear that wasn't against the phone, in order to hear better.

'Benvartis,' the faint voice floated down the line. 'I've found him for you.'

'Where is he?' said Peter, perking up like a hound that has smelt blood.

'Coming to London,' continued Geoffrey's barely audible tones. 'He's looking after the ex-president now, on security – it was the worst job the Adminstration could think of. Their idea of a ghastly punishment.'

'When?' said Peter, barely able to breathe from excitement.

'They're running the marathon,' said Geoffrey. 'As a good-will gesture to the people of Britain. Arriving Thursday night.'

'What should I do?' said Peter.

'Give Benvartis a witness summons the minute he hits British soil,' replied Geoffrey.

'Can I do that?' asked Peter. As a young barrister, Geoffrey had been his mentor and he was grateful to be able to turn to him now, when he needed him most.

'Of course you can,' Geoffrey sounded as if he was laughing. 'You know what to do, Peter. Just get on with it. And let me know. Sounds fun.' With that, he was gone.

Peter frantically tried to call the number Geoffrey had used but it rang and rang until eventually it was picked up by a brusque Dutch man who told Peter quite clearly to get stuffed. Knowing it would be useless to try and call Geoffrey on any of his official numbers, Peter resigned himself to the fact that he had been given as much information as he needed. The rest would be up to him.

24

From what had threatened to be a no-show event as far as useful witnesses were concerned, Fleur's preliminary hearing was set to be a far more exciting day than anyone had bargained for. And yet it started very quietly. A couple of bored-looking journalists poked their noses in but that was only as a diversion from a huge murder case in full swing in court number 1. Like tennis watchers at Wimbledon, the court reporters were always alert to whether a better spectacle was unfolding in a different location and liked to check occasionally they weren't missing out on the best action. And yet not one of the supposedly razor-eyed rat pack noticed that the rather short and somewhat elderly man entering court number 2 was none other than legendary rock star Sir Jed Harris, on his way to attend what would turn out to be the most exciting session of the day, if not year. Had any of the hacks thought to follow him, they would have found themselves in possession of a very great scoop. But none did and Jed's presence passed, for once, unremarked and unfeted.

Fleur's father was among the first to enter the empty public gallery and take a seat overlooking the darkly wood-panelled courtroom at the Old Bailey, with its air of solemnity and occasion. Arriving just a heartbeat behind him came Fleur's mother, Rowena, looking very wholesome and motherly in her linen suit and flowered scarf, her long blonde hair caught up in a fat bun on the nape of her neck. Her husband, Richard, nodded tightly to Jed but didn't speak to him. Richard, who had never been impressed by Jed's behaviour, fame or money, had little inclination to exchange pleasantries with the dried-out old rocker.

'I'll just say hello,' Rowena murmured.

'If you must,' Richard muttered, shooting Jed a dark look.

'I'm so grateful for all you've done for Fleur,' said Rowena, accosting Jed.

'Oh, darling,' said Jed, wrapping her in an enormous hug. 'I've missed you, baby,' he whispered in her ear.

'No, you haven't,' said Rowena firmly. She would not, she told herself, get bamboozled by his charm once more.

'The original and the best,' said Jed, rubbing her arm. 'That's you, darlin'.'

'Rowena.' Richard was by her side. As he gently guided her away, a bird of paradise burst into the viewing gallery, long turquoise and gold feathers decorating her ebony locks, floor-length fuchsia brocade coat swirling about her ample figure. She rushed to Jed's side and gave him a hug which nearly drowned the much smaller man. When he managed to drag his nose from her alabaster cleavage, he looked rather dazed.

'Darling,' she crooned into his ear, cupping his head in her broad hands. Looking down at him, she gave Jed the most enchanting smile.

'Oh, hi, Greta,' stammered Sir Jed, for once stripped of his savoir faire. Suddenly feeling his age, he sat down rather meekly with Greta coming gracefully to land beside him.

Below the public gallery, Peter walked to the front of the courtroom, ruffled some papers on his desk, looked up at the audience and walked straight out again. It was strange what a sense of excitement pervaded the court, as if a show was about to begin, only this time the live players were gambling for real stakes. It brought out the gladiatorial instincts of even the most pure-hearted spectator, the perverse glamour of the situation giving the humblest of participants in the drama a certain aloof grandeur.

Alice, who by now was settled on a bench, whispered to Ben, 'Peter's quite dishy in his robes.'

'No getting any ideas,' said Ben fiercely, one protective hand on her knee.

'Have you seen Roz today?' asked Alice.

'Look, there she is,' said Ben. 'Talking to Peter.' There was something about the angle of Peter's head and the way his shoulders turned towards Roz that indicated a protective and affectionate stance.

A tall, thin man, immaculately turned out in a soft brown and grey pinstripe suit, walked up to Roz and Peter and politely accosted them.

'Could you give this note to Fleur?' he asked them pleasantly.

'Do you mind if I read it?' asked Peter.

'Not at all,' said the man, turning to leave the courtroom. The note that Peter opened read, 'Dear Fleur, I think it rather drastic of you to attempt to go to prison to avoid coming to work for me. However, I would like you to know the offer of a job still stands, whenever you wish to take it up. If, on the other hand, life with another antiques dealer fails to appeal, I have an idea for something that might suit you. Please call me when this debacle is over and until then, all my best wishes are with you, love, Matthew.'

'All rise,' intoned the usher as the judge, a venerable figure in his crimson robes, white wig snugly fitted over his almost entirely bald pate, tiny little eyes like chips of blue flint peeking out from the layers of skin folded round them, entered the courtroom. When he extended his neck forward from his hunched shoulders or pressed his dry lips together, Judge Hargreaves looked exactly like a tortoise, but Peter had warned Fleur that this dim, distracted look was misleading as Hargreaves was as sharp as a stiletto and missed little that passed before him.

'So,' said the judge, chomping his lips as though on a piece of tasty lettuce, 'I am to hear a submission from the defence in the matter of Bonner. The defence holds that Bonner has been wrongfully accused of arson with intent and wishes to present evidence to that effect. Am I correct? I have been asked – given the somewhat exceptional nature of the evidence – that the defence should be allowed to present it. Is this correct?'

'Yes, my lord,' said Peter, standing up to speak and then sitting down again.

'Yes, my lord,' parroted the prosecution, standing up and sitting down in exactly the same manner, which made her and Peter look like a pair of jack-in-the-boxes in wigs and gowns.

Peter's opposing number from the Crown Prosecution Service was a rather attractive woman who set her face in a mask of severity for court but let it lapse quickly into twinkling dimples when her 'court face' was not needed. Roz hated her on sight.

'How can you fraternise with the enemy?' she had scolded Peter after she caught him having a joke with the other barrister.

'It's not like that,' said Peter patiently. 'It's not personal.'

'It jolly well is!' flared Roz. 'She's trying to get Fleur put away.'

'No, she's acting for the prosecution,' said Peter. 'The police are trying to get Fleur locked up but you can't blame the barrister.'

'Hmph,' said Roz crossly. 'I suppose that's how you all sleep at night.'

'Well, this is most unusual,' grumbled the judge. 'I'm tempted to say out of order but apparently, Mr Greyson, your evidence is time-sensitive and may only be available today. Extraordinary. Hmph.'

'Yes, my lord,' said Peter, standing up again.

'If, Mr Greyson, I feel you have wasted my – and the court's – time, the penalty for you and your client will be quite serious, you do understand that?'

'I do, my lord,' said Peter calmly, although a frisson of horror went through the public gallery at the judge's words. Fortunately, Roz wasn't inside the courtroom to hear this exchange or she probably would have had a mini cardiac arrest, being the only one apart from Peter who knew that their key witness had not yet arrived. Peter, with his years of training in presenting an impassive façade, managed not to flinch at the judge's words, but his razor-sharp brain went into overdrive, making a contingency plan for the awful eventuality that his star player wouldn't show. Success for Peter – and of course for Fleur – he knew would now rest on how skilfully he could spin out what he had to say until such time as his most important witness appeared. He wasn't so much playing for time as attempting to prevent the whole matter from being slung out of court or adjourned to another day. They didn't have another day, he knew with total certainty. This was their one shot and if he messed it up now, Fleur could be lost for ever.

Fleur, sitting in the dock, looked down at her feet. She couldn't bear to look out at the courtroom where she saw familiar faces as though through a blur of tears. She couldn't believe the hearing was actually happening – all too literally, the day of judgement had arrived.

'Mr Greyson, perhaps, without further delay, you would like to proceed,' said the judge, snuffling a little and casting around for a handkerchief. An usher handed him a box of tissues.

'My lord,' began Peter as Judge Hargreaves loudly blew his nose, 'my client, Fleur Bonner, has been the victim of a vicious and deliberate fraud, set up to take the blame for a crime she did not commit, would never contemplate committing and has absolutely no connection with whatsoever. As I will show, a false trail of evidence has been laid, a trail which the police have been only too eager to follow and which led directly, for reasons I will come to later, to my client.'

'Yes, jolly good,' said the judge. 'Get on with it.'

'Let us first of all deal with the allegations made against my client by her former boss, Brinley Boulden,' said Peter with consummate confidence. 'Unfortunately, having originally made himself available to the police, he has now disappeared. Unless the prosecution can enlighten us as to his whereabouts?' Peter sneered at his colleague who returned his glance with a theatrical cold glare.

'Can you?' said the judge.

The prosecution barrister got to her feet, the hisses and boos from the gallery forming a malicious backdrop to her words. As she stood, Peter sat down again.

'My lord, that is correct. Urgent business has taken Brinley Boulden to New Zealand. However, he remains fully cooperative.'

'Does he have plans to return?' said the judge.

'When a trial date is fixed, I am sure he will make himself

available.' She sat down once more as Peter leapt to his feet. 'Rubbish!' he cried. 'Brinley Boulden has fled the country.'

'My lord!' said the prosecution in tones of muted outrage, half getting to her feet.

'Sustained,' said the judge.

'Your lordship, clearly Mr Boulden has left the country.' Peter modified his words. 'I wish to bring out Defence Exhibit One,' Peter nodded and *To the Sea* was produced. 'As you can clearly see, this painting was not burnt in the warehouse fire of 17 March and yet Mr Brinley Boulden, currently of Auckland, New Zealand, has entered it as part of his insurance claim. Not only has he submitted a claim to his insurers for a substantial sum for this painting, he also sold it recently at a private auction in London. I suggest this throws considerable doubt on all the evidence provided by Brinley Boulden in the matter of Crown versus Bonner.'

'My lord,' the prosecution was up once again, forcing Peter to bob down, 'I would like to know how this painting came into the possession of my learned friend and why he has not informed the police of its existence.'

The judge looked severely at Peter.

'All will become clear,' said Peter temptingly, 'if I am allowed to finish.'

'Mr Greyson, I will let you continue for now,' said the judge. 'But I agree with the prosecution that we have some queries about your methods in this case.'

'Then I will be happy to answer them,' said Peter politely, crossing his fingers under his gown. His methods were unusual, to say the least, and one of his big fears for today was being dismissed from the court because of them. But unbeknown to Peter, he had a guardian angel in the shape of a benevolent judge on his side. From The Hague, Sir Geoffrey had been keeping an eye on the proceedings, and when he found out that Peter would be appearing in front of Hargreaves he had sent that judge a message asking him to hear Peter out. The community of judges was tightly knit enough for one to take very seriously the request of another, which was why Hargreaves hadn't thrown Peter out of court already. Without Geoffrey's intervention, it was likely that Peter would have lasted five minutes.

'Let us consider the night in question,' said Peter, moving gamely forward. He hadn't yet seen Roz come into the court-room, which would be the sign that the man who held the answer to the riddle of Fleur and the burning building had arrived. 'My client visited the warehouse in question in the early evening to check in a delivery – three paintings which had arrived from Belgrade. I would like you to note that these paintings had never been officially verified or valued – my client had seen them in Belgrade where she was pushed into naming a figure for them. But we have no guarantee that the paintings that arrived in London were the same ones she had seen in Serbia, nor can we be sure they were originals in the first place. The three works were due to be checked over but, as we know, the warehouse burnt down before this was possible. Yet on the insurance claim they have been listed as original works of high value. Someone stands to be make a lot of money out of this unfortunate event.' He flipped over some paperwork. 'My client left the warehouse and attended a party at the Tate, given in honour of the artist Greta Raynar.'

'Is that the rude girl?' the judge interrupted. As Greta had once made a blow-up version of her own private parts for an exhibition, Peter had to conclude that yes, it was. He ran quickly through the events that followed Fleur's arrival at the party, the mysterious text message, Denny's seemingly psychic knowledge that she needed to leave, the taxi driver whose insistence on dropping her at the garage made sure she was caught on CCTV, the petrol canister placed in the hallway where she was likely to trip over it, the anonymous call made to the fire brigade which coincided with the time of Fleur's arrival at the riverside warehouse and Fleur's missing mobile phone.

Peter paused. So far, Fleur had heard nothing she didn't already know and she was starting to feel very anxious. She had been hoping that Peter had unearthed some crucial evidence which would show beyond any reasonable doubt that she was innocent, bringing this whole nightmare to a speedy close. Disloyally, she was even beginning to wonder if her unorthodox method of hiring a barrister had been somehow rather rash when Peter spoke up again. He wasn't going to disappoint her after all.

'This man, Denny,' Peter leaned forward and practically spat the name. Watching him, Fleur knew these were no courtroom theatricals. Peter genuinely hated Denny, 'is without doubt involved in framing my client for the crime of arson. He followed her around London, he took up jogging in the same park as her, he feigned an infatuation with one of her friends to get closer to her, doubtless he sent her the text message telling her to visit the warehouse, arranged for a driver to be ready to pick her up to take her down to the river, called the fire brigade . . .' Finally, Peter breathed, much to the relief of his audience. 'Not only that.' He left an impressive silence before launching in again. 'But he also visited Brinley Boulden at his shop in Piccadilly *after* the time of the warehouse fire. Fingerprints from the man, Denny, taken on the night of the party are an exact match for those found on a whisky tumbler at Boulden's!' Peter's triumphal ending was well earned, as was the ripple of applause that went through the viewing gallery. Greta, who had been responsible for lifting Denny's fingerprints, first from the wrapping paper on the small gift Denny had given Roz on the night of her party and second from a sweep of Brinley's office while Fleur was in jail, stood up. Assuming the applause must be for her, she curtseyed in a balletic manner.

The prosecution raised her hand. 'Speculation.'

'I think this is all speculation,' huffed the judge. 'But I am now curious. Mr Greyson, I have a question for you myself.'

Peter raised an eyebrow. This was unusual.

'How can you possibly know these fingerprints were left at Boulden's after the time of the warehouse fire?'

'Er, well, my client,' said Peter softly, 'did the washing up at work the day of the fire. So any fingerprints must come from a later date.'

'I see,' said the judge thoughtfully. 'Or do I?'

'Yes, your lordship,' said Peter firmly. 'Brinley Boulden has fled the country, possibly in fear of his life after a visit to his office by this mysterious character Denny, who no doubt also persuaded Boulden to give a very bad character reference for Fleur and to claim he had sacked her when he had not. Perhaps in the immediate aftermath of the fire, Mr Boulden hoped to make some financial gain for himself from the incident. But later on, I suggest, he just wanted to save himself by any means possible.'

'So,' said the judge, wig askew over one eye in the excitement. 'Are you suggesting that Brinley Boulden burnt down the warehouse himself?'

'Absolutely not,' replied Peter. 'What I am saying . . .' He was interrupted.

'Objection,' came a clear male voice from the back of the public gallery. In the accused box, Fleur started. She knew that voice only too well.

'I beg your pardon?' said the judge, looking round. Standing up in the balcony was a tall man, soberly dressed in a dark suit, by whose side sat a pale-faced woman with wavy chestnut hair, her eyes closed with nerves.

'I said objection,' the man persisted. 'I have something to add.'

Down in the courtroom, Peter was furious. The last thing he needed was more irregularity.

'My name is Sean Duvall,' continued the man in the gallery. 'I have worked for Brinley Boulden for several years and I believe it is entirely possible he burnt down the warehouse – in fact, it may have been his only option.'

'Excuse me,' said the judge, pushing the wig out of his eyes. 'Mr Greyson, did you know about this?'

'I had no idea,' said Peter hotly. The judge smirked. He was quite pleased to see Peter as wrong-footed as the rest of them had been so far.

'Mr Duvall, why are you only coming forward now?' he asked, looking up into the viewing gallery. This was turning out to be a most enjoyable day after all.

'I have just returned from a trekking holiday in Patagonia,' said Sean. 'Late last night. So this is my first opportunity to speak.'

'Very good,' said the judge, making a note. 'Kindly explain yourself further.'

'Brinley asked me to restore an icon he had bought,' said Sean. 'But I decided to double-check it with the Art Loss Register, to make sure it wasn't a stolen item. At first they told me the work, Saint Sava at Zvornik, was on their list of missing items and I should hand it over to them immediately. But the next day, they called back and said they had made a mistake.' Sean paused. 'They told me to finish restoring the icon and send it back to Belgrade, as planned, which all seemed very strange. I called Fleur many times – I wanted to warn her there was something odd about the icon. But she didn't call me back until after she'd been to Belgrade when it looked as if everything was okay after all. It didn't seem worth mentioning.'

In the dock, Fleur nodded to herself. She had been very stupid. All that time when Sean had been so desperate to get in touch with her and she had foolishly ignored him, he had wanted to pass on a vital piece of information which might have stopped her from getting into trouble. Instead, she had indulged herself in a daft fantasy that something as broken and bespoilt as her relationship with Sean could be mended. She felt like weeping.

'Why would this encourage Mr Boulden to burn down his warehouse?' said the judge.

'Because as a result of my call, the Art Loss Register were planning a full stock check of Brinley's shop and warehouse,' said Sean. 'When I heard there had been a fire, my first thought was that Brin had done it himself rather than let Art Loss see what he really kept in there.'

'How intriguing!' commented the judge. 'I long to know what was really in the warehouse at the time of the fire. Well, well, this has all been most helpful. I am an avid art collector myself and shall avoid Mr Boulden quite carefully in future. Mr Greyson?'

Only a few moments before, Peter had been looking black-faced with anger. Suddenly, his face cleared and he almost laughed out loud. The one thing he hadn't understood had just been explained to him.

'Thank you, my lord,' he said politely. 'Thank you, Mr Duvall. Perhaps you would be seated? The missing piece of my jigsaw puzzle has just become clear.' He saw Roz walk into the back of the court and give him the prearranged signal, at which he nodded. 'Now, your lordship,' he addressed the bench once more. 'As I previously requested, I would like to introduce Martin Benvartis to the court and ask that we listen to what he has to tell us.'

A blond man of medium height, dressed in city clothes – dark suit, smart long wool coat, polished shoes – walked forward, but his physique and his outfit were not a happy mix. With his short haircut, broad shoulders and big hands, he looked as if he was in fancy dress when he would be happier in fatigues or on a horse. Stone-faced, he bowed slightly to the judge before giving Peter a bone-crushing hand-shake.

'Your lordship!' uttered the prosecution, staggering up from her seat. While Sean spoke, she had seemed stunned into silence, seemingly unable even to frame the words to protest at the absolute overturn of anything approaching normal procedure. The arrival of Benvartis seemed to bring her back into the land of the living and restore her power of speech, of which she was now making use quite vociferously. 'I must object in the strongest possible fashion.'

'Sustained,' roared the judge. 'But at the same time, over-ruled,' he added.

'What?' said the prosecution in sheer disbelief.

'Mrs Martin,' said the judge, leaning over the bench to talk to her. 'There is a time for everything. A time to adhere rigor-ously to the rules, a time to interpret them. This is a time to be flexible until we have heard what this man has to tell us. Sir, please inform the court of your name and position.'

Marty walked forward and, with Peter's prompting, entered the witness box.

'Martin Theodore Benvartis the second,' he began. 'From Phoenix, Arizona. I am a former CIA operative with special responsibility for the Balkans, currently on security detail in London with former president Ted Harvie. Although one person here knows me better by the name of Striker.'

25

The evening before his surprise appearance in the British courts, Martin Benvartis had been sitting rather glumly in the Dorchester hotel, attempting to drink weak tea out of a tiny porcelain cup, when he had received a most surprising pair of visitors. The pale yellow stuffed sofas, the boldly striped wallpaper, the framed hunting prints of the hotel were all anathema to this man who loved the smoke and chaos of war, the unpredictability of the chase, the devious winding machinations of the sharp end of international foreign policy at work. To find himself demoted back to civilisation was a horrible shock and he was not enjoying his new post as Deputy (not even Head) Security Adviser to the previous American president, Ted Harvie. He liked the man himself – it was impossible not to. He had been a successful and charismatic president, standing down only when he had run his maximum two terms in the Oval Office. His legendary charm was such that all who came into contact with him left feeling as though they had been warmed to their very soul by the brief encounter. Coming to London to run the marathon had been a private initiative on the part of Harvie. A great Anglophile, he had been upset by how badly damaged the US-Brit relationship had been by the Iraq war and hoped to spread some goodwill among the British people by arriving on their shores to take part in their race. Recently recovered from heart surgery himself, he saw it as a personal challenge as well. But with only a few years separating him from holding the reins in the world's most powerful country, he was still unable to travel without extra security and his visit had been kept under wraps, only to be publicly announced on the morning of the marathon itself. When Ted went jogging, his security men did too, meaning Benvartis was now facing the prospect of running the London marathon without having had much chance to prepare, another thought which was adding to his melancholy aspect as he munched on quite the smallest, thinnest sandwich he had ever seen. How much lower, Marty wondered to himself, could he possibly fall? All for one rash statement made on camera.

In normal circumstances, two unexpected visitors arriving to try to gain entry to the ex-presidential suite would have been wrestled to the ground by men with ear pieces and then deported to Guantanamo Bay. But the message relayed to Marty told him they had come about Fleur Bonner, the one person for whom Marty's much under-used conscience had a soft spot. Since he'd been brutally stitched up himself by the television documentary crew, he had fallen to wondering what had happened to that girl and whether she'd survived her inadvertent part in his great scheme. What his two visitors, a lawyer and his plump lady friend, had told him indicated that she hadn't. Unwilling to let someone else's life be ruined in a way too similar to his own, Marty rose to the occasion and agreed to save the day.

'I met Fleur Bonner on the plane to Belgrade,' he told the court, his drawling cowboy tones bringing the sound of desert wind across red mountains into the rarefied air of the court-room.

'Where you knew she would be,' put in Peter.

Marty nodded. 'Oh yes. Using the name Striker McCullum, I posed as an NGO worker travelling to Kosovo in order to meet Fleur and get access to the icon she was carrying.'

'Can you explain to us how you knew she had an icon and why this should interest you?' said Peter. The courtroom was so still, not a rustle, not a breath was heard.

'We've been hunting some of these guys in the Balkans for years,' said Marty baldly. 'With very little success. They're smart – they don't use mobiles, they don't communicate by e-mail, we can't penetrate their inner circles. Everywhere we looked, we drew a blank. But the pressure's been rising – the big cheese wanted Namanic and the others brought in from the cold. So we started getting imaginative.' He linked his hands together and cracked his knuckles with a sound like bullet shot. 'It was my idea to keep an eye on Art Loss – they're looking for people in strange places, just like we are. We, um, well,' he paused. 'I won't go into detail. Let's just say if you use a computer, I can find out a whole bunch of stuff about you. So we compiled a list of key words or phrases for each person we're after – mother's maiden name, known pseudonyms, past history, general perversions, that kinda thing, and fed them into our monitoring systems. If any of the organisations we were . . . supervising,' he said, rather delicately for a man of his build, 'used one or more of these search terms, we knew about it straight up. When Art Loss looked up Saint Sava and Zvornik on their database, we got a red alert. Saint Sava,' he continued, looking at Fleur in the accused box, a white, trembling version of the confident girl he'd derailed in Belgrade, 'is the patron saint of Sava Namanic, a heinous killer we have been seeking for years now. Zvornik is his birthplace. When we found this icon had been bought by a dealer in Belgrade, we realised there was a very small –

but very real – chance its eventual destination was Namanic. We had to do a bit of negotiating with Art Loss – they weren't keen on letting the icon out of the country. But I can be very,' he looked down modestly, 'persuasive. That's why they gave you the all clear for Saint Sava at Zvornik.'

'I don't believe it!' Fleur looked up, her blue eyes turned milky with the shock.

'Fleur.' Peter held up a hand. 'Let Marty speak. He may be the only man who can help you.'

'Namanic is supported by a party of ultra-religious ultra-nationalists in Serbia,' continued Marty, 'who are very, very clever. If we had delivered the icon ourselves, using one of our own operatives, there was a chance they would bust us. We had to let an innocent person with no history act as the courier.'

'Why, thanks,' muttered Fleur.

'I'm sorry, Fleur,' said Marty. Having followed the maxim 'never explain, never apologise' all his working life, he found confrontation with the human victims of his handiwork a new and uncomfortable experience. He now spoke as though to her and her alone.

'When you arrived in Belgrade with no one to meet you, it was because we had deliberately messed up your travel arrangements. One of my female operatives had called Zoran Lazarevic, posing as your secretary, to tell him she had booked you into the Hyatt and that he should collect you from there the next morning rather than from the airport as originally planned. I took you to the Hyatt where the room he expected to find you staying in had been pre-reserved for you from London. I drugged your wine and while you slept that night I broke into your room and fitted a microscopic transmitter to the icon which was so small and so state of the art that Zoran had no hope of detecting it.' Even while he related this awful tale, Marty couldn't hide his evident pride in his work.

'Poor Spook,' said Fleur in a daze, thinking of how cross she had been with her hapless secretary, thinking it was her latent dyslexia which had caused the mix-up, leaving Fleur stranded at Belgrade airport.

Marty continued with his tale. While Fleur, he told the court room, travelled back to London to resume her normal life, the icon set off on a strange and disrupted journey of its own. The tiny transmitter embedded in the icon gave off a signal which allowed the CIA to track its progress although monitors watching the screen were astonished by quite how slowly the flashing red dot, indicating the icon's journey, inched across it. The dot plodded along for days, zigzagging through ravines, up steep hills where only scree and scrub bushes covered the bare slopes, past abandoned burnt-out villages filled with roofless houses, through lusher, lowland wooded land and small farms worked with agricultural methods more akin to the middle ages than the twenty-first century. Eventually, just as it seemed the dot on the screen would carry on inching its way east for ever, it stopped and stayed stopped. The satellite picture showed the icon's destination was a little monastery, clinging to a rock face in one of the most remote and forgotten spots in Europe. It was on this minuscule house of God that just hours later a phalanx of Black Hawk helicopters descended, filling the sky with their angry screams like the wrath of divine judgement being rained down from the very heavens above. Inside, they found a monk praying in front of the icon of Saint Sava at Zvornik, an enormous man with long, ragged hair and a huge beard who smelt so rank that some of the CIA gagged when they had to grab hold of his torn robes. It was Sava Namanic, the Killer.

'Excellent – how exciting!' exclaimed Judge Hargreaves,

rubbing his hands. 'How very *Boy's Own*.' He was loving this court session – for years, he had been just filling in time, mouldering away slowly on the judge's bench, hoping his contribution to posterity would be a few more criminals locked up, a few more innocent people spared. And yet here he was, having a whale of a time. He must remember to thank Geoffrey for the top tip. Even the prosecution had binned all her objections and seemed absolutely riveted.

'We thought we had rounded up all the monks and taken them with us,' said Marty, who obviously spared no compassion for those who had harboured Namanic. 'But later we learnt that one had got away and run, barefoot, to the nearest monastery to pass on the message about Namanic's capture.'

'Could you estimate the distance that the monk ran?' asked Peter, more out of curiosity than professional necessity.

'About fifty miles,' said Marty. 'Across mountainous terrain.' A little murmur of respect rose from the various members of the Runners' Club dotted around the room.

'Right,' said Hargreaves. 'Let's wrap this up.' It was a phrase he'd heard in popular culture but never yet been able to use in court. 'Mr Greyson, could you draw your final evidence together?'

'With pleasure,' said Peter. 'Marty, the paintings sent to England – why?'

'The ultra-nationalist party needs money,' said Marty. 'Maybe the paintings were real but I'm gonna say they sent fakes with the intention of burning down the warehouse to collect the pay-out. Maybe Fleur saw originals in Belgrade but then they sent copies to London.'

'What about framing Fleur?'

'Revenge is a big deal in the Balkans,' said Marty. 'Matter of honour. They'd have worked out pretty quickly it was the icon that led us to Namanic so Fleur would be their number one target. If they planned to set light to the warehouse anyway, why not go one step further and make Fleur the culprit.'

'Why not just kill her, if they hated her that much?' said Peter.

'An eye for a eye,' said Marty. 'Remember, Namanic's gone all Old Testament, thinks he's some kind of prophet. The order probably came from him. He'd want Fleur to face a false trial and be unfairly imprisoned for ever, which is exactly what he thinks she's done to him.'

'Anything else?' said Peter as a collective shiver of horror ran through the courtroom.

'I expect they threatened her boss as well – this Denny character, probably all part of some inter-European mafia set-up,' said Marty, also known as Striker McCullum. 'But I don't think we'll ever really know. Or,' the former operative added thoughtfully, remembering his now cancelled security access to high-level international intelligence, 'someone somewhere will know. But it won't be us.'

'Well, goodness gracious,' said Hargreaves, taking off his wig and giving his bald head a quick wipe with his hanky. This session would certainly provide him with some spanking tales to tell at the next judges' jolly, even if he feared he would spend the next few months trying to untangle all the pro-cedural hitches. 'This has been a very productive session, if most irregular,' he went on, regretfully deciding it was prob-ably time to bring matters to a close. 'However, all good things come to an end so, with no further ado, I dismiss the case of the Crown versus Bonner and find Miss Bonner to be acquitted entirely of the charges laid against her. You are,' he beamed in Fleur's direction, 'free to go. All other matters,' he gave Peter a very stern look, 'will be dealt with by me at a later

date, although I would like to see you in my chambers immediately, Mr Greyson. And I mean immediately. I am going to
rise.'

'All rise,' said the usher. 'All rise.'

26

The morning of the marathon dawned clear, bright and sunny, much to the disgust of many of the 30,000 runners taking part who had believed the Met Office when they had forecast a chilly day of overcast gloom with scattered showers. As the nervous crowds of hopeful marathoners, many of whom had never before subjected their bodies and minds to such an awesome task, trudged up Shooter's Hill to the mass start, those dressed in cold weather running gear complained bitterly to their friends. Those who had, as tradition demands, ignored the forecast and chosen their day's outfit after looking out of the window that morning, trotted along in their shorts and singlets, looking a little smug. All shapes and sizes, ages and fitness levels were represented, some already sweating in the unexpected sunshine, some cool as cucumber, strolling along munching jelly babies, chatting on their mobile phones, their forearms decorated with biro marks indicating at what time they intended to reach which mile.

Blithely swinging her kit bag by the string handles, Fleur skipped up the hill, her runner's number safety-pinned to the front of her vest. When her court case had finished, she had been astonished to find she was still entered for the marathon, the other members of the Club having taken the precaution of registering her earlier in the week. When asked quite how they had managed to do such a thing without her knowledge or consent, there had been a little shuffling of feet before Ben had burst out laughing and admitted it had been him. Her letter, with her registration number, had been sitting in her post box so he had purloined it, forged a letter with Fleur's signature giving him the right to register her and taken along as proof of ID a copy of her birth certificate, helpfully printed out by Roz.

'Given everything else that happened,' he had pointed out quite logically, 'it didn't seem such a very great fraud.'

Fleur wasn't angry, more relieved. When the judge had handed her back her freedom, so cruelly and wrongly taken from her by a series of sinister events, she had been elated beyond belief. The elation hadn't lasted very long, however, as it didn't take much time for the realisation to hit her that once more she would be starting again from scratch. Finding she was running the marathon after all meant she could put off worrying about the rest of her life for at least another couple of days until that too was over.

'Right, group hug,' said Ben as they reached the numbered ranks of lorries waiting to take their kit bags and deposit them at the finish. The five runners, Alice, Ben, Roz, Peter and Fleur, gathered round, arms locked about each other's shoulders as though in a rugby scrum.

'Now, team,' said Ben, who was sounding rather emotional. 'Training with you guys has been an incredible experience. When I put the Lifestyle Checklist through your doors, I hardly expected that anyone would take the statement on it, Let The Marathon Change Your Life, quite so seriously. But it has, and I'm glad it has.' He squeezed Alice's shoulder and gave her a smile. Peter and Roz exchanged affectionate glances and Fleur just looked at the ground.

'I'm really sorry,' she muttered, 'that you got caught up in all that.'

Peter let out a bark of laughter. 'I can assure you, my dearest Fleur, I wouldn't have missed it for the world. My life before now seems very dull.'

'I for one,' said Alice, 'have to thank you, Fleur.'

'Thank me?' said Fleur. Had all that porridge turned Alice's head? 'What for?'

'You set me on the right path,' said Alice. 'You told me about Mikhail and the paintings. And then you were so brave about your court case – I don't feel so afraid now of what I might have to face.'

'Good girl!' said Roz approvingly. 'I'd like to thank Fleur for being the best friend I've ever had and tell her that when she does meet Mr Right – which she will . . .'

'Look!' Ben interrupted, pointing to where a man was struggling into costume. 'There's Scooby-Doo – perhaps he's Fleur's soul mate?'

'I'm always available for weddings,' finished Roz firmly.

'And I, too, am always available for criminal court cases,' said Peter, laughing. 'Although I rather hope Fleur will never need me in that context again.'

'Roz, where's your costume?' asked Ben, remembering Roz's furry rabbit outfit.

'Oh, that,' said Roz. 'I only wanted to wear it so I'd have somewhere to put my cigarettes. But I've given up properly now so I don't need it.' She smiled coyly at Peter.

Over the tannoy came the announcement that runners were to take their places, according to their allotted number.

'That's us at the back,' said Ben. 'Anyone need Vaseline before I check my bag in? No? Toes? Nipples? Peter?'

'Thank you, Ben,' said the barrister politely. 'All my moving parts are well oiled.'

'In that case,' said Ben, 'may your legs be strong and your toilet breaks few. Good luck, Runners. I'm so proud of you.'

He broke off, giving a strangled sob. Alice turned to him and hugged him, a hug that looked as if it could have lasted the duration of the marathon, if the voice from the tannoy had not urged them into their places once more.

A cheer went up from the massed ranks of runners, waiting in the fat queue to reach the starting line.

'Why are we cheering?' Fleur asked Ben. His runner's number actually placed him much nearer the front but he didn't want to abandon his team, all of whom as first time runners with no known marathon time were starting right at the back, only just in front of the street sweepers. Next to Fleur stood a man carrying so much technology with him – iPod strapped to his arm, mobile phone with special running attachment, bum bag, rucksack with drinks dispenser – it looked as though he intended to do a day's work between miles one and twenty-six. Fleur, who had nothing but shorts, singlet and trainers about her person, had been amazed by how many people had asked her if she would be running with a mobile phone. She supposed there would be some novelty value in phoning friends up to say 'Hi! I'm running the marathon!' but she could see that the fun of that would quickly wear off.

'We're cheering because we've started,' said Ben. They were standing stock still in the crowd.

'We have?' said Fleur.

'It'll take us about twenty minutes to get past the start,' said Ben. 'But the Championship Chip on your shoe won't start your time until you cross the line – it won't count in your official time.'

'I just want to finish,' said Fleur. 'That's all.'

'Give yourself a target to beat for your next marathon,' put in Peter, whose running gear was surprisingly sleek, Roz having taken him out shopping.

'No thanks,' said Fleur. 'Once'll be enough.'

'That's what I said.' A very ancient, very small, white-bearded gentleman in front of her turned round. 'But you'll change your mind. I've done twenty-two marathons now.'

Roz nudged her as they shuffled forward, excitement mounting as all the runners found themselves moving at last. 'Scooby-Doo's just over there,' she said, pointing. 'Why don't you see if you can chat to him while you're going round? He looks very nice.'

Fleur sighed. Her main motivation in finding a boyfriend now would be to stop Roz from attempting to set her up with any man who strayed across her path, even if he was dressed as a cartoon dog.

A light breeze brushed across the runners' heads, fluttering the leaves on the trees. The pace was picking up – they were walking faster and faster and suddenly they were running, moving towards the park gates which signalled that finally, after all their troubles, dramas, tears, squabbles, arguments and despair, for the Battersea Park New Runners' Club, their marathon had begun.

'This is an extraordinary day,' a BBC commentator was enthusiastically informing the nation via the medium of television. 'This – the silver anniversary of the London marathon – promises to be a record-breaking day in all respects.'

'Oh, quite, Bob,' Wanda, the square-jawed ex-shot putter turned female presenter cut in, her strident tones totally overwhelming her male counterpart. 'Leading the women's race, we've got Andrea Miller, the best athlete this country has ever produced. Back on form, she's looking terrific. Wonderful weather, sunshine, blue skies . . .' Through her ear piece, the producer tersely informed her to shut up about the bloody weather as they'd had over a thousand complaints already about last night's forecast's getting it totally wrong.

Quickly taking advantage of Wanda's pause to get back into the commentary, Bob jumped in. 'And we've got a surprise celebrity running today – we've just been informed that none other than Ted Harvie, ex-US president, is taking part in today's London Marathon. Let's see if we can catch him on camera.' As the screen showed pictures shot from the helicopter hovering over the head of the runners, Wanda threw Bob a nasty look. She'd been looking forward to breaking the news about Ted Harvie and now Bob had stolen her thunder. She'd be holding him in a head-lock later in the BBC canteen.

Bob carried on happily, oblivious of the fate that awaited him. 'It's an extraordinary sight.' He used his favourite adjective again and yet he wasn't far wrong. Seen from the air, the marathon looked like a river of multicoloured humanity, flowing through the streets of London. As the television cameras showed the swift-footed early runners rounding the corner past the *Cutty Sark*, the grand old tea clipper brought to dock with a brass band alongside playing merry tunes to speed the athletes on, a strange vision hove into view. From above, it seemed as though a band of black, like a Politburo armband for a dead comrade, stretched across the road, moving in perfect synchronicity. In the middle of the funereally clad runners ran one man in white. 'And there's Ted!' said Wanda with great excitement. While the cameras were off the studio, she had given Bob a tactical biff with her strong right arm. 'Running with his security cordon – of course, given his prestige and the difficult political climate, he can't be too careful. But what a wonderful man,' she enthused, one hand now clamped firmly over Bob's mouth. 'Major heart surgery just six months ago and here he is, keeping up with the best of them. Already at the *Cutty Sark*, well, well.' She hoisted the other presenter into a fireman's lift.

'Wanda, get off Bob,' the producer said evenly into her ear

piece. Threatening to sack her, his normal procedure with wayward presenters, was too terrifying a prospect so he had to cajole her another way. 'Or I'll give him the breaking story, not you.' Quelled, Wanda put Bob back in his chair, where he sat rather white and shaky.

'And now we have some incredible news!' Wanda shouted at the camera. 'Let's go to the head of the race to see . . . Andrea Miller has pulled out of the race . . . she's gone under the barrier at a drinks station and it looks as if she is giving up again. Andrea Miller is OUT of this year's marathon, she has done it again, she is . . . oh, no, she's not, she's . . .' The screen suddenly returned brusquely to the airborne helicopter camera. 'She's just having a pee,' said Wanda, slumping back into her chair in great confusion as Bob, her harried co-presenter, burst out laughing.

At mile eleven, Fleur was still going strong. The atmosphere was electric, the crowds massed along the route roaring the runners on, the sun beating down from overhead, the small smiling children shyly offering jelly babies on their outstretched hands. The pubs lining the racecourse had all opened early, giving punters a fabulous excuse to come out and get pissed on a Sunday morning while having the satisfaction of supporting athletics at the same time. Elvis impersonators, go-go dancers, Japanese drummers, jogging Jehovah's witnesses and mobile discos provided entertainment while serious-faced St John's ambulance men and women held out latex-clad hands with lumps of Vaseline on for runners in need to slick on to their friction burns. At each water stop, the road was covered in half-empty water bottles where runners had taken a swig and thrown the rest into the crowd, often covering them in a shower of Vittel as they did so.

In the distance, as she ran towards Tower Bridge, Fleur heard the strains of a familiar melody. She overtook a pair of Wombles who were fading a little in the heat. She'd lost the other members of the Club, Alice and Ben being quite a bit faster than her, Roz and Peter rather slower. Getting closer to what looked like a band on an enormous roadside stage, she caught the chorus line of the song, picked up by the happy crowd. 'Flower . . . you're my flower . . .' they were bellowing as the silver-haired man on the stage strummed his guitar and made love to the microphone.

'Here she comes!' His blonde backing singer had spotted Fleur, running up the road towards them. 'Fleur,' she shrieked into her microphone. 'We're singing your tune!' Waving violently and jumping up and down, the girl reprised the melody in a beautiful, high clear voice. 'Flower . . . you're our flower.' Tears sprang to Fleur's eyes and her legs gained extra power as she pounded past her dad onstage, singing the song he'd written when she was born, the gorgeous Tibby harmonising madly behind him. 'Fleur!' he bellowed into the mike as she ran past him. 'Fleur! You're my hero!' For once, and she realised probably it would be just the once, her dad was in the crowd cheering her and not the other way round. Suddenly, it all seemed worth it after all.

'And for yet another surprise today,' Bob the commentator had regained some ground in the BBC studio as Wanda was still sulking. She wasn't at all amused that she had just announced with great excitement to nine million viewers that Andrea Miller was taking a toilet stop, 'Sir Jed Harris is giving a performance at mile thirteen, singing "Flower", the song he plans to release next week in support of a children's charity. With him is new soul sensation Tiberia, giving it her all for this magnificent occasion. What a heart-warming day the marathon is, wouldn't you say, Wanda?' Wanda growled and flexed her muscular hands.

After the knee-buckling excitement of crossing Tower Bridge, the tour around the Docklands was long and harsh, the crowds now somnolent and subdued from hours of main-lining lager in the brilliant sunshine, the road sticky from discarded Lucozade, the runners struggling to maintain momentum.

'Come on, you can do it.' Scooby-Doo, who'd been pacing Fleur for several miles now, ran alongside.

'Oh, bugger,' said Fleur in despair as they approached the seventeen-mile marker. 'I thought this would be eighteen.' Her heart sank as she realised she still had 9.2 miles to run, a tall order at the best of times.

'Think of Jimmy Savile,' ordered Scooby. 'If he can do this, so can you. It's under ten miles now. Together, we'll crack it.' And on they ran, on and on and on, the seemingly never-ending road carrying them forward until the magic moment when they turned back towards London, on to the homeward straight. Putting one foot in front of the other, one foot in front of the other, Fleur just kept going, over bridges, round corners, through tunnels, until emerging on to the packed Embankment she suddenly saw her mother, waving like mad and almost crying from excitement.

'Fleur!' Her mother was running with her. 'You're brilliant! You can do it!' Her stepfather, in a heavy jumper and over-coat, was jogging along with her mum.

'Richard, don't run!' said Fleur in alarm. 'You'll have a heart attack.'

'Thanks, Fleur!' His amused voice floated behind her. 'I'm entering next year!'

*   *   *

The last mile of the marathon was the longest. Big Ben came into view, telling Fleur her time was better than she could have imagined in her wildest dreams. 'I'm going to make it,' she told herself. 'I'm actually going to make it.'

'Energy is your friend!' hollered a man, pressing one last carton of Lucozade into her hand. Neck and neck, she and Scooby pounded along, turning right towards the Houses of Parliament, to Birdcage Walk, the tree-lined route that led to Buckingham Palace whose fluttering Union Jack showed the Queen herself was inside, probably watching the marathon via a pair of racing binoculars. The crowd were ecstatic – 'You're nearly there, you're nearly there,' they chanted, a swaying, hyped-up, adrenalised mass of screaming people.

'Run, run, run,' the race marshals were yelling, clapping their hands. 'Run – this is the end, keep running.'

But suddenly, Scooby was down.

'Get up, Scooby-Doo,' the spectators roared. 'Get up.'

'Don't stop,' he yelped as Fleur faltered. 'Keep going. I'll see you later.' With no thought in her mind now but the finish, Fleur lengthened her stride and from somewhere very deep inside herself forced out a sprint to the finish and passed the line. Her marathon endeavour was over.

It wasn't easy to meet up with the others but eventually they found each other – the panting, sweating, dazed, medal-wearing Battersea Park Runners' Club coming together on the Mall to hug, cry and congratulate each one another.

'I can't believe I did it.' Roz hadn't been that far behind after all. 'I thought I'd be out there for twenty-four hours.'

Ben, who'd finished in four and a half hours, a time slower than his best because he had refused to abandon Alice, was lying on the ground under the shade of a tree with his eyes closed while Alice stretched his hamstring.

'My God my God my God.' Peter was walking in small circles. 'I've run a marathon. I've run a marathon. I've run a marathon.'

From their kit bags, which lay in a pile on the ground, came a tinkling noise. Roz started. 'Oh!' she exclaimed. 'I must have forgotten to turn my phone off.' She reached inside her bag and fished out her mobile. 'Hello, Rosalind Squires, marathon runner,' she squeaked with a huge smile which was hastily wiped off her face. 'Yes, of course, yes, put him through . . .' Her tone changed completely. 'Your highness!' she said reverentially. 'But . . . but . . . I would be so honoured . . . my sincerest congratulations . . . I am overwhelmed . . . I shall do my utmost to ensure that you have the very happiest day of your lives . . .' She rang off with a stunned look on her face.

'You'll never guess what,' she said, her eyes taking on a far away aspect. 'That was . . . to let me know before the official announcement this afternoon . . . there's going to be a royal wedding . . . in Windsor . . . and they want *me* to marry them . . .'

'That's amazing!' said Fleur after a moment's stunned silence. 'But how come they've asked you when you work at the Chelsea office?'

'He,' Roz put great and reverential emphasis on the pronoun. She sighed happily, 'said he had heard I was simply the best . . .' She beamed at the others, her brown eyes brimful of tears. She held out her arms and Fleur hugged her tightly.

'And so you are,' said Peter firmly, putting his hands on both their shoulders. 'And so we all are.'

26.2

Peter, who fell hopelessly in love with Roz the first time he saw her, had wanted to drop to his knees after they crossed the starting line of the marathon to ask her to marry him. But instinct told him it would be better to wait until she felt totally secure and confident in his affections. He is planning to surprise her next year instead.

Gregor Besaronovich tracked Ben down and offered him a very highly paid job as his UK business manager, which Ben immediately refused. Gregor, however, was very determined and in the end Ben negotiated a lower salary as head of Gregor's charitable foundation. Being charitable does not come naturally to Gregor so Ben doesn't have the world's easiest job but he likes a challenge so he's sticking with it for now.

Alice sold her house in Battersea at the same time as Ben put his bachelor flat on the market. Together, they bought a big house in East Dulwich where Alice, her children and Ben all live together, Mikhail and his dirty dealings being nothing more than a nasty memory. After much legal wrangling, ownership of the painting, *To the Sea*, was restored to Alice who promptly sold it, paid off her immediate debts and made a large donation to the children's hospice. Sadly, her other painting was never recovered but Alice has other matters on her mind. She is pregnant with Ben's baby and has never been happier.

Brinley Boulden is still living in New Zealand, which he hates.

Somewhere in a military warehouse in northern Bosnia lie several crates, containing the paintings taken from Tito's villa in the Adriatic after his death. Whether these valuable works will ever see the light of day again is anyone's guess.

Greta, with her iron will and unshakable self-confidence, took on Sir Jed, his entourage, his habits, his children and everything else that comes with a life spent in rock and roll. She has him completely under her thumb.

After the marathon and her court case finished, Fleur found herself once more unemployed. She didn't take up Matthew's offer of a job but, with his help, instead she set up on her own as a private art consultant and now has a lucrative new career advising very rich clients. She hadn't intended to take on any staff but she couldn't bear to leave Spook behind so she hired her, although she does insist Spook uses spell-check on all her correspondence. Much of Fleur's business concerns supplying extremely wealthy yacht owners with paintings – rapper Ritz-ee is one of her best and most faithful clients, although it seems he has hopes of becoming more than just a customer. Every week, he sends her a large bunch of pink roses with a note saying that whenever she's ready he'd like to take her out for dinner. Fleur can't decide whether one rock star in her life is quite enough so she hasn't yet accepted. But she's thinking about it. Perhaps in the future she will say yes, but for now she's free of prison and free from her past and that feels like enough.

LUCY HAWKING

Jaded

William Gadget has his life on a plate – money, success, sharp clothing, an interior-designed apartment, a collection of platinum credit cards and even his own personal manservant. But he's about to find out the price of the one thing you can't buy.

Dragged into the sudden drama that erupts in William's life, causing him to flee his Notting Hill flat in the middle of the night, clad only in his pyjamas, are his friends: Jemal, reluctant producer of television's most popular gardening show, DIG IT!, Dallas, a pot-smoking actor, freelance mercenary Mac, and Ambrosia, nomadic heiress, photographer and William Gadget's oldest friend. In the wake of the mysterious disappearance of their dear friend Will, they are forced to pool their resources to find out why he went and whether they can save him . . .

Warm, witty and deliciously unpredictable, JADED is a must for anyone who's winced in recognition at THE OFFICE, laughed at NOTTING HILL or longed for a more anarchic view on FRIENDS.

0 7553 0696 1

headline
review

ISLA DEWAR

Secrets of a
Family Album

Obsessively neat Lily, a writer who writes about writers, is asked to interview the enigmatic journalist and photographer Rita Boothe. Leafing through a book of Rita's from the early seventies, Lily notices a picture of an incandescently sexy young woman sitting in a limousine swigging Jack Daniels. It's her mother, Mattie.

Lily isn't shocked. She's jealous. She wants to be like that, beautiful, abandoned. But Mattie is no longer meltingly gorgeous. In their neglected house, she and her husband scrape by and bicker. Upstairs, Grandpa flirts on the Internet. Marie, Lily's sister, is facing a custody suit and her brother Rory avoids coming home.

Lily is usually the one to sort the family out, but she's tired of being boring and dependable. She wants to let go, be a woman of wicked mystery and intrigue. Like the one in the photograph.

Praise for Isla Dewar's novels:

'Observant and needle-sharp – very funny' *The Times*

'Both wise and funny' Shena Mackay

'Breathless . . . appealingly spirited . . . sparkiness, freshness and verve' *Mail on Sunday*

'Genuinely moving and evocative' *Scotland on Sunday*

0 7553 0082 3

headline
review

6. M

Now you can by any of these other bestselling
Headline Review titles from your bookshop
or *direct from the publisher.*

FREE P&P AND UK DELIVERY
(Overseas and Ireland £3.50 per book)

Secrets of a Family Album	Isla Dewar	£6.99
Atlantic Shift	Emily Barr	£7.99
On Dancing Hill	Sarah Challis	£6.99
Passion	Jude Morgan	£7.99
All is Vanity	Christina Schwarz	£7.99
The Distance Between Us	Maggie O'Farrell	£7.99
The Woman on the Bus	Pauline McLynn	£6.99
Havoc, in its Third Year	Ronan Bennett	£7.99
Play it Again?	Julie Highmore	£6.99
Single Men	Dave Hill	£7.99
The Homecoming	Anna Smith	£7.99
Despite the Falling Snow	Shamim Sarif	£7.99

TO ORDER SIMPLY CALL THIS NUMBER

01235 400 414

or visit our website: www.madaboutbooks.com

Prices and availability subject to change without notice.